John Wycliffe, Edward Harris

**Johannis Wyclif Tractatus de Benedicta Incarnacione**

John Wycliffe, Edward Harris

**Johannis Wyclif Tractatus de Benedicta Incarnacione**

ISBN/EAN: 9783337424459

Printed in Europe, USA, Canada, Australia, Japan

Cover: Foto ©Raphael Reischuk / pixelio.de

# Tractatus de Benedicta Incarnacione.

"Wyclif's" "De Benedicta Incarnacione".
MS XV Oriel Coll: Oxford. leaf 225 d.
(Page 113 line 16, of this book.)

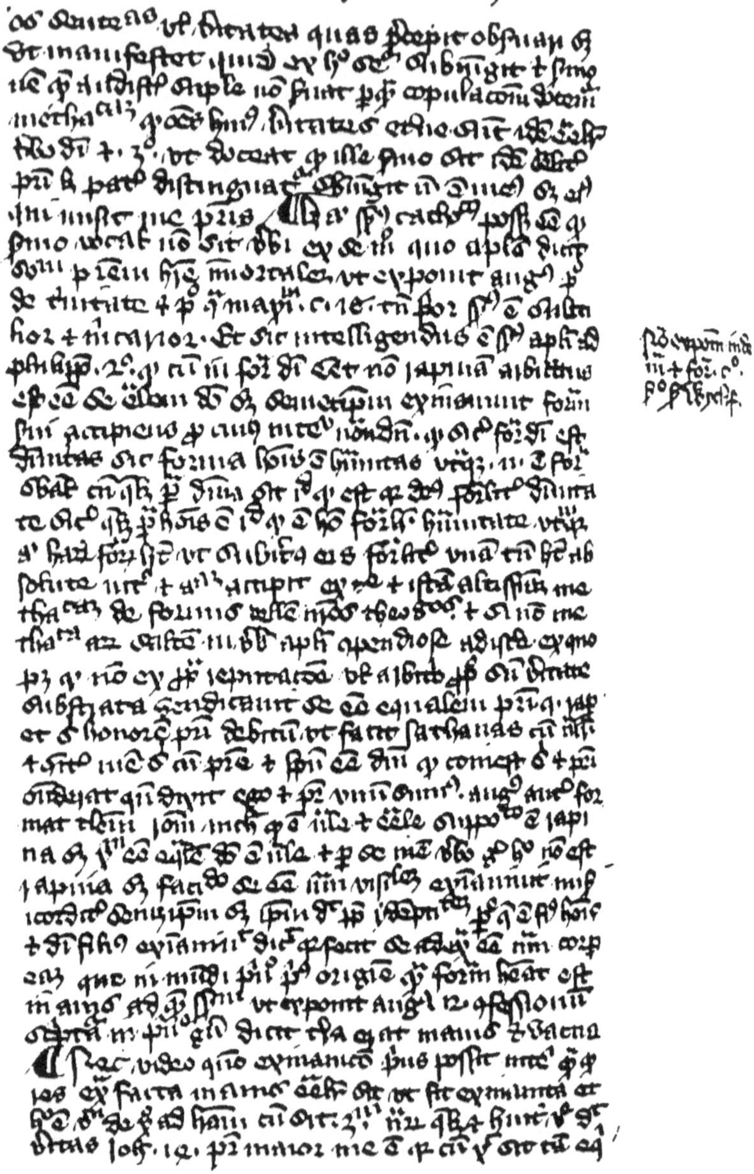

# Johannis Wyclif

# Tractatus de Benedicta Incarnacione

NOW FIRST PRINTED
FROM THE VIENNA AND ORIEL MSS.

AND EDITED
WITH NOTES AND INDICES
BY

EDWARD HARRIS, M.A.
LINCOLN COLLEGE, OXFORD.

LONDON:
PUBLISHED FOR THE WYCLIF SOCIETY,
BY TRÜBNER & CO., LUDGATE HILL, E.C.

MDCCCLXXXVI.

HERTFORD:

PRINTED BY STEPHEN AUSTIN AND SONS.

[redacted]

[redacted]

# CONTENTS.

# PREFACE.

I. The treatise *De Incarnatione Verbi* now first printed in this volume is the unquestioned work of Wyclif. The style is unmistakeably his, the phraseology often identical with that used by him in other works, and the substance agrees with what he maintains elsewhere. Moreover, besides the quotations of this book in the *De Veritate S. Scripturae* and the *De Universalibus*, noted by Dr. Shirley in his Catalogue, it is expressly referred to in the *Trialogus* (p. 225, Lechler), and is quoted in the *De Ecclesia*, p. 126 in Dr. Loserth's recently printed edition. Furthermore, Walden, in his *Doctrinale Fidei*, writing within forty years of Wyclif's death, quotes several passages from various parts of the book. These and other coincidences will be found in the Notes at the end of this volume.

By way of more direct external evidence the three Vienna codices bear Wyclif's name in the Incipit or Explicit or in both. In the margin of the Oriel codex '*W. de Incarnatione Verbi*' is written in the top right-hand corner of each leaf, in a hand contemporary or almost contemporary with the copyist's, *i.e.* about A.D. 1400; and there are besides in the margin of the same MS. two special notes of the same date connecting the text with Wyclif. One is a marginal note on fol. 225*d*, on a line with page 113, line 28, in this edition, 'Nota exposicionem in de materia et forma cap° secundo secundum Wyclif,'[1] which is the

[1] See facsimile specimen page at the beginning of this volume.

only appearance of the author's name in full in the Oriel codex; and the other, also a marginal note, fol. 234*a*, on a line with page 221, line 18, in this edition, 'sententia Johis.'

The absence of Wyclif's name from the beginning and end is probably due to prudential reasons, in view of the Lollard persecution: just as a similar cause led to the strange misplacement of the letters in the several words of the Incipits and Explicits in many of the Polemical Tracts, as shown by Dr. Buddensieg.

II. The treatise then being unquestionably written by Wyclif, to what time of his life does it belong?

There is no reason to question that Shirley was right in assigning it to the group of works written before A.D. 1367. The absence of any allusion to political matters, of any reference to reforming ideas as to the hierarchy or the religious orders, and the Eucharistic theory here adumbrated, all point to an early date. The author is still the theologian of the schools; he is not yet the politician, or the reformer. But some of the views which he propounds are already branded as heretical, *e.g.*, page 25 top, *Obicitur quod dico horribilius Arianis quia dico Christum esse materiam primam et sic abiectissimam creaturum.*

This figures as the fifth of the 'haereses quas primo jactavit in aera,' but which, according to Fasciculi Zizaniorum, p. 2, did not attract notice until their author became Doctor of Divinity at Oxford. Besides the fifth in this list those 'haereses' numbered 3, 4, 6, and 7, are all enunciated in this treatise, and all maintained by Wyclif in the face of opposition. If Walden, or whoever may be the author of the narrative in Fasc. Zizan., is right in stating that these doctrines of Wyclif were not opposed until their author became doctor of divinity, 'cathedram doctoris audax arriperet,' it seems to follow that the treatise in its present form belongs to the early days of his doctorate. Shirley, in his Preface to Fasc. Zizan., gives good reason for fixing the date of the doctorate at about A.D. 1363. This year then will be the earliest possible date for the treatise. And this conclusion is confirmed by the position taken up here on the Eucharist. Wodeford, quoted by Shirley, Fasc. Zizan. p. xv, note 4, and by F. D. Matthew, English Works, p. xxiii, notes three stages of opinion in Wyclif on this subject. 'Alias dum esset praedictus magister Johannes sententiarius Oxoniae, ac etiam baccalarius responsalis, publice tenuit et in scholis quod licet accidentia sacramentalia essent in subjecto, tamen quod panis in consecratione desinit esse. [This is the then prevalent Roman doctrine of Transubstantiation pure and simple.] Et cum multae quaestiones essent sibi factae quid esset subjectum illorum accidentium, primo per tempus notabile respondit quod corpus mathematicum. [This was an attempt to reconcile the received doctrine with reason and such science as he possessed.][1] Et posterius post multa argumenta sibi facta contra hoc respondit quod nescivit quid fuit subjectum illorum accidentium, bene tamen posuit quod habuerunt subjectum. [This is pretty much Wyclif's position in this treatise, page 190, line 23 seqq., although in the same passage he adopts the word 'transubstantiatio,' and still speaks of the celebrant priest as 'conficiens,' page 44, line 2.] Nunc in istis articulis et sua confessione ponit expresse quod panis manet post consecrationem, et est subjectum accidentium.' This is open denial of Transubstantiation. Dr. Shirley says: "We have here three stages of opinion; the first while he was Master of Arts and Bachelor of Divinity; the second when he became Doctor of Divinity; the third from the Confession of A.D. 1381." All this points to the conclusion that this treatise belongs to the beginning of Wyclif's doctorate: and for the reasons given by Shirley this cannot be later than A.D. 1367. It belongs therefore to the four years immediately preceding that date. There being cross references between the *De Universalibus* and our

[1] Compare p. 191, ll. 10-16.

treatise, it is not possible to state their relative dates: and as yet that treatise is unedited. Possibly when this and the *De Anima* and other early philosophical treatises are edited, more precision may be attainable. This much is certain that our treatise is the work of the Oxford Realist theologian, whose mind is already awakening to great difficulties underlying current conceptions, but has not yet been urged forward by conviction or circumstances to any direct opposition to them. And there is this special point of interest in this book that it is a specimen from a period of Wyclif's development hitherto unrepresented in any printed work.

III. How and in what form has this treatise been transmitted to us?

So far as is known at present the following extract from Shirley's Catalogue, p. 6, exhausts the list of existing codices:—

1. Vienna, ccclxxxiv.[1] ff. 75-104.
2. ,, ccclxxxvii. ff. 37-110.
3. ,, cccciv. ff. 115-157.
4. Oriel Coll. Oxford, xv. ff. 117-235.
5. Bib. Reg. 7. B. iii. imperfect.

These five codices have all been made use of for this edition. They are referred to henceforth as follows:—

1. Vienna as **A.**
3. ,, **B.**
2. ,, **C.**
Oriel **O.**
Bib. Reg. **M.**

I proceed to give some account of each. And first of the three Vienna MSS., the following report is supplied by Dr. Herzbergfraenkel, who kindly undertook to examine them for the purpose.

[1] Since Shirley's catalogue the Vienna Library of MSS. has been renumbered.

**A. Cod. Vindob. 1387,** membranaceus, fol.; 215 folia. Singula folia in quaternas columnas, paginae in binas, divisa sunt. In fol. 75*a*—104*c*. Tractatus de Incarnacione continetur. Pulchra scriptura unius per totum tractatum manus, seculi 14[i] exeuntis vel ineuntis 15[i] esse videtur. Notae et glossae in marginibus variis manibus adjectae sunt. Praecedunt prologum haec verba rubris scripta litteris: *Prologus mgri Johīs de Incarnacione.* Eodem colore titulus ipsius tractatus excellit. *Explicit prologus. Incipit de Incarnacione Capitolum primum.* Litterae initiales capitulorum sunt omissae vel potius nondum depictae, in lacunis enim parvula signa miniatori litteram ponendam indicant.

Notarum marginalium triplex distinguo genus praeter paragraphos A, B, etc., quibus capitulum primum in minores dividitur partes: (**a**) correcturae, voces in textu omissae vel a textu discrepantes saepe alia manu scriptae; (**b**) argumenta brevia textus vocabulum significantissimum repetentia; ad exemplum fol. 75b. (cap. I. p. 3, ll. 9, 10) in margine *Homo perfectus, Augustinus:* vel etiam (**c**) argumenta majora in tractatu dicta paucis verbis exprimentia et haud raranter quasi glossantia; ad exemplum ad Cap. I. p. 3, l. 21 seqq. *Creaturam Christum asserentes sicut et negantes quomodo sunt intelligendi;* ad p. 8, l. 8 seqq. *Persona hominis si fiat ex corpore et anima non videtur distincta ab (h)unitate integra et completa facta ex eisdem.*

Notae sub (**b**) et (**c**) specificata diversis et inter se et a textu manibus scriptae sunt; nonnullae speciei glossae in pedibus foliorum ita positae sunt, ut, si eas legere velis, codicem perverse tenere cogaris.

Cod. 1387 praeter tractatum de Incarnacione haec continet: ff. 1-75. Wycliffi De Eucharistia (2° tract.), et De Trinitate: ff. 104-215 ejusdem Epistolae octo, De Mendaciis, Descripcio fratris, Conclusio de officio regis, De IV imprecacionibus, De solucione Satane, De purgatorio, De Clavibus ecclesie, De tribus partibus ecclesie, De sentencia incarcerandi, De condemnacione 19 questionum, De vaticinatione, De dotacione ecclesie, Speculum secularium dominorum, De paupertate Christi, Ad parliamentum regis, Super Matthaei 21, De Antichristo super Matthaei 24, Dialogus, Trialogus.

**B. Cod. Vindob. 4307** chartaceus, folia 242, 4to. Folia 115-157 tractatum de Incarnacione continent. Scriptura parva sed distincta: ut in fine elicitur anno 1433 exaratus est. Titulus rubris scriptus litteris: *Incipit tractatus de incarnacione mgrī Jo. Wykleph.* In margine; *Prologus.* In fine prologi: *Capitolum primum.* Multae paginae in frontibus *d'incarnacōe m*[ri] *Jo. W*[y]. vel numeros capitulorum exhibent. Litterae initiales prologi et primi capituli variis coloribus sed pessimi gustus depictae; ceterae plerumque desunt et eodem ut in **A**. codice 1387 modo indicatae sunt. Notae marginales rarae et nullius momenti non consonant glossis Cod. 1387.

Codice 4307 continentur Johannes Ssarp Tractatus De Anima: Joh. Wiclef De Composicione hominis. Idem De Universalibus. Idem de Incarnacione. Tractatus De ente in communi. Tractatus De Ente in particulari.

**C. Cod. Vindob. 4504** chartaceus. 153 foll. 4to. Fol. 37–110*b* tractatum de Incarnacione continent. Scriptura codici 4307 fere coaeva. Titulus, litterae initiales, notae, marginales desunt. *De Bened. Inc. Jo. Wiklif* a manu sec. 17 in initio tractatus scriptum ex *Explicit* desumptum est. Capitula partim alia manu numerata, partim numeris carent. In marginibus paucas invenis correcturas, in f. 60a *corrige* in margine scriptum est. Codicem nihilo minus diligentem definitivamque perscrutationem evitasse multae textus lacunae non expletae satis demonstrant. Duodena folia quaternionem constituunt; in fine folii 12[i] numerus ponitur, primus fol. 48*b*, secundus 60*b*, etc.

Codex 4504 continet infra scriptos Joh. Wiclefi tractatus: De Simonia, De Incarnacione, Sermo super illud probet autem se ipsum homo, Epistola pape Urbano missa, De Composicione. In folio non numerato inter thecam et fol. 1, manu seculi 15[i], *Hic de composicione hominis non est examinatus.*

Ex *Explicit* hujus codicis R. Beer titulum tractatus in *De Benedicta Incarnacione*[1] transformavit. Sed optimus codex **A**. 1387, ut etiam **B**. 4307, *De Incarnacione* tantum scribunt, et nullam video causam quare notulae illi sine dubio non ab auctore factae sed a scriba additae, major fides sit attribuenda.

De codicum **A, B, C** affinitate.

Cum tres codices Viennenses tractatum De Incarnacione continentes per omnes suas partes verbo tenus conferre magnum opus et inutile esset, capitula tantum in paginis impressis 1–13 et 65–70 contenta et hic ibique nonnullos locos minus extensos diligenter et accurate comparavi. Quae inde resultent, paucis verbis dicam.

Codices **A**, et **B**, et **C** unam textus recensionem repraesentant a codice Oxoniensi non mediocriter discrepantem. **A** veracissimum esse ex comparacione cum reliquis manu scriptis facile demonstratur; omnes enim fere **B** et **C** differenciae aut nullius momenti sunt, aut

[1] v. Note, p. 233.

sensum deteriorant. Sed qualis horum trium codicum sit affinitas, minus evidenter definiri potest. **B** et **C** ex **A** desumptos esse haud probabile mihi videtur. Nam in **A** *gradum* (p. 3, n. 7), *sic* (p. 4, n. 5), *infirmum* (p. 6, n. 3), *finaliter* (p. 12, n. 14), *pure* (p. 12, n. 15), *racionabiliter* (p. 66, n. 13 et saepius), *similibus* (p. 69, n. 1), ita distincte scripta sunt, ut scriba codicis **B** nullo modo *gaudium, sicut, infirmius, faciliter, purus, racionaliter, substancialibus* legere potuisset. Ex quibus concludo codices **A** et **B** ex eodem exemplari descriptos esse, **A** majori cura, **B** minori diligentia adhibita.

Codex **C** nondum finaliter correctus paucis locis ab **A** differt, quarum lectionum variantia ex defectu manus corrigentis sufficienter explicari potest. Nihilo minus et hic probabilius mihi e communi cum **A** et **B** fonte derivari videtur."

The following account of the codex in the British Museum is supplied by Mr. F. D. Matthew, who kindly collated my proofs with this MS., and thereby gave valuable assistance in cases of difficult readings. Moreover, the knowledge of the contents of this abstract or summary proved to me of great assistance in finding the main thread of the argument, and in breaking up the text into paragraphs.

**M. Bib. Reg. 7, B. iii.** Casley's Catalogue gives the contents thus:—

1. Gulielmi Wodeford de Sacerdotio Novi Testamenti Liber. ἀκέφαλος. chartaceus.
2. ———— Quaestionum 72 de Eucharistia Liber.
3. Johannis Wycliff de Incarnatione Verbi Liber.
4. ———— Confessio de Eucharistia.
5. ———— Assertiones ejusdem 24 damnatae.
6. Thomae Winterton contra Confessionem Wiclevi, Liber.

It will be seen that all the contents relate to Wyclif; they have probably been always together, and are not a fortuitous concourse of tracts, although the present binding is only about a century old.

The volume is a folio of 85 leaves, about 11½×8 in. Casley describes it as 'chartaceus'; it is in fact made up of quires of 7 or 8 leaves, in each of which the outer leaves are parchment, the rest stout paper. The only exception to this arrangement is that at the end of the tract *Quaestionum* 72, only two leaves (64, 65) are of paper, and the *De Incarnatione* begins a new quire with a leaf (66) of parchment.

The book is incomplete, having on its last page the beginning of a tract on the poverty of Christ.

The writing varies very much in the volume; some parts being much clearer and more careful than others. The worst is the *De Incarnatione*, which is written very hurriedly, with excessive contractions. The lines are generally crooked and very close together. Some parts of the first treatise (*De Sacerdotio*) are almost as bad.

The relation of the MS. to the text of our tract is curious. Very much is omitted, and the joining words and clauses of sentences are commonly altered, while on the other hand long passages are given verbatim from a good text.

I was at first inclined to hope we had here the notes of a pupil who had heard the *De Incarnatione* as lectures, but I now take this copy to be a summary made from a MS. for the use of the writer. The parts copied contain the main course of the argument, the omissions being chiefly of illustrations and authorities cited. A listener would be less choice in his selection and less full in the pieces given. Moreover, the best judgments I can obtain say that the writing is not of Wyclif's time, but of the fifteenth century.

**O. Cod. Oriel. XV.** The Oriel MS. is found in a volume thus described in Coxe's Catalogus Codd. MSS. Oriclensis:—

XV.

Membranaceus, in folio grandiori, ff. 279, sec. xiv. exeuntis, binis columnis exaratus.

1. Ricardi Radulphi, Armachani, opus in P. Lombardi Sententias, in quaestiones xxix. distributum, praevio sermone super idem, f. 1.

. . . . . . . .

2. Roberti Holcoth quaestiones in Sententiarum libros.
   in calce
   Laus tibi sit Christe quoniam liber explicit iste,
   Mentem scriptoris salvet Deus omnibus horis.
3. Quaestiones duodecim magistri Nicholai Aston Oxoniae disputatae, fol. 202.
4. Tractatus de communicatione idiomatum in capitula viginti distributus, fol. 214b.
5. W. [an Jo. Wycliffe] tractatus de Incarnatione Verbi, capitulis tredecim, fol. 217.
   Incip. "Prelibato tractatu de anima qui introductorius est propter incarnacionis mesterium."

6. [Rogeri ?] Swineshead Quaestiones super Sententias; in calce mutil, fol. 235.

This copy is undoubtedly of the date assigned in the Catalogue, *i.e.* about A.D. 1400. The ornamentation and handwriting is distinctly English as one would expect. The initials are delicately drawn and of simple design, consisting of leaves of flowers, but no heads of animals; and there is no pretence to a high standard of illumination. The material is vellum, and is in good preservation, but little stained. The height of the page is $42\frac{1}{2}$ centimetres, the breadth 30: the height of column 31, breadth $8\frac{3}{4}$; interval between columns $1\frac{3}{4}$ centimetres. This gives a handsome margin. There are 72 lines in each column, written on very faint lines ruled in red. The large initial beginning the treatise, extending with its flourish, from the top to the foot of the column, is in blue and vermilion: as also are the smaller initials at the beginning of each chapter. Paragraphs are marked with coloured initials alternately blue and vermilion. At the top of right-hand margin of each leaf is written *W. de incarnatione Vbi*; there is no other title. There is in the margin in parts a fitful kind of analysis of the text; but this is not continuous, nor always correct. Besides this, occasionally the name of some author quoted in the text is written in the margin, and such remarks as 'nota bonam rationem,' 'argumentum bonum.' To two such comments of special interest I have called attention above, pp. vii, viii. From the top of fol. 229 (p. 194, l. 30 of this edition) the numbers of the imperfect numerical analysis are framed in red, thus Caᵐ 12ᵐ', and from the same point the longer notes are generally underlined in red.

The punctuation is scanty and worthless, except in the case of paragraphs, which generally correspond with a new sentence. Only fresh chapters begin with a new line: there is no other break in the text; and the breaking up in this edition has been done on my own responsibility, and was a matter often of doubt and difficulty. This MS., kindly lent me on two occasions for considerable periods by the Provost and Fellows of Oriel, I copied carefully; and have since collated my copy, and lastly the printed text and notes with it.

The Vienna Codex A. was copied for me with great care by Mr. Rudolph Beer, who also collated B and C, and supplied me with their variations: my proofs have been returned to him for a second collation. In this respect, therefore, everything has been done which which could be done to secure the result aimed at, that is, that this edition should place the reader in possession of the facts.

As to the construction of the text, although naturally inclined to lean on the one English copy O, with which alone I was personally familiar, yet after comparing its readings in many places with those of A, B, C, I did not feel justified in taking the easier and less responsible course of printing the text either of O or of any one of the codices, and appending the variant readings of the rest in the margin: but it seemed best to select from all the materials at command, including the fragmentary Codex M, what appeared to be in each case of discrepancy the best reading, and to place that on the page, noting at the foot the alternatives supplied by the other MSS. And in this I had Lechler's Trialogus as a precedent. In very few instances, never without a statement at the foot, have I departed from the authority of the MSS. entirely. Hence, wherever I am right, the reader's purpose is served; he has before him the best text; where I am wrong, he has at hand the materials for a more correct judgment.

For the sake of completeness I have made no distinction between important and unimportant variations, and have placed all readings of A, B, C, O not embodied in the text into the notes at the foot of the page, with the exception of the numberless alternative readings of 'ille' and 'iste,' and a few unimportant variations in the order of the words. I have endeavoured also to give the spelling, I must not say the orthography, of the MSS., even when it is manifestly incorrect, *e.g. methaphisica, anthitesis, dyabolus*. Editions like this, besides their interest to students of theology or philosophy, contribute material also to the students of language. It is noticeable in this connection that there is scarcely any Greek word which is not misspelt.

As to the relative value of the MSS., I think O is the best, as probably it is the oldest; but the contributions to a good text, furnished by Mr. Beer and Mr. Matthew, are invaluable. A careful analysis of the various readings will, I think, establish this one point, the only one to which I can see a clue, as to the relation between O and A, B, C, viz. that O is more nearly allied to C than to either A or B. Besides numerous smaller coincidences peculiar to O and C, there is a remarkable omission (p. 68, ll. 19-25) common only to these two codices.

There is a strange historical ignorance displayed in A, B, and less distinctly in C, on page 155, line 21, where the two former insert 'Nestorius,' the latter 'n,' in the text to explain the 'clericus in fide devius' against whom St. Anselm wrote his treatise on the Incarnation. Of course it is Roscellinus who is referred to (v. Note ad loc. cit.).

Besides the short omission on page 68, just mentioned, as common to O and C, there are two longer passages wanting in O, and in O only. The former of these, page 134, line 31, to page 136, line 25, contains the statement of a metaphysical objection to Wyclif's doctrine, which is also the Catholic doctrine, that Christ did not become a person by the Incarnation, and the answer to that objection. The omission is cleanly made, and does not seem to be due to a copyist's carelessness; rather the passage appears to be an addition to the original treatise. The argument in it is somewhat involved, and there is a remarkable sentence at the foot of page 135, which bespeaks so much greater freedom in the use of Greek metaphysical terms than Wyclif usually displays, that one feels almost inclined to follow O in rejecting it. However, the existence of the passage was known to the annotator of O, who writes in the margin 'deficit multum.'

The other omission on page 168, line 25, to page 170, line 15 is curious. The omitted passage consists of a quotation from a Decretal and the application of it to Wyclif's argument: and there is no hint in the margin of O of any omission. I can only suggest that perhaps a Lollard copyist or his employer did not set much store by a papal anathema. It is even possible that Wyclif himself in his later years may have preferred to withdraw an argument which rests on the dictum of one Pope Alexander III., the patron of Thomas à Becket and adversary of Henry II., and which had been reissued by another Gregory IX., the oppressor of Henry III. On the other hand, the only other reference to a Decretal in this book (page 122, line 15) stands in all the four codices alike. And it is quite possible that O, instead of being from a later, may be from an earlier 'edition' of the treatise, and A, B, C may be from a later one to which the author had added as subsidiary arguments the additional passages not found in O.

It is perhaps remarkable that so many copies of this treatise should survive, especially when we remember on the one hand the attempts to exterminate the works of Wyclif, and on the other the nature of the treatise. It has not the popular interest of the English sermons or of the polemical tracts, still less of the English Bible. And it is among the works, copies of which were publicly burnt at Prague on July 16, A.D. 1410. Dr. Johann Loserth has given us the following interesting account of the condemnation and burning of the Wyclif books in his valuable monograph, 'Wiclif and Hus,' English ed. 1884, p. 114 :—

"A papal bull was issued by Pope Alexander V. December 20, 1409, conferring on Zbinco, Archbishop of Prague, the commission to take measures against the heretical doctrines. . . . The commission, which he had called together in accordance with the papal bull, pronounced the judgment . . . which was likewise proclaimed by Zbinco at the summer Synod of 1410—that the books of Wyclif should be burnt. . . . Of the books of Wyclif the following were mentioned by name :—1. Dialogus ; 2. Trialogus ; 3. De Incarnacione Verbi Divini ; 4. De Corpore Christi ; 5. De Trinitate ; 6. De Ideis ; 7. De Hypotheticis ; 8. Decalogus ; 9. De Universalibus Realibus ; 10. De Simonia ; 11. De Fratribus Dyscolis et Malis ; 12. De Probacionibus Proposicionum ; 13. De Attributis ; 14. De Individuacione Temporis ; 15. De Materia et Forma ; 16. De Dominio Civili ; 17. Super evangelia sermones per circulum anni.

Against this decision the university was the first to raise its voice, on the 21st of June : then Hus, who, four days later, in conjunction with seven others belonging to the university, addressed a solemn appeal to John XXIII. (who had meanwhile succeeded Alexander V. as Pope) . . . .

As regards the prohibiting of the possession of Wyclif's books, the appeal points out that only a fool, who is entirely devoid of acquaintance with the Bible and with canon law, could consign to the flames the logical, philosophical, moral, mathematical, theophysical books ; as also those on matter and form, on ideas, etc., which contain many noble and glorious truths, but not a single error. Moreover, Hus urged, by the death of Alexander V., the authority entrusted to Zbinco for this prosecution had lapsed.

The university had meanwhile invoked the mediation of the King ; and at his intervention the Archbishop consented to postpone the execution of the sentence until the Margrave Jost should have come to Prague from Moravia. As, however, the arrival of the Margrave was delayed, Zbinco caused Wyclif's books to be burnt on the 16th July. This *auto-da-fé* was carried into effect in the court of the archiepiscopal palace on the Hradschin, in the presence of the Cathedral Chapter and a great multitude of priests. More than 200 MSS. were consumed, containing the works of Wyclif. Stress has been laid upon the fact that several of them were sumptuously bound. Yet only the smaller proportion of Wyclif's books which were to be found in Bohemia fell victims to the Archbishop's injunction; for, as is related by Stephen of Dolein, the Wyclifites publicly boasted that the Bishop had burnt indeed some very renowned books of Wyclif, but not all. "We still have most of them, and are collecting others from every quarter to transcribe and then possess them."

It is due to this bold resolve not to lose the works of Wyclif, which the Hussites at any rate highly valued, that we owe these Vienna codices.

The Oriel MS. has been in the possession of the College since A.D. 1454. The following extracts from the Treasurer's books have been kindly supplied me:—

1454. Feb. 14. Sol. pro uno libro operis Wyclyffe de dominio civili et blasfemia & ligatura certorum & cathenatione librorum vii^s vi^d

„ April 18. Sol. pro libro empto a Johanne More continente Armacanum Holkot & Wyclyff super sententias xlii^s

Of these volumes the former has slipped its 'chain,' the latter is the volume containing our treatise, for which the College paid 42*s.*—a large sum considering the value of money in those days.

IV. This description of the treatise of Wyclif as 'super sententias,' as also its place in a volume of treatises on the work of Peter the Lombard, indicate the point of view from which it must be regarded. It is a Scholastic treatise; it treats its subject from the Schoolmen's point of view; its method is that of the Schoolmen. It is necessary to bear this in mind, or readers will be disappointed or will fail to follow the author's argument. The doctrine of the Incarnation as expressed in the Catholic creeds is assumed; the author endeavours to establish to the reason this article of the faith. But he is not so much concerned with unbelievers as with what he considers the partial or inaccurate definitions of other 'modern doctors.' William of Occam (died A.D. 1349) had about the time of Wyclif's birth revived the great Nominalistic controversy. "Universals, said Occam, bear the same relation to the infinite number of individuals that signs do to the things signified. The universal, be it a thought or a word, is nothing but a sign which by *suppositio* is beforehand taken to denote a number of individual things, and is thus the common noun denoting them all." Now Wyclif was from the beginning to the end of his life a thorough Realist. In the unprinted treatises, *De Universalibus, De Ideis, De Materia et Forma*, he sets himself to prove and support the Realistic hypothesis. In our treatise he assumes it as proved and constantly (v. Index IV. Realism, Universals) inveighs against the 'doctores signorum,' 'non ponentes universalia praeter signa,' 'negantes universalia,' etc., although he nowhere quotes or names Occam. Indeed, the theory is necessary to his view of the Incarnation. The Word, Wyclif says, assumed Man, not the person of any individual of the species Man, nor yet abstract Humanity, but Man the 'res communis' by virtue of which the individual supposites are what they are; assumed Man as he is in the 'forma exemplaris,' in the Divine idea. Christ took on himself in the Incarnation the nature not of a man, or of many men, but the 'communis humanitas' of all men, so that he is at once 'communis homo' and 'unicus homo,' *The* Man (ch. xiii.). And lest this should seem to place 'the Man Christ Jesus' at a distance from his brethren 'the sons of men,' Wyclif constantly repeats that, to the Realist, it only brings Christ nearer, nay, identifies him with other men: for the 'forma' and the 'formatum,' the individual and the universal, are identical. Although he would not deny the extreme Realistic position 'universalia ante rem' in the sense of priority in thought and causation, 'universalia in re' is Wyclif's favourite formula. 'Every universal is identical with each and all of its supposites' (page 145, line 19). Therefore 'unica communis humanitas est quelibet persona hominis' (page 20, line 10), *i.e.* the one common Humanity is identical with any individual man: again (page 218, line 8) 'hic communis homo . . . est idem singularis homo, omnium hominum quilibet.' Christ is the 'homo communis,' the idea of Man; by the Incarnation he is objectively 'unicus homo' · he is 'eadem communis humanitas que est quilibet frater suus' (page 101, line 28). Certainly here was a brave and subtle effort to give to the understanding a reason for the faith that Christ is one with all his brethren. It is another conspicuous instance of our author's desire to fix his foundations deep and solid. He was not content with metaphorical expressions about membership in Christ; he essays to establish that union on a metaphysical necessity, and to bring it home to others as a logical sequence. Different minds will estimate differently the value of the attempt; and if few in our day can accept Wyclif's argument as a settlement of the question, no one who studies the treatise from the author's standpoint will fail to admit the power and subtlety of his reasoning. This identification of the Eternal Word with the idea of Man, and at the same time by reason of the metaphysical oneness of idea and reality, by reason also of the logical identity of universal and particular, the identification of Christ the Incarnate Word with each individual man, is the keystone of the treatise, and is, so far as I know, in this form peculiar to Wyclif. The Realistic position is essential to his argument and, even, as with much plausibility he asserts, to the very existence of catholic doctrine (page 144).

But Wyclif has more than a scholastic, more even than a theological interest, in vindicating the reality of Christ's humanity. At times his style glows, his heart seems to throb beneath the words, as he struggles to express the intensity of his conviction. The literal reality of Christ's human nature is a 'most precious jewel,' 'absoluta humanitas Christi illud jocale preciocissimum' (page 54, line 20), which he will not surrender. Hence his labour in Chapters i. ii. v. to establish as catholic truth that 'Christ is a creature': hence he argues that 'Christ did not cease in the three days and never can cease to be man,' in Chapters iii. iv. v. viii.: the Jesus of the Gospel narrative is the same yesterday, to-day, and for ever. Moreover, Christ and the Humanity of Christ are henceforth one never to be divided: this is the contention of Chapter x.: that Christ is man in the plain sense of the word 'man' is the gist of Chapter vi.: that he is liable to all the ills that flesh is heir to (mobilis) is the argument of part of Chapter vii. Wyclif will have no unreal, equivocal, histrionic humanity, not a God come down to us in the likeness of men, but our 'brother,'[1] 'univoce homo cum aliis hominibus,' 'frater cum fratribus suis,' living as we live, suffering, dying, being buried as other men. And the Evangelical Doctor often loses the stiffness of his Latin style, the scholastic fetters fall off him, and he rises into a real beauty and eloquence of expression when possessed by this thought, *e.g.* page 64, lines 24 seqq.; page 26, line 13; page 184, line 6. Yet with all his clinging to the humanity of Christ, Wyclif does not yield to any one in his assertion of the other side of the Catholic creed. Christ is three natures—Deitas, anima, corpus: two forms, God and Man. His doctrine of the Word is that of the orthodox Fathers and Schoolmen, but he brings into prominence the ideal and potential existence of all things in the Word (page 12, line 13). The Word is both Deity and all ideas, *i.e.* all the truth (page 113, line 21). This doctrine of the Realist doctor, as Lechler has shown, is based on St. John i. 4, according to the punctuation of the Vulgate: 'All that was made in Him was life;' and it is supported by the traditional identification of the

[1] 'The Christ of Aquinas is after all not our brother, not a man, but only a ghastly simulacrum.'—Bruce, Humiliation of Christ, p. 79.

'Word' of St. John with the 'Wisdom' of Proverbs and the Book of Wisdom, which our author enlarges upon, pp. 11, 12, and chapter vii.

But the treatise being obviously controversial, he does not dwell long on points like this, then generally admitted. He is controversial, but he is more concerned to establish positive truth than to establish or refute various negations rife in the schools. He can agree to most men's affirmations: their sweeping negations he may perhaps admit with limitations (page 13, line 10). He takes his stand on the plain literal meaning of Holy Scripture. The facts vouched for there are enough for him. Hence he is impatient of the numberless questions which arise out of hypotheses which the Schoolmen had propounded. The question as to the necessity of the Incarnation he does not directly handle; but, in contrast to the generality of the Schoolmen, he clearly would answer the question in the affirmative. Only through the Incarnation is the Divine Idea in Man realized. Peter Lombard had raised the question whether the Incarnation could have been accomplished by the Father or the Holy Spirit. Towards the end of the treatise Wyclif replies in the negative, Chapter xiii.

Likewise he shrinks from admitting with Aquinas the possibility of the Word assuming many humanities: to this he replies that in assuming the 'communis humanitas,' he assumed not one or many, but all humanities. He makes what seems to us unseemly mirth (page 65, line 10) over the Scotist hypothesis of the possibility of the assumption of a non-human animal nature.[1] In the concluding chapters xi. xii. xiii. he

[1] Lest any hasty modern reader should dub the Schoolman 'dunce' for such a thought, he may find in Wilberforce on the Incarnation, ed. iii. 1850, p. 209, the same hypothesis glanced at. "Had God been pleased to employ the organs of some inferior animal . . . for the expression of His will, such nature had not been susceptible of that personal union with Him which is set forth in the Incarnation of Christ." And near parallels to the Scholastic hypotheses and questions on this subject may, I believe, be found by the curious in the controversy which took place some forty years ago among the Christians commonly called 'Brethren' on the Very Humanity of Christ.

allows himself to handle some of these 'vermiculate questions,' but his general attitude is that of impatience with them. He wistfully regrets that the days are past 'ante Petrum Lombardum,' when men abstained from these futile hypotheses. He denies the wisdom, he even fears the sinfulness (page 228, line 15) of discussing them. Thus, although with one foot he stands in the Scholastic age, the other is seeking a resting place elsewhere. He has no patience with the puerile vanity, the love of novelty, the ambition, the manifold discordances of the 'moderns': he cares for reality, fact, truth. What God, in fact, has done, that alone is real, is possible, is true (page 228). God's word must be taken, and taken literally 'de vi vocis,' 'de virtute sermonis': the logic of Scripture transcends all other logic. First, What saith the Scripture? and, secondly, What is the 'concors sententia' (page 159), what is the voice of the Catholic Church in its interpretation? Listen to this rather than to the frivolous and swollen disputations of the 'novelli,' the new-fangled doctors. Thus we see in our author, while still only a disputant in the schools at Oxford, the germs of his future revolt from medieval routine. He leans upon the Bible (canonica) absolutely: next, St. Augustine as 'subtilissimus explanator' is made most use of. St. John of Damascus, St. Bonaventura, Hugo of St. Victor, are never questioned, but quoted as absolute authorities: but St. Thomas Aquinas may be mistaken (Chapter xiii.), Duns Scotus and the modern Doctors with their endlessly divergent hypotheses have not been free from sin (page 228), the Nominalists from Roscellinus downwards 'ille clericus in fide devius' (page 155) would render Christian faith impossible.

On the Eucharistic question there is the like nascent indication of the attitude which he afterwards took up. It is still *miraculosa transubstantiatio,* but Wyclif is not unaware of or unwilling (p. 186, l. 10) to recite the opinions of certain of the saints (quotlibet dicta sanctorum, p. 190, l. 25), which seem to mean (sonant), that even after consecration the bread and wine are bread and wine. He makes a praiseworthy effort (ll. 26-29) to explain their words away in what seems to him the orthodox sense, but gives up the attempt to define the Eucharistic change as unnecessary to a 'pilgrim's' faith.

It must be confessed that Wyclif's mind is as yet a strange medley: he uses the very methods which he condemns; he wanders into hypotheses where in the attempt to follow him one finds oneself 'moving about in worlds not realized,' and for me, at any rate, the attempt to analyse his meaning breaks down (*e.g.* Chapter xi. pp. 194-199): the width and variety of his knowledge tempts him to combine incongruous materials: Aristotle and Euclid, Averroës and Avicenna are brought to bear on a doctrine of revelation. He makes the hazardous claim that all Christian truth may be established on grounds of reason, even the miracles explained 'lumine naturali' (page 159), even the Catholic faith as to the Eucharist philosophically sustained by parallels from the natural sciences. In much of this treatise there is crudity and confusion; but yet there is also the germ of the revolt from medieval Rome, and the prophecy of the English Bible. The greater part of the treatise, now for the first time generally accessible, will continue to be unread: and those who follow his reasoning will come to the inevitable conclusion which we almost start to find that Wyclif himself had reached, that human thought and language are, after all, unequal to the task of dealing absolutely with such themes. Seldom has this sense of 'knowing only in part' been more boldly expressed than in these words of Wyclif (page 115, line 20), "Imo si non fallor omnis locucio nostra de Deo est figurativa—Non enim habemus nomina quae sine figura Deum signent." This is scarcely less distinct than two contemporary utterances with which I venture to conclude this subject. "The assumption of human nature by the Creator of it brings us to a point where conception absolutely fails—where the light of imagination goes out—where language moves without ideas—where all is lost in one vast and vague emotion of awe." (Archer Butler, Lectures on Ancient Philosophy, vol. i. p. 143.) And again,

"Our little systems have their day;
They have their day and cease to be:
They are but broken lights of Thee,
And Thou, O Lord, art more than they."
—Tennyson, *In Memoriam, Introduction.*

It is not then to be wondered at if Wyclif's treatise on the Incarnation leaves the reader unsatisfied. That he will rise from it without increased respect and liking for its author, I do not think possible: and to that end the labour spent upon this edition has been willingly bestowed. No critic will know better than myself how incompletely the work has been done. At a distance from libraries of reference, with other occupation which has left only occasional leisure for the work, and above all with knowledge insufficient for an adequate performance of my task, I have done what I could.

The zealous cooperation of Mr. Rudolph Beer, of Vienna, the readiness of Mr. F. D. Matthew to give me his continual assistance and highly skilled counsel, the patience and encouragement of Dr. Furnivall have made the task a pleasant one, and my hearty thanks are here tendered to them. To the Provost and Fellows of Oriel College for their exceptional indulgence in lending and prolonging the loan of their MS.; to Mr. R. S. Poole for several useful suggestions, and for a skilled opinion on the writing, etc., of the Oriel codex; to Dr. Herzbergfraenkel for his report on the Vienna Codices; and also to various private friends for loans of books and other assistance, I also desire to express sincere acknowledgments.

Parting with what has been the companion of my leisure for many a month, whilst I regret the many imperfections, of which I am conscious in the work, yet I do venture to hope that even as it is it may contribute something towards the truer appreciation of John Wyclif, and may even aid in what was the supreme purpose of his life—to win for himself and his race 'increase in the knowledge of God.'

8, Wellswood Park, Torquay,
*September* 9, 1886.

# CORRIGENDA.

| | | | |
|---|---|---|---|
| Page 8, line 25 | for *non est* | read *est non.* | |
| ,, 9, ,, 26 | ,, *Dicit, " deus* | ,, *dicit " Deus.* | |
| ,, 11, ,, 22 marg. | ,, 308 | ,, 3. 8. 9. | |
| ,, 14, ,, 2 | ,, *Dist.* 2ª | ,, *Dist* 11ª. | |
| ,, 15, ,, 20 marg. | ,, *John* xi. | ,, *John* x. | |
| ,, 21, ,, 17 | ,, *verbum* | ,, *Verbum.* | |
| ,, 28, ,, 8 | ,, *Christum ?* | ,, *Christum ?'* | |
| ,, 28, ,, 10 | ,, *Jeronimus* | ,, *Ieronimus.* | |
| ,, 32, ,, 13 marg. | ,, *Heb.* viii. | ,, *Heb.* vii. | |
| ,, 42, ,, 27 | add *unquam* after *Deus.* | | |
| ,, 48, ,, 29 | for *patre* | read *Patre.* | |
| ,, 64, note 6 | ,, *om.* | ,, *om. O.* | |
| ,, 74, line 15 marg. | add *John* v. 39. | | |
| ,, 74, ,, 25 marg. | for *John* v. 35 | ,, *John* x. 35. | |
| ,, 88, ,, 14 | ,, *Grossteste* | ,, *Grosseteste.* | |
| ,, 101, ,, 6 marg. | ,, 1 *Cor.* xv. | ,, 1 *Cor.* xiii. | |
| ,, 101, ,, 16 | ,, *affeccione* [*et*] *conglutinio quodam proprio,* read *affeccione conglutino, quodam proprio.* | | |
| ,, 107, ,, 17 | ,, *Physicorum : Ymaginatur motum* read *Physicorum ymaginatur : 'Motum.* | | |
| ,, 111, ,, 10 | ,, *illa illa* read *illa.* | | |
| ,, 111, ,, 29 | ,, *audacter, licet quod* read *audacter licet, quod.* | | |
| ,, 136, ,, 10 | dele , | | |
| ,, 163, ,, 10 | for *ad* read *aliud* | | |
| ,, 167, ,, 9 | ,, *esset ? Unde* read *esset, unde.* | | |
| ,, 190, ,, 30 | ,, *accidenta. Illa* ,, *accidentata ; illa.* | | |

"*Fateor quod propter altitudinem materiae ignoro plurimum; sed credo quod in patria videbo clare sententiam quam modo balbutio.*"—Wyclif, *Trialogus*, page 61.

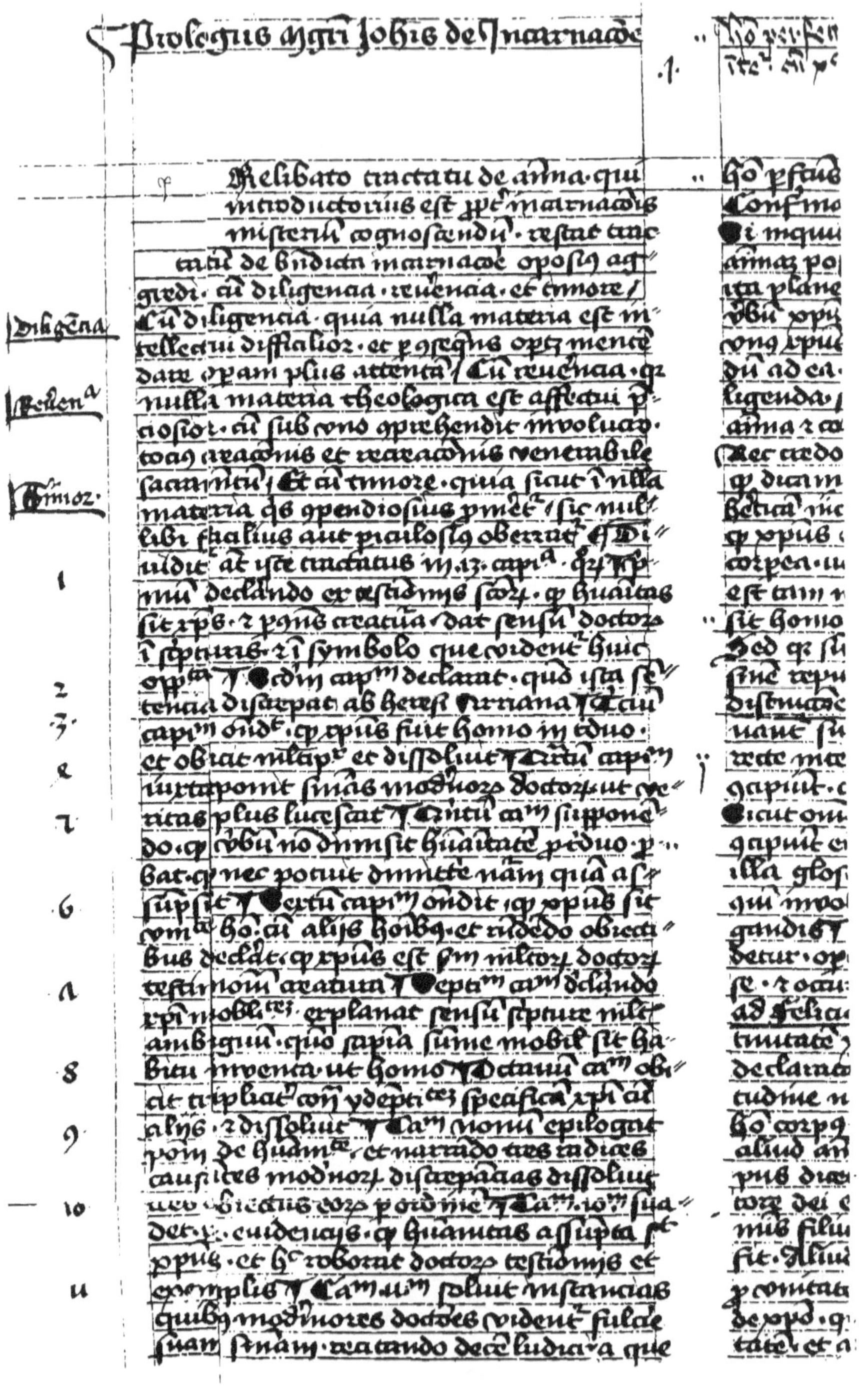

Photolith M. JAFFE Vienna.

Wyclifs De Incarnatione Verbi
Imperial Library Vienna. Ms. 1387 Fol. 15 a.

# Johannis Wyclif

## Tractatus de Benedicta Incarnacione.

---

[A 75a]
[B 115a]
[C 37a]
[O 217a]

### Prologus.

The treatise *De Anima* has prepared the way for the present treatise (cf. infra, p. 7, line 21).

The Incarnation requires to be treated with careful attention because of its difficulty; with reverence as an all-embracing mystery; and with awe as involving risk of dangerous error.

Prelibato[1] tractatu *De Anima* qui introductorius est propter incarnacionis misterium[2] cognoscendum, restat tractatum *De Benedicta Incarnacione* operosius aggredi cum diligencia,[3] reverencia, et timore. Cum diligencia,[3] quia nulla materia est intellectui difficilior, et per consequens oportet mentem dare operam plus attentam: cum reverencia, quia nulla[4] materia theologica est affectui preciosior, cum sub uno comprehendit involucro tocius creacionis[5] et recreacionis venerabile sacramentum: et cum timore, quia, sicut in nulla materia quis compendiosius promeretur, sic nullibi facilius aut periculosius aberratur.[6]

It consists of 13 chapters.

Dividitur autem tractatus iste[7] in[8] 13 capitula.

i. The statement that Christ is Man and therefore a creature, is not contrary to Holy Scripture nor to the Creed.

Quorum primum, declarando ex testimoniis sanctorum quod humanitas sit Christus et per consequens creatura, dat sensum dictorum[9] in scripturis et in[10] symbolo[11] que videntur huic opposita.

ii. Nor identical with the Arian heresy.

Secundum capitulum[12] declarat quomodo ista sentencia discrepat ab heresi Arriana.

iii. Christ really Man in the 'three days' between his death and resurrection.

Tertium capitulum ostendit quod Christus fuit homo in triduo et obicit multipliciter et dissolvit.

*Prologus.* Codex A. *habet colore rubro superscriptum:* Prologus magistri Johannis de incarnacione.
Codex B. Incipit tractatus de incarnacione Mgi. Jo. Wykleph. Prologus.
Codex C. *manu recentiore:* De Benedicta Incarnatione Jo. Wielif.
Codex O. *in ipso textu nullum titulum habet, sed in exteriore angulo ad summum uniuscujusque folii haec addita sunt:* W. de incarnacione V'bi.

[1] *Litera initialis* (P) *om.* A B C. [2] mesterium O. [3] dilligencia B. [4] nulla *om.* O. [5] creacionis *om.* O. [6] oberratur A B C. [7] ille C. [8] in *om.* O. [9] doctorum A B C. [10] in *om.* O C. [11] simbolo O. [12] capitolum A B C *ut fere semper.*

iv. The opinions of modern doctors; Bonaventura, Duns Scotus, Thomas Aquinas, Anselmus.

Quartum capitulum iuxta ponit sentencias modernorum doctorum, ut veritas plus lucescat.

v. The Word did not and could not lay aside the human nature in the three days.

Quintum capitulum, supponendo quod Verbum non dimisit humanitatem pro triduo, probat[1] quod nec potuit dimittere naturam quam assumpsit.

vi. Christ is Man in the simple sense of the word *man*: and a creature.

Sextum capitulum ostendit quod Christus sit univoce homo cum aliis hominibus;[2] et respondendo objectibus[3] declarat quod Christus est, secundum multorum doctorum[4] testimonia,[5] creatura.

vii. Discussion of Wisdom vii. 24, with its bearing on the Incarnation.

Septimum capitulum declarando Christi mobilitatem explanat sensum scripture multis ambiguum,[6] quomodo sapiencia summe mobilis[7] sit habitu inventa ut homo.

viii. Three objections to the position of c. vi. refuted.

Capitulum octavum obicit tripliciter contra ydemptitatem specificam[8] Christi cum aliis et[9] dissolvit.

ix. Restates Wyclif's position and accounts for modern divergence of opinion.

Capitulum nonum epilogat posicionem de humanitate; et,[10] narrando tres radices causantes modernorum discrepancias, dissolvit tres objectus eorum per[11] ordinem.

x. Twelve proofs that the assumed humanity is Christ, with confirmatory authorities.

Capitulum decimum suadet[12] 12 evidenciis quod humanitas assumpta sit Christus; et hoc[13] roborat doctorum testimoniis et exemplis.

xi. Modern objections (Duns Scotus) lead to impossible conclusions.

Capitulum undecimum solvit instancias quibus moderniores doctores videntur fulcire suam sentenciam, recitando decem ludicra que concedentes possibilitatem dimissionis annuunt consequenter.

xii. In what sense Christ took Man's nature upon him:

Capitulum duodecimum recitando opiniones varias de assumpcione creature declarat quod, si assumeret multas humanitates, foret[14] multi homines, sicut dictat sentencia sancti Thome.

xiii. Not a man's or many men's, but all men's. This statement reconciles divergences, and is the teaching of Holy Scripture and of the Church, and the truth about the Incarnation.

Capitulum tredecimum confirmat [15]aliorum sentencias quod[15] tunc nec foret unus homo nec multi homines, sed[16] et unicus atque multi; et sic concordat modernorum sentencias cum antiquis.[17]

[1] probat *om.* O. [2] hominibus *om.* O. [3] objectionibus O. [4] doctorum *om.* C. [5] testimonium A B. [6] ambigue O. [7] mobilis *om.* C. [8] specificam *om.* C. [9] ac O. [10] ut C. [11] in O. [12] swadet B C. [13] hoc *om.* B O. [14] forent A B. *altera manu* C. [15-15] dicta aliorum quod A B C. [16] set O, *et sic saepe.* [17] Cod. A. *addit haec rubro colore*: Explicit prologus. Incipit de incarnacione capitolum primum.

## Cap. I.

[*Declarando ex testimoniis sanctorum quod humanitas sit Christus et per consequens creatura, dat sensum dictorum in scripturis et in symbolo que videntur huic opposita.*

*Discussion as to the sense in which it is catholic truth to say: Christ is a creature.*]

[C 37b] Quia autem spiritualiter viantibus in discendo necesse est primo removere prohibens disciplinam; ac in scriptura sacra et [1]sacris doctoribus de Christo[1] sunt multa scripta[2] que videntur inperitis contraria; ideo pro solucione eorum in primis supponitur[3] quod Christus sit tres nature incommunicantes: scilicet, deitas, corpus, et anima. Patet sic. Christus est Deus et homo perfectus, ut ex fide supponitur: omnis [A 75b] Deus est deitas: omnis | homo perfectus est tam corpus quam anima: ergo conclusio. Confirmatur per Augustinum super Ioh. Omc. 47.[4] 'Si, inquit, caro animam posuit, quomodo Christus animam posuit? numquid[5] caro Christus?' Et respondet: 'Ita plane et caro Christus et anima Christus et Verbum Christus: nec tamen hec tria[6] tres Christi, sed unus Christus. Hominem interroga et de eo fac gradum[7] ad ea que super te sunt, et[8] si nondum intelligenda, saltem credenda. Quomodo enim unus homo anima et corpus? sic unus Christus Verbum et homo.' Nec credo quod nos ignari ad tantum desipimus quod dicamus hunc sanctum tam crebro sentenciam hereticam inculcare.

The difficulties which arise from apparent contradictions in Holy Scripture concerning Christ may be removed by remembering that the Person of Christ is twofold. He is God and Man: and Man consisting of body and soul, there are in Christ three 'natures': Godhead, body, and soul; as St. Augustine often teaches.

Ex istis plane[9] sequitur quod Christus est creatura. Nam omnis natura corporea vel spiritus creatus est creatura: Christus est tam natura corporea quam spiritus creatus, cum sit homo perfectus: ergo Christus est creatura. Sed quia sunt multe scripture que videntur isti sentencie repugnare, ut recitat Magister 3° Sentenciarum Dist. 2ª, ideo ut omnes communiter[10] dissolvantur[11] sub uno epilogo; dicitur quod omnes recte intelligentes Christum non esse creaturam

Christ, being perfect man with body and soul, is a creature.

Peter Lombard fixes the sense in which Christ is a creature: not in his divine

[1] et sacris doctoribus de Christo *om.* A B C. [2] scriptura O. [3] supponi oportet A B C. [4] 4 A B C; 41 O. [5] numquam C. [6] tria hec O. [7] gaudium, B; gradum fac C; gratiam O. [8] et si dum non O. [9] palam O. [10] consequenter B. [11] dissolva- *ad finem lineae* -tur *om.* O.

concipiunt quod Christus secundum deitatem non est creatura: sicut omnes recte concipientes[1] Christum esse creaturam concipiunt eum secundum humanitatem esse creaturam. Et ista[2] glosa, si non fallor, satisfacit sub communi involucro omnibus auctoribus in oppositum allegandis.

*but in his human nature:*

Sed ut illa[3] materia particularius denudetur, oportet primo fundare sentenciam huius glose. Et occurrit michi[4] primo disputacio Augustini ad Felicianum hereticum; ubi post duplicem nativitatem Christi et duplicem eius substanciam vel naturam declaratam tam ex scriptura sacra quam similitudine naturali, sic[5] ait inter cetera: 'Non[6] alius homo corpus, alius animus, quamvis aliud corpus, aliud animus; unus tamen atque idem homo et corpus dicitur et animus. Sic, inquit, in mediatore[7] Dei et hominum: aliud Dei filius, aliud hominis filius, unus tamen Christus Iesus ex utroque fit: aliud, inquam, pro discrecione[8] substancie, non[6] alius pro unitate | persone.' Et per hoc solvit scripturas de Christo,[9] [B 115b] quarum alique locuntur de ipso secundum deitatem et alie secundum humanitatem. Et posiciones[10] secundum habitudinem[11] concedit simpliciter; unde subdit: 'nec ideo dicimus non pacientem quia ipse faciebat celos,[12] nec ideo non facientem quia non alius tollerabat. Nam si dominice incarnacionis misterium consideremus,[13] idem sibi in hac humilitate et auctor[14] et opus | est.' Unde et post declaratur esse possibile [C 38a] quod eadem | persona simul et semel sed secundum diversam [O 217b] naturam mortem paciatur et vivat, sicut idem sol secundum diversos situs simul tempore diem causat et noctem.

*and so St. Augustine*

*explains apparent discrepancies in Holy Scripture.*

Secundum testimonium Augustini est in Ep. 12[15] ad Pascencium et in Epistula 40 ad Dardanum ubi cap. 7° ita inquit: 'Cum enim Christus sit Deus et homo, Deus utique est; unde dicit: "Ego et Pater unum sumus" Ioh. 10: homo autem; unde dicit: "Pater maior me est," Ioh. 14: idemque Filius Dei unigenitus a Patre, et filius hominis ex semine David[16] secundum carnem est. Utrumque in illo consideran-

*e.g. John x. 30, 'I and my Father are one,' compared with John xiv. 28, 'My Father is greater than I.'*

[1] concedentes O. [2] illa A B C; 'ille' *et* 'iste' *variantur saepissime in codd.*
[3] in ista O. [4] michi *om.* O. [5] sicut B. [6] est *add.* B. [7] meditatore O.
[8] distinccione O. [9] de Christo *om.* O. [10] ꝑpcones A; ꝑciones B; ꝑ̈ces C.
[11] predicaciones secundum humanitatem O. [12] celos *om.* C O. [13] consideres A B C.
[14] autor B. [15] 125 O M. [16] davit O.

dum est cum loquimur vel cum scriptura de ipso loqui- [A 75c] tur: et quid et[1] secundum quid | de illo dicitur intuendum est. Nam sicut unus homo est anima rationalis[2] et caro, sic unus Christus est Verbum et homo. Proinde quod ad Verbum attinet, creator est Christus; "omnia enim per ipsum facta sunt;" quod vero[3] ad hominem attinet, Christus creatus est; "factus enim est[4] ex semine David secundum carnem," et "in similitudinem hominum[5] factus est."' Et post diffuse prosequitur declarando que scripture sibi conveniunt secundum deitatem et que secundum humanitatem.

*Christ as the Word is Creator; John i. 3, as man is created. Rom. i. 3. Phil. ii. 7.*

Nec est maior color quod sit creator quia secundum deitatem, quin per idem sit creatura quia secundum humanitatem, specialiter cum sit illa completa humanitas. Quia certum est ex testimonio[6] Augustini ad Felicianum quod totus homo assumptus passus est mortem, sicut sola caro iacuit in sepulcro, ut testatur Augustinus Omc. 47 ubi super: '[7]Confiteris, inquit, in illum[7] Christum credere qui est mortuus et sepultus: ergo et sepultum esse Christum non negas. Et tamen sola caro sepulta est: si enim erat ibi anima, non erat mortuus: si autem vera mors erat, ut vera sit eius resurreccio,[8] sine anima erat in sepulcro, et tamen sepultus est Christus. Ergo Christus erat etiam sine anima caro, quia non erat sepulta nisi caro.' Unde paulo ante ipse Christus dictus est sola caro. [9]'Quomodo, inquit, probas? Audeo dicere: sola caro[9] Christi dictus est Christus;' et probatur[10] per hoc, quod Christus iacuit in sepulcro.[11]

*Christ is as truly creature in his human nature, as he is creator in his divine nature.*

*St. Augustine urges that in saying 'Christ was buried' we mean Christ in his bodily nature only.*

*Much more, therefore, may we use the term Christ for his complete humanity of body and soul.*

Tercium testimonium Augustini est Omc. 8. super illud Ioh. 2°. 'Quid michi et tibi, mulier? nondum venit hora mea.' 'Dominus,[12] inquit, Iesus Christus Deus erat et homo: secundum quod Deus erat,[13] matrem non habebat: secundum quod homo erat, matrem habebat. Mater ergo erat carnis, mater humanitatis, mater infirmitatis quam suscepit propter nos. Miraculum autem quod facturus erat

*Augustine discussing John ii. 4, 'Woman, what have I to do with thee? mine hour is not yet come.'*

[1] et *add.* M. [2] ratio O. [3] enim O. [4] enim est *om.* A B C. [5] hominis O. [6] testimoniis A B C. [7-7] confitens, inquit, unum A B C. [8] resureccio O. [9-9] quomodo . . . caro *om.* O. [10] probatur *om.* A B C. [11] sepulchro B. [12] deus A B C. [13] deus erat erat et homo C.

[1]secundum deitatem facturus erat et[1] non secundum infirmitatem;[2] secundum quod Deus erat, non secundum quod in- 1 Cor. i. 25. firmus natus erat: sed "infirmum[3] Dei forcius hominibus." Miraculum autem[4] exigebat mater: at[5] ille tanquam non

draws out the distinction between acts of Christ in his divine, and acts in his human, nature.

cognosceret[6] viscera humana operaturus facta divina, tanquam diceret; "quod de me fecit miraculum non tu[7] genuisti: sed quia | tu[8] genuisti infirmitatem meam, tunc te[9] [C 38b] cognoscam, cum ipsa infirmitas pendebit in cruce:" hoc est enim, "nondum venit hora mea." Unde et commemorans illam nominacionem extraneam "mulierem" qua[10] vocavit matrem in nupciis Galilee, pendens in cruce dixit matri: John xix. 26. "Mulier, ecce filius tuus!" Ioh. 19. Non quod Christus aliquando non cognoscit matrem; in predestinacione, inquit Augustinus, noverat matrem, eciam[11] antequam ipse Deus eam crearet, de qua ipse homo crearetur: tunc tamen in effectu[12] agnovit, quando illud quod peperit moriebatur.[13] [14]Non enim moriebatur per quod facta erat Maria, sed moriebatur[15] quod factum erat ex Maria:[14] non moriebatur eternitas divinitatis, sed moriebatur infirmitas carnis: filius itaque virginis secundum quod creator celi et terre et dominus mundi creator fuit Marie, Deus[16] fuit Marie; secundum Gal. iv. 4. autem quod dictum est "factum ex muliere, factum sub lege:" ipse enim[17] dominus Marie est filius Marie; ipse creator Marie creatus ex Maria. Noli mirari: nam ideo David est filius, quia Marie est filius. Audi apostolum Rom. i. 3. dicentem "qui factus est ei[18] ex semine | David secundum [A 75d] Ps. cx. 1. carnem": audi eum et dominum David, 'dixit dominus [Acts ii. 34.] domino[19] meo: "sede a dextris meis." Unde[19] et ipse Iesus[20] Matt. xxii. 42-45. hoc proposuit Iudeis et eos inde convicit.'

Et isti regule innititur Augustinus utrobique, ut in libris contra Maximinianum; sicut Ieronimus in Epistula ad Paulam

[1]-[1] *om.* A B C. [2] sed secundum A B C. [3] infirmius B. [4] autem *om.* A B.
[5] ac C. [6] agnosceret A B C; cognoscit O. [7] tu *om.* O. [8] tunc B.
[9] te *om.* A B C. [10] mulieris quam O; mulierem quia B. [11] et A B C.
[12] affectu A B C. [13] mirabatur A B C.
[14]-[14] Non enim moriebatur per factum erat ex Maria A B; non enim moriebatur per quod factum erat ex Maria C. [15] per *add.* O. [16] dominus O.
[17] idem O. [18] ei *om.* O. [19]-[19] domino etc. Unde B. [20] Christus O.

et Eustochium, et alii probabiles doctores. Unde libro primo contra Maximinianum sic loquitur Augustinus: 'Dicis B 116a] Patrem in|factum quasi Filius factus sit, per quem facta sunt omnia. Scito factum esse Filium sed [1] in forma servi, qui in forma [1] Dei usque adeo non est factus, ut per illum facta sunt omnia.' Unde et [2] infra 2° dicit quod Deus Pater non creatorem creavit, sed creatorem [3] constituit iuxta illud Ps<sup>l.</sup> 8<sup>l.</sup> quod [4] secundum apostolum et secundum Augustinum [4] ad litteram verificatur de Christo: 'minuisti eum [5] paulo minus ab angelis, gloria et honore coronasti eum, Domine,[6] et constituisti eum super opera manuum tuarum: omnia subiecisti sub pedibus.[7]'

St. Augustine elsewhere, as well as St. Jerome and other authorities, maintain this distinction.

Ps. viii. 5, 6. Heb. ii. 7.

Nec dubium quin ex principiis beati Augustini plane sequitur Christum esse creaturam. Quia iuxta suam infringibilem sentenciam Christus nedum est completa humanitas assumpta, sed tam corpus quam anima. Et quis dubitat de ista sequela? Christus est corpus creatum sicut et [8] spiritus creatus. Ergo Christus est creatura et secundum illam creatus. Nec aliter esset univoce homo nobiscum: [9] cum omnis alius homo sit duarum naturarum utraque. Nec credo sine [alta] [10] illa philosophia *De Anima* nos posse recte concipere incarnacionem Verbi. Ideo Augustinus [11] Epistula 3ª ad Volusianum sic loquitur: 'Nunc vero inter Deum et homines mediator apparuit ut in unitate [12] persone [13] copulans utramque naturam et solita [13] sublimaret insolitis et insolita solitis temperaret. . . . [14] Ille ergo sine seminibus operatus est hominem, qui in rerum natura sine seminibus operatus [C 39a] est semina.[14] Ille in suo corpore numeros temporum | mensurasque servavit etatum qui sine ulla [15] mutabilitate mutando ordinem contexuit seculorum.[16] Hoc [17] enim crevit in [18]

Christ then being perfect man, is created body and created spirit, which, in the *De Anima*, are shown to constitute man: and to this St. Augustine gives confirmation.

[1] informam servi qui formam Dei O. [2] et *om.* O. [3] creaturam A B C.
[4]-[4] servi appellacionem (applm̄) Augustinus ad O. [5] eum *om.* O. [6] domine *om.* O.
[7] petibus O. [8] sed et C. [9] cum aliis hominibus A B C.
[10] sine "alta" philosophia *in marg.* illa *man. pr.* A; sine alta 1ª philosophia B; sine 1ª philosophia C O; *an* prima *legendum*? [11] Augustinus *om.* O. [12] unitatem O.
[13]-[13] copulaus utraque et solita A B C; copulam utramque naturam solita O.
[14]-[14] Ille ergo sine seminibus temperatus est semina A B C.
[15] ista A B C; illa O; ulla *Aug. ut sensus poscit.*
[16] seclorum O. [17] homo O. [18] ex B (with mark above).

tempore quod cepit ex tempore: Verbum autem in principio, per quod facta sunt omnia tempora, tempus elegit quo susciperet carnem, non tempori[1] cessit ut verteretur in carnem: homo quippe Deo accessit, non Deus a se recessit.' Et sequitur ad propositum. 'Sic autem quidam[2] reddi sibi | [O 217c] racionem flagitant, quomodo Deus homini permixtus sit, ut una fieret persona Christi, cum hoc[3] semel fieri oporteat. Sed quam racionem reddant ipsi de re quae cotidie[4] fit, quomodo anima misceatur corpori ut una persona fiat hominis? Nam sicut in unitate[5] persone anima unitur corpori ut homo sit, ita in unitate[6] persone Deus unitur[6] homini ut Christus[7] sit. In illa ergo persona mixtura est anime et corporis, in hac persona[8] mixtura est Dei et hominis. Si tamen recedat, [9]auditor a consuetudine corporum qua[9] solent duo liquores ita misceri ut neutrum servet suam integritatem.' Et sequitur. 'Quia ergo non oportebat ut in plenitudine temporis novum faceret[10] mundum, nova[11] fecit in mundo. Homo enim de virgine procreatus et a mortuis in eternam vitam resuscitatus et super celos exaltatus potencius[12] fortasse opus[13] est quam mundus.' Quotlibet[14] sunt talia dicta hujus boni hominis, ex quibus aperiri[15] potest sensus scripture loquentis vario de ipso[16] | [A 76a] et controversia doctorum sequencium concordari.[17]

And this is the doctrine of the Athanasian Creed;

Et patet quod in simbolo Athanasii quando dicitur 'Filius a Patre solo non est factus nec creatus sed genitus' loquitur de eo pure secundum deitatem.[18] Aliter enim contradiceret sibi ipsi, cum secundum humanitatem conceptus est a tota Trinitate ex substancia matris: ut dicit idem simbolum quando post introducit Christi incarnacionem secundum quam dicit verissime quod Christus est minor patre.

Et idem patet in alio simbolo ecclesie; ubi primo loquens

[1] tēpalī O. [2] quidam *om.* B. [3] hoc *om.* O. [4] quotidie A B; cottidie C.
[5] unitatem A C. [6] unitatur O. [7] deus B. [8] persona *om.* A B C.
[9] auditor a consuedudine corporum quomodo A; auditor a consbbetutine corporum quomodo B; audito a⁹fne^ue q^a O.; qua *Aug.* [10] fieret A B C.
[11] novam C. [12] competencius A B. [13] omnipotens A B C.
[14] quota O. [15] apparere A B C. [16] Christo A B C.
[17] concordare O. [18] divinitatem A B C.

de eo secundum quod Deus est vere dicit 'genitum non factum, consubstancialem Patri per quem omnia facta sunt.' Sed post loquendo de Christo ut homine dicit quod 'incarnatus est de Spiritu Sancto ex Maria virgine et homo factus est.' Ideo in talibus attendendum est ad regulam beati Augustini 'quid et secundum quam naturam de Christo dicitur:' et facile videtur quotquot auctoritates occurrerint[1] concordare. Cum enim sit Christus multorum singulum, sicut essencia divina, species humana, vel aliud universale; patet quia, sicut non repugnat Deum esse genitum et eundem Deum esse ingenitum, sic non repugnat eundem Christum esse creatorem et tamen ex tempore esse creatum.

*and of the Nicene Creed.*

*We must hold then the diversity of natures, but no less*

Sed oportet in istis diversas[2] naturas subintelligere[3] cum ydemptitate persone. Unde in primitiva ecclesia quando Christi divinitas fuit minus cognita,[4] ordinaverunt apostoli [C 39b] quod fideles baptizarentur | in nomine domini Iesu Christi, ut patet Actuum 8. ut vel sic Christiani elevarentur in animo[5] ad credendum Christum esse supremam naturam possibilem[6] scilicet deitatem. Sed postquam sancti doctores ecclesie ut Augustinus, Ieronimus et ceteri cultores assidui scripturarum intellexerunt quod Christus fuit gigas gemine substancie, scilicet[7] tam divina substancia quam humana, concesserunt copulative Christum esse tam creatorem quam[8] creaturam.

*the unity of Person in Christ.*

*Acts viii. 16, 37.*

*This explicit statement as to the Person of Christ gradually attained after the first age of the Church.*

Unde beatus Ieronimus in fine primi libri super Epistolam ad Galat,[9] 'Quia semel,[10] inquit, ad nomen creature venimus et sapiencia in Proverbiis Salomonis Dicit, "deus creavit me[11] in inicio viarum suarum antequam quidquam[12] faceret, [B 116b] a principio ab eterno | ordinata sum,[13] et ab antiquis antequam terra fieret"; multique timore ne Christum creaturam dicere compellantur,[14] totum Christi misterium negant, ut dicant non Christum in hac sapiencia [15]sed mundi sapienciam significari:[15] nos libere proclamamus non esse periculum cum

*St. Jerome plainly calls Christ a creature:*

*Prov. viii. 22.*

*identifying Christ with Wisdom whom God created.*

[1] occurrerunt A B C. [2] diversitas O. [3] sub *om.* A B C.
[4] nimis incognita O. [5] anima O. [6] possibile O.
[7] scilicet *om.* O. [8] quam eciam O. [9] galath. O; Gall. A B C.
[10] solum A B C. [11] me *om.* O; in *om.* A B C. [12] quitquam C; quicquam O.
[13] sunt C. [14] ne Christum eere compellantur B; appellantur O.
[15-15] sed mundum per sapienciam signari A B C.

dicere[1] creaturam, [2]quem verum esse hominem[2] et crucifixum et maledictum tota spei nostre reverencia profitemur."

And yet St. Jerome does not confuse this creation with the eternal generation of the Son, as do the Arians: for creation is making out of nothing;

Nec credo quod sanctus iste intellexit Christum esse creaturam sub racione qua eternaliter genitus; propter tria. Primo quia tunc concederet[3] Christum eciam secundum deitatem esse creaturam; et cum creatura dicitur abstractive, sicut substancia vel essencia, tunc Christus esset alia substancia vel essencia quam Pater; quod est heresis Arriana. Et ad tantum non licet catholico laxare terminos, cum omnis creatura secundum Augustinum in Dialogo ad Felicianum et in De Questionibus[4] Veteris et Nove Legis 122, sit de nichilo facta essencia. Sed constat quod Christus secundum deitatem non est factus ex nichilo; ergo nec secundum deitatem est creatura. Non est ergo de intencione huius sancti et profundi doctoris baptizare et[5] tam extraneare[6] a scriptura significacionem huius nominis 'creatura.'

nor did he doubt that Christ was of the substance of the Father (adintra) begotten before the worlds (eternaliter): only this does not refer to his humanity, nor interfere

Secundo movet me causa quam beatus Ieronimus innuit. | [A 76b] Videtur enim loqui de fidelibus sui temporis negantibus [7]adverbia scripturarum loquencium[7] de Christo secundum humanitatem. Sed quis queso fidelium trepidaret concedere[8] Christum esse genitum[9] eternaliter de Patre? cum puri philosophi diu ante incarnacionem hoc professi sunt, ut declaravi[10] in tractatu *De Trinitate*.[11] Non ergo timebat concedere Christum [12]esse genitum vel genitum[12] eternaliter adintra; sed non secundum hominem assumptum et[13] racione cuius concedimus de Christo predicata et gesta hominum ut sanctus doctor exemplificat et clarebit posterius.[14] Unde evidencia Ieronimi est quod concedendum est Christum esse creaturam eo quod concedimus ipsum verum[15] esse

[1] esse A B C.
[2] quem verum est et hominem A B; quod verum esse hominem C; quem verbum esse et hominem O.
[3] concederem A B C.
[4] in de q. veteris A B; in de veteris C; in questionibus veteris O.
[5] et *om.* A B C.
[6] extrance A B C; extranie O.
[7] ad verba scripturam loquentem A B C; adverbia scripturam loquentem O.
[8] contendere O.
[9] non *add. in marg.* A.
[10] declarat O.
[11] eternitate B.
[12-12] esse genituram vel genitum A B C; genitum vel genitura O.
[13] esse O; et M; et *om.* A B C.
[14] post A B C.
[15] concedimus esse vermem hominem A B C; concedimus ipsam esse v$^{m}$ ē hominem O.

hominem et cetera huiusmodi que humanitatem concernunt.

Tercio movet me quod nec iste sanctus sapiens nec scriptura alia canonica, si non fallor, alicubi[1] accipit creari[2] pro gignicione eterna. Supposito ergo quod scriptura tam Salomonis quam Ecclesiastica loquatur de sapiencia increata que est Verbum Dei, ut testatur Ieronimus, et beatus Augustinus [C 40a] Ep 31 declarat | ex textu Proverbiorum 8 et 30 quod intencionis Salomonis est dicere, quod Deus habet Filium sapienciam increatam: patet quod de ipsa loquitur nunc secundum O 217d] deitatem ut eternaliter adintra | genita non creata, et nunc ut creata vel creanda: ut nunc dicit secundum deitatem, 'cum eo eram cuncta componens,' et nunc 'ab eterno ordinata sum:' primum ad deitatem sapiencie referens, et secundum ad eius humanitatem, ut patet Proverbiorum 8. Unde de eius humanitate dicit infra 30.[3] 'Quis ascendit in celum atque descendit etc?[4] Quod nomen eius aut quod nomen filii eius, si nosti?' Et isti sensui alludit Apostolus secundum exposicionem Augustini ad Eph.[5] 4, quando[6] dicit: 'qui descendit ipse est qui et ascendit super omnes celos.'

Et istum sensum[7] declarat Ecclesiasticus 24 cap. loquens de eadem sapiencia: primo sic: 'ego ex ore altissimi prodii primogenita ante omnem creaturam,' et sic[8] de multis que conveniunt divinitati. Sed post prosequitur quoad eius humanitatem: 'tunc precepit et dixit mihi creator omnium, et qui creavit me requievit in tabernaculo[9] meo:' dixit, inquam, in plenitudine temporis quando misit me incarnandam; iuxta[10] illud Psalmi 31 iuxta exposicionem Apostoli ad Hebre. 10. 'holocaustum et propeccato non postulasti; tunc dixi, ecce venio' scilicet incarnandus; et sic deitas creavit me secundum essenciam corpoream ante omnia secula: que quidem essencia transivit honorata[11] a patribus veteris testamenti nunc in gentibus et nunc in patribus, ut patet

with its reality.

Creation nowhere confused in Holy Scripture with eternal generation.

'Wisdom' in Proverbs and Ecclesiasticus is twofold:

(a) The uncreated wisdom or the Word;

Prov. viii. 22. which should become incarnate:

(b) The created wisdom of Christ's humanity

Prov. xxx. 4, 5. as explained by St. Paul. Eph. iv. 9.

This twofold reference also in Ecclesiasticus xxiv. 30s.

(a) The uncreated Divine wisdom:

(b) The wisdom Incarnate in the fulness of time:

to which also applies Ps. xl. 6. as explained in Heb. x. 5, 6.

[1] alicubi *om.* A B C. [2] creari *om.* O. [3] 30 *om.* C. [4] et A B C.
[5] epheseos O. [6] qui O. [7] sensum *om.* A B C. [8] cetera A B.
[9] thabernaculo A *ut infra saepius.* [10] sed B. [11] transit onerata O.

*The hypostatic union in the Incarnation fulfilled these prophecies.*

alibi. Sed in plenitudine temporis quando erectum est tabernaculum ex carne assumpta de beata virgine et forma humanitatis copulata ypostatice, tunc requievit tota Trinitas in assumpto corpore iuxta illud Colos. 2.[1] 'In ipso, inquit Apostolus, habitat omnis plenitudo divinitatis corporaliter.' Nam tota Trinitas est eadem divina essencia que est Christus existens illud corpus. Unde et illud tabernaculum figuratum est per quelibet tabernacula veteris testamenti. Et ad istum sensum[2] loquitur apostolorum capitaneus de corpore quod est ipse: 'iustum, inquit, arbitror quamdiu sum[3] in hoc tabernaculo suscitare vos in commonicione, | certus quod velox est [B 117a] deposicio tabernaculi mei.' 2 Petri 1° capitulo.

*Col. ii. 9.*

*In him, in the tabernacle of his human body, dwelleth all the fulness of the Godhead.*

*2 Pet. i. 13.*

Sic ergo, intelligendo[4] per sapienciam Verbum Dei quod est tam deitas[5] quam raciones quotlibet exemplares | et per con- [A 76c] sequens veritates, quae [6]terminant creatam sapienciam[6] obiective, ac ultimo ipsa sapiencia incarnata; [7]possunt dicta in libris Sapienciae[8] optime verificari ad litteram de eadem sapiencia incarnata:[7] ut testantur Augustinus et Ieronimus duo[9] non parvi pugiles scripturarum.

*Wisdom then is the Word of God: i.e. 1. Deity. 2. The idea of created wisdom really existing (in the Logos). 3. Wisdom incarnate in Christ.*

Tercio autem, declinante scola ab antiqua logica[10] de universalibus et a recta metaphisica[11] de formis substancialibus, negarunt doctores moderniores concorditer quod homo est anima, vel Christus humanitas, et[12] consequenter quod Christus est creatura, intelligentes autonomatice[13] Christum solum secundum excellentissimum | quod est Christus; et sic [C 40b] licet verum concipiant, multum tamen degenerant a logica scripturarum.

*The want of precision in language which makes men shrink from saying 'Christ is a creature,' arises from bad 'logic': i.e. from giving up the true doctrine of 'universals.'*

Ego autem finaliter[14] concordo cum quocunque catholice loquente in illa materia, concedens cum fidelibus primitive ecclesie quod Christus est purissimus homo possibilis: verumtamen non pure[15] vel tantum est homo, cum sit assumpta

*So to sum up, 1. Christ is very Man, according to the doctrine of the primitive church;*

[1] colocf. in C; coloc°. ¶ 2°. in O. [2] sensum *om.* O. [3] sunt O.
[4] intendo O. [5] divinitas A B C. [6] terminantâ sapienciam O.
[7-7] possunt . . . incarnata *om.* A B C. [8] lib; *add.* O; *pro* libris *per errorem iterato.*
[9] non duo A B C O. [10] loyca C. [11] methaphisica O; *et sic saepius.*
[12] et *om.* A B C. [13] authonomatice A B C. [14] faciliter B.
[15] purus B.

humanitas; et cum plene sit divinitas, patet quod est aliud sed non alius quam illa humanitas.

but not only man, but very God in the same Person.

Concordo 2° cum approbatis doctoribus ut Augustino Ieronimo et ceteris concedens quod Christus nedum est creator et essencia que nullo[1] modo creari poterit vel moveri, sed eciam[2] creatura.

2. Christ is the creator, and cannot be created or changed; but also a creature, as Augustine, Jerome, and others maintain.

Concordo 3° cum novellis quod Christus secundum deitatem non est creatura, nec minor Patre, corporalis, mobilis, visibilis, subicibilis, et sic de quocunque quae scriptura ascribit sibi humanitus. Et[3] ad istum sensum concedo[4] affirmativas, modifico negativas.

3. Christ, as later writers teach, is not a creature, nor has he any attributes of a creature. But this holds good only of his divine not of his human nature.
What the 'moderns' affirm is true: their denials require qualification.

---

## Cap. II.

[*Declarat quomodo ista sentencia discrepat ab heresi Arriana.*

*The assertion of the reality of Christ's humanity, by maintaining that as man he is a creature, gives no support to the errors of Arius, Sabellius, or Nestorius.*]

Ex istis per modum corollarii elucescit quomodo ista posicio[5] differt ab opinionibus[6] hereticorum de Christo heretice senciencium.

As a corollary to Chapter i. follows the distinction between that position and the heresies on the Person of Christ.

Et primo de opinione[7] Arrii de quo narrat Eusebius in Ecclesiastica Historia li° 10° ca. 13. 'Arrius, inquit, pergens ad[8] ecclesiam episcoporum et populorum frequencia constipatus, humanae necessitatis causa[9] ad locum publicum[10] declinavit; ubi cum sederet, intestina eius atque omnia viscera in secessu[11] cumulorum[12] defluxerunt, et ita in apto

That of Arius, whose miserable death is related by Eusebius;

[1] non A B C. [2] est A B C; eciam O M. [3] et *om.* A B C.
[4] concedens O. [5] proposicio A B C. [6] posicionibus B. [7] oppinione C.
[8] ad *om.* A B C. [9] tam C. [10] pupcul O. [11] secessus A B C.
[12] cumulorum O ? *cuniculorum*; tumulorum B.

loco dignam mortem blasfemie[1] [2]et fetide mentis[2] exsolvit.' Et quia secundum Magistrum Senteneiarum in 3°. Dist. 2a. Arrii hec fuisse perfidia[3] legitur ut Christum esse[4] creaturam fateretur, ut capit a beato Ambrosio primo libro de Trinitate cap. 9°. 'Ideo, inquit Ambrosius, diffusa sunt Arrii viscera et crepuit medius prostratus in faciem ea, quibus Christum[5] negaverat, feda ora[6] pollutus.'

*and St. Ambrose quoted by Peter Lombard,*

Quando[7] ergo illa[8] opinio videtur Arrio in hoc consentire bonum videtur differenciam[9] declarare. Nam propterea videtur Magistro et ipsum sequentibus potissime quod non debet concedi simpliciter Christum esse creaturam vel factum sed cum determinacione[10] quod fuit factus secundum hominem. Primo ergo notandum quod nunquam fuit hereticus quin in aliquo dixit verum: omnes enim concesserunt Deum esse: et ideo valde inconsonum est doctori imponere alteri[11] heresim Arrianam, nisi prius diligenter notaverit in quibus et quomodo talis heresis est fundata.

*who shrinks from saying that Christ is a creature from a needless fear of being involved in the Arian heresy.*

Stetit ergo heresis Arriana in his tribus precipue. Primo in hoc quod negavit Christum esse Deum deorum et magnum Deum, cum posuit eum[12] esse non eiusdem substancie cum Patre, sed ipsos differre ab invicem eciam secundum deitatem substancialiter sicut[13] differunt personaliter.

*This heresy consists of three errors. i. Denying the consubstantiality of the Son with the Father.*

Unde Augustinus Epa. 33 ad Bonifacium, 'Ut, | inquit, [O 218a] breviter[14] insinuem dileccioni tue quid inter Arrianorum[15] et Donatistarum intersit errorem: Arriani Patris et Filii et | [A 76d] Spiritus Sancti diversas esse substancias dicunt; Donatiste autem non hoc[16] | dicunt, sed unam Trinitatis substanciam [C 41a] confitentur.' Dixit itaque[17] Arrius quod summa essencia que est Christus sit citra essenciam Dei Patris, ut est essencia angeli vel hominis quos scriptura sacra vocat deos pluraliter, ut allegat Salvator Iudeis Ioh. 10. 'Nonne scriptum est in lege vestra, 'Ego dixi dii estis?' Si igitur eos vocat deos,

*Augustine notices this in distinguishing between the error of the Arians and that of the Donatists.*

*John x. 34. Ps. lxxxii. 6.*

[1] blasfeme O; blasphemie C. [2-2] debitam M. [3] profidea O.
[4] esse *om.* O. [5] Christum *om.* A B C. [6] hora O. [7] Cum A B C.
[8] ista O. [9] drām A B C. [10] declaracione O.
[11] doctori alteri imponere A C; doctori altius imponere B. [12] ipsum O.
[13] sic C. [14] breviter *om.* O. [15] arriarrorum O.
[16] hoc non A B C. [17] autem O.

ad quos sermo Dei factus est, et non potest solvi scriptura; quem Pater sanctificavit et misit in mundum, quomodo et vos dicitis 'blasfemas,'[1] quia dixi 'Filius Dei sum'[1]?' Et forte ex isto dicto capta est heresis Arriana. Unde dicit Augustinus Omo 48.[2] quod Iudei audientes illud Ioh. 10. 'Ego et Pater unum sumus,' et intelligentes Christum intendere quod sit eadem substancia cum Patre, 'Iudei, inquit, intellexerunt quod Arriani non intellexerunt; quoniam sense-

[Arian heresy possibly arose from misunderstanding our Lord's quotation, John x. 30, "I have said, 'Ye are gods.'"]

117b] runt non posse dici "ego et | Pater unum sumus," nisi ubi equalitas est Patris et Filii. Sed Dominus videns Judeos pre ira non ferre splendorem veritatis, cum temperavit in verbis eis allegans illud Psi. 81.[3] "Ego dixi dii estis etc."' Nec est putandum quod Veritas illuserit[4] Iudeis[5] sophistice in hoc dicto, sed dulciter manuduxit mitigando eorum rancorem ex[6] scriptura patriarche David plus eis autentica[7] inter omnes. [8]Cum enim non fuit in Christo *EST* et *NON*, et dixit[8] eis superius Ioh. 10. quod ipse est omnipotens et eadem substancia cum Patre: patet quod illam sentenciam postmodum non retractat. Minor patet notato textu illius capl. Nam ibi dicitur: 'oves mee vocem meam audiunt et ego vitam eternam do eis, et non rapiet eas[9] quisquam de manu mea' et cetera que secuntur. Probatur illa trimembris conclusio ex ibi positis. Nam ibi[10] dicitur, 'Pater meus quod dedit michi maius omnibus est:' ergo Pater meus[11] est omnipotens, et per consequens 'nemo potest rapere de manu Patris mei,' et ultra sequitur[12] 'nemo potest rapere de manu Patris mei;[13] et 'Ego et Pater unum sumus;' ergo 'nemo potest rapere oves de manu mea.' Istam itaque connexionem subtilissimam Iudei conceperant quam ignorabant Arriani. Ex quo patet quod in deduccione sequenti eandem conclusionem intenderat sed medio plus occulto.

[But the Jews made no such false inference.]

[2 Cor. i. 18 Vulg.]

[John xi. 27-29.]

[1-1] blasfemias quia filius dei sum B; blasfemia etc. C; blasfemo O.
[2] ep. 49 A B C. [3] 81 *om.* A C. [4] illusit O.
[5] iudeos A B. [6] ex *om.* O. [7] illis authenticata O.
[8] cum enim non fuit in christo est et non dixit A B: cum enim non fuit in christo non est et non dixit C; cum non fuit in christo est et non dixit O.
[9] [illegible] *sic in cod.* A; eas *in margine* C. [10] ubi A B C. [11] meus *om.* A B C.
[12] sequitur *om.* O. [13] mei *om.* O.

Discussion of Ps. cx. 1, Ps lxxxii. 6, by our Lord.

Matt. xxii. 41.

Ps. cx. 1.

Pro quo notandum quod sicut Judei multum appreciati [1] sunt prophetam [2] David, sic [3] ex eius textu cognoverant quod Messias venturus ex eis foret tam Deus quam homo. Hoc videtur evidens ex argumento Salvatoris facto Phariseis, Mt 22. ubi sic congregatis Phariseis interrogat ab eis [4] Jesus dicens,[5] 'Quid vobis videtur de Christo? cuius filius est? dicunt ei, 'David:' [6] ait illis, 'quomodo ergo David [7] in spiritu vocat eum dominum dicens: 'dixit Dominus Domino meo, 'sede a dextris, donec ponam inimicos tuos scabellum pedum tuorum.' Si | ergo David vocat eum Dominum quomodo [C 41b] filius eius est? Et nemo poterat ei respondere verbum, nec ausus est quisquam ex illa die eum amplius interrogare.' Non enim contendebant [6] illi legis periti in ampliacione [8] verbi de presenti scientes ex sensu scripture quod apud Deum

Three inferences drawn by the scribes:

sunt cuncta [9] presencia. Ideo sciverunt Christum vel Messiam esse filium David pro quodam tempore. Sciverunt 2do illud Psalmi 109 quod Veritas allegavit dictum esse de Christo. | [A 77a] Sciverunt 3° quod propheta tam eximius non vocaret filium suum tam pauperem et abiectum Dominum suum secundum naturam [10] ab eo assumptam sed secundum naturam [10] superiorem. Ideo non affuit eis vel ullum [11] coloratum subterfugium evadendi. Unde pro 2° argumento Salvatoris supponitur quod Verbum vel Sermo Dei quod idem est, sit

three consequences follow:

Ps. xxxiii. 6.

1. The consubstantiality of the Word;

Ps. cvii. 20.

2. The Incarnation of the Word:

3. The extension to mankind of the divine nature through the Incarnation.

Ps. lxxxii. 6.

eternum idem substancialiter Deo Patri. Patet hoc per illud Psalmi 32 [12] 'Verbo Domini celi firmati sunt.' 2do supponitur quod dictum verbum fuit incarnandum. Patet hoc per illud Psalmi 106 [13] 'misit verbum suum et sanavit eos.' Unde et dictum Verbum vocaverunt prophete concorditer Messiam vel Christum eis promissum. 3° supponitur quod dicti Verbi participacione sit multitudo hominum [14] in Christum directe [14] credencium deificanda participative, sicut carbo ex ignis participacione est ignitus. Patet hoc per illud Ps. 81.[15] 'Ego dixi dii estis.'

[1] appresciati O. [2] prophetiam O. [3] sicut A C; sicud B. [4] interrogavit ex eis O.
[5] Jesus d. A. [6-6] David etc. Non enim contendebant B. [7] David *om.* A.
[8] amplificacione O. [9] omnia sunt B. [10-10] ab eo . . . naturam *om.* O.
[11] ullum *om.* O. [12] 22 O. [13] 108 A B C.
[14-14] in ipsum debite A B C. [15] 81 *om.* O.

Statement of our Lord's argument in John x. 34-36:

Istis suppositis formetur racio sic ex sentencia Salvatoris: Ille Sermo vel Verbum, in quo concordant omnes prophete de operibus miraculosis, de tempore et aliis circumstanciis, et illis quibus mittitur salvandis et deificandis, est verus Messias, et per consequens Deus et homo iuxta textus propheticos: sed in me omnia ista conveniunt: ergo sum [1]Deus et homo: et per consequens non solum[1] participacione deificatus.[2]

with Augustine's comment:

Ideo hic[3] dicit Augustinus; 'Si Sermone[4] Dei facto ad[5] homines fiunt ipsi dii, [6]tunc participando fiunt ipsi dii[6]; et per consequens Sermo ille, quo participant, erit Deus. Si lumine luminati dii sunt, lumen quod illuminat non est Deus? si calefacti igne salutari[7] dii efficiuntur, ignis unde calefiunt non est Deus?'

from which it follows that the Word is One God with Him who speaks it.

Oportet ergo [8]quod Sermo, quo[8] fontaliter deificantur homines ex unitate substancie cum suo eternaliter adintra dicente, sit eadem deitas cum dicente; et per consequens non blasfemat[9] dicendo se naturalem filium Dei esse. Et ex ignorancia huius sensus literalis scripture exciderant[10] Arriani, sicut et Sabelliani, ut recitat Augustinus Omc. 47.

ii. The second error of the Arians lies in the statement that Christ assumed human flesh without a human soul:

Secundo stetit[11] error Arrianorum in hoc quod dicunt
[O 218b] Christum sine anima | solam carnem suscepisse[12]; | ut meminit
[B 118a] [C 42a] Augustinus libro suo De Heresibus | Heresi 49. 'Arriani, inquit, dicti ab Arrio in eo sunt notissimi[13] errore, quo Patrem et Filium et Spiritum Sanctum nolunt esse eiusdem substancie vel nature; sed Filium dicunt creaturam, Spiritum vero creaturam creature; hoc est, ab ipso Filio creatum[14] volunt.

as Augustine stated, who found the Apollinarists

In eo autem quod dicunt Christum sine anima solam carnem sumpsisse minus noti sunt. Sed hoc verum esse[15] Epifanius[16] non tacuit, et ego ex eorum scriptis et collocucionibus certissime comperi.' Et in hoc conveniunt cum Appollinaristis[17]; de quibus scribit Augustinus Heresi 55

[1]–[1] deus et per consequens homo non solum A B C.
[2] deificus *codd. omnes.* [3] hic *om.* A B C. [4] sermonem B; sermo dei factus C.
[5] ab B. [6]–[6] tunc . . . dii *om.* B. [7] salutarii O.
[8]–[8] oportet ergo sermo quo O; oportet ergo quod sermo primo quo A. B.
[9] blasfemant C. [10] excidarant B. [11] stat B M.
[12] suscipere O M. [13] notissimo A B C. [14] esse *add.* B.
[15] Et hoc utrumque esse A C; et hoc utrumque est B. [16] Ephifanius O.
[17] Apolinaristis B.

fallen into the same misunderstanding of Scripture.

quod de anima Christi ab ecclesia catholica[1] differunt[2] dicentes, sicut Arriani, [3]Dominum Jesum Christum sine anima carnem suscepisse,[3] et Verbum fuisse pro anima: et sic glosant scripturas loquentes de anima Christi et Verbum in carnem[4] fuisse conversum, non carnem sumpsisse de virgine.

Augustine's refutation is not obsolete: for Scripture is to be understood literally; but the distinction is to be borne in mind between what is said of Christ *in the form of a servant* and what *in the form of God*.

Et illam heresim[5] elegantissime destruit Augustinus Ep. 127[6] et duabus sequentibus ad Pascencium episcopum Arrianum; cuius dicta utinam hodierni atttenderent! Scribit enim capcioso heretico, non [7]puto quidquam inprovide de quo calumpniam formidaret.[8] 'Quia, inquit, Dei Pa|tris unigenitus Filius Dominus et Deus noster Jesus Christus, post- [A 77b]

Gal. iv. 4. quam "venit plenitudo temporis" opportune[9] "formam servi

Phil. ii. 7. suscepit" ad diem salutis [10]nostre; de illo multa[10] in scripturis

Phil. ii. 6. sacris[11] secundum "formam Dei" dicuntur, multa secundum "formam servi": quorum exempli gracia duo commemoro,[12] ut singula ad singula referantur.[13] Secundum formam Dei ait

John x. 30. "ego et Pater unum sumus": secundum autem[14] servi ipse

John xiv. 28. de se ait "Pater maior me est."' Nescivit[15] enim ille[16] sanctus negare scripturas illas[17] de virtute sermonis, cum personam[17] Filii concedit[18] esse multorum quodlibet.

For Augustine knew that Christ was a composite person.

God has given us, as Augustine notices, two illustrations of unity combined with diversity; which throw light both on the doctrine of the Trinity and on that of the Incarnation.

1. A man consisting of body and soul,

Et ponit ad hoc consequenter duplicia exempla quibus Deus hucusque non[19] dignatus est ostendere hominibus meliora, per que tam in noticiam Trinitatis quam eciam incarnacionis posset[20] hereticus manuduci. Primum sic. 'Cum corpus, inquit, et anima sunt unus homo, quamvis corpus et anima non sunt[21] unum; cur non multo magis Pater et Filius sunt unus Deus? cum Pater et Filius sunt unum secundum illam Veritatis vocem "ego et Pater

John x. 30. unum sumus." Cum, inquit, homo exterior et interior homo non sunt unum, neque eiusdem nature est exterior cuius

[1] katholica C, *ut saepe*. [2] discesserunt A B C; disserunt O.
[3–3] deum christum sine anima carnem suam sumpsisse A B C.
[4] verbum in carne A B, verbum carnem fuisse C. [5] eresym B.
[6] Ep 21 vel 5 O. [7] heretico. Non puto A B C. [8] formidarem A B C.
[9] oportune A B C. [10–10] nostre. Multa de istis A B C. [11] sanctis A C.
[12] comemoro O. [13] referuntur O. [14] formam *add.* O. [15] Restitit B.
[16] iste sanctus negare istas istas (*sic*) scripturas O. [17] persona A B C.
[18] concedat O. [19] non *om.* A B. [20] potest A B C. [21] sint O.

est [1]interior; quia exterior cum corpore nuncupato[1] dicitur homo; interior autem sola anima racionali[2] intelligitur; utrumque tamen illorum simul non[3] duo homines sed unus dicitur: quanto magis Pater et Filius unus Deus est?'

*i.e. of an outer and an inner man, is yet one man.*

Secundum exemplum est de natura universali. 'Homines, inquit, per consorcium et communionem[4] unius eiusdem nature [C 42b] qua omnes homines unum erant, et si aliquando | secundum diversitates voluntatum et sentenciarum opinionum et morum dissimilitudines[5] non erant unum, [6]erunt tamen perfecte plenceque unum[6] cum perventum fuerit ad eum finem ut sit "Deus omnia in omnibus." Et sic non est possibile homines esse unum in caritate vel alio accidente, nisi prius sint unum in substancia vel natura: ut declarat libro primo et[7] 3° contra Maximinianum 22° capitulo. Quod autem multi homines sint unum in substancia vel natura[8] probat[9] per illud Apostoli ad Cor. 3° dictum[10] de Paulo et Appollo "qui plantat et qui rigat unum sunt." Unde Veritas Joh. 17.[11] [12]"Non (dixit) rogo ut ipsi et nos unum simus;"[12] sed "ut ipsi unum sint, sicut et nos unum [13]sumus:" non solum natura quod iam erat verum, sed et perfecte[13] caritatis atque iusticie[14] pro sue[15] capacitate nature, quantum[16] in Dei regno esse poterit,[17] ut sic ipsi summe unum sint in natura sua, sicut Pater et Filius summe unum sunt incomparabiliter[18] meliori natura. Nunquam, inquit, de aliquibus rebus legimus quod unum sunt, nisi sint eiusdem substancie vel nature.'

*2. Man, i.e. mankind, consisting of many diverse individuals, is yet one in nature, and will be perfectly one at the consummation of all things when 'God is all in all.'*

*1 Cor. xv. 28.*

*1 Cor. iii. 8.*

*John xvii. 21.*

*Those who deny the real existence of Universals are prone to various heresies,*

Et indubie[19] in illo errore de universalibus cecati sunt Arrius, Sabellius, et quam plures heretici. Ideo Anselmus De Incarnacione primo vocat[20] negantes universalia ex parte rei extra signa[21] dialectice hereticos. Unde Pascencius Arrianus post-

*as Anselm has expressly stated: and Pascencius*

[1–1] interior cum corpore nuncupato A B, interior comunia (? *quia*) exterius cum corpore nuncupato C. [2] racionabiliter A B C, racionali O. [3] sunt *add.* B. [4] et communionem *om.* B. [5] dissimiles O. [6] erant A B C; erant . . . unum *om.* O. [7] 23° A B C. [8] vel natura *om.* A B C. [9] probatur O. [10] est *add.* O. [11] Joh. 11°. O. [12–12] Non dicit ut et nos unum sumus A B; simus C; sumus O. [13–13] sumus. Sumus enim non solum unum natura quod verum est iam sed et perfecte A B C. [14] iusticia O. [15] sua A B C. [16] quod A B C. [17] esse potuerunt A B C. [18] comparabiliter A B. [19] dubie O. [20] vocant B. [21] signum O.

the Arian is a case in point: for he could not understand how unity of nature could co-exist with distinction of persons:

quam vocaverat[1] Augustinum succensum errore tanquam aqua cenosa se ingurgitantem et ut arborem curvam et nodosam que nichil rectitudinis in se habet, scribit quid moveat[2] cum ad depravandum senteneiam Augustini confitentis sibi in[3] scriptis fidem | suam. Nam[4] inter alia beatus Augustinus [B 118b] scripsit sibi Patrem et Filium et Spiritum sanctum esse unum Deum, 'Quis, inquit, Pascencius e[5] tribus personis est unus Deus? an forte | una est persona triformis que hoc nomine [A 77c] nuncupetur?' Si iste hereticus cognovisset quomodo[6] unica[7] communis humanitas est quelibet persona hominis; vidisse potuisset[8] faciliter quomodo unica deitas, essencia, substancia, vel natura divina, est tres persone et quelibet earundem.

nor could Sabellius.

Sabellius eciam si vidisset quod cum unitate nature stat distinccio personarum, sic quoque[9] non fuisset cecatus[10] in isto turpissimo paralogismo[11]—Petrus est natura specifica: Paulus est eadem natura specifica: ergo Petrus est Paulus—vidisset quod non oportet quod Pater sit Filius, quamvis utrumque sit eadem simplicissima substancia. Et sic de aliis heresibus pullulantibus propter defectum logice scripturarum.

And many nowadays do not apply Augustine's rule: (*i.e.* to ask first whether the words in each passage refer to Christ as God or as man, *cf. p.* 9. *l.* 6.

Multi enim[12] cupiunt autorizare novam logicam extraneam a scriptura et hinc dicunt[13] se ipsam corrigere tanquam impossibilem[14] de vi vocis. Et illud meminit Augustinus contra dictum Pascencium. [15]Nam contra[15] negantes scripturas de Christo sic loquitur: 'Homines, inquit, minus intelligentes quid propter quid dicatur | precipites | volunt habere sentencias: [C 43a] [O 218c] et scripturis non diligenter scrutatis arripiunt [16]defensionem[17] cuiuscumque[18] opinionis[16] et ab ea vel[19] nunquam vel de difficili deflectuntur, dum docti atque sapientes magis putari quam esse cupiunt. Ea quippe, que propter formam[20] servi

[1] vacaverant vocaverant (*sic*) O. [2] movet O. [3] in *om.* O.
[4] nam *om.* A B C. [5] a O. [6] quomodo *om.* B. [7] una A B C.
[8] posset O. [9] quod *omnes codd.* [10] cecitatus O. [11] Peraloysmo A B.
[12] autem A B C. [13] dicunt *om.* B. [14] impossibile O.
[15-15] nam consequenter contra A B C; nam consequenter O.
[16-16] defensionem cuiuscunque opinionis *om.* B; defensionem *add. iterum* C.
[17] defencionem O. [18] oppinionis A. [19] vel *om.* A B. [20] formam *om.* B.

dicta sunt, volunt transferre ad formam Dei. 'Hoc, inquit, nomen Jesus Christus ex dispensacione misericordie[1] susceptoque[2] humanitatis assumptum est, quia ipse Filius Dei factus est filius hominis, non mutando quod erat, sed[3] assumendo quod non erat.' Et probat diffuse ex scripturis[4] quod tam Christus quam Spiritus Sanctus[5] est idem Deus cum Patre et specialiter per illud Apostoli ad Cor. 8. 'Scimus quoniam nullus Deus nisi unus: nam etsi sunt qui dicantur dii[6] multi et domini multi, nobis tamen unus Deus Pater ex quo omnia et nos in illo: et unus Dominus[7] Jesus Christus per quem omnia et nos per illum.' Ex isto plane sequitur non protervo quod Christus sit idem Deus cum Patre. Unde dicunt periti scripture quod deus et dominus per se sumptus[8] dicitur authonomatice de Deo et Domino dominorum. Scio tamen quod protervus potest,[9] ut hodie, negare quamlibet partem scripture de virtute sermonis, et dicere quod Deus erat verbum nuncupative, et quod per Christum non sunt omnia facta sed omnia citra ipsum, [10]et sic est Deus ac animatus,[10] sed nec Deus deorum nec animatus[11] nobiscum univoce. Sed non sic sophisticati sunt eciam heretici, non sic negantes[12] scripturam ut hodie, quia melius fundati in logica et methaphisica quam nostrates.

which rule he exemplifies in many places, and asserts plainly both the humanity

1 Cor. viii. 4-6.

and the divinity of Christ.)

So they surrender the literal sense of Scripture through their ignorance both of logic and of metaphysic.

Tercio autem stat opinio Arrii in his que ex predictis erroribus sequuntur[13]: ut puta[14] quod Christus nedum[15] est univoce homo cum aliis sed non est homo simpliciter, cum non potest esse homo si non sit anima intellectiva; et per consequens non est passus[16] mortuus aut sepultus, et sic de quibuscunque predicatis humanitatem Christi concernentibus.[17] Quamvis enim dici possit quod angelus, coniunctus nature corporee tanquam motrix, sit homo; verumtamen est alterius speciei quam totus vel completus homo, id est,

iii. The third error of Arius is a corollary from the above: that Christ not having a human soul was not very man.

For an angel in human form

[1] nunc B; m̃ic A C O, *i.e.* misericordie. [2] suscepte quia A B C. [3] et B.
[4] scripture O. [5] sanctus *om.* A B.
[6] sive in celo et in terra siquidem sunt dii *add.* A B C.
[7] deus A B C. [8] sumpti B. [9] posset O.
[10–10] ac *om. sed in loco habet rasuram duarum litterarum* A; et sic . . . animatus *om.* B.
[11] anima O. [12] mutantes A B C. [13] sequentur A B C. [14] puta A B C; pũ O.
[15] nedum non A B C. [16] mortuus passus B. [17] consernentibus O.

is not very man.

natura integra ex corpore et anima composita: homo enim est racione spiritus eiusdem speciei cum angelis et non racione nature corporee.

Augustine teaches that for very man, body and soul, *i.e.* the three elements of flesh, intellect, and spirit, in Luke xxiii. 43, combination, are necessary:

Et per hoc patet quod quidam minus intelligentes Augustinum putant ipsum contradicere sibi ipsi, quando dicit quod anima non completus aut | totus[1] homo: nam[2] verum dicit ad [A 77d] sensum[3] expositum. Unde Epistola 40 ad Dardanum solvendo questionem de dicto Salvatoris[4] Luc. 23 quo[5] promisit | latroni quod foret secum illo die in paradiso; [C 43b] 'antequam, inquit, sciatur utrum secundum deitatem[6] vel[7] secundum humanitatem intelligatur promissio Veritatis, oportet videre quomodo sit loquendum de homine. Non, inquit Augustinus, sicut quidam heretici dicunt, Verbum Dei[8] et carnem sine anima humana[9] suscepit, sic quod Verbum esset carni pro anima; vel Verbum Dei carnem et animam sine mente, ut Verbum Dei esset anime[10] pro mente. Sed accipis, inquit ad Dardanum, hominem Christum; sicut[11] superius aisti quod Christum Deum non crederes nisi perfectum hominem credidisses. Profecto, inquit, cum dicis hominem, perfectam totam illic naturam humanam vis intelligere. Non est[12] autem homo perfectus si vel anima carni vel anime ipsi mens[13] humana defuerit.'[14] Et illam naturam complete ex anima et corpore compositam vocat super Joh. Omc. 47[15] totum hominem: quam[16] notum est ex

which is also shown in the *De Anima*:

dictis *De Anima* distingui tam a corpore quam anima[17] licet omnia ista tria sint eadem persona hominis. Sic ergo[18] intelligendus est Augustinus quandocunque videtur dicere | [B 119a] quod corpus vel anima non est homo; id est, non est[19] tota vel completa natura ex corpore et anima composita. Sed pro solucione Dardani questionis videtur Augustino catholicum quod promissio facta latroni intelligatur secundum

[1] totus aut completus O. [2] non O. [3] sermonem A B C.
[4] salvatore O. [5] quō = quomodo A C. [6] divinitatem O.
[7] aut B. [8] deā O. [9] humana *om.* A B C.
[10] anima C. [11] sicud A B C. [12] est *om.* O. [13] meus O.
[14] deseruit O. [15] 40 A B C. [16] quanquam O. [17] anima *om.* O.
[18] igitur A C. [19] non est *in margine* C.

humanitatem Christi: [1]sed cum corpus Christi[1] sepultum sit solum in orto, ut patet Ioh. 19,[2] relinquitur quod sue anime in parasceue erant simul; quia modicum felicitatis fuisset animam latronis fuisse cum solo corpore Christi mortuo in sepulcro. Et cum vera mors fuit in Christi corpore, cum aliter non fuisset vera resurreccio; querendum est—quo devenit anima[3] Christi in illo triduo? Quod cum evangelium non reserat, supplet[4] beatus Petrus Actuum 2° probans ex illo Psalmi 15 dicto de Christo 'quoniam non[5] derelinques animam meam in inferno, nec dabis sanctum tuum videre corrupcionem,' quod anima Christi descendit in illo triduo ad limbum patrum, quem Veritas Luc. 16. vocat 'sinum Abrahe,' ubi patres veteris testamenti feliciter quieverunt. [6]Quamvis enim dictum psalmiste sit negativum, impertinenter tamen menti prophetice diceretur, nisi intenderet Messiam secundum mentem visitare inferos et statim sine media incarceracione corpori reuniri.[6] Et hinc fundatus est de Christo articulus fidei, quod 'descendit ad inferos.' Cum ergo paradisus generale nomen est ubicunque feliciter[7] vivitur, quid obest animam latronis fuisse cum anima Christi in regione quiescencium congaudendo et non in regione inferiori dolencium,[8] inter quas est 'magnum chaos' secundum veritatem evangelicam interceptum?[9]

yet Augustine rightly admits John xix. 42. that there is a sense in which the soul is man:

Acts ii. 31. Ps. xvi. 10.

and it was in this sense that the penitent thief

Luke xvi. 22, 26.

was with Christ in Paradise, *i.e.* with Christ's disembodied human nature.

Redeundo[10] ergo ad propositum patet ex dictis quantum differt ista posicio ab heresi Arriana. Ideo est michi verisimile quod doctores moderni[11] cum non ydemptificarent que [C 44a] minus intelligunt,[12] | locuntur michi temptative, yronice, vel iocose. Yronice quidem, quia Arrius negavit Verbum Dei esse idem substancialiter Deo Patri, sed creatum esse secundum supremam substanciam, que est Christus. Ego autem dico

Thus my original position (ch. i.) that Christ is a creature differs widely from that of Arius.

Yet through want of precision in thought and language, some confuse the two.

1. Arius denies the consubstantiality of the Word with the Father.

I affirm it;

[1] sed . . . Christi *om.* O. [2] 29 O. [3] deveniet Christi B, *om.* anima.
[4] suplet O. [5] non *om.* O.
[6-6] quamvis enim dictum psalmiste sit negatum impertinenter tamen diceretur menti prophetice nisi intenderet Messiam visitare inferos ac statim sine mera incarnacione corpori uniri A B C. *Cod.* O. *habet* quam enim dictum . . . incineracione corporis veniri; *cetera ut supra in textu.* [7] bene B.
[8] dolencium *om.* A B C. [9] interceptum *codd. omn. Qu. interseptum?*
[10] respondendo A. [11] mei B C *om.* O. [12] intelligunt minus O.

*and in this sense deny that Christ, as the Word, is, or can be, a creature.*

quod Christus | absolute necessario[1] est eadem deitas que est [O 218d] Pater,[2] nec posse secundum supremam naturam, que est Christus, | creari vel fieri. [A 78a]

*2. Arius denies in Christ the existence of a human soul saying that its place was supplied by the created spirit of the Word. I affirm that Christ has, and is, a human soul; and that only thereby is the hypostatic union possible.*

2° autem dixit Arrius quod Christus non habet animam sed pure carnem; spiritu illo creato[3] supplente vicem anime non ypostatice, sed ut motrice, corpori copulato. Ego autem dico quod Christus nedum habet animam, sed est anima, nec posset[4] carni nisi mediante anima ypostatice copulari.

*3. Arius denies the real humanity of Christ. I affirm that he is very man in the plain sense of the term.*

3° ubi posuit[5] Christum non esse hominem nisi equivoce, nec proprie passum[6] esse, mortuum, et sic de aliis que fides evangelica de Christo predicat. Ego autem[7] dico Christum esse[8] verissime, completissime, et univoce hominem cum quolibet fratre suo; et vere de virtute sermonis conversatum esse in terris, ut canit processus evangelicus.

*Thus, whereas Arius sinned against both the divine and the human nature of Christ; I cordially acknowledge both, neither confounding natures nor distinguishing persons in Christ.*

Et sic, ubi Arrius peccavit in deitate Christi negando eum verum Deum[9] eundem cum Patre; ubi eciam peccavit in humanitate Christi negando ipsum esse verum hominem; ego utrumque[10] pleno corde confiteor non confundendo naturas nec[11] distinguendo personas in Christo. Et patet quod non, quia dixit Christum esse creaturam, censetur hereticus[12]; sed, quia dixit Christum esse puram[13] creaturam meliorem homine; et non hominem passum abiectum et ab hominibus reprobatum.

*The Arian heresy consists not in saying 'Christ is a creature': but in making the word 'creature' in that statement include more or less than 'man': as Augustine perceived, whose rule (pp. 9, 18, 20) would save many of our modern confusions.*

Et utinam nostri loquentes attenderent ad regulam Augustini 'quid propter quid de Christo dicitur,' allegando complete scripturam vel determinaciones ecclesie non truncate. Ut primo libro contra Maximinianum ca° 11. 'Audi, inquit, Maximiniane, auctoritatem synodice[14] locucionis: Si quis ex nichilo Filium dicit non ex Deo Patre, anathema sit.' Quis ergo color, si dico—Christus est creatura—sed et Arrius dixit Christum esse creaturam, quod coincido in heresim Arrianam? Vere non plus quam sequitur, si uterque nostrum dicat Christum esse aliquid[15] sive Deum.

[1] intus O. [2] eadem deitas cum patre B. [3] increato M A; creato B C O.
[4] potest A; oportet C. [5] ut possuit B.
[6] proprie ~~passum~~ esse (*sic*) A; tibi posset esse B; posset esse C.
[7] autem *om.* A B O. [8] ipsum esse A C; esse *om.* B. [9] verbum domini A B C.
[10] utraque B. [11] non B. [12] esse Christum censetur creaturam hereticus B.
[13] pure O. [14] siuodice O, *ut saepe post.* [15] aliud C.

Sed obicitur quod dico horribilius Arrianis, quia ipsi dixerunt Christum esse primam et optimam creaturam; ego autem dico Christum esse materiam primam, et sic[1] abiectissimam creaturam. Hic dicitur quod non sequitur. Nam Christus est optimus homo possibilis, inter omnes creaturas particulares optima, in tantum quod est melior B 119b] [2]angelo; et per consequens melior[2] illa creatura, si esset, | quam[3] finxit Arrius nimis stolide esse[4] primam creaturam Dei, mediante qua[5] Deus creavit Spiritum Sanctum et consequenter alias creaturas. Nam illa creatura non foret melior creato angelo: de Christo autem dicit Apostolus ad Hebr. 1° quod 'est tanto melior angelis effectus quanto differencius pre illis nomen hereditavit.' Et si obicitur per illud Ps. 8[6] dictum de Christo ad litteram[7] 'minuisti eum [C 44b] paulo minus | ab angelis'; dicitur quod Christus, sicut est natura increata et natura creata, sic secundum naturam creatam est simul[8] tam natura corporea quam natura incorporea; [9]secundum autem naturam corpoream[9] est 'paululum minoratus ab angelis,' sicut[10] sentenciat satis[11] psalmus; et secundum creatum spiritum per graciam unionis angelos[12] antecellit. Conceditur tamen[13] quod abiectissima creatura que est Christus Deus, licet sit natura inferior quam angelus vel anima humana, est tamen optima et suprema persona possibilis: cum omnis natura que est filius[14] Marie virginis hominis[15] est et[16] Filius Dei; et e contra omnis natura, que est Filius[14] Dei, est filius hominis; quia natura divina est filius hominis, ut patet ex confessione beati Petri Mat. 16. querente Veritate, 'Quem dicunt[17] homines esse filium hominis?' et respondente Petro de eadem humanitate que [A 78b] est | Christus, de qua fit questio. 'Tu es, inquit, Filius Dei vivi,' intelligens indubio filium naturalem. Unde Veritas

Objection. 'I am a worse heretic than Arius: for Arius said that Christ was the highest creature: whereas I make him the lowest.'

Answer. As a man Christ was the best possible man; *i.e.* among creatures the best creature. For it is only in his bodily nature that he is 'lower than the angels': by the grace of union even in his created spirit, he is 'better than the angels.'

Heb. i. 4.

Heb. ii. 9.

Ps. viii. 5.

But even, if it be granted that in nature he is 'lower than the angels,' because of his human body; yet in his compound person, as Son of God and Son of Man, he is the best and highest person possible. And Scripture says that he is both Son of God

Matt. xvi. 13, 16.

[1] sic *om.* A B C.
[2] angelo . . . melior *om.* O.
[3] qm̄ A B O.
[4] esset A B C.
[5] quam B.
[6] dictum 8 *om.* A B C.
[7] ad litteram *om.* B.
[8] filius B.
[9–9] secundum . . . corpoream *om.* O.
[10] sicut *om.* O.
[11] sacer O.
[12] angelos *om.* A.
[13] tamen *om.* C.
[14–14] Marie . . . filius *om.* B.
[15] virginis *om.* O M; *forsitan aut* virginis *aut* hominis *omittendum.*
[16] et *om.* A.
[17] ducunt O.

and Son of Man.

approbando responsionem[1] adiunxit premium, et monet eum[2]:

Matt. xvi. 17.

'Beatus es, inquit, Symon Bariona, quia caro et sanguis non revelavit tibi, sed Pater meus.'

This doctrine of diversity of natures and unity of person is the answer to the Nestorian heresy, as Anselm

Et per hoc destruitur heresis Nestoriana arguens ex diversitate naturarum in Christo quod sit diversitas personarum. Nesciunt enim quomodo humanitas assumpta et natura divina tam dispares sunt utraque[3] eadem persona cum Verbo Dei, ut ostendit Anselmus de Incarnacione Verbi cap. 6.[4] et sic posuit alium esse filium hominis et alium Filium Dei; sicut aliud est filius hominis et aliud Filius Dei; sicut dicit

and Augustine show.

superius Augustinus. Et patet quantum differt ista posicio ab heresi Arriana et Nestoriana, cum quibus videretur minus intelligentibus maxime concordare.

If it is still objected that I am worse than Arius in saying that Christ is the lowest of creatures; I grant

Et si obicitur quod non tollitur, quin Christus sit creatura [5]et abiectissima, quod[5] non posuit Arrius; concedo conclusionem. Unde inter alia, que accenderent[6] virtutes theologicas in nobis[7] viantibus, maxime videtur mihi debere gignere[8] illa summa minoracio,

Phil. ii. 7, 8.

illa summa exinanicio, illa summa[9] obediencia vel humiliacio

the conclusion; and gratefully hail, as a help in our Christian pilgrimage, the consideration

qua[10] Verbum, manens substancialiter complete et eternaliter quod erat, assumpsit ypostatice quod prius non erat. 'Nusquam[11] enim angelos apprehendit' secundum Apostolum ad

Heb. ii. 16, 17.

that Christ thus emptied himself;

Hebr. 2°. sicut ficte garriunt Arriani; sed 'semen Abrahe'[12] tam secundum naturam corruptibilem quam secundum[13] naturam immortalem 'ut fieret per omnia fratribus similis':

Heb. ii. 11, 12.

dicente Apostolo ubi supra, 'non confunditur[14] fratres eos vocare, dicens "narrabo nomen tuum fratribus meis"': et

in taking on himself not an angel's but man's nature, for our sake. This is an incentive a) to our faith,

sequitur 'nusquam enim angelos apprehendit, sed semen Abrahe apprehendit: unde debuit per omnia fratribus similari, ut misericors fieret et fidelis pontifex ad Deum.' Ex quo textu patet quod fides nostra viresceret ex hoc quod naturam nostram fragilem non pure angelicam dignatur

[1] confirmando questionem B. [2] et moneutem *codd. omn.*
[3] utrumque O. [4] 6. *codd. omn.* [5] est abiectissima quomodo A B C.
[6] attenderent A B C. [7] nube A B C. [8] giuguere O.
[9] sublima A B; *om.* C. *cum lacuna.* [10] quia A C; quam B.
[11] nunquam O; nusquam A B C *ut in Vulg.* [12] habrahe O. [13] secundum *om.* O.
[14] confundetur O; confunditur A B C *ut in Vulg.*

suscipere. 2° cum non [1] potest frustrari, patet quod ex assumpcione nostre nature, quos vocat [1] fratres suos passus et temptatus [2] ad nobis auxiliandum, invalesceret spes [3] [C 45a] humana. Et 3° visa humiliacione | qua Dei Patris primogenitus naturalis dignatus est naturam nostram fragilem et abiectam assumere fortificaretur caritas ad ipsum et fratres [O 219a] suos in ipso [4] car|ius diligendum. Non ergo iniuriatur nobis nec debet vilescere quod nos sic univit, non angelos; nec ab honore Patris degenerat, nec [5] fundatur in ipso [6] remissior nobis diligendi racio. [7] Sed per omnia e converso. Unde Ioh. 14. vere dicit, 'si diligeretis me, gauderetis utique quia vado ad Patrem.' Pro cuius declaracione suppono: primo quod Christus, hoc dicens [8] secundum humanitatem assumptam, [9] sit eiusdem nature nobiscum. 2° suppono [10] quod apostoli, quibus locutus est et alii sermones eius servantes sint nedum servi Domini sed amici. Patet per [11] illud Ioh. 15 [12] 'Vos amici mei estis si feceritis que precipio vobis: iam non dicam vos servos etc.' 3° suppono quod de racione amicicie sit, cum amicus sit alter ipse, congratulari de prosperis coamici, specialiter si exinde [13] speratur amicicie fructus uberior. Patet per Aristotelem 8 Ethic 5. [14] Ex istis sic arguitur. Quilibet amicus debet gaudere de eventu prospero coamici amiciciam confirmante; sed Christo amico aposto- [A 78c] lorum ascendente in celum | et collocato a dextra [15] Dei Patris advenit summa felicitas: ergo de eius transitu fuit apostolis congaudendum. [16] Et hinc dicit apostolus ad Hebr. 7 'quod [17] Iesus accedit per semet ipsum ad Deum, semper vivens ad [B 120a] interpellandum pro nobis.' Cui conformiter | scribitur prima [18] Ioh. 2° 'sed et si quis peccaverit [19] advocatum habemus apud [20] Patrem, Iesum Christum.' Unde Augustinus super illo textu Omelia 78 sic scribit: 'humane nature congratu-

b) to our hope,

and c) to our charity.

In taking man's nature rather than that of angels, he neither dishonours the Father nor offers a weak incentive to our love: as he himself testifies, John xiv. 28.

This passage implies

1. Identity of nature between him and ourselves.

2. That his apostles and followers are his friends, not servants. John xv. 14, 15.

3. That 'friends' share in a happiness which befalls their friend, as Aristotle says, especially when by that happiness the friendship is made more fruitful.

Heb. vii. 25.

And this was the result of Christ's ascension: for now he intercedes for us. 1 John ii. 1.

[1]–[1] potest . . . vocat *om.* O. [2] temperatus O.
[3] species B C O; spes *cum rasura supra* A. [4] in ipso *om.* C.
[5] vel O. [6] in nobis A B C. [7] pō (*potencia*) O. [8] hic docens O.
[9] assumptam *om.* A B C. [10] supponantur O. [11] per *om.* A B C.
[12] *lacuna in loco numeri* C. [13] inde B. [14] 11° A B C.
[15] dextris A B C. [16] con- *om.* A B C [17] hebre qui O; 7 *om.*
[18] scribitur prima *om.* O. [19] peciaverit O. [20] aput A B.

*Thus, as Augustine says, Christ's return to the Father is the exaltation of the mortal into immortality, which, already fulfilled as to 'universal' humanity, is the hope of the individual believer.*

*1 Cor. xv. 53.*

laudum est eo, quod assumpta est a Verbo ut immortalis[1] constitueretur in celo, atque ita fieret[2] terra sublimis, ut[3] incorruptibilis pulvis[4] sedeat ad dextram Patris; et sic Christum ire ad Patrem et recedere a nobis est mortale, quod ex nobis suscepit, levare in celum[5] et facere immortale. Quis ergo non hinc gaudeat ut et suam naturam iam immortalem gratuletur in Christo, ac[6] illud se speret esse futurum per Christum? Nec dubito, quin omnes moderni scholastici nescirent impugnare istas logicas de vi vocis.

*This is an irrefragable conclusion from the words of Scripture, as Jerome and others rightly understand them, viz. that Christ is in plain terms our brother.*

Et sic intelligit Jeronimus et alii rectiloqui quod tota spes et consolacio nostra est in summa humiliacione Christi, qua naturam nostram assumendo et nobis exemplum conversacionis tribuendo fecit se non angelum vel naturam alienam ab homine, sicut fabulantur heretici, sed verissime et univoce fratrem nostrum, ut post[7] declarabitur.

---

## Cap. III.

[*Ostendit quod Christus fuit homo in triduo, et obicit multipliciter et dissolvit.*

*Christ's humanity was not suspended during the three days' entombment.*]

*The position that Christ was man in the three days is thus proved. A man's body and soul are each of them the same man: Christ's body and soul remain during the three days: therefore during that time Christ is very man. This statement is enough for me; but for the sake of reconciling apparent discrepancies, it is well to examine further.*

Ex[8] istis plane consequitur quod Christus fuit verus homo in triduo inter eius mortem et resurreccionem. Probatur sic. Cuiuslibet[9] hominis tam corpus | quam anima est insepara- [C 45b] biliter idem homo: sed tam corpus Christi quam eius anima per dictum triduum manet: ergo Christus fuit per dictum triduum verus homo. Maior patet ex dictis. Nam quomodocunque scriptura vel alii doctores catholici hoc intellexerunt sive figurative sive aliter, suppono me intelligere; sic tamen quod maneat verum de virtute[10] sermonis: et sic oportet me concedere aliqua[11] que secuntur. Nam licet illud argumentum det michi plenam fidem ad conclusionem propositam, verumtamen pro intellectu scripture et veritatum annexarum huic

[1] immortalis *om.* A B C. [2] in terra A B C. [3] et C. [4] pulius O.
[5] in celum *om.* B. [6] at A B C. [7] post *om.* A B C.
[8] *littera initialis om. ut fere semper* A B C. [9] cuiuscunque O.
[10] de vi sermonis A B; de Christo sermonis C. [11] alia O.

materie cum dictis doctorum oportet illam materiam ulterius triplici medio[1] dilatare. Veritas enim testatur omnimode sibi ipsi, nec aliquid ex veritate consequens offenderet pias aures. Quicquid ergo ex hoc principio perfectus[2] philosophus sciret deducere concedi debet tanquam catholicum, et oppositum abici[3] tanquam dissonum fidei Christiane.

*If the converse be true, Christ did not 'descend into hell,' nor lie buried in the tomb.*

Ut primo sequitur ex eius opposito quod Christus non descendisset ad inferos, nec iacuisset sepultus in sepulcro, sicut tamen[4] superius allegatur ex fide. Si enim descendit ad inferos, vel secundum deitatem vel secundum humanitatem. Non secundum[5] deitatem, cum non secundum illam sit mobilis; et si secundum humanitatem, tunc illa fuit servata[6] pro tunc descendens ad inferos. Nec sufficit hoc, nisi illa pro tunc fuerit sibi ypostatice copulata: quia persone non est attribuenda pars[7] denominacionis[8] pro tempore pro quo ipsa non est pars persone: cum tunc omne corpus racione materie foret perpetue,[9] et omnis homo racione anime eque post mortem viveret sicut ante. Quod negant illi, quibus non sapit, quod Christus vixit humanitus in dicto triduo: unde dicunt quod est impossibile de vi vocis quod Christus fuit mortuus aut sepultus vel quod descendit ad inferos: sed sic [A 78d] in|telligitur: corpus, quod quondam fuit Christi, sepultum est, et anima, que quondam fuit Christi, descendit ad inferos, sed non Christus, [10]cum tunc non fuit ita quod Christus est.[10]

*For this must have happened to his human nature; and if he was not then man, it could not have happened at all.*

*The hypostatic union was not severed, nor is there need to correct the common saying, 'Christ died and was buried' into 'the body of Christ died,' etc.*

Sed revera ista ficticia superaddit perfidiam Iudeorum. Nam turba Iudaica Ioh. 12. dixit Iesu: 'nos audivimus ex lege quod Christus manet in eternum': quia Iesaie[11] 9° scribitur: 'super solium David et super regnum eius sedebit, ut confirmet illud et corroboret a modo[12] et usque in sempiternum,' id est, a tempore quo 'puer natus est nobis.' Probatur sic. Iesus natus est rex humanitus, ut patet Ioh. 18[13] 'Tu dicis quia rex sum ego: nam ego[14] in hoc natus sum.' Cum ergo per mortem non fuit intercisio regni sui, cum fuit spirituale

*John xii. 34.*

*Isa. ix. 7.*

*For 'Christ abideth ever.'*

*Isa. ix. 6.*

*John xviii. 37.*

*His royalty was not interrupted by death; it was spiritual and in-*

[1] 3ci A B C O. *Qu.* modo *legendum pro* medio? [2] factus O. [3] hiti B.
[4] tamen *om.* A B; tum C. [5] secundum *om.* A B C. [6] incarnata A B C.
[7] partis *codd. omn.* [8] denominandum O. [9] perpetuo O.
[10-10] cum tunc non ita quod Christus fuit B [11] ysae O.
[12] año A B C; a m° O, *i.e.* a modo. [13] Ioh. 18 *altera manu* C. [14] ego *om.* B.

*dependent of the body; but still in relation to his human nature, it was the royalty of his 'inner man,' and not separable from his royalty as divine: not a corporal but a spiritual royalty, as Augustine testifies.*

a corpore independens; ergo mansit perpetuo. Confirmatur: *Dan. vii. 14.* quia Daniel 7 scribitur de humanitate Christi: 'potestas eius eterna que non auferetur,[1] et regnum eius quod non corrumpetur.' Non ergo potest ille Dominus eciam[2] secundum humanitatem perdere regnum suum: quia *Mic. iv. 7.* Michee 4[to]. dicitur, 'regnabit super eos ex hoc[3] nunc | et usque in seculum.' Et [O 219b] patet[4] ex hoc quod non est[5] alia regnacio hominis | interioris[5] [C 46a] in Christo nisi que est[6] regnacio Christi Dei: sed anima regnavit a principio sue creacionis continue: ergo Christus. Non enim dictus rex Israel secundum humanitatem ut corporaliter regnet sed spiritualiter super illos: ut exponit *John xii. 13.* Augustinus Omc. 50 [7]exponens illud[7] Ioh. 12 'Benedictus qui venit | in nomine Domini, rex Israel.' 'Non enim,[8] [B 120b] inquit Augustinus, rex Israel fuit Christus ad exigendum tributum vel ferro exercitum armandum hostesque[9] visibiliter debellandos; sed rex Israel, quod mentes regat, quod in eternum consulat, quod in regnum celorum credentes sperantes amantesque perducat.' Cum ergo illa[10] potestas spiritualis, existens subiective in anima independenter[11] a corpore, non fuit spoliata ab anima Christi in morte; videtur quod eciam[12] in morte fuit humanitas vel spiritus[13] Christi rex Israel[14] sicut ante.

*As this spiritual royalty continued, the human spirit also continued: which proves the position of this chapter.*

*Ps. xxiv. 7.* Unde et illud Ps[i]. 23 'attollite portas etc.'[15] exponitur a beato Augustino et Ieronimo de anima Christi descendente ad inferos: ac si angeli preconizantes[16] Christi[17] descensum[18] ad inferos dicerent principibus tenebrarum; 'O principes mundanorum! attollite[19] portas vestras, et introibit rex glorie cum captivitate ducta ab inferis, portas aperiens[20] eternales.' Et sic in scripturis dirigitur liberacio patrum ab inferis ad personam Christi, quod ipse humanitus immediate ipsam perficeret.[21] *Luke i. 79.* Ut Luce 1°. 'Illuminare his[22] qui in tenebris et in umbra mortis sedent.' Quod,[23] cum sequitur de

*In Scripture the entry into hell and the liberation of 'the spirits in prison' is performed by the person of Christ, which in one aspect is human.*

[1] aufertur A B C. [2] et A B C. [3] super hoc ex hoc B. [4] quod O.
[5] aliqua potestas hominis ynterioris B; aliqua A C. [6] est *om.* B.
[7–7] exponendo O. [8] enim *om.* B. [9] quia A B C.
[10] illa *om.* A B C. [11] independenter *om.* C *cum lacuna.*
[12] eciam *om.* O. [13] pars O. [14] israhel C. [15] etc. *om.* O B.
[16] preconisantes A B C. [17] eius B. [18] descensus A B C. [19] attolite B.
[20] apperiendo A; aperiendo B C. [21] proficeret O. [22] illis B. [23] et O.

virtute sermonis ex dicto principio, est catholice concedendum.

He did not delegate to his created spirit, in a state of hypostatic separation from himself, the completion of his work for man.

Item nemo sapiens et plene potens incipit opus laudabile in propria persona perficere; et, dum perfecerit[1] in propria persona rudimenta[2] operis,[3] committit suo subdito operis complementum. Cum ergo edificacio ecclesie et liberacio patrum[4] ab inferis sit opus summe laudabile; sequitur quod Christus in propria persona non perficiet imperfectam disposicionem, et committet spiritui creato ypostatice separato belli victoriam, que est operis complementum. Indignius namque[5] est temptari a dyabolo, pati, et corporaliter disponere ad edificacionem ecclesie, quam[6] potenter spoliare Tartara[7] a dyabolo devicto.

As he was tempted and suffered in his own person, so also in his own person he 'went down into hell.'

Si ergo Christus in propria persona passus fuerat et temptatus, quia in carne et[8] anima ypostatice copulata: per idem in A 79a] | propria persona spoliavit infernum[9] extrahendo patriarchas ab inferis, specialiter cum non reliquit unionem anime vel corporis quod assumpsit: dicente Augustino Ome. 47. 'Si enim dixerimus quod Verbum Dei posuit animam suam et iterum sumpsit eam, metuendum est, ne subintret[10] prava cogitacio et dicatur:—Ergo[11] aliquando anima illa separata est a Verbo, et aliquando Verbum illud, ex quo suscepit illam animam[12] fuit sine anima.—Video enim fuisse sine anima humana Verbum cum "in principio erat Verbum;" [13]sed ex quo "Verbum[13] caro factum est et habitavit in nobis;" et susceptus est[14] a Verbo totus homo, id est,[15] anima et caro. Quid fecit passio, quid fecit mors, nisi corpus ab anima separavit, animam vero a Verbo non separavit?' Et sequitur. 'Fidelis latronis animam[16] non deserebat? et deserebat[17] suam? Absit.' Et quia minus intelligens potest[18] ex dictis intelligere quod Verbum solum per graciam affuit illi anime et non hypostatica[19] unione

Augustine rightly says that the Incarnation was not interrupted by death: John i. 14. all that death did was to separate the human soul from the body.

[1] perficerit O. [2] redimenta O. [3] operis *om.* C.
[4] parentum O. [5] nanque A; nam O. [6] quantum A.
[7] creaturam A B C. [8] vel C M. [9] in infernum O.
[10] subintret *om.* O. [11] ergo *om.* B. [12] utcumque O.
[13]–[13] sed . . . verbum *om.* O. [14] est *om.* O; suscepit est B. [15] id est *om.* C.
[16] fidelis animam latronis animam B. [17] et deserebat *om.* O. [18] posset O.
[19] apostatica O.

subdit [1] differenciam: 'latronis vero [1] animam custodivit, suam vero inseparabiliter habuit.' [2]

Further, a creature, such as the human spirit of Christ would be apart from the person of the Word, could not have released the fathers from their prison.

Et potest illud confirmari ex hoc, quod aliter patres in limbo [3]tantum tenerentur creature, que non est Deus, spoliando [3] eos de manu dyaboli, sicut Christo secundum humanitatem: quod est impossibile. Cum ergo persone debetur accio, anima fuit tunc anima persone agentis.[4] Unde sicut anima Christi non fuit [5] spoliata gracia per mortem, et per consequens non [6] gracia unionis; sic non fuit spoliata potestate spirituali regia, caractere,[7] vel sacerdocio, quod est qualitas indelebilis secundum doctores. Unde sanctus Thomas concedit [8] quod Christus fuit sacerdos secundum animam in triduo iuxta textum Apostoli ad Hebre 8. 'Iesus autem eo quod maneat [9] in eternum sempiternum habet sacerdocium.'

This action is the action of a person, and the spirit is that of the person who performs the action.

Heb. viii. 24.

The human spirit of Christ did not lose the grace of union (with the Word), which endowed it with its royalty and priesthood. And to this both St. Thomas and Duns Scotus agree: and it would be absurd to suppose that without the hypostatic union a human spirit could perform acts of redemption.

Et revera non sapit [10] quod illa anima sit rex et sacerdos, nisi sit persona; quia actus huius officii sint signantissime personales. Et Doctor Subtilis vere dicit quod Christus mansit Christus in illo triduo. Sicut ergo nichil quod non est Deus sufficit genus humanum redimere, sic nichil quod non est Deus suffecit tam potenter de manu inimici patres eripere. Sed si hoc posset [11] in virtute Dei creatura ab eo ypostatice separata; per idem posset passio vel meritum cuiuscunque hominis a Deo personaliter seiuncti auctoritate Dei pro quocunque peccato | hominis facere recompensam. [B 121a]

Scripture also consistently assigns the triumph in hell to the person of Christ.

Ps. lxviii. 18.

Unde videtur michi scripturas insolubiles appropriate [12] tribuere persone Christi descensum [13] ad inferos et spoliacionem fidelium de potencia inimici. Nam Psalmo 67 dicitur ad litteram [14]de Christo dividente spolia 'Ascendisti [14] in altum' sed prius 'cepisti captivitatem,' et 3°. 'dedisti dona hominibus.' Cui [15] sensui alludit Apostolus ad Ephes. 4.

[1] dr̄am latronis. Vero A B; dr̄am latronis. Non C. [2] habuit *om.* O.
[3–3] *locus corruptus.* *Qu.* tenerentur, tantum creatura . . . spoliante?
[4] persona agens A B C. [5] est A B C. [6] non *om.* A B C.
[7] correctere O; *nempe* charactere. [8] concessit A B C.
[9] manet A B C; moneat O; maneat *Vulg.* [10] non sapit *om.* B; sapit *om.* O.
[11] potest A B C. [12] apropriate A B C. [13] descensus C.
[14] "de Christo" dicente. Sola ascendisti A; de Christo solo ascendisti B; dicente de Christo: Spolia ascendisti C. [15] Illi A B C.

'Ascendens,[1] inquit, Christus in altum,[2] captivam duxit captivitatem.' Et sequitur: 'quod autem ascendit, quid[3] est, nisi quia descendit primum ad partes inferiores terre?' Et ut ostenderet nobis quod eadem sit persona, que hec cuncta [C 47a] perficiat, subiungit: 'qui descendit ipse est et qui | ascendit super omnes celos ut impleret omnia.'

Eph. iv. 8–10.

and this triumph was effected in his humanity; and in his divinity;

Ex istis verbis Apostoli patet primo quod loquitur de Christo secundum humanitatem, secundum quam solum ascendere et descendere sibi conveniunt.[4] 2°. probat illum hominem esse Deum, cum post ascensionem dedit spiritualia dona hominibus mittendo eis Spiritum Sanctum, ut testatur [O 219c] utrumque testamentum et rei eventus probaverat | in effectu. [A 79b] 3°. intendit | quod eadem persona secundum humanitatem eandem descendit [5]et taliter[5] ascendit. 'Qui descendit, inquit, ipse et non alius ascendit,' racionem autem subiungit 'ut impleret omnia.'

in the unchanged personality, wherein he descended and ascended and filled all things.

Cum enim tres sint[6] regiones mundi notabiles,[7] in quibus oportuit Christum humanitus possessionem accipere vel sesinam,[8] scilicet celestium, terrestrium, et infernorum; proporcionaliter[9] descendit tripliciter benefaciens et repetens omagium de[10] subiectis. Primo descendit per inanicionem secundum infirmitatem carnis, [11]et cum mundus infirmus sibi similis in carne[11] et anima eciam genus proprium non cognovit. 2°. Descendit ad patres in limbo qui erant [12]tantum in spiritu post triumphum sed proporcionaliter in anima,[12] et indubie fuit in illo triduo in sinu Abrahe per 36 horas, quibus passio[13] continuata fuerat, non parva exaltacio capite coniuncto membris cum multitudine angelorum. Sicut enim sexto die creatum est genus humanum,[14] sic sexto senario, qui est numerus perfectus ex ductu eius in se circu-

As there are three regions, viz. heaven, earth and hell, of which Christ was to become Lord; so there was a three-fold descent, viz. 1. By the Incarnation; 2. By the descent of his soul into hell;

John i. 11.

[mystical interpretation of the three days.]

[1] ascendit A B C; ascendens O. [2] et *add.* B. [3] quidem O.
[4] convenit O. [5–5] taliter et A B C. [6] sint *om.* O.
[7] nobiles A C; mobiles B. [8] se'suram A; sessuram B C.
[9] proporcionabiliter A B C, *ut infra.* [10] a C O.
[11–11] et tunc cum mundus infernus similis in carne A B C.
[12–12] tamen post triumphum *om.* in spiritu O. *An ita corrigendum?*—qui erant tunc tantum in spiritu sed post triumphum proporcionaliter in anima.
[13] possessio A B C. [14] humanum *om.* A C; hominum O.

lariter, fuerat recreatum; ut[1] per tantum tempus clarere[2] posset veritas et excludi[3] ficticia mortis Chrsti. Resurrexit autem, ut confortaret ecclesiam de fide resurreccionis future, ut patet ad Cor. 15[4]; et ut 'primatum teneat' ut abbas ordinis Christiani aperiendo[5] patribus completo purgatis ianuam eternalem. Tempus autem continens purum integrum diem et duas seminoctes significat quod simpla mors Christi,[6] que integraliter fuit lucida proporcionaliter ad vitam, fuit medium sufficiens ad nostram duplicem mortem semiplenam. Tercius vero[7] fuit descensus[8] corporis in sepulchro,[9] qui nedum ostendit corpus vere mortuum anima ab eo[10] elongata, sed per omnia factus nobis consimilis sanctificavit subterraneas requies beandorum.

I Cor. xv. 12.

3. By the descent of his body into the grave.

Et correspondenter tres maneries hominum eripuit, et tres[11] dimisit. Extraxit enim, quasi mordens infernum, patriarchas prophetas et fideles alios, quorum peccata sunt plene purgata, relictis purgandis in purgatorio et dampnatis in inferno; sive sint infantes solis originalibus, si sit possibile, irretiti; sive adulti peccatis actualibus maculati.

So likewise *three* kinds of men were set free, and *three* 'dismissed.'

Sed 3°. post | privatam instruccionem apostolorum 40 diebus, [C 47b] ut patet Actuum 1°, ascendit gloriose in celum secundum utramque naturam summe beatus, ducens secum numerum insensibilem suo tempore captivorum; et sic tenendo primatum multiplicem inter omnia supposita humani generis, sicut est prior vel abbas omni dignitate: iuxta illud Baptiste: 'qui post me venit ante me[12] factus est,' Ioh. 1°. sic habuit primatum resurgencium, et virtute sui solius ascendentis omnia genera hominum ad se trahentis[13] fuit primus celum intrancium. Nemo enim sufficit[14] suo imperio portas huius[15] aperire[16] nisi filius [17]hominis, qui notus hostiariis prius descenderat.[17] Et sic indubie sicut illuminavit istas tres

After the forty days he ascended in triumph,

John i. 30.

the unique conqueror,

[1] et A B C O. [2] clare A, *pr. manu.* clarere A *corr. alt. manu.* B C O. [3] concludi O. [4] ad corum. 3°. O. [5] apperiendo A. [6] mors Christi simpla B; simplani—oris (*sic*) Christo O. [7] Tercio non C; 3°. vero O. [8] decensus O. [9] sepulcris A B. [10] a deo O. [11] et tres *om.* O. [12] prior *add.* C. [13] trahentes O. [14] suffecit A B C. [15] huiusmodi B. [16] apperire A O. [17–17] hominis hostiarius prius descenderet A B C; hominis qui notis hostiariis prius descenderat O; hostiarius *pro* ostiarius.

machinas sua humanitate impletas, ita suscepit omagium[1] vel obsequium utrobique: cum secundum Apostolum ad [B 121b] Philipp. 2°. 'oportet quod in nomine | Iesu omne[2] genu flectatur celestium, quos restituit, terrestrium, quos redemit, et infernorum,' quos spoliavit.

Omnia quidem hec fecit humanitas Christi. Et ideo post tantum honorem triumphalem individui humane nature prohibuit nimirum Iohannem angelus seipsum vel[3] dulia adorare, [A 79c] ut[4] patet Apoc. ultimo capitulo | : ante quidem satis permiserant,[5] ut patet Gen. 18 et Iosue 5. Omnia quidem hec fecit idem filius hominis secundum eandem humanitatem continue[6] ypostatice copulatum: qua unione habita patet quod oportet Christum esse continue creaturam et aliquid quod prius non fuerat. Sed quid, rogo, si non homo? Ipsa ergo humanitas fecit[7] hec omnia, id est, 'in opus ministerii, in edificacionem corporis Christi,' ut dicit Apostolus ad Ephes. 4°., quia Ioh. 4°. dicitur: 'meus cibus est ut faciam voluntatem eius, [8]qui misit me, ut perficiam opus eius,' id est,[8] ut perfecte usque ad consummacionem faciam: inter que hoc videtur principium,[9] descendere ad inferna et extrahere patres captivos in limbo, sicut ante promiserat. Et huic consonat[10] illud Zacharie[11] 9°. ubi post propheciam Messie quod veniet salvator et ipse 'pauper et ascendens super asinam et super pullum asine' alloquitur eundem Messiam in hec verba: 'Tu quoque in sanguine testamenti tui emisisti vinctos tuos de lacu in quo non est aqua.' Quod[12] exponitur ad litteram de patribus incarceratis in limbo. Et[13] idem sonat illud Osee 13. verificatum ad litteram de Messia: 'ero[14] mors tua, o mors; ero morsus tuus, inferne.'[15]

Qui ergo sumus,[16] ut impugnemus [17]tenorem verborum fidei vel scripture,[17] specialiter cum sanctioribus et approba-

and received universal homage.

Phil. ii. 10.

All this was the work of Christ's humanity; and

Rev. xxii. 9.

thereby exalted

Gen. xviii. 2. Josh. v. 14.

human nature above angels.

But he is still a creature in his humanity, which is united by the hypostatic union

Eph. iv. 12.

John iv. 34.

with his Divinity, as various prophecies testify.

Zech. ix. 9.

Hos. xiii. 14.

We dare not, therefore,

[1] homagium C O. [2] Jesu omne *om.* B. [3] vel *om.* A B; se *om.* O.
[4] ut ut C. [5] permiserat A B C; promisserant O; permiserant *sc. angeli.*
[6] continue *om.* A. [7] fecit bis O. [8]–[8] qui . . . est *om.* O.
[9] primum A B C. [10] et *add.* O. [11] zekarie O. [12] sed B.
[13] ad *add.* O. [14] ero *om.* B. [15] in inferno O. [16] quum ergo nescimus O.
[17]–[17] vel tenorem verborum scripture A B C.

contravene the concurrent testimony of Holy Scripture, the creed, the fathers and doctors, that Christ was man in the three days.

tioribus[1] doctoribus visa sit illa[2] logica subtilis et de virtute sermonis verissima?[2] Pro certo per idem possemus innovando falsificare reputacione totum corpus biblie[3] scripture. Ideo expedit obstare principiis | erroris[4] ne error intollerabilis[5] [C 48a] consequatur.

If Christ ceased to be man in the three days, it follows that there was a second Incarnation at the resurrection.

Item iuxta sic loquentes sequitur quod Christus bis factus fuit homo, bis eciam incarnatus. Nam semel fuit incarnatus et humiliatus[6] in utero virginis et in morte desiit[7] esse homo et caro, et post pro instanti[8] resurreccionis incepit | esse homo [O 219d] corporeus: ergo conclusio. Si enim[9] homo pro quacunque modica[10] morula reticens post loquelam reloquatur,[11] bis loquitur; multo evidencius persona, que 33 annis[12] est homo et post per[13] intercisum triduum non est homo ac tercio post est homo, bis evidenter est homo.

Three reasons against this. 1. It would lead to the absurd conclusion, that his resurrection and birth (or generation) were identical.

Sed consequens videtur[14] falsum tripliciter.[15] Primo ex hoc quod tunc resurreccio Christi foret eius nativitas vel generacio. Et sic Christus haberet triplicem nativitatem et generacionem multiplicem: nativitatem unam eternam et duas alias temporales.[16] Nam generacio Christi prima[17] in utero ideo est generacio quia est produccio a non esse hominem ad esse hominem. Cum ergo sic sit pro instanti[18] resurreccionis, sequitur quod illa sit generacio, et per idem nativitas ex[19] sepulcro, sicut foret posito quod semen virginis esset per se positum[20] in sepulcro, et[21] successive vel subito[22] lineatum, ac creata anima copulata.[22] Nec est locus nativitati corporali pertinens, nisi forte racione conservacionis, sicut nec est pertinens nativitati ex spiritu, de qua Ioh. 3°., sed utrobique habita generacione renati consequitur proporcionaliter[23]

John iii 6.

[1] approbatis A B C; approbatoribus O.
[2] lingva (lingbba B) subtilis et de vi verbi sit vera A B C.
[3] biblic *om.* O.
[4] erorum A B C.
[5] intellerabilis O.
[6] humanitus A B C.
[7] desivit O.
[8] et post tempore A B C; pro $\Theta^{ti}$ O, *ut saepe infra.*
[9] ergo A B C.
[10] monica B.
[11] reloquendo O.
[12] annis *om.* B.
[13] per *om.* A B C.
[14] verbi B.
[15] dupliciter A B.
[16] eternas B.
[17] prima est B C; persone O.
[18] vel instanti resurreccionis A; pro tempore sibi instanti resurrectionis B; pro Φ resurrectionis C; pro $\Theta^{ti}$ resurreccionis O.
[19] in A B C.
[20] esset suppositum A B; esset persuppositum C.
[21] ut A B C.
[22] creatum (lineatum *in margine*) ac creata anima, anima copulata A; creatum ac creata anima copulata B; lineatum ac creata anima anima copulata C.
[23] proporcionalis A B C.

nativitas. Oportet ergo ad resurreccionem persone quod eadem persona, que cecidit sopore mortis sive[1] intercisione humanitatis, resurgat; cum spiritus racionalis persone[2] sit humanitas et sic homo.

Secundo obicitur contra dictum consequens per hoc, quod mundus per mortem Christi esset quantumlibet imperfectus: quod est impossibile, cum illa fuit mors iustissima preciosissima et utilissima perficiens[3] totum mundum: et consequencia [A 79d] probatur. Christus, in quantum homo, est | pars mundi, ut patet eciam modernis loquentibus, qui concedunt Christum, in quantum homo est, esse creaturam: et mundus est universitas creaturarum. Cum ergo Christum esse hominem plus perficit mundum quam totum usque[4] celum vel quecunque alia pars mundi; videtur quod, hoc ablato, plus proporcionaliter imperficitur ille mundus: quod est impossibile; [B 122a] | cum tanta perfeccio, quanta ad humanitatem Christi attinet, servatur in anima et corpore incorrupto. Ideo cum totum[5] sit sue partes, patet quod mansit idem homo in triduo.

2. His death, by withdrawing out of the universe of created things one created thing (the man Christ), would have inflicted loss, not conferred boundless gain.

Tercio confirmatur illud ex[6] testimonio scripture. Nam Ioh. 19 scribitur: 'ad Iesum autem cum venissent,[7] ut[8] viderunt eum iam mortuum, non fregerunt eius[9] crura; sed unus militum lancea[10] latus eius[11] [12]apperuit, et exivit sanguis[12] et aqua: et qui vidit, inquit Iohannes, testimonium perhibuit;[13] et verum est testimonium eius.' Rogo, quomodo [C 48b] venissent ad Iesum | mortuum,[14] nisi ille homo mortuus esset Iesus? aut quomodo miles lancea latus eius Iesu aperiret,[15] si non tunc fuerat latus Jesu? Numquid credimus quod evangelista, tam signanter asserens [16]se ista vidisse ultra omnia alia[16] gesta Christi, finxit mendacium? Et si dicatur quod littera occidit, sensus autem spiritualis et rectus vivificat,

3. Scripture speaks of him John xix. 32, 33. during the three days as Jesus: and we must take Scripture literally.

[1] sine A B C. [2] species racionalis per se O. [3] utillissima et totum *om.* perficiens O.
[4] usque *om.* A B C. [5] toum *sic* C. [6] ex *om.* B. [7] perveuissent B.
[8] et A B C O, ut *Vulg.* [9] eius *om.* B. [10] lancia O. [11] eius *om.* O.
[12–12] perforavit et sangwis C. [13] perhibet O. [14] venissent *add.* B
[15] apperiret (*sic*) A (uit written above the underlined "iret"); aperuit B. [16] se vidisse omnia ista ultra omnia alia B.

If we introduce finedrawn philosophical glosses into Scripture, we reach absurd conclusions:

cuiusmodi est talis?—cum venissent ad illud corpus mortuum, quod [1]non potuit esse Iesus, sed[1] prius, non tunc fuit corpus Iesu; tunc unus militum, non latus eius, nec univoce latus alicuius aperuit, sed partem unius corporis mortui, quod non tunc fuit Christus vel pars eius[2]; et exivit, non sanguis redempcionis et aqua baptismatis de latere Christi, quia tunc non fuit Christus. Et sic spiritus, aqua,[3] et sanguis non sunt nec fuerunt testes humanitatis Christi, quia non simul fuerunt, sicut videtur Iohannes dicere I Ioh 4°. Nec est verum ad verba illud quod dicit Apostolus ad Ephes. 5°. quod 'Christus sic dilexit ecclesiam quod tradidit semetipsum pro illa, ut sanctificaret[4] mundans eam lavacro aque in verbo vite;' cum ecclesia per totum triduum fuit cum sponso vel capite Christo.[5] Nec est illud Apostoli ad Ephes 5°. verum ad verba, quando illud Gen. 2.[6] [7]dictum ad sensum litteralem de primo Adam et de uxore[7] sua, exponit ad sensum misticum de Christo et ecclesia: 'hoc, inquit textus, nunc os ex ossibus meis et caro de carne mea: propter hoc [8]relinquet homo patrem et matrem suam et adherebit uxori sue, et erunt duo in carne una.' 'Sacramentum,[8] inquit Apostolus, hoc magnum est: ego autem dico in Christo et in ecclesia.' Illa autem exposicio Apostoli est impossibilis, scilicet quod,[9] sicut ex costa Adam resoluti[10] in soporem[11] edificata est sponsa eius secundum membra ossea solida et tenera, sic ex apertura[12] lateris secundi Adami edificata est ecclesia sponsa Christi secundum varietatem[13] membrorum ecclesie. Nec reliquit[14] Christus Patrem semetipsum[15] exinaniendo[16] et exeundo a[17] Patre, ut dicitur Ioh. 16°.; et 'matrem synagogam in qua natus' est Isa. 50[18]; et adherebit uxori sue scilicet ecclesie, ut dicitur Osee 2°. Nec erant duo coniugata in eadem natura communi tam secundum carnem[19] quam

1 John iv. 6, 9.
Eph. v. 26.
as several examples show.
Eph. v. 31, 32.
Gen. ii. 24.
John xvi. 27.
Isa. li. 1.
Hos. ii. 16, 19.

[1–1] non potuit . . . sed *om.* A B C. [2] eius *om.* O. [3] a quo B.
[4] eam *add.* A B C. [5] Christo *om.* O. [6] 3° A B C. [7–7] dictum . . . uxore *om.* O.
[8–8] relinquet etc. Sacramentum B. [9] quod *om.* A B.
[10] resoluta A B; resoluto C. [11] sopore B. [12] appertura A B C; aptura *pro* aptura O.
[13] veritatem A B C. [14] requirit O. [15] seipsum O. [16] exauiniendo A B C.
[17] de O. [18] Isa. 7 A B C. [19] naturam *in margine corr.* carnem B.

spiritum ac[1] affeccione tam sensitiva quam intellectiva concordes; ut exponit Augustinus et alii sequentes Apostolum. Sed quelibet illarum particularum est impossibilis de vi vocis, cum Christus non passus est mortem in cruce; quia pro[2] instanti mortis Christus non est Christus, nec fuit illud [A 80a] sacramentum in Christo et ecclesia: cum pro toto tri|duo non fuit Christus, sed sponsa exspectavit usque ad instans resurreccionis sponsalia. Deliramenta sunt ista et verbis puerorum similia.[3]

Unde omnes moderniores doctores, quorum scripta memini me legisse, dicunt concorditer quod in triduo corpus illud fuit corpus Christi sicut et anima fuit tunc anima Christi: quia manentibus extremis unionis[4] Verbi ad naturam assumptam, [C 49a] manet eadem unio. Unde dicunt, | quod est syncedochica[5] locucio, sepelierunt Iesum, id est, corpus Iesu. [6]Sed ego [O 220a] non video, quomodo foret tunc corpus Iesu,[6] | nisi Iesus tunc foret Iesus corporeus, habens omnes partes illius corporis partes suas, iuxta illam[7] Veritatis vocem Mt 26°. 'mittens hec unguentum[8] hoc in corpus meum ad sepeliendum me fecit.' Pro certo ego credo quod ipse Christus sicut et[9] quelibet pars corporis sui sepultus est.

Not only was the body of Christ buried, but

Matt. xxvi. 12.

Christ himself was buried,

Ideo hoc[10] concedo cum istis doctoribus in prima parte, cum sit de fide, et concedo de summa virtute sermonis [B 122b] Christum iacuisse in sepulcro; cum illud corpus mortuum fuit | persona[11] Verbi: non quod[12] quelibet pars quantitativa illius corporis generaretur[13] pro instanti mortis, sic quod Christus tunc generaretur assumendo novam naturam: sed manens continue idem[14] corpus prius vivum et[15] post mortuum subiectum est perpetuo[16] eidem ypostatice unioni. Nam per totum triduum Christus mansit homo tam secundum corpus quam secundum[17] animam; et vere passus est mortem pro

Christ lay in the tomb, the hypostatic union with the Word remaining;

[1] et B; *om.* O. [2] per C. [3] puerorum dissimilia A B C. [4] unionibus A B C.
[5] synochica A; sinodochia B; sýnodogica O; syndochica C. *pro* syncedochica *i.e. per synecdochen.* [6–6] sed . . . Iesu *om.* O.
[7] illud O. [8] hec *om.* A B C; hunguentum B. [9] in O.
[10] hoc *om.* A B C; ideo *om.* O. [11] Christi *add.* O. [12] quod *om.* O.
[13] generabatur A B O. [14] continuo A B C; illud C. [15] et *om.* A B C.
[16] perpetue B. [17] secundum *om.* C O.

In virtue of which his death and the water and the blood from his side were effectual.

instanti separacionis; cum caro mortua, que tunc[1] fuit Christus, passa est privacionem vite: et vere de latere Christi exierunt aqua et sanguis Christi pro mora exitus; quia Christus pro toto triduo est idem corpus mortuum, cuius sanguine et spiritibus effluentibus, ut anima naturaliter separetur, reservata est miraculose subtilior pars sanguinis cum ichore[2] ad sponsalia celebranda inter sponsum viventem gloriose in triduo post triumphum et corpus suum misticum,

Isa. xi. 10.

quod est ecclesia. Nam Isae 11°.[3] scribitur: 'radix Iesse[4] in signum populorum, ipsum gentes deprecabuntur; erit sepulcrum eius gloriosum.' Et sic intelliguntur alie scripture de Christo ad litteram tam novi quam veteris testamenti. Oportet enim interpretari[5] scripturas de Christi humanitate secundum sensum, quem in eis sancti doctores sunt sedulo scrutati.

It is not a valid objection that, in speaking of a dead body or separate soul as a 'man,' we use

Et si[6] obiciatur,[7] quod ista posicio, vocando 'hominem' corpus mortuum et animam separatam, sequitur sentenciam plebeiorum,[8] et per consequens est erronea, ut multa alia dicta vulgaria; dicitur quod non est color in consequencia; cum dicta vulgaria a prima veritate communitati[9] hominum inspirata

John xii. 35.

popular not philosophical language.

non possunt in toto esse falsa. Unde Salvator Ioh. 12°. approbat turbe[10] sentenciam, que dixit: 'Nos audivimus ex lege quod Christus manet in eternum. Adhuc, inquit, modicum lumen in vobis est; ambulate dum lucem habetis, [11] ut

The multitude may speak truth:

non tenebre vos comprehendant; dum lucem habetis,[11] credite in lucem, ut filii [12] lucis sitis.' Quasi diceret [12] iuxta exposicionem beati Augustini Omc. 52. 'Verum est principium

Christ himself acknowledged that they did, when they said, "Christ abideth for ever."

quod de Christo concipitis, scilicet quod ipse eternaliter manet humanitus cognoscendo. Sed oportet ultra procedere, quod non obest eundem hominem [13] esse mortuum corporaliter et cum hoc mente vivere. Ambulate, inquit Augustinus, attendite et totum intelligite tam moriturum[14] Christum quam

[1] que tunc *bis* O. [2] iecore A B C: ÿcore O. [3] 7° A B C.
[4] qui stat *add.* A B C [5] impleri A B C O. [6] si *om.* O.
[7] obicitur A. [8] plebeorum A B C; plebiorum O.
[9] communitate C; a primis veritate communicati hominem O.
[10] turpe O. [11–11] etc. et A B C. [12] sitis lucis q. d. iuxta B; scitis O.
[13] eundem hominem *bis* O. [14] mortuum O.

victurum in eternum. Cum aliquid, inquit, verum habetis, C 49b] non sitis comprehensi | tenebris ignorancie[1] contempnendo A 80b] mortuum et occisum[2] | hinc trahentem ad se omnia, et sic offendatis in lapidem offensionis et petram scandali.' Unde Ome. 78[3] super istud[4] Ioh. 14. 'non turbetur cor vestrum:[5] declarando Christum esse duplicem formam, scilicet humanitatem et deitatem, subdit de eius humanitate. 'Non, inquit, homo Christus, non dixit[6] "Filius Dei," quod eciam sola caro eius in sepulcro meruit appellari?' Probat. 'Cum,[7] inquit, credimus in Dei Filium qui sepultus est, profecto et Filium Dei dicimus carnem que sola sepulta est.' Et post declarando quomodo ad verba [8]est verum, 'Pater[8] maior me est,' per hoc quod est duarum formarum utraque, ita subdit: 'Quid ergo, heretice?[9] cum Christus sit Deus et homo, loquitur ut homo; et tu calumpniaris Deo?[10] Ille in se commendat naturam humanam; et tu in illo audes deformare divinam? Infidelis, ingrate,[11] nonne tu minuis eum qui te fecit, quia ille dicitur [12]factus sic[12] propter te? Equalis enim Patri est Filius per quem factus est homo; ut minor esset Patre, factus est homo; [13]quod nisi fieret, quid esset homo?[13] agnoscamus, inquit, geminam substanciam Christi: divinam[14] scilicet, qua equalis est Patri; et humanam, qua minor est Patre. Utrumque autem simul; non duo, sed unus est Christus, ne sit quaternitas non Trinitas Deus.[15] Sicut enim unus est homo, anima racionalis et caro, Christum, inquit, in omnibus istis et[16] singulis confitemur. Probat hoc. Quis est ergo, per quem factus est mundus? Christus Iesus; sed in forma Dei. Quis est sub Poncio Pilato crucifixus? Iesus Christus; sed in forma servi. Item de singulis ex quibus[17] homo constat. Quis non[18] derelictus est in inferno? Christus

Augustine explains this saying

John xiv. 1.

with its context of the combined human and divine nature of Christ.

John xiv. 28.

[1] et *add.* O.
[2] ocasum C.
[3] Unde act. 78 B.
[4] istud *om.* O.
[5] etc. *add.* A B.
[6] dixit *om.* A B C.
[7] probat tamen A B C.
[8]–[8] est vero non pater C.
[9] heretici O.
[10] ut deo B.
[11] infidelis vel ingrate A B; infideliter, Nonne C.
[12]–[12] factus est homo ut minor esset patre sic O.
[13]–[13] quod . . . homo *om.* B.
[14] divinarum O.
[15] deus *om.* O.
[16] et *om.* O.
[17] de singulis quibus O.
[18] enim A B C.

Iesus; sed in anima sola. Quis resurrecturus in triduo iacuit in sepulcro? Christus Iesus; sed in | carne sola.' [B 143a]

And, to understand this, we must bear in mind that Christ is any of three natures (cf. p. 3, l. 6).

Hec sentencia huius sancti que, sicut non potest dissolvi, sic non cognosci, nisi viso quod Christus est trium naturarum incommunicancium quelibet. Qui ergo voluerit illam materiam[1] verissimam de virtute sermonis infringere, incipiat communicacionem persone[2] Christi multis naturis, non multis personis, ut deitas, improbare. Parcant igitur emuli huic vie quod naturali instinctu a vulgo sit cognita; quod a scriptura sacra et sanctis doctoribus sit tam assidue declarata; et quod mentes fidelium substrata sentencia non fallaci sed veridica excitat pro cura mortuorum, ut sepultura cum aliis exequiis devocius peragenda. Eadem enim persona hominis, que heri viva conversata est cum proximis, deportatur hodie mortua ad ecclesiam, et deponitur in sepulcro.

Thus Scripture, authority, and the common instinct of men, shown in their care for the dead, support our thesis that a dead man is a man;

and the sophistical objections to miracles wrought by relics and to invocation of saints, have no weight.

Nec oportet timere ampullosas[3] | instancias sophisticas [O 220b] quibus nituntur istam sentenciam impugnare dicendo, quod frivolum est credere racione corporum mortuorum vel personarum sanctarum in celo Deum facere miracula: cum, ut false garriunt, non est corpus sancti mortuum,[4] nec sunt reliquie | sanctorum, nec est possibile Petrum Iacobum vel [C 50a] Iohannem ante resurreccionem orare, sicut in letaniis[5] canit illusa ecclesia per ignoranciam logice[6] minus caute. Quicunque ergo sophista logicus[7] vel naturalis vel methaphisicus vere voluerit ista defendere vel probare, si dicta factis compensat,[8] est simul [9]excellencior philosophus et objector[10] quam Deus hucusque dignatus est sensibus mortalium | propalare.[9] [A 80c]

Objection.

Nec credo sophistam ad tantum desipere quod credat, si sola caro Christi fuit Christus in sepulcro et sola anima fuit Christus in inferno, quod[11] tunc sola caro vel sola anima fuit

[1] senteneiam O. [2] persone *om.* A B C.
[3] Nac . . . appullosas B; ampulosas O. [4] mortuorum A B C.
[5] letariis B; lataniis C. [6] loyce C. [7] loytus C. [8] dictis facta compenset O.
[9–9] excellencior vel abiectior philosophia (philosophus C) quam deus unquam hucusque sensibus mortalium voluit propalare A B C.
[10] abicôr O. abiectior *non* abieccior A B C. [11] quod *om.* O.

Christus. Ac si sic[1] argueretur solus Petrus est homo [2]in domo ista: ergo solus Petrus est homo[2] alicubi tenendo quidem diccionem exclusive, sicut facit Augustinus quando dicit[3] quod nec sola caro nec sola anima fuit Christus, sed humanitas completa, que differt a parte qualitativa: patet decepcio sophistica introducta; et sicut dixi superius, quando Augustinus dicit quod pars qualitativa non est homo, exponit se ipsum quod non est completus homo, id est, natura composita[4] ex corpore et anima: et sic intelligit 17[5] de Trinitate ca. 7. exponens se ipsum quod intelligit 'hominem' ut veteres diffinierunt[6] per 'animal racionale mortale,' vel iuxta descripcionem suam 'substanciam racionalem constantem ex corpore et anima.' Et[7] per hoc distinguit inter triplicitatem naturarum in homine et trinitatem anime ac Trinitatem increatam. Affirmative itaque sue sunt concedende et negative modificande.

"When flesh and spirit are separated, neither alone is Christ."

As Augustine shows in his definitions of Man, there is a distinction between complete humanity and a qualitative part of humanity.

Ulterius si queratur, utrum verum sit in triduo quod hoc est corpus Christi et hec anima Christi pro nunc; dicitur[8] quod sic: cum[9] Christus vere sit tam corpus quam anima pro triduo, quo simul iacet mortuus et descendit vivus ad inferos, et sic persona viva est mortua secundum diversas naturas. Et movent me tria. Primo auctoritas scripture et exposicio beati Augustini superius recitata.[10] Secundo quod aliter non esset concedendum quod Christus sit homo per illud triduum, quod nimis invaderet fidem meam. Et tercio quod doctores tam priores sapienciores quam moderniores capaciores[11] dicunt concorditer quod Christus nichil de humana natura dimisit quod[12] assumpsit, sed mansit per triduum unitus tam carni[13] quam anime sicut ante. Cum igitur unione ypostatica, que non est per accidens unio ypostatica, fuerat antea copulatus[14]; sequitur quod per illud triduum manet tam caro quam anima sicut prius. Unde

In the three days the body and the soul were the body and soul of Christ: for three reasons. 1. The authority of Scripture and of Augustine as above. 2. The continuity of the humanity of Christ. 3. The continuity of the hypostatic union.

[1] sic *om.* C. [2-2] in domo . . . homo *om.* O. [3] dicitur O. [4] complesita O.
[5] 19 O. [6] definierunt O. [7] et *om.* C.
[8] christi. Pronunc dicitur A B C. [9] quod B. [10] recita O.
[11] capciosiores A B C. [12] quam C O. [13] corpori A B C.
[14] perante copulata A B C; añtea copulatus O.

dicunt loquentes nostri temporis concorditer quod sacerdos conficiens pro illo triduo conficeret dicendo verba sacramentalia corpus mortuum. Sed quomodo, queso, per verba falsissima[1] quibus diceret 'hoc est corpus meum' vere conficeret, nisi corpus confectum pro tunc fuerit corpus Christi?

St. Thomas quoted, to the same effect. But his doctrine of substantial forms requires modification, as shown in the *De Anima*: else three difficulties arise.

Unde sanctus Thomas de Christo ca°. 50 videtur dicere[2] quod idem sit corpus Christi mortuum[3] pro illo triduo quod[4] fuit corpus Christi post et ante; et hoc racione unionis ad Verbum; licet quelibet pars quantitativa[5] illius corporis racione forme substancialis substancialiter | variatur. Teneo igitur[6] primam [C 50b] partem huius sentencie et vario in 2a.; cum oportet | formas [B 123b] substanciales esse subordinatas anime, ut patet ex dictis *De Anima*. Nec video quin, si ad omnem punctum corporis Christi generata sit nova forma[7] substancialis preter quamcunque formam substancialem que infuit Christo vivo, foret aliud novum corpus mortuum secundum quamlibet eius partem quantitativam quam fuerat corpus vivum. Nec video 2°. quomodo illud esset tunc corpus Christi, [8]nisi tunc Christus esset Christus, et[8] esset illi novo[9] corpori nova unione ypostatice copulatus.[10] Nec video 3°. quomodo illud corpus sit mortuum, cum sit per totum noviter generatum, et nunquam antea fuit vivum. Dico ergo quod idem corpus in numero tam secundum materiam quam secundum[11] formam corporis, quod prius participative vixit, est in triduo corpus mortuum et cum hoc Christus Deus noster. | [A 80d]

My doctrine is that both in matter and form it was in the three days the same body of Christ as before.

Three objections considered.

Sed contra illud obicitur. Videtur primo quod corpus mortuum [12] sit corpus vivum; quia Christus, qui est corpus mortuum[12] in dicto triduo, est corpus vivum post et ante: et sic, cum corpus animatum et corpus inanimatum distinguuntur in specie, videtur quod illa non sunt idem corpus in numero, cum differencia specifica presupponit differenciam

[1] falsisima O. [2] dicere *om.* B. [3] quod *add.* C. [4] quam O.
[5] quantitativa *om.* A B C. [6] itaque O. [7] form) O.
[8-8] nisi christus tunc esset christo et A; nisi illud tunc esset christus et C.
[9] novi B. [10] computatus O.
[11] quam secundum *om.* O. [12-13] sit . . . mortuum *om.* O.

numeralem.[1] Hic dicitur quod corpus vivum et animatum est idem corpus in numero mortuum et inanimatum, licet non simul et semel; nec differt corpus in quantum [2]animatum specifice ab inanimato[2] corpore. Pro quo notandum quod dupliciter[3] dicitur corpus animatum, scilicet, ab extrinseco participative, vel ab intrinseco qualitative[4]; ut corpus compositum ex corpore et anima est animatum anima, que est eius forma et quiditas, et illud non potest esse inanimatum: sed corpus, quod est altera pars qualitativa hominis, est animatum participacione anime; que, cum non sit forma eius intrinseca, potest abesse a corpore manente eodem in numero; sicut homines, qui participative dicuntur dii possunt manere iidem[5] Deo absente ab eis per graciam.

Objection i. "A dead body is a living body."

Answer. A body remains the same body, although the extrinsic quality of animation be withdrawn.

2°. obicitur sic. Si Christus in dicto triduo habet corpus et animam, [6]tunc Christus est animatus; et per consequens tam corpus quam anima[6] est pars[7] Christi; et per consequens Christus in illo triduo componitur ex corpore et anima; et per consequens non iacet mortuus in sepulcro.

Objection ii. "If Christ had body and soul in the three days, he was not dead."

Hic dupliciter[8] dicitur. Primo quod tam [9]corpus quam anima[9] eius[10] est pars Christi, sed non in dicto triduo; quia non tunc qualitative componunt Christum, sed alias pro suo tempore. Unde posito quod essemus in dicto triduo, vere sciremus quod hec[11] anima que nunc est anima Christi, sed non nunc pars Christi, est pars Christi optima post et ante;
220c] et correspondenter | de corpore. Ex quo patet quod hec non est synecdochica[12] locucio: 'hoc corpus' vel 'hec anima est nunc Christus:' sed, sicut homo est essencia substancia vel quiditas sua intransitive intelligendo, sic Christus est tunc hoc corpus et hec anima, que sunt sua ad[13] sensum intransitivum, ut supra. Unde hec anima, licet non nunc animat corpus illud quod iacet mortuum, animat tamen Filium Dei;

To which there are two answers. Answer 1. The body and soul were then the body and soul of Christ, but not in composition.

[1] materialem A B C.
[2]–[2] inanimatum specifice ab animato A B; inanimatum specifice abianimato (*sic*) C.
[3] dur O.
[4] quiditative O.
[5] idem A B C.
[6]–[6] tunc Christus . . . quam anima *bis* A.
[7] corpus O.
[8] duplicitur A; communiter O.
[9]–[9] anima quam corpus B.
[10] eius *om.* A B C.
[11] licet A B C.
[12] sinodica A B C; synodogica O, cf. p. 39, n. 5.
[13] ad *om.* O.

sicut caput[1] denominat hominem capitatum: et patet quod[2] animare est equivocum ad corpus subiectum vivificare et ad denominare personam cui copulatur ypostatice habentem[3] animam, quam[4] per se animat, cum ad invicem[5] consequuntur[6] vires inferiores sicut passio ad subiectum.

Answer 2. The body and soul are each a part of Christ, but neither a 'qualitative' nor 'quantitative' but a 'discretive' part.

Secunda responsio dicit quod tam corpus quam anima Christi est in triduo vere pars Christi, sed nec qualitativa nec quantitativa, cum non tunc [7]componuntur ad idem,[7] sed est pars discretiva. Et sic intelligit Damascenus, quod Christus descendit totus ad inferos, sicut totus iacuit in sepulcro, sed non totum; quia persona fuit homo in utroque loco, sed non secundum ambas naturas; et sic in triduo habuit omnes partes [8]quas habuit[8] post resurreccionem, sed[9] tunc defecit unio vel[10] composicio. Sed nullum absolutum[11]: nec pono vim in illa variacione, quia utraque sentencia est satis[12] catholica ad sensus equivocos.[13]

Objection iii. "Christ was neither a mortal nor an immortal man during the three days, and therefore not man at all."

Sed 3°. obicitur ex hoc, quod Christus in illo triduo nec est homo immortalis nec homo[14] mortalis; et omnis homo est mortalis vel immortalis: ergo Christus pro illo triduo non est homo. Maior patet eo quod Christus tunc passus est mortem: ergo iuxta Apostolum 'mors illi ultra[15] non dominabitur.' Et quod non sit homo immortalis videtur ex hoc quod iacet mortuus in sepulcro et nondum consecutus | [A 81a] est dotem[16] immortalitatis, sed primo in resurreccione sequente iuxta communem doctorum sentenciam.[17]

Rom. vi. 9.

Answer. He was both mortal

Hic dicitur quod Christus pro hoc[18] triduo est tam homo mortalis quam eciam[19] homo immortalis. Est homo mortalis quia corpus, quod moritur et[20] iacet mortuum in sepulcro. Pro quo notandum quod mori, cum sit privari vita, vel potest intelligi ut dicit subitum actum privacionis vite a corpore, vel ut dicit absolute[21] carenciam vite a corpore prius[22] vivi-

[1] capud B C. [2] quomodo A B C. [3] habente B. [4] quomodo O.
[5] inbicem C; mentem O. [6] consequitur A B C. [7–7] componunt ad invicem O.
[8–8] sicut A B C. [9] et A B C. [10] seu A C; sive B.
[11] ab^tū=absolutum A B C. [12] satis *om.* A B. [13] equivoces O. [14] homo *om.* O.
[15] ultra *om.* A B. [16] dotem & mortalitatis O. [17] sentencias C.
[18] per hec O. [19] quan et C. [20] et *om.* A B.
[21] absolute *om.* O. [22] prius *om.* A B C.

ficato. Primo modo[1] est mors Christi subita non possibilis iterari licet Christus eternaliter potest mori. 2°. modo est[2] mors triduana, sicut corpus incorruptibile per triduum caret vita, sicut aer habet tenebram triduanam, et sicut pater semper gignit[3] filium, sol semper producit lumen et medium per tempus privatur lumine, licet quodlibet istorum complete continue sit[4] productum. Sic Christus ad sensum expositum[5] continue moritur per istud triduum et habet simplam mortem triduanam, sicut dampnati habent mortem perpetuam. Est ergo Christus mortalis pro illo triduo cum moritur in effectu: non potest tamen nisi solummodo semel mori. Est eciam immortalis pro illo triduo[6] quia est spiritus Iesus,[7] qui nec potest mori corporaliter nec spiritualiter. and immortal.

Et si obicitur quod hic predicatur oppositum de opposito; homo mortalis pro hoc instanti[8] est homo immortalis; dicitur quod verum est. Ideo conclusio est impossibilis. Nec est color in isto paralogismo:—ergo homo mortalis est homo immortalis — iste homo Dominus Iesus est nunc homo [C 51b] mortalis, | et iste idem homo est nunc homo immortalis;— Non enim sequitur, si persona que est commune ad ambas naturas illas est utraque illarum, quod ex hoc una sit reliqua; sicut non oportet, licet tantum sit unus Deus et ille sit copulative[9] tam Deus genitus quam Deus ingenitus, quia tam Pater quam Filius, quod exinde Pater sit Filius vel Deus genitus sit Deus ingenitus, quod est idem. Nec sequitur, si Petrus sapiens et salvatus sit natura humana specifica, et Paulus insipiens et dampnatus sit eadem natura specifica, quod Petrus sapiens et salvatus sit Paulus insipiens[10] et dampnatus. Et patet [11] ex simili modo [11] nutritis in rectis principiis. Sicut enim natura divina est trium personarum quelibet, et species humana personarum hominum quelibet; et tamen tantum est una natura divina sive

And there is no real contradiction here.

[1] modo *om.* C. [2] est *om.* A B. [3] gnignit O. [4] sit *om.* A B.
[5] secundam exposicionem O. [6] pro illo triduo *om.* C O. [7] Iesu A B C.
[8] per hoc instans A B C. [9] copulate C. [10] incipiens O.
[11–11] similitudo A B C; ex silido O.

[1]species humana:[1] sic persona Verbi Dei est trium naturarum quelibet et tamen una persona Verbi.

*Peter Lombard's denial accounted for by the ambiguity of the terms employed.*

Quod autem Magister Distinctione 22 aliter loquitur cum modernis est propter equivocacionem, cum non admittit aliquid pro quacunque mensura esse hominem, nisi tunc componatur ex corpore et anima. Nos autem sequentes[2] scripturam non ficte sed philosophice[3] dicimus quod eadem persona Petri vel cuiuscunque sancti prioris, que conversata est hic corporaliter in terris, manet iam beata in celis; et ubicunque est spiritus ille creatus sive in corpore sive extra corpus est idem homo in numero, et solum, ubi est corpus vel anima, est persona humanitus. Ut patet Ep. 40 ad Dardanum. Et cum certum sit quod Christus pro illo triduo non componitur qualitative[4] ex corpore et anima, eo quod unio illorum dissolvitur; patet quod tunc nec est sic homo mortalis nec homo immortalis, quia non ad illum[5] sensum tunc est homo. Si autem vocatur[6] vere corpus et anima separata utrumque homo, sicut vocat Hugo de sancto Victore sequendo Augustinum, scripturas, et philosophicas raciones; tunc respondendum est sicut superius ad obiectus. Nam anima est per se homo et corpus | nuncupative; et sic utrumque non [A 81b] duo homines, sed unus tantum. Si autem Magister intelligit hominem collective pro[7] duabus naturis ad[8] invicem et Verbo ypostatice copulatis, non est color quod tunc sit homo nisi utraque natura sit homo: et sic esset homo immortalis sicut anima fuit a sua[9] origine immortalis; et per consequens partim mortalis, quia mortuus, et partim immortalis, quia anima. Hoc autem concedendum est de quolibet alio homine.

*He will only use the term 'man' when body and soul are united.*

*The author, following Scripture, Augustine, Hugo de St. Victor, and true philosophy, uses 'man' for body and soul of man, even when separated.*

*Thus Christ remained true man and a creature in the three days, although the parts of his human nature were then separated.*

Mansit ergo Christus pro triduo minor patre quid|quid fuit [O 220d] ante et sic suppositum humane speciei licet non tunc com- po|nebatur qualitative ex anima et corpore. [B 124b] Unde tunc complevit obedienciam Trinitati[10] ministrando secundum naturam assumptam.

[1]–[1] specifica humana C; specifica *om.* humana O.
[2] consequentes A B C.
[3] sophistice B.
[4] qle^{te} O.
[5] ad id' = idem C; illum *om.* O.
[6] vocentur O.
[7] per O.
[8] ab O.
[9] suo A B C.
[10] trinitati *cum lacuna om.* C.

## Cap. IV.

[*Iuxta ponit sentencias modernorum doctorum ut veritas plus lucescat.*

*The opinions of Bonaventura, Duns Scotus, and St. Anselm, as to the nature of Christ during the three days' entombment, examined.*]

Sed ut magis appareat, quomodo communicacio ydiomatum pro triduo Christo conveniat, iuxta posite sunt sentencie modernorum.

Bonaventura distinguishing three kinds of predication: 1. actualis; 2. aptitudinalis (or habitudinalis); 3. mixtim; rightly describes the statement—Christ was man in the three days—as a mixed predication; being 'actualis predicatio' inasmuch as the Word was united to both soul and body; 'aptitudinalis predicatio' in that the natural and habitual union between the human soul and body, which is the 'form' of humanity, was suspended.

[C 52a] Scribit enim Bonaventura | super Distinccionem 12.[1] 3[ii] Sentenciarum, quod triplex[2] est predicacio, scilicet actualis, aptitudinalis,[3] et mixtim. Actualis, quando subiectum est ens actu et forma predicati sibi inest; ut cum dicitur homine existente 'homo est animal.' Predicacio secundum puram aptitudinem est, quando nec subiectum nec forma predicati est in actu, sed necessaria[4] est ordinacio unius ad alterum fundata super principia nature; sicut nulla rosa existente 'rosa est flos.' Quando subiectum autem est in actu, et forma predicati non inest sibi actualiter sed secundum necessariam ordinacionem fundatam super principia nature, tunc est predicacio mixtim, id est, partim actualis et partim aptitudinalis. Et sic concedit quod Christus fuit homo in triduo, quia subiectum, quod est Verbum Dei, tunc fuit in actu, et forma humanitatis servata fuit in aptitudine coniunccionis anime ad corpus. Nec vidi planiorem sentenciam alicuius doctoris in illa materia; quia indubie, quicunque concedit quod corpus et anima fuerunt partes Christi in triduo, habet concedere consequenter quod Christus habet correspondenter esse hominis ex eisdem.

But Duns Scotus,

Sed Doctor Subtilis dilatat[5] ibidem[6] amplius istam materiam. Dicit enim quod in triduo fuit ita; quod 'Christus est Christus, et quod Verbum habet tam corpus quam animam

[1] 22 O. [2] duplex O.
[3] habitudinalis *codd. omn. Quae sequuntur lectionem in textu confirmant.*
[4] natu O. [5] dilitat O. [6] ibi B.

sibi unitam, et tamen non tunc fuit ita quod Christus est homo; quia humanitas dicit ultra naturas imperfectas et ultra unionem respectivam unitatem[1] absolutam, sicut est in numeris. Et illa unitas non componit cum aliis; quia tunc esset[2] processus in infinitum. Et sic in triduo corruptum est aliquid absolutum, quia humanitas; sic quod nulla pars eius remanserat, cum sit [3]forma totalitatis[3] non habens partes quantitativas vel qualitativas. Racio autem quare non sequitur—Christus est Christus: ergo Christus est homo—est ista. Christus secundum Damascenum ca°. 49 est nomen ypostaticum[4] duarum naturarum[5] completarum singulatim,[6] scilicet humanitatis et deitatis. Cum ergo oportet racionem subiecti talis esse in se veram, antequam aliquid de eo enuncietur; quia aliter esset hec vera—maius Deo[7] est—quod est falsum,[8] cum subiectum includit repugnanciam: patet quod hec—Christus est homo—[9]formata pro triduo[9] foret falsa; quia humanitas non tunc infuit Verbo Dei. Ideo, sicut,[10] nullo homine existente, homo albus[11] est homo albus, [12]nec ex hoc sequitur quod homo sit homo albus[12]: sic pro triduo Christus est Christus; sicut Deus-homo est[13] [A 81c] Deus-homo, | et tamen Deus non est tunc homo.'

quoting John of Damascus to define the term 'Christ,' denies that Christ was man in the three days; since the unity of the human composite nature was not then present in Him.

Ulterius quo ad denominacionem Verbi ab illis partibus ita scribit: 'Verbum, inquit, quamvis in triduo habuit[14] corpus et animam sibi unitam a quibus potuit denominari: non placuit tamen doctoribus quod denominetur ab eis, et forte non sine causa: cum partes non denominant, nisi ut subsistunt naturaliter in suo toto. Sed tunc defuit humanitas:| [C 52b] ideo non denominavit eum carneum vel carnalem. [15]Verumptamen si essent[15] nomina imposita, posset denominari ab illis; sed[16] oporteret quod essent denominativa, que non saperent vicium. [17]Unde sicut substancia[17] non sufficit denominari [18]alba ab albedine,[18] nisi mediante subiecto: sic

The Word, says Duns Scotus, had body and soul, but not united so as to make up the whole — humanity: therefore the Word cannot be called 'man;' or be said to be 'in the flesh.'

[1] humanitatem A B C. [2] est C. [3–3] totalitas A B C.
[4] ypostasis O. [5] coniunctaturum *add.* B. [6] significancium A B C.
[7] de eo A B C. [8] factum O. [9–9] pro triduo formata A B C.
[10] sicut *om.* O. [11] aj? O. [12–12] nec . . . albus *om.* B.
[13] est *om.* O; *sed in margine adnotatur* hô ô de°. [14] habet A B C.
[15–15] verumptamen esset O. [16] si O. [17–17] *bis* O. [18] alba albedine C O.

nec Christus denominari carnalis, nisi mediante humanitate: ut, si Christus assumpsisset solum quantitatem, adhuc[1] non esset quantus propter defectum subiecti materialis.' Hoc Latinum huius doctoris est michi[2] et forte aliis difficilius [3]quam sentencia Augustini.[3]

*The author finds the Latin of Duns Scotus difficult: so he applies to it an admitted logical maxim of the same doctor,*

Sed pro eius intellectu notandum quod ipse admisit predicacionem secundum habitudinem[4] sicut Doctor alius.[5] Et illud antiquitus est famosum,[6] ut: 'Quandocunque predicatur idem de se vel per se superius[7] de suo per se[8] inferiori [9]est predicacio vera,[9] licet neutrum extremum sit in actu. Ut verum est, dicit Doctor, quod—Cesar est homo—eciam nullo homine existente.' Sed quando predicatur formaliter res alterius generis, tunc limitat ad predicacionem actualem; ut, 'si homo est qualis,[10] quantus, pater, agens, et cetera; tunc est actu.'

*in the application of which Duns Scotus is supported by St. Anselm.*

Et cum illo concordat Anselmus in De Concordia 5° ca°. ita dicens: 'Quippe non idem est, rem esse preteritam, et, rem preteritam esse preteritam; aut, [11]rem esse presentem, et, rem presentem esse presentem; aut,[11] rem esse futuram, et, rem futuram esse futuram: sicut non est idem, rem esse albam, et, rem albam esse albam: lignum enim non[12] de necessitate semper est album, quia[13] aliquando antequam fieret album, potuit non fieri album; et [14]postquam fieret album,[14] potest fieri non album: sed lignum album de necessitate semper est album, quia non potest[15] fieri, ut album simul sit non album.'

*Their logical theory cannot be successfully impugned;*

Volunt ergo isti doctores quod necessaria sit predicacio aptitudinalis secundum esse possibile in causis secundis, quandocunque predicatur idem de se vel per se superius de suo per se inferiori. Nec ex hoc concluditur existencia talis rei. Nec contendo multum circa hanc logicam, cum nescio[16]

[1] ad hoc A B C. [2] michi *add. in margine* B. [3–3] quam ē aug⁹ sen^{as} O.
[4] *An potius legendum* aptitudinem? *cf. p.* 49 *passim.*
[5] alius doctore A B C [6] famosus A B C. [7] vel *add.* A B C.
[8] ꝑe C. [9–9] est . . . vera *om.* A B C. [10] est equalis C.
[11–11] rem . . . aut *om.* O. [12] non *in margine* C. [13] quoniam A B.
[14–14] postquam est album A B C; postquam fieret est album O.
[15] poterit O. [16] nequeo B.

but it does not apply to the case in point. From the author's logical standpoint it follows that Christ was man in the three days.

cam efficaciter | impugnare. Sed considero quod si moderni [B dignarentur [1] attendere ad scripturas patrum priorum, non tantum mirarentur de hoc quod dico: Omne preteritum vel futurum esse pro suo tempore: quia ex illo dicto sequitur nedum omne preteritum vel futurum sed eciam omne possibile esse [2] pro semper. Et sic videtur quod infiniti homines, sicut quelibet signanda individua, sunt ubique; nam mille homines sunt mille homines, et sic infinitum,[3] nullo homine existente. Nec videtur | racio quare [O semper, quin [4] per idem ubique et sic quilibet [5] infinitum bonus foret infinitum bonus, et sic de quacunque denominacione possibili.

Sed dimittendo istud argumentum, ad propositum quod sequitur: Christum fuisse [6] hominem in triduo. Nam Christus est per se in specie humana, ut patet posterius: ergo est per se homo: et per consequens, si est Christus, tunc est homo. Confirmatur. Sicut conceditur quod Christus | [A est Christus, sic concedi debet quod iste homo est iste homo, demonstrando Iesum.[7] Sed impossibile est istum hominem esse istum hominem, nisi iste homo sit [8] homo. | [C Ergo concesso quod Christus est Christus pro triduo, concedendum est ipsum esse hominem pro eodem. Unde dicit Doctor quod, † [9] 'si hec esset per se Christus est homo et sufficiens quod causet inherenciam predicati ad subiectum, sine hoc quod subiectum dicat compositum unum hoc Christus est homo fuisset semper vera. Sed magis, inquit, credo quod requiritur hoc et plus.' [9] †

If Christ was Christ, Christ was man in the three days.

Item sicut conceditur quod pro triduo ille homo est ille homo, ita concedi debet ut convertibile per se, quod ille

[1] dedignarentur O. [2] est O. [3] infinito O. [4] quando C.
[5] cuilibet A (*prima manu*) B C; quelibet A (*altera manu*). [6] esse B.
[7] îhŝ O. [8] iste *add.* A B.
[9–9] *Locus difficillimus et valde corruptus, ut crebrae rasurae et variae lectiones codicum indicant. Edidi supra lectionem codd.* A B C; *hic codicis* O *lectio subjungitur.* Si hic esset per se Christus est homo et sufficiat quod causet inherenciam predicati ad subiectum cum hoc quod subiectum dicat conceptum unum hic Christus est homo fuisset semper vera sed magis inquit credo quod requiritur hoc et plus.

homo componitur ex hoc corpore et hac anima. Ex quo plane sequitur quod ille homo sit homo, sicut ille homo est Deus-homo. Nam Christus et Deus-homo convertuntur [1] simpliciter et ex equo: [1] et per consequens, sicut conceditur quod Christus est Christus, sic concedi debet quod Deus-homo est Deus-homo. Sicut ergo conceditur quod rosa est flos propter possibilitatem [2] licet nulla existat; sic evidencius videtur concedendum quod hec persona est homo, posito quod essemus in triduo cum sit nedum remota potencia, sed disposicio propinqua et necessaria, ut resurgat. Unde propter essenciam materialem perpetuam videtur Ieronimus [3] in Ep. ad Paulam et Eustochium concedere quod Christus a principio seculi erat Christus: sed Doctor ille concedit ad sensum alium.

Which follows also from the fact that Christ and God-Man are convertible terms.

Christ is (S. Jerome says, ever has been from the beginning of the world) the same Christ.

Item cum Christus secundum illum doctorem habet omnes partes [4] quas habet post resurreccionem, non deficit ad hoc quod tunc [5] sit homo nisi unio respectiva: sed nullum tale respectivum est de essencia substancie ut patet alibi *De Continuacione*: ergo corpus et anima unita Verbo pro triduo sufficiunt [6] denominare ipsum esse hominem. Minor patet ex hoc: quod addita unione illa ad alia principia existencia [7] pro illo triduo, [7] foret consequens formaliter, quod Christus sit homo: ergo tunc non deficit [8] nisi [9] dicta unio; nec valet dicere quod humanitas deficit; [8] quia humanitas est quod ipse est homo: ergo non est previe requisita [10] ad hoc quod ipse sit homo, quia tunc idem esset previe requisitum ad se ipsum.

The absence of 'union' in the elements of the human nature does not invalidate the true humanity of Christ in the three days.

Item vel est dicta unio causa humanitatis vel e contra; cum distinguuntur ut absolutum et respectivum, et non sunt impertinencia. Si humanitas sit causa dicte unionis tanquam [11] passionis que consequitur ad subiectum: tunc

Union is not the cause of

[1]–[1] ex equo simpliciter B; simpliciter et e contrario O.
[2] possibilem O.
[3] Ieronimum A B C.
[4] personas B; ptes (*sic*) C.
[5] tunc *om.* B.
[6] faciunt A B C.
[7]–[7] *om* B.
[8]–[8] nisi . . . deficit *om.* C.
[9]–[9] nec O.
[10] requisita *codd. omn.* sc. unio.
[11] tanquam *bis* O.

humanity for three reasons: 1. Continuation is not identical with cause.

unio non requiritur ad humanitatem, et e contra [1]pro dicto triduo sunt omnes cause posite, que requiruntur ad humanitatem Christi;[1] et per consequens tunc est homo. Si e contra unio sit causa dicte humanitatis, hoc[2] videtur tripliciter esse falsum. Primo per[3] hoc quod continuacio per idem foret causa corporis; quod improbatum est alibi. 2°. per hoc quod unio illa, cum dependeat ab extremis, non est essenciale principium hominis, eo quod posset manere idem homo variato corpore vel ablata eius parte quantitativa. Non ergo est illa unio causa beatitudinis, sciencie et [4]aliorum accidencium[4] hominis que insunt racione anime; et multo minus est causa[5] humanitatis, que est prior illis accidentibus. 3°. per hoc quod illa unio nedum dependet ab illis extremis absolute, sed ut copulantur qualitative ad invicem; et per consequens presupponit perfectum hominem: et sic non est previe requisita sed accessoria.

2. A man remains a man although changes pass over his body.

3. Union is an accessory not a necessary previous condition.

The fact is that the whole humanity and personality are preserved in the soul: and so Christ's complete perfect humanity existed, and perfected the world, in the three days.

Tales multas evidencias | feci alias cum testimoniis sancto- [C 53b] rum, quod tota humanitas et personalitas servatur in anima; aliter enim nimis esset mundus peioratus per deperdicionem absolute | humanitatis Christi succedente[6] loco illius iocalis[7] [A 82a] preciosissimi sola morte. Oportet ergo plenam perfeccionem humanitatis Christi servari[8] in composito discretive ex corpore et anima, quod plus sic perficit mundum quam prius perficit qualitative compositum, sicut contingit de Sampsone.

Judges xvi. 30.

Consideration of Duns Scotus' statement (p. 50, l. 21) that the name 'man' cannot refer to body or soul separately united to the Word. At any rate the Holy Spirit uses such language, when in Holy Scripture Christ is said to 'descend into hell' (*i.e.* in his soul) to 'lie in the tomb' (*i.e.* in his body),

Ulterius quoad denominacionem Verbi pro illo triduo ex corpore et anima resultantem, videtur responsio multum literalis, quando dicit quod 'non placuit doctoribus ipsum denominari ab illis.' Nam semper[9] Spiritui sancto auctori[10] scripture placuit quod denominetur pro illo triduo | 'descen- [B 125b] dens ad inferos'[11] secundum animam, et 'iacens in sepulcro' secundum corpus: et sic de sepultura et aliis ministeriis[12] ad sepulturam pertinentibus, ut condimento mixture mirre et aloes, involucione in sindone, posicione in monumento.

[1–1] pro . . . Christi *om.* A B C. [2] hoc *om.* O. [3] ex O.
[4–4] rerum accedencium A B C. [5] sunt cause O. [6] sic sedente O.
[7] vitalis A B C. [8] servare A B C. [9] semper *om.* A B C.
[10] auctore C. [11] ad inferna B. [12] misteriis *pro* mîsteriis O.

Et racione anime denominatus est 'rex spolians tartara,'[1] regens spiritualiter suum exercitum pacificando rebelles tam intraneos quam extraneos:[2] et sic de omnibus actibus regiminis, que ad regem spiritualem pertinent, longe efficacius quam antea fecit vivus[3]: tunc enim habuit exercitum plus unitum.

*and to 'triumph over hell.'*

Item cum tam corpus Christi quam anima fuerunt secundum Doctorem tunc partes Christi, et nichil dicitur pars, nisi in comparacione ad aliquod totum: videtur quod fuit unum totum continuum vel discretum, cuius erant partes, ut dictum est superius: et illud discretum, cum non deficit in aliquo substanciali quod fuit in humanitate, quando affuit qualitativa composicio: videtur quod tunc,[4] sicut mediante[5] illo toto et unione sufficiunt partes ille[6] denominari partes Christi, sic sufficiunt denominare Christum denominacionibus naturaliter[7] consequentibus ex eodem.

*Christ lacked no essential of man when the parts of his humanity were in separation.*

Et quantum ad[8] exemplum Doctoris de albedine dependente a subiecto ut causante et non substantivante[9]: patet quod ymaginacio[10] est ficta ex falso principio, scilicet quod albedo potest primo[11] esse ad omnem[12] punctum subiecti sui informans; [13] 2°. conservata[13] ab eo sine hoc, quod informat; et 3°. nec informans nec conservata ab eodem.
[O 221b] Albedo | enim, cum sit subiectum esse album, non potest esse sine subiecto.

*The instance of Duns Scotus (p. 50, l. 30), that 'whiteness' makes nothing 'white' without the help of a substance, is invalid; since the idea of whiteness includes a substance.*

Item de hoc quod dicit Christum posse denominari ab illis partibus ut sic 'Si essent nomina imposita;' miror de istis verbis tam realis philosophi et subtilis, cum constat[14] quod denominacio rei extra est impertinens imposicioni[15] nostrorum nominum, ut albedo eque denominaret[16] simplum[17] album, nullo signo artificiali hominum[18] existente; sicut quotlibet talibus positis secundum varia ydiomata. Unde denominaciones, quas Augustinus, Hugo de Sancto Victore,

*Also his objection (p. 50, l. 28) to applying to Christ terms which belong strictly to only a part of his being, is not tenable. S. Augustine and others*

[1] tarthara A B. [2] externos A B C. [3] vivus *om.* A B C; vn⁹ O.
[4] tunc *om.* A B C. [5] mediate A B C. [6] ille *om.* A B C.
[7] naturalibus A B C. [8] 2m. *add.* O. [9] subiectante O M.
[10] ymago O. [11] primo potest A B C. [12] hominem O.
[13] 2° conservatum O. [14] cum stat A B C. [15] imposicionem A B C.
[16] denominari O. [17] ipsum A B C. [18] hominem O.

*before Peter Lombard freely used these terms.*

et alii precedentes Magistrum Senteneiarum imposuerunt Verbo Dei secundum illas[1] partes pro illo triduo, scilicet | [C 54a] quod est caro, quod est anima, et sic de ceteris, non sonuerunt in vicium. Nec valet dicere quod ille denominaciones sunt synecdochice[2]; quia, ut patet alibi, construccio synecdochica[3] est, quando parti quantitative attribuitur primo denominacio accidentalis, et consequentur toti secundum illam partem ut;—homo est[4] albus faciem et sanus thoracem.[5] Cum ergo nec corpus nec anima Christi sit pars eius quantitativa; sequitur quod hic non est construccio synecdochica[6]—Christus est anima—sicut nec—Hic homo est tibia.

*Discussion of the difference between these expressions and others in which (κατὰ συνεκδοχήν) the part is put for the whole.*

Item si pro dicto triduo corpus et anima sunt partes Christi, tunc denominant[7] ipsum habere partes illas tanquam partes suas: quia constat quod non sequitur[8]—Hec[9] res est mea et est pars; ergo est pars mea—quia quelibet pars creature esset pars | Trinitatis increate; et, ut sophiste[10] [A 82b] arguunt, homo[11] monstruose haberet multa capita asinina. Ideo concedit doctor[12] quod Christus potest vere denominari pro illo triduo habens partes illas ut partes suas, sed non carneus vel carnalis: ut si solum[13] assumpsisset[14] quantitatem, adhuc[15] non[16] esset quantus propter defectum subiecti materialis: sic licet habeat carneam partem suam, adhuc[17] non est carneus, eo quod deest humanitas. Sed miror de ista similitudine propter tria. Primo cum impossibile sit quantitatem per se esse. 2°. cum hoc posito per impossibile Verbum esset quantum per ypostaticam unionem. Non enim est unio vel assumpcio personalis sine communicacione ydiomatum nature specifice assumpte[18] Verbo vel persone assumenti: assumptum enim ypostatice oportet terminari suppositacione[19] aliena et non esse suppositum proprie speciei,

*Duns Scotus allows that Christ had 'caro,' but denies to him the term 'carneus' or 'carnalis.'*

*Three reasons why he is wrong.*

[1] alias O. [2] sinodochice A B C; sýnodotice O; *cf. p.* 39, *n.* 5.
[3] sinodochica A B C; synodotica O. [4] est *sec. man.* A; *om.* B.
[5] serenus thoracem A B C; sanus secundum thoracem O.
[6] sinodochica A B C; sýnodogica O; *cf. n.* 2 *supra.* [7] denominat A B C.
[8] sequitur *om.* O. [9] hoc A B C. [10] sophistice A B C; so[te] O.
[11] hoī O. [12] doctor *om.* C. [13] solus B. [14] sumpsisset A B C.
[15] ad hoc C. [16] non *om.* O. [17] ad hoc C O. [18] assumpti O.
[19] suppōne A B C.

ut eciam[1] dicit doctor. 3°. videtur similitudo[2] impertinens; cum natura illa non dependet ab humanitate, cum manet naturaliter sine illa, et posset fuisse assumpta sine assumpcione humanitatis. Si enim Verbum posset pure assumere quantitatem, multo evidencius carnem mortuam per se de natura possibilem.

Item pari[3] evidencia, qua Christus habet corpus mortuum tanquam partem suam pro illo triduo, habet quamlibet partem illius corporis partem suam, ut latus, [4]caput, et pedes,[4] sicut scriptura sacra patenter asserit. Sed concesso consequente, cum non possunt poni nisi partes quantitive Christi, cum sint partes quantitative corporis, sequitur quod sunt partes quantitative Christi. Et cum omnis pars quantitativa rei componit ut sic quantitative[5] omne totum cuius est pars, sequitur quod dicte partes quantitative componunt Christum quantitative,[6] et per consequens sic componunt,[7] ut sit maius[8] sua parte quantitativa. Sequitur quod Christus sit[9] pro triduo mole magnus, ut puta septipedalis, in tumulo, cum ibi habeat partes extra partes: et cum nichil sit quantum nisi substancia materialis, sequitur quod Christus fuit pro dicto [B 126a] triduo substancia corporea; | et per hoc est verisimile[10] Doctorem debere concedere, cum dicit quod Christus potest denominari pro illo triduo homo mortuus a tota natura, cui [C 54b] discrete | copulatur. Et abreviator suus Cowtonus[11] dicit quod fuit pro illo triduo homo mortuus[12] sed[13] non homo. Sed videtur michi quod si quis est homo mortuus,[12] tunc est animal et corpus mortuum[14] et sic corpus, quamvis enim mortuum[14] per se circumlocutum cum verbo equivaleat verbo ampliativo. Ita[15] quod non sequitur—ista bestia nunc est mortua; ergo illa nunc est—Tamen si ista bestia nunc sit[16] bestia mortua, ista nunc est bestia, que moritur

In the three days Christ not only had a body, but was

a bodily substance.

In Cowton's summary of Duns Scotus it is stated that Christ in the three days was 'homo mortuus,' but not 'homo': but this will not hold.

[1] eciam *om.* A B C. [2] illa *add.* C. [3] per C. [4-4] pedes et capud B.
[5] quantitative *om.* B. [6] quantitative *om.* A B C.
[7] componit O *ut om.*. [8] magis B; mag° O. [9] sit *om.* C.
[10] verissimilem O. [11] colton A; carton B; cantori C; cowtonus O.
[12-12] sed . . . mortuus *om.* O. [13] et B. [14-14] et . . . mortuum *om.* O.
[15] ampleatiō ĭ O. [16] ~~est~~ (*sic*) sit *in marg.* A.

aut[1] moriebatur. Si ergo res sit mortua secundum partem quantitativam ut[2] manum aridam[3] vivente residuo, quanto magis erit mortua per totum, si quelibet pars quantitativa sui sit mortua? Patet ergo quod si Christus unquam[4] fuit mortuus,[5] hoc fuit in triduo, et indubie tunc fuit persona mortua: et cum oportet dare[6] naturam unitam, secundum quam passus est mortem, que natura subiectet mortem; patet quod tunc fuit corpus sibi unitum sicut subtiliter[7] dicit Doctor. Non enim fuisset mortuus, si pro primo instanti non-actuacionis corporis post vitam Christi tam corpus quam anima adnichilata[8] fuerunt; quia tunc omnis mors esset adnichilacio.[8]

The created spirit of the Word, being in the three days the soul (anima) of Christ, animated, not the body, but Christ; not of course in his divine, but in his human nature:

Item omnis anima, in quantum huiusmodi,[9] | animat, ut [A 82c] patet 2° *De Anima*. Si ergo ille spiritus creatus fuit pro illo triduo anima Christi, tunc animavit; et, cum non animavit tunc corpus, relinquitur[10] quod tunc animavit Christum[11]; et per consequens ipse fuit tunc animatus ad sensum expositum. Et cum[12] non secundum naturam divinam pocius quam[13] in mundi principio: ergo servata est unio nature create precedens animam, que non potest fingi nisi humanitas. Non enim sortiretur[14] animacionem cum illo creato spiritu, nisi ypostatice uniretur; sicut habet denominacionem humanitatis propter ypostaticam unionem. Confirmatur. Si Christus uniretur ypostatice primo illi spiritui separato tunc esset aliquid quod prius non fuerat, cum fieret alicuius speciei in genere substancie, cum aliter non esset unio personalis. sed modo unitus est eadem unione qua tunc uniebatur[15]: ergo manet Christus illud pro triduo. Minor patet ex hoc, quod alterius racionis fuit unio, qua[16] Christus uniebatur spiritui suo pro triduo, quam[17] unio non ypostatica[18] solum per graciam: eo quod aliter non denominaretur Christus tunc habere animam, descendere ad[19] in-

[1] ac A B C. [2] aut *codd. omn.* [3] aridum O. [4] nunquam C.
[5] per totum *add.* A C. [6] dari B. [7] subiecti O.
[8] anichilata anichilacio A. [9] modi *om.* O C. [10] requiritur O.
[11] Christum *om.* O. [12] cum *om.* O C. [13] quoniam A C.
[14] sortitiretur O. [15] uniretur A B C. [16] quam C.
[17] quoniam A. [18] ypostaica O. [19] in A B C.

fernum, et ministrare Patri ut sibi subditus, pocius quam Spiritus Sanctus dicitur minor Patre secundum columbam; quod est contra Augustinum primo Contra Simplicianum. Sicut ergo Christus fuisset tunc spiritus create speciei, ita est modo propter consimilem unionem: et cum ille spiritus non esse[1] potest nisi humane speciei, quia tunc posset [O 221c] transire de specie ad speciem, et sic species solum | per accidens sibi inexistens foret sibi non species: nam[2] corrupto omni corpore et servatis spiritibus illis, qui quondam erant anime, forent ipsi individua racionalis nature; quia per se [C 55a] denominati agere acciones personales; | et per consequens individua speciei non alterius quam humane, ut olim fuerant: ergo relinquitur quod forent homines: haberent enim unam[3] naturam communem, in qua convenirent pari evidencia qua[4] alia supposita speciei, et talis communis natura, cum sit prima quiditas[5] illorum individuorum, foret illis species specialissima. Et illud facit michi evidenciam quod humanitas servatur in anima; cum individuum non potest exuere formam specificam, et olim fuit in specie humana non solum indirecte,[6] sed habuit propriam quiditatem.

Christ was therefore human in the three days;

Propter tales evidencias declinant moderniores loquentes [7]superficialiter more[7] legis ab istis principiis dicentes quod Christus non habuit in dicto triduo corpus vel animam; et sic nec fuit mortuus nec mortem passus, cum nulla fuit mors Christi; nec iacuit sepultus, nec descendit ad inferos; et per consequens, cum tunc non fuit unio ypostatica Christi ad naturam creatam, Christus non liberavit in persona propria patres de limbo, sicut nec Pater; cum tunc fuit secundum [8]omnem naturam[8] tunc habitam equalis[9] Patri et non minister.

and the moderns, who say that Christ then had neither body nor soul, are in error; and practically cancel his death, burial, and descent into hell.

Nec intelligende sunt [10]dicte locuciones[10] synecdochice,[11] cum Christus tunc non habuit partem: et non est synecdochica[12]

[1] esset O. [2] a *add.* O. [3] unam *om.* B. [4] quum B.
[5] deitas B; quantitas C. [6] indirecem A C. [7-7] superficienter nrē (nostre) O.
[8-8] semē nīī (*Qu.* semen et naturam ?) O. [9] essencialis C.
[10] de vi locucionis A B; de ēē (esse) locucionis C.
[11] synodochice A B C; sýnodotica O; *cf. p.* 39, *n.* 5.
[12] synodochica A B C; synodotica O *ut saepissime*.

locucio tocius per partem nisi pro mensura pro qua[1] est pars propter inconsequencia,[2] que secuntur. Sed hos deliros a scriptura a fide et a sanctis doctoribus vocat Magister Senteneiarum Distinccione 21 'hostes veritatis.' Nec inveni in scriptis[3] | alicuius doctoris probabilis istam[4] sentenciam; sed fingunt eam recentissimi correctores. Unde doctor Bonaventura[5] putat super Distinccione 21. 3[ii] Senteneiarum quod sit de substancia fidei credere quod tam corpus quam anima | fuerunt in triduo partes Christi; et allegat[6] ad hoc tam Augustinum quam Iohannem Damascenum dicentes[7]: 'Anathema sit, qui dicit Verbum deposuisse quod semel assumpsit.' Unde consequenter declarando quod triplex[8] est unio, scilicet accio agentis, passio uniti vel unitorum, et 3°. unitorum relacio, dicit quod eadem[9] unione activa continue unitum est[9] Verbum carni et anime sicut eadem tencione tenemus equum et frenum. Unde et sanctus Thomas super D^e. 21 dicit quod deitas fuit coniuncta in dicto triduo tam corpori quam anime; non quod Verbum fuit tunc corpus vel anima, sed quod tunc fuit corpus Christi [corpus][10] et anima eius anima, et solum[11] talis fuit unio ypostatica post et ante. [B 126b] [A 82d]

*i. Peter Lombard condemns them; and so does Bonaventura,*

*who quotes both Augustine and John of Damascus;*

*with whom St. Thomas also agrees.*

*ii. The creed also, in stating that Christ lay in the tomb and descended into hell, implies that he possessed body and soul.*

Arguitur[12] autem de racione supposita fide catholica ad probandum propositum. Nam, supposito quod essemus in triduo, patet quod corpus Christi iacet in sepulcro et anima descendit ad inferos: nam hoc iacet in sepulcro et hoc est corpus Christi post et ante hoc triduum; ut patet ampliantibus presens tempus: ergo corpus Christi iacet in sepulcro. Et idem est argumentum de anima. Ex quo videtur quod[13] dicte partes sunt partes Verbi in triduo, quia[14] Verbum habet in triduo illas partes.

Sed quia non omnes conveniunt in illo | principio, ideo [C 55b]

[1] mensura que *om.* pro O. [2] inconveniencia O. [3] scripturis O.
[4] illam scienciam A B C. [5] bonaventure O. [6] alligat O.
[7] dicentes *om.* O. [8] z^x (duplex) B.
[9] unione (acciva *vix legitur in rasura*) unitum A; unione anima quo unitum B; unione ac͡ca 9° (activa conclusio) C.
[10] corpus *in codd. omnibus omissum restitui.* [11] solam B.
[12] aliter O. [13] cum O. [14] et quod A B C.

iii. These arguments from authority supplemented by a third. Continuous personality implies the continuous possession of the parts which constitute the person.

arguitur 3° sic. Eo ipso quod persona manet[1] per tempus et[2] habet per idem tempus omnes [3]subiectas partes[3] sibi proprie servatas, que erunt postmodum[4] partes[5] sue, habet pro illo tempore partes illas: sed sic fuit de corpore et anima Christi pro dicto triduo: ergo tunc fuerunt[6] partes sue. Maior patet eo quod aliter manus arida vel membrum mortuum non esset pars persone: quod est contra scripturam et communem modum loquendi. Imo, ut patet in *De Anima*, partes extreme[7] longe cicius moriuntur ipso corde: et sic in[8] media vita est dare aliquas partes mortuas mixtas cum vivis.[9] Ad cuius conformitatem locuntur Morales, quod[10] membrum corporis Christi mistici[11] per privacionem gracie mortuum, non exinde desinit esse membrum, cum tunc omnis[12] expers gracie foret ut sic[13] infidelis. Et confirmacio illius est, quod tunc continuacio non est de essencia substancie materialis. Ex quo videtur quod manus abscisa ab homine supervivente remanet quodammodo manus sua. Et per idem, cum persona Filii Dei mansit per totum triduum habens a proprietate[14] et specialiter idem corpus aliter quam alia, videtur quod[15] tunc fuerat corpus suum.

[As, by analogy, members of Christ's mystical Body, even though spiritually dead, are still members and not heathen men.]

Item logice[16] potest deduci illud, posito quod solum[17] Christus[18] sit [19]mortuus de specie humana: tunc Filius Dei est mortuus, licet non sit homo ut conceditur[19]: ergo Filius Dei est persona mortua. Consequencia videtur tenere,[20] eo quod persona est superius ad hominem secundum tenentes istam sentenciam, et in talibus eodem distrahente addito conformiter utrobique tenet consequencia, ut: Si Petrus est homo mortuus, tunc est animal mortuum et corpus mortuum. Si ergo Christus sit persona mortua, cum non superest que persona nisi persona Verbi, sequitur quod sit persona Verbi

Again, if the person of the Word died,

[1] nunquam (*Qu. pro* nunc habet = naturam habet ?) O. [2] ut A B C. [3-3] substancias O. [4] postmodo C. [5] parte O. [6] fuerant O. [7] extere O. [8] in *om.* O. [9] cum vivus C. [10] quia A B C. [11] mixti A B C; mistici (*i.e.* mystici) O. [12] omnis *om.* O. [13] sit O. [14] appropriate A B C. [15] quantum O. [16] loyce A B C *ut fere semper.* [17] solus A C. [18] sic *add.* B. [19-19] mortuus licet non sit homo ut conceditur de specie humana tunc filius dei est homo mortuus ergo O. [20] tenere *om.* O C.

*It was Christ who died: but by the hypostatic union his body escaped corruption;*

mortua; et per consequens est persona Verbi, quo moriebatur; et sic persona Verbi est Christus. Si enim caput pedes et alia derelicta pro triduo sint partes hominis mortui, et solum Filius Dei sit homo mortuus; sequitur quod sunt[1] partes Filii Dei. Unde propter istam unionem ypostaticam Verbi ad[2] illud sanctum corpus sepultum in triduo dicit Doctor Solempnis | 12° Quodlibeto: quod illud servatum est nedum [A 83a] incorruptum sed incorruptibile iuxta illud Psalmi 15 'Non dabis sanctum tuum videre corrupcionem.' Nec video quomodo esset naturaliter inditum[3] homini timere mortem, nisi poterit pati mortem. Non enim ordinat natura hominem timere eventum, qui[4] non potest sibi accidere.

*as Henry of Ghent (doctor solemnis) maintains.*

*Ps. xvi. 11.*

Item si anima Christi desiit esse anima Verbi Dei, cum tunc et ante scivit omnia, sequitur quod hoc scivit continue. Queritur[5] utrum voluntarie[6] reliquit corpus in morte vel non. Quod sic patet: quia fuit obediens usque ad mortem inclusive et post perpetuo. Nec illud debet | verti in dubium[7] [O 221d] cum scivit hoc esse de necessario Dei beneplacito ad exaltacionem sui et sui generis. Unde Augustinus Omc. 119. [8]'Quis, inquit, ita dormivit quando voluit sicut Christus?'[8] Oblatus est | enim, quia voluit, ut dicitur Is^e. 52. Si volens [C 56a] [9]fuerit ypostatice[9] separata, cum | ex hoc perdidit graciam [B 127a] unionis; sequitur quod sic volendo peccavit, quia voluntarie defecit a gracia; quod nephas [10]est dicere. Et consequencia videtur ex hoc[10]: quod anima propior[11] est Deo, cum est anima Dei, quam foret ab eo ypostatice separata: quia aliter esset possibile Deo[12] plus vel tantum diligere ipsam animam alterius sicut suam: quod non puto. Cum ergo anima Iesu gratis elongavit se a Verbo postquam fuit sibi carior ypostatice copulata: sequitur quod de tanto graciam perdidit et per consequens sic peccavit. Nam nulli dubium, quin maxima gracia possibilis creature est quod sit pars qualita-

*The soul of Christ voluntarily and with foreknowledge left his body.*

*Isa. liii. 10.*

[1] sunt *om.* C. [2] ubi *add.* B. [3] ruditum B.
[4] que C. [5] ergo *add.* O. [6] volupta^e O. [7] indubie B.
[8–8] quod inquit ideo (cita C) dormivit quando voluit sicud (sic B) Christus A B C.
[9–9] ypostatice fuerat B. [10–10] est . . . hoc *om.* B.
[11] prior B O. [12] deum O.

tiva vel humanitas Dei sui. Si enim magna gracia est quod Deus velit[1] adoptare hominem in filium et heredem, longe maior est quod velit creaturam eternaliter predestinare in suam propriam animam vel humanitatem.

Item iuxta sepe dicta et diffusius declarata impossibile est aliquam substanciam esse[2] materiam vel[3] formam vel ex eis compositam, nisi sit singularis essencia vel persona per se supposita speciei: sed tam corpus Christi quam eius anima fuit pro illo[4] triduo individua substancia: igitur[5] fuit essencia vel persona per se supposita speciei: et cum nullum suppositum potest manere aliud[6] suppositum, sequitur quod utraque illarum naturarum manet idem suppositum quod fuit,[7] anima et corpore, copulatum[7]: [8]sed tunc fuit suppositum hominis,[8] cum cuiuslibet hominis personalitas sit supposicio utriusque partis qualitative: igitur[5] utraque natura manet adhuc idem[9] suppositum hominis, et per consequens eadem persona Verbi. Et illa racio foret evidens cuicumque cui assumptum principium est famosum: 'Unde quia de virtute sermonis': sequitur ex hoc principio cum veritate fidei quod tam corpus Christi quam eius anima quantumlibet a se invicem[10] separata sint, utrumque[11] eadem persona hominis, que fuerant,[12] copulata. Ideo concedendum est quod pro triduo ypostatice sint unita et patet quomodo Verbum non potest assumere corpus mortuum, nisi mediante assumcione anime naturaliter precedente. Nec alteram illarum naturarum potest assumere,[13] nisi faciat se esse [14]illam naturam, cum nulla tali distinguit[15] essencialiter vel specialiter suppositacio a natura. Et patet 3°. quod Verbum non posset assumere corpus et animam separata, nisi faceret se esse[14] eandem personam que fuerunt tam corpus

Either nature of Christ remained in the three days;

and they remained united to one another.

[1] vult A C. [2] esse *om.* C. [3] sive A B C.
[4] illo *om.* A B C. [5] ergo O. [6] illud B.
[7–7] anima in corpore copulantis O.
[8–8] sed . . . hominis *suppletum in marg.* A.
[9] adhuc *om.* O. [10] inbicio C. [11] utraque C.
[12] fuerat O. [13] assumpnere B.
[14–14] illam . . . esse *om.* A B C. [15] *An* distinguitur *legendum* ?

And it is unnecessary to consider the consequences of absurd hypotheses in this matter.

quam anima copulata. Ideo non sollicitor quid sequeretur,[1] si Verbum assumeret unione[2] ypostatica tam corpus quam animam proditoris et dimitteret ipsa[3] supposittacioni proprie in finali resurreccione. Nam certum videtur michi[4] quod peccatum inde foret penitus deletum, eo quod ypostatica assumcio esset[5] efficacius medium ad tergendum | peccatum [A 83b] quam lavacrum baptismale: sed istud delet omne peccatum suppositi vel nature: ergo multo | magis personalis assumcio. [C 56b] Et ex alio latere puto me esse securum quod peccatum finalis impenitencie[6] subiectatum in anima proditoris[7] non potest deleri, [8] vel post eius incorrupcionem[8] redire. Ideo non superest nisi fugere tales casus. Nec est negandum, quin illud corpus mortuum [9] sit suppositum, sicut et spiritus; cum utrumque[10] habet supposibilem operacionem secundum idem suppositum;[9] quia persona Filii est utrumque.[10]

The thought, that God was a body, or even a corpse, is no shock to piety;

Et si obiciatur quod pie aures abhorrent quod Deus universitatis[11] sit corpus vel cadaver mortuum; dicitur quod Deus non est cadaver, cum non sit mortuum corpus et putidum[12] sed ad sensum proprium incorruptum. Quamvis enim laceratum sit lancea et flagellis causantibus solucionem[13] continuitatis, non tamen crura eius fracta per milites, nec carnes eius canibus[14] aut avibus[14] laniate; quia

Exod. xii. 46.

Exod. 12 mistice est preceptum; 'os non comminuetis ex eo.'

but rather is it an incentive to love and gratitude that, without seeing corruption, he lay dead in the tomb:

Nec horreret, sed accenderet pias mentes[15] quod Dominus celi et terre, qui[16] dignatus est nasci parvulus, vagiens in cunabulis,[17] ac reponi coram bestiis in presepe, dignatus[18] est idem et non alius iacere mortuus in sepulcro. Sed quia putrefaccio et incineracio corporis mortui non profuisset suo generi, cum corpus mortuum non mereretur[19] sibi vel aliis: ideo inconsonum et superfluum fuisset quod dictas infirmitates

[1] sequitur A B C. [2] unionem O. [3] ipsam A B C.
[4] michi, *om.* B. [5] est O. [6] impunie A B C.
[7] prodicoris A. [8]–[8] vel post eius corrupcionem A B C; post eius *om.*
[9]–[9] sit suppositum . . . suppositum *om.* A B C. [10] utraque O.
[11] pietatis *add.* A B C. [12] putridum A B C. [13] sollucionem A B.
[14]–[14] aut avibus *om.* A B C. [15] aures B. [16] qui *om.* A B C.
[17] cunibulis O. [18] quia *add.* A B C.
[19] non *om.* A B C; meretur O.

post completam victoriam assumpsisset. Nec auderem[1] dicere quod corpus mortuum foret Deus, nisi scriptura sacra tam patenter illud assereret, Ioh. 19: nec crederem[2] capiti meo de exposicione sensus litteralis eius scripture, nisi Augustinus, Hugo de Sancto Victore, et ceteri superiores doctores illud patenter assererent: nec diligerem Verbum Dei pro tunc ut Deum meum, nisi pro tunc esset spiritus [B 127b] descendens ad inferos et cum hoc natura divina gu|bernans omnia.[3] Nec video quomodo posset sumpsisse naturam [4] porci, serpentis,[4] vel alterius creature quam hominis, ut patet posterius. Nam si aliquid potuisset[5] esse monstrum, potissime fuisset[6] chimera vel tragelaphus habens caput asininum, caudam equinam, pectus leoninum.[7] Et sic [8] esset veracissime[8] de Iesu nostro in casu, quo omnem naturam aliam[9] assumeret et post assumpcionem continuaret. Vacuum ergo[10] et periculosum est raciones tales asserere.

*and this is the literal statement of Holy Scripture, not in my judgment only, but as expounded by Augustine, Hugo de St. Victor, and other leading doctors.* John xix. 38-42. *And the Word in the three days was also spirit descending into hell as well as a divine nature ruling all things; and did not assume any monstrous animal nature, but retained his humanity.*

---

## Cap. V.

[*Supponendo quod Verbum non dimisit humanitatem pro triduo, probat quod nec potuit dimittere naturam quam assumpsit.*

*Assuming as already proved that the Word did not as a matter of fact in the three days lay aside the human nature which he had taken up; it is here proved to be impossible that he should so lay it aside.*]

[11] Viso quod Verbum non dimisit de facto in sancto triduo corpus vel animam: restat ostendere quod Deus non potuit dimittere naturam hominis quam assumpsit.

[O 222a] Probatur tripliciter. Primo sic. Deus non | potest dampnificare naturam aliquam sine suo demerito[12] precedente: sed

*As the Word did not lay aside either body or soul; so likewise, although God, he could not lay aside the humanity which he had assumed.* *Threefold proof of this position.*

[1] auderunt B; audire O. [2] credissem O. [3] animas B. [4]–[4] porci secundum presentis C. [5] poterit A C O. [6] foret A C O. [7] bovinum A B C. [8]–[8] esse veracissime B; (e͞e͞) essent variatissime O (*sc.* nature *vel* sentencie). [9] animalis O. [10] vanum igitur O. [11] *Littera initialis om.* A B C. [12] merito B.

Proof I. God cannot inflict loss on any nature without any antecedent demerit on the part of that nature.

si dimitteret naturam assumptam, eam sic dampnificaret: ergo et cetera.[1] Maior patet ex hoc, quod dampnificacio est creature racionali [2] mali illacio inutilis,[2] | que non potest [C 57a] sibi inexistere nisi oriatur principaliter a se ipsa, iuxta senteneiam beati Iohannis Chrisostomi et aliorum doctorum communiter. Confirmatur. Si Deus aufert creature racionali bonum aliquod, iustum et pulcrum est illud auferri et per consequens non sonat[3] in malum inutile: et sic[4] servata immunitate peccati non est dampnum. Nam si Deus dampnificat hominem, quia facit eum iuste carere bono possibili; tunc infinitum multum dampnificaret quamlibet beatificabilem creaturam; et, ut communiter deducitur, infinitum impediret | quodlibet opus suum. 2°. Confirmatur[5] ex [A 83c] hoc, quod inflieeio[6] pene perpetue pro peccato non dampnificat sed meliorat dampnatum in tantum quod, si esset in eleccione[7] sua sic dampnari post peccatum vel vacare[8] impunem,[9] eligeret racionabiliter sic dampnari: ergo a maiori vel pari, si Deus aufert ab aliquo [10] sine suo demerito[10] quodvis bonum, cum sit pulcrum et bonum quod ita faciat nedum toti universitati[11] sed persone, que aliter frustratorie[12] occuparet; sequitur quod talis ablacio non sit dampnificacio; cum nec pro illa ablacione nec pro eius causa racionabiliter[13] sit dolendum. Ex quo[14] videtur 3°. quod innocens hoc videns eligeret[15] racionabiliter sic privari: et cum nemo [16] potest racionabiliter eligere[16] dampnificari, sequitur quod Deus non dampnificat creaturam, sed solum ipsamet[17] seipsam[18] vel aliud alliciens ad peccandum. Ymo si bene consideretur, omnis dampnificacio sapit iniuriacionem, que non potest per se bono et iusto competere, quin pocius bonificare et corrigere. Minor autem argumenti sic

[1] etc. *in marg.* A. [2-2] inutilis illacio *om.* mali O. [3] soluat O.
[4] sic *om.* O. [5] idem *add.* O. [6] influecio A B C.
[7] elleccione O. [8] viare *cum litura in medio verbo* A; viare B: vitare C.
[9] impune O. [10] sine suo demerito *om.* A B C. [11] universo O.
[12] frustracione O. [13] racionaliter *et sic postea* B. [14] quo *in margine* O.
[15] debet eligere B: eligeret A *sed addit in margine* debet eligere.
[16] sic (sit B) racionabiliter eligeret A B C. [17] ipsam A B C.
[18] se ipsam *om.* O.

probatur. Humanitas assumpta a Verbo non potest demereri previe suam dimissionem: ergo, illa dimissa, hoc sibi contingeret sine suo demerito. Antecedens patet per hoc, quod non potest demereri stante unione, quia tunc Verbum peccaret: et si pro instanti dissolucionis vel post peccaret, patet quod demeritum [dimissionem] sequetur[1]; et per consequens non dampnificaretur ex suo demerito precedente. Quod autem dimissio[2] foret dampnosa humanitati Christi ex hoc evidet, quod deperdicio gracie unionis foret deperdicio maximi boni possibilis intrinseci creature[3]: et per consequens tum[4] loco illius non succederet tantum bonum: sequitur quod humanitas ipsam perdens foret notabiliter peiorata, et per consequens dampnificata. Valorem autem ypostatice unionis suppono[5] ex dictis et dicendis: per illam enim fuit homo assumptus idem personaliter Verbo Dei. Magna ergo peioracio sua foret quod dimitteretur sine suo demerito tanquam extranea. Non enim pertinet ad dictum Cesarem semper Augustum[6] sic peiorare sine suo demerito carissimam[7] creaturam: quia indubie creatura dimissa pro instanti dimissionis posset racionabiliter conqueri de ingratitudine Dei
[C 57b] sui, cum continue ante fecit quidquid debuit, | et finaliter reciperet pro 'retribucione [8]mercedis' tantum dampnum.[8] Non ergo foret spes[9] in tali Deo. Et hinc nimirum[10] dicit Augustinus Omo. 47: 'Absit[11] quod Christus pro triduo animam suam dimiserit[12]: ipsam enim inseparabiliter habuit:' unde indubie, si post peccaret, dimissio gracie unionis preservantis ne peccet foret causa principalis peccati: quia si affirmacio sit causa affirmacionis, negacio est causa negacionis, ut absencia naute est causa periclitacionis navis ex 2° Physicorum. Illud ergo peccatum, ex dimissione originatum, esset Deo principaliter imputandum, cum non ex parte creature, sed Dei, causatur talis absencia: talis[13] ergo

The human nature of the Word could not sin whilst still united to the divine; could not therefore incur demerit; could not therefore suffer loss.

It is contrary to the justice of the Supreme Ruler (Cæsar semper Augustus) that he should inflict such undeserved loss on (the human nature of Christ, which is) his dearest creature, as the dismissal of the human nature by the Word would be.
Heb. ii. 2.

Augustine shudders at the thought: and indeed it would stifle hope in God to think that by withdrawing himself thus he should cause (Aristotle Physics ii.) a sinless being to sin,

'T' 'I'
[1] sequetur *et in margine* suple dimissione A; sequitur O; sequetur B C.
[2] dimissa B. [3] a creatura O. [4] tum *om.* O. [5] suppo° A B C.
[6] augustutum O. [7] kr̃aȝ B; bm̃aȝ (*i.e.* beatissimam) O.
[8–8] mercedis tantum premium A B C; mercedem O. [9] species B O.
[10] mimirum A. [11] absit *om.* O. [12] dimiseret O. [13] talis *om.* O.

and make our God more spiteful than the (evil) god of the Manicheans.

Deus excederet | in malicia deum Manicheorum,[1] qui sine[2] [B 128a] demerito servi sui absentaret se pro temptacionis tempore non iuvando. Unde et illam racionem tangit sanctus Thomas De Christo,[3] articulo 70.[4]

Proof II. If 'dismissal' could befall the human soul of Christ, sin might also befall it: and this would place the king of saints on a lower level of bliss than any other saint:

Item quilibet beatus in celo est tam insolubiliter Deo connexus quod repugnat illi statui miseriam peccati in anima succedere vel[5] coesse: sed Christus ab instanti unionis fuit perfeccius beatus secundum animam quam alius, cum fuerit sanctus sanctorum: ergo multo magis repugnat animo sue peccatum succedere vel[6] coesse: sed | si[6] dimissio foret [A 83d] possibilis,[7] hoc potuit contigisse[8]: ergo illa[9] dimissio non fuit possibilis. Maior probatur ex hoc. Omnes beati sunt immortales et impeccabiles, sicut omnes rectiloqui[10] confitentur: non quia non possunt peccare, quia multi prius tempore suo peccant; sed sunt in gracia confirmacionis et glorie, cui repugnat peccatum vel miseriam coexistere, vel post illam succedere: patet ergo quod beatitudo est qualitas implicans securitatem perpetuitatis pleni gaudii et exclusionis miserie. [11][Eciam [12]securitas perpetuitatis pleni gaudii[12] et exclusionis miserie est per seipsum securitas talis, cum sit deveniendum ad ultimum formale, quo formaliter et non alio est quis securus de perpetuitate pleni gaudii et exclusionis miserie.

for the bliss of heaven is continuous, everlasting, and secure.

Sed contradiccionem implicat tali coexistere in subiecto suo vel post illam in ipso subiecto suo miseriam succedere: igitur etcetera.][11] Unde omnes theologi concorditer confitentur, quod [13]contradiccionem claudit aliquem esse[13] vel fuisse beatum cum hoc quod fiat postmodum non beatus.

[In reply to a logical objection that bliss may exist not only 'per se,' but also 'per accidens';

Nec valet dicere quod beatitudo *per accidens* sit beatitudo, quia ipsa est ultima forma abstracta, qua quis est beatus formaliter. Ideo, si illa non sit *per se* beatitudo, non superest quid aliud *per se* foret.

[1] manichiorum O. [2] sint B. [3] Aquino C.
[4] 50 O. [5] vel *add. altera manu* O.
[6–6] coesse. Secundo Christus si A B C. [7] possibiliter O.
[8] contingisse O. [9] alia A B C. [10] reliquie A B C.
[11–11] *Locus uncinis inclusus in codd.* C. O. *prorsus deest.*
[12–12] securitas . . . gaudii B *in marg.* [13–13] contradiccionem anime esse C.

Sicut ergo iusticia non potest esse non iusticia et de formis similibus;[1] sic status beatitudinis non potest esse non huiusmodi[2] status. Unde notum est methaphisicis quod tales forme abstracte non suscipiunt sic[3] predicacionem per accidens ut concreta: si enim beatitudo sit *per accidens* beatitudo—cum non sit processus in infinitum; sed, cum *omne per accidens* sit reducibile ad *aliquid*[4] *per se*, est devenire ad [O 222b] ultimum formale, quo | quis est beatus—et *illud per se* et *non per accidens* est beatitudo: et de tali est michi sermo. Confirmatur. Si *A* qualitas[5] sit nunc beatitudo et potest manere et[6] desinere esse beatitudo; per idem post esse [C 58a] potest reincipere esse beatitudo. Quo concesso, | patet quod preter *A*, quod non sufficit denominare hominem beatum, requiritur forma superaddita; et sic non *A*, sed forma sibi adveniens,[7] foret beatitudo. Patet ergo, quod cum beatitudo et confirmacio non possunt esse, nisi sint perpetue; nec possunt esse nisi huiusmodi quod, eo ipso quod insunt, reponunt hominem in statu cui repugnat miseriam succedere vel cessse; nec dependet beatitudo pocius a futuro, quam qualitates alie absolute[8]; tunc enim non forent beati de sua beatitudine securati. Minor ergo argumenti patet generaliter omni professori fidei incarnacionis: cum anima Christi ab instanti sue creacionis fuit plena omni genere carismatum, habens clariorem[9] visionem divine essencie quam alia creatura, et per consequens plenam fruicionem ad tantam noticiam naturaliter[10] consequentem. Cum ergo 'vita eterna sit[11] sic cognoscere Deum Patrem ac Dominum Iesum Christum,' ut testatur Veritas Ioh. 17; patet quod anima Christi ab instanti sue creacionis perpetue est beata.[12] Nec audivi hoc negatum ab aliquo, cum palam sequitur ex incarnacione. Si enim homo solum [13]intelligit quod intelligit mens[13]

It is replied that bliss is an abstract form, and only concretes admit predication 'per accidens.']

That of all creatures Christ is the most blessed is obvious to all who hold the doctrine of the Incarnation.

S. John xvii. 3.

[1] substancialibus B. [2] h̶ı̶¹ (*sic*) C. [3] sicut A; sed C.
[4] aliquod A B C. [5] a qüˡⁱˢ O. [6] manere et *om.* O.
[7] a deveniens O. [8] *forsitan* abstracte *legendum*.
[9] cariorem O. [10] generaliter A C.
[11] sic sit A B; ~~sic~~ sit C; sit sic O. [12] beatificata A B C.
[13] intelligit (*rasura*) mens A; intelligit mens B; intelligit quod mens C.

ypostatice copulata; per locum a sufficienti similitudine spiritus Iesu cognoscit quidquid cognoverat[1] ipse Iesus specialiter cum sit personaliter Verbum Dei.

The assumption of the humanity carries with it the blessedness of that humanity,

Ex istis colligitur talis racio. Tam determinatum et necessarium est ipsum hominem fuisse assumptum, quam necessarium est mundum vel aliquid aliud prefuisse: sed non potuit fuisse assumptus | nisi fuisset exinde beatus: ergo [A84a] tam necessarium est ipsum fuisse beatum quam necessarium est aliquid prefuisse: sed preterieiones huiusmodi non possunt solvi: ergo nec beatitudo vel assumpcio Domini nostri Iesu Christi. 2°. confirmatur ex hoc; quod anima Christi actu elicito vidit clare in Verbo omnia preterita vel futura; et per consequens clare vidit perpetuitatem sue beatitudinis; et ultra, cum illa visio[2] non potuit defuisse vel verti in ignoranciam aut[3] aliud genus entis; sequitur quod illa anima non potuit desinere esse beata vel Verbo ypostatice copulata. 3°. confirmatur ex testimonio Leonis Pape in quodam sermone dicentis: 'tanta fuit unicio[4] Dei et hominis ut nec supplicio posset[5] dirimi nec morte distingui.' | Nec [B128b] obest isti sentencie divina dispensacio, qua voluit Verbum suum ad tempus esse corpus, non plene sed quasi arraliter tunc[6] beatum, et per consequens esse animam secundum actuacionem corporis et racionem, qua[7] ipsam respicit, quantumlibet dolorosam.[8] Nam ille homo est multarum naturarum quelibet,[9] secundum quarum unam[10] fuit ad tempus abiectus viator, et simul secundum aliam perfectissimus comprehensor: et sic simul summe gaudens et summe tristis secundum vires et raciones dispares, [11]ut ostenditur consequenter: et dico[11] quod arraliter habuit in via dotes corporis, cum dote subtilitatis exivit sponsus de clauso utero,[12] dote | [C58b] agilitatis ambulavit super aquas, dote incorruptibilitatis et claritatis in transfiguracione emicuit.[13]

and the continuity of that blessedness;

as Pope Leo witnesses:

although whilst Christ was 'a pilgrim' and 'in the body,' that blessedness was only experienced by way of earnest (arraliter).

3°. per deducens ad impossibile patet idem.[14] Nam si

[1] cognoverit O. [2] visus o B. [3] vel A B. [4] unio A B C.
[5] potest A B C. [6] esse *add.* A B C. [7] quam O. [8] dolosam O.
[9] qualibet B. [10] una A. [11–11] ut ostenditur ut dico A B C.
[12] uthero B. [13] enituit O. [14] illud A B C.

Proof III. If the humanity of the Word can be dismissed, it becomes when dismissed liable to sin: *i.e.* the Word can sin: which is impossible.

humanitas ypostatice copulata posset dimitti et sic dampnari pro peccato, et tam caro quam anima est personaliter ipsum Verbum; sequitur quod Verbum Dei peccare [1] poterit et dampnari; quod nephas [2] est dicere. Patet consequencia supposito fundamento, cum arguitur ab inferiori ad suum superius personale, cui per se competit accio personalis. Sequitur ergo—hec humanitas potest peccare: hec humanitas est persona Verbi: ergo persona Verbi potest peccare—. Nam persona Verbi nedum est hec [3] humanitas, sed aliquid aliud [3] quia divinitas; ideo est superior [4] vel communior quam [4] est hec [5] humanitas. Unde, sicut sequitur quod Filius Dei fuit natus humanitus, conversatus,[6] passus, mortuus, et sepultus, et ascendit, eo quod humanitas, que fuit dictus Filius, sic se habuit; ita eciam sequeretur quod Verbum peccaret, si humanitas, que fuit dictum Verbum, peccaret.

The moderns admit that sin in the humanity of the Word implies sin in the Word.

Confirmatur ex testimonio moderniorum [7] dicencium quod hec humanitas non posset [8] ypostatice copulari peccando nisi Verbum exinde peccaret [9]; et, quod plus est,[10] racione unionis prioris Verbum denominatum est secundum moderniores jacuisse pro triduo in sepulcro, et ad sensum consimilem peccasse in casu, quo [11] natura dimissa pro tunc peccaverit. Que, rogo, causa diversitatis sensus Spiritus [12] Sancti in isto articulo fidei 'Christus descendit ad inferos, fuit mortuus et sepultus;' hoc est, non illa persona, sed pars eius pro tempore quo [13] non fuit pars vel ypostatice copulata,[14] sic se habuit; quin ad sensum simillimum concederet, quod natura dimissa et postmodum reassumpta, si peccaret interim, denominaret Filium sic peccare? [15]

And from this follow consequences so absurd,

Ponatur ergo quod in die parasceues anima Christi [16] perfecerit liberacionem patrum a limbo,[16] et pro tunc agitetur [17] corpus a demone multos homines conquassando et quod in

[1] dei deprecari B. [2] nefas B. [3]–[3] humanitas . . . aliud *om.* B
[4] quam communior quam B. [5] ista; *om.* est O. [6] conversatus *om.* B
[7] modernorum O. [8] potest B C. [9] peccaverit O.
[10] est *om.* O. [11] qua A B C. [12] spiritus *om.* O.
[13] qui O. [14] copulativa O. [15] peccaret O.
[16]–[16] perfeceret libacionem patrum a libo O. [17] agetur C.

as to prove that the hypothesis of the peccability of the human nature of the Word after dismissal is untenable.

sancto[1] sabbato † reuniatur[2] anima corpori suspensa ypostatica unione, et peccet ante nonam adulterio, homicidio, blasfemia, et omni genere peccatorum; et post nonam peniteat, et procreet legitime, ac juste condempnet multos ad mortem, assumpta humani|tate in prima sabbati in unitatem [A 84b] suppositi Verbi Dei: quem casum | moderni admittunt et [O 222c] magis mirabiles tanquam necessario possibiles; in quo casu videtur juxta glosam quam dant[3] articulis fidei quod[4] omnes dicte operaciones in triduo redundarent in Christum vel aliter fingeret[5] ex instinctu Spiritus Sancti sensum impossibilem et insolitum. Certum est itaque Christum non istos homines suffocasse,[6] virginitatis laureolam[7] ex procreacione seminis perdidisse, irregularitatem incurrisse, vel remansisse in eo vestigia peccatorum. Et | conformi racione nec iacuit [C 59a] sepultus nec descendit ad inferos, nisi conformi racione denominaciones predicte in casu [8]posito sibi insint,[8] vel aliter dicatur sentencia supradicta, quod mansit pro dicto triduo unio ypostatica ad utrumque.

If peccable men by grace have such bliss as to be inseparably united to God, much more is Christ by the hypostatic union inseparably united:

Ex istis colligitur quod, si beatus alius tantum adheret Deo quod non potest post beatitudinem dissolvi unio, qua est unus spiritus cum eo[9]; multo magis natura Christi, que ultra hoc ypostatice est unita: ut si homo, qui potest peccare, habet per graciam quod sit impeccabilis, immortalis, et sic de aliis que peioracionem sapiunt: quanto magis natura humana in fine bonitatis possibilis exaltata, que omnino peccare non poterit, ab illa gracia dimitti non poterit. Unde, quamvis Mt. 27 secundum naturam completam creatam clamet Christus; 'Deus meus, Deus meus, utquid me dereliquisti?' non tamen dimisit ypostaticam unionem, sed dereliquit illud 'infirmum Dei,' quod est suppositum 'forcius' ad tempus, inconservatum a [10]persecucionibus et flagellacionibus Iudeorum; sed[10] nun-

nor does the cry, 'My God, my God, why hast thou forsaken me?' Matt. xxvii. 47, imply a dissolution of the hypostatic union.

1 Cor. i. 25.

[1] isto C.
[2] reniatur A C; revivatur B; revinatur *in margine* C; renunciatur O; *certe aut* revinciatur *aut* reuniatur *legendum*.
[3] dant autores A B; dat autores C.
[4] quod *om.* O.
[5] finge (*lacuna*) ex instinctu C; fig[t] O.
[6] suffocare O.
[7] aureolam A B C.
[8-8] sibi posito insunt A B; posito sibi nisunt (*sic*) C.
[9] cum eo *om.* O.
[10-10] a persecutoribus et flagellacionibus; sed *om.* iudeorum A B C; a persecucionibus in flagellacionibus iudeorum sed O.

quam dimisit vel simpliciter dereliquit, quia dimissio dicit existenciam dimissi et separacionem ypostaticam ab eodem, quod non fuit in triduo.

Quod si quis in evidenciam huius veritatis olim famose expectat testimonium scripture, ecce Veritas Ioh. 10. alloquitur [B 129a] Phariseos: 'non potest, inquit, solvi scriptura, | quem Pater sanctificavit et misit in mundum.' Pro cuius intellectu sunt tria notanda per ordinem.[1] Primo quod Veritas non loquitur de scriptura nostra artificiali aggregata ex ficturis[2] atramenti et pellibus mortuorum; tum quia talis scriptura cottidie per artifices potest solvi; tum eciam quia illi non competit sanctificacio et missio in mundum: sed illa scriptura est 'liber vite' cui inscribuntur omnia, cum sit intrinsecus Sermo Dei. Et ad illum sensum exponit Augustinus Omc. 44.[3] 'Forte, inquit, aliquis dicit[4]: Si pater eum sanctificavit, [5]ergo aliquando non erat sanctus; sed si sic eum sanctificavit,[5] quomodo genuit? ut enim sanctus esset, gignendo ei[6] dedit, quia sanctum eum genuit.' Et respondet posterius ad obiectum. 'Si, inquit, quod sanctificatur aliquando, non erat sanctum; quomodo dicimus Deo Patri —"sanctificetur nomen tuum"—?' Ille ergo, qui est absolute necessario in se sanctus, fit sanctus[7] in nobis per prevenientem graciam, noticiam, et operacionem, et confessionem meritoriam.[8] Unde Spiritus Sanctus ad relinquendum nobis exemplar, quod loquitur de scriptura vitali, subdit in genere masculino — '*quem* Pater sanctificavit' — innuendo nobis relacionem faciendam ad Filium. Mos[9] enim est scripture et Augustini per [10]adiectivos masculinos personas concipere et per neutros[10] naturas. Et isti modo[11] loquendi alludit Apostolus ad Gall. 3°; 'non, inquit,[12] dicit *seminibus* quasi in multis, sed *semini* tuo, qui est Christus.' Indubie, sicut [C 59b] sanctus | Apostolus notavit[13] numerum, sic et genus.

The possibility of the dissolution of the compound nature of the Word into its elements is expressly denied in Holy Scripture, S. John x. 35, 36: where (in the Vulgate) in the words 'non potest *solvi scriptura, quem* Pater sanctificavit, *etc.*' (1) '*scriptura*' refers not to writing with ink on parchment;

Phil. iv. 3.
Rev. iii. 5.

Math. vi. 9.

for the masculine '*quem*' proves that *scriptura* is equivalent to *Sermo Dei*, *i.e.* the personal Word of God:

Gal. iii. 16.

[1] pro ordine O. [2] figuris A B C. [3] 48 O.
[4] diceret A B C. [5–5] ergo . . . sanctificavit *om.* A B C.
[6] et A B C. [7] firmius O. [8] meritoriam. Ad. Unde (*sic*) C.
[9] mous O. [10–10] adiecciones masculinas—neutras A B C.
[11] moi A B. [12] enim A B C. [13] numeravit C M.

and (2) '*solvi*' refers not to the separation of (*a*) the human soul from the body, S. John ii. 19. or of (*b*) the Father from the Son: but 2 Cor. i. 18.

2°. supponitur quod Veritas non loquitur de solucione mentis a corpore vel Patris a Filio in hoc dicto: de prima non, quia supra Ioh. 2°. dicit Veritas Iudeis | prophetice quod solverent [A 84c] templum corporis sui ab anima et ipse in tribus diebus excitaret illud. Cum ergo 'non fuit in eo *EST* et *NON*,' patet quod hic non intellexit corpus non posse solvi ab anima. Nec alius sensus est pertinens; tum quia ligacio[1] et solucio est duarum naturarum ad invicem et non personarum eiusdem summe indivisibilis essencie; tum eciam, quia ille sensus fuisset dictis impertinens, non eis ambiguus. Ideo relinquitur 3°. per locum a sufficienti divisione quod intellexit insolubilitatem deitatis ab humanitate, quas expressit nomine 'scripture,' ut vel sic scrutarentur scripturas, que testimonium perhibent[2] de istis duabus naturis sic ypostatice copulatis. Unde et Ioh. 5. dicitur[3] 'scrutamini[4] scripturas in quibus vos putatis vitam eternam habere, et ille sunt que testimonium perhibent[2] de me.' Non enim haberent evidenciam dicere quod blasfemat dicendo se esse Dei Filium naturalem apposito sufficienti scrutinio scripturarum. Nam si in lege scriptum sit de Messia vel Christo futuro in duabus naturis et una ypostasi[5]—quod vinculum propter unionem[6] ypostaticam ad infinitam personam non potest includi[7] fine temporis, sicut potest unio participative deificatorum per Sermonem Dei[8] factum ad eos et non eis personaliter copulatum—quomodo est color concludendi blasfemiam[9] ex assercione filiacionis naturalis? Medium autem per quod tenet ista inveccio est veritas quod 'non potest solvi' hec 'scriptura' ad sensum expositum. Nam ex illo[10] sequitur quod sit natura increata in supposito Verbi, et cum[11] hec natura creata temporaliter sed[12] insolubiliter copulata. Unde signantissime Veritas dicit negativam quod 'non potest solvi scriptura;' quia, licet sancti in patria sint Deo inseparabiliter copulati, tamen contingentissime possunt solvi, cum sint pro

(3) to the separation of the deity from the humanity of Christ.

To his possession of these natures,

and to their indissoluble union, the Scriptures, which Christ bade the Jews to search, bear ample witness:

S. John v. 35.

[1] ligamentum O; pertinens. Cum ligacio C. [2] prohibent O.
[3] dicit A B C. [4] scruta num A C; scruta in B. [5] ypostasis B.
[6] unione O. [7] concludi A B C. [8] domini A B C.
[9] blasfemia A B C. [10] 2°. A B C. [11] tamen C. [12] scilicet A B C.

tempore suo viantes[1] peccabiles. Homo autem assumptus [O 222d] a Verbo Dominus Iesus Christus pro nullo tempore peccare | poterit. [2]Et patet conclusio.[2] Nec[3] aliter haberent sancti doctores evidenciam imprecandi anathema eis qui concedunt dimissionem vel solucionem huiusmodi naturarum.

and the doctors of the church rightly anathematize those who teach otherwise.

Sed contra illud obicitur. Quicquid Deus contingenter et libere contradictorie facit, potest alias eciam adnichilando[4] destruere: sed libere contradictorie assumpsit hominem: ergo potest nedum ipsum dimittere sed adnichilando[4] destruere.

Objection. God being as free to destroy, as he is to create, having freely assumed man, he can as freely annihilate, much more dismiss him.

Confirmatur tripliciter. Primo ex hoc, quod idem est iudicium de una creatura et qualibet, cum tanta sit utrobique divina libertas: sed aliquam creaturam Deus potest adnichilare: ergo[5] quamlibet. 2°. per hoc quod aliter Deus esset [C 60a] necessitatus ad conservandam dictam unionem, | et sic non libere contradictorie eam servat. 3°. ex hoc quod Deus non esset omnipotens, nisi posset tam contingentem et fragilem[6] nedum dissolvere, [7]sed et adnichilare.[7] Tales[8] sunt multe[8] instancie, que omnes currunt sub uno circulo quod Deus non esset omnipotens nisi posset in talia. Vel taliter[9] arguunt per locum a simili;— | Si Deus creare poterit et utrobique [B 129b] [10]tanta est[10] distancia; ergo per idem[11] adnichilare poterit.

Threefold confirmation. 1. Based on the unlimited range of the Divine freedom.

2. If God cannot dissolve, he cannot freely maintain this union.

3. God would not be omnipotent, if he could not dissolve, nay, annihilate so contingent a union.

[4.] God's power is equally near for creation or for destruction.

Pro isto dico sicut alias sepe dixi quod ad omnipotenciam Dei consequitur perficere construere et non destruere, creare[12] et non adnichilare; et sic de actibus positivis privacionibus repugnantibus separatis. Unde sicut repugnat[13] [A 84d] pure creaturam esse et non posse deficere, sic repugnat | omnipotencie Creatoris posse adnichilare peiorare dampnificare vel de[14] se destruere creaturam. Peccatum autem[15] quod non est creatura Deus destruit, peccantes solum per accidens racione peccati punit vel meliorando consumit.[16]

Answer. Omnipotence acts constructively, not destructively, positively not privatively.

[1] cuantes O. [2–2] ut patet oculo A B C. [3] nam C.
[4] anichilando *ut infra saepius* A B C. [5] in *add.* O.
[6] nedum *prima manu* nodum *altera manu* A C; nodum B; nedum O; nisi posset creaturam tam contingentem dissolvere M; *et certe aut* creaturam *supplendum aut* unionem *subaudiendum est.* [7–7] sed et adnichilare *om.* O M; et *om.* B.
[8–8] sunt multe *om.* A B C. [9] aliter O. [10–10] est tanta B C. est carifata A.
[11] perinde O. [12] creare *om.* O. [13] repugnant O.
[14] per O. [15] autem *om.* O. [16] consumat C.

Et sic ex omnipotencia Dei sequitur oppositum predictorum et patet quod assumptum est inpossibile.

*Threefold exemplification of the author's theory of omnipotence. 1. Logical. God produced time: Ps. lxxiv. 17. but he cannot destroy it.*

Pro cuius[1] intellectu pono triplex exemplum ut alias posui. Primum logicum. Nam Deus produxit tempus perpetuum, sicut testatur scriptura et sepe meminit Augustinus. Nam Ps. 73.[2] dicitur 'estatem et ver tu plasmasti ea.'[3] Et idem est iudicium de [4]toto tempore,[4] et signanter dicit Veritas Marc. 2° quod 'Filius hominis est dominus sabbati' et sic Deus. Et tamen notum est quod Deus de potencia absoluta non potest tempus perpetuum[5] adnichilare sive destruere, ymo, quod plus est, tempus vel motum finire ante finem sue periodi naturalis. Modicus ergo color est concludere, si Deus libere contradictorie datum effectum produxerit, quod potest ipsum destruere.

*Mark ii. 28.*

*2. Natural. God created the world, but he cannot destroy it, or any other substance: else he would create a want in himself.*

2m exemplum [6]naturale est de hoc[6] quod Deus libere contradictorie produxit mundum ex nichilo et tamen non potest ipsum destruere nec aliam substancialem essenciam ut patet in materia *De Adnichilacione*, ne fiat vacuum vel defectus in Deo formaliter.

*3. Metaphysical. God cannot annul the past truth that I existed.*

3m exemplum est methaphisicum. Nam Deus produxit veritatem talem, de preterito me fuisse, et hoc liberrime contingenter; et tamen [7]notum est quod[7] de potencia sua absoluta non potest ipsam destruere vel eius desicionem[8] permittere.

*God's action is necessarily towards good, advancing towards actual existence, not declining towards non-existence or evil in any form.*

Talia quotlibet exempla reliquit nobis Deus, ut consideremus eius bonitatem et naturalem condicionem ad positive posse bene agere et non male. Sicut enim est actus purus non admixtus [9]potencia ante[9] actum, sic potest per se proficiendo tendere in esse positivum, et non deficiendo per se tendere in[10] non esse, ut, licet modicum sit, mentiri vel aliter peccando male agere; Deus tamen ex omnipotencia hoc non potest.

Et utinam nos[11] scolastici, nescientes probare vel

[1] protinus C. [2] 25 A B C; 72 O. [3] eam B.
[4–4] causa creature A B C. [5] perpetuum *om.* O. [6] "est" naturale hoc A B C.
[7–7] notum . . . quod *om.* A B.
[8] desicionem A B C M; designacionem O; *an* destruccionem *legendum?*
[9] potencia ad A B C. [10] et O. [11] nō (*non*) O.

[C 60b] sophistice secundum vivacem[1] scintillam evidencie | tales casus, insisteremus circa noticiam et deteccionem[2] substrate necessarie veritatis a nobis hodie plurimum occultate propter inanem occupacionem circa conclusiones impossibiles, que ex principiis impossibilibus consecuntur[3]: ut patet specialiter de casibus quibus ponitur Deum creaturam suam adnichilare, vel Verbum naturas prius assumptas dimittere ac alias personas in eisdem naturis assumendo communicare. Conceditur ergo quod, sicut libere contradictorie et per consequens contingentissime assumpsit hominem, sic potest absolute necessario nunc et semper facere vel[4] causare quod neminem assumpsit, et quod non est vel[5] fuit vel erit aliqua creatura, ymo quod ipsummet non fuit vel[6] erit amplius Verbum Dei. Patet hoc, posito quod non sit tempus. Sed absit ex isto concludere quod Deus potest quidquam adnichilare, vel facere tempus aut unionem predictam cessare. Talis enim non foret potencia contradiccionis ut ad affirmacionem et negacionem, sed potencia adnichilacionis,[7] destruccionis, sive privacionis. Et patet solucio ad primam confirmacionem cum secunda. Deus enim necessitat se volicionibus[8] eternis ad omne quod efficit, et tamen non potest efficere nisi summe libere contingenter, cum necessitas illa non sit coaccionis a causa superiori limitante; et per [A 85a] consequens nec pure naturalis inclinacionis, | sed necessitas supposicionis, ut alias diffuse exposui. Et patet ad terciam quod Deus non est omnipotens, si posset vinculum dicte corrigie denodare.

Et quoad argumenta fundata in loco a simili, vellem quod sic arguentes attenderent et stabilirent sufficientem similitudinem argumentis,[9] et non quererent questiones novas induendo habitum responsalis vel dicendo negativas, quod ipsi nesciunt racionem diversitatis et alia multa verba preter

We schoolmen ought to abandon sophistical discussion, and earnestly search for necessary truth, now-a-days much lost sight of because of our futile efforts to track impossible conclusions from impossible premisses: *e.g.* If time be not (*i.e.* if the category under which every possible predication is made be annulled), and if God willed otherwise than he actually has willed, there might follow the possibility of the non-assumption of humanity, of the non-existence of any creature, even of the non-existence of the Word. But this only amounts to the possibility of inserting or withdrawing negations in a logical arrangement of *words*: not to the actual power of annihilating *things*. And it does not follow that God can annihilate anything at all, or cause time or the aforesaid union to cease. For God necessitates his own action by his own eternal purposes: and this necessitation, arising from his own being, is no limitation of his absolute freedom. Thus the objection and the confirmations of it (p. 75, ll. 6-20) 1. 2. 3. are answered: and as to [4] (p. 75, l. 21) it rests upon an unproven analogy;

[1] unitatem O.
[2] decepcionem create *in marg.* A; vel detepcionem substracte B: et deteccionem substracte C.
[3] con- *om.* A B C.
[4] vel *om.* A B C.
[5] vel *om.* O.
[6] nichil O.
[7] adilacōnis (*sic*) O.
[8] volucionibus A B C O.
[9] argumenti A B C.

and is a mere begging of the question.

scolastica. Unde quando assumitur quod tanta est distancia inter terminos creacionis sicut inter terminos adnichilacionis, pure petitur quod antea probaretur. Oporteret[1] ergo primo fundare existenciam adnichilacionis vel eius possibilitatem, et post sollicitari de eius terminis. Sed hoc non probabitur antequam | humanitas Christi sit soluta.[2] [O 223a]

Corollary I. Neither created nature could be the humanity in Christ, unless it were assumed in hypostatic union by the word.

Ex istis videtur corelarie[3] sequi primo quod neutra natura creata in Christo posset esse humanitas, nisi a Verbo ypostatice sit[4] assumpta. Patet ex hoc quod aliter | natura, que [B 130a] est Christus, dampnificari[5] poterit; et sic Christus: si enim humanitas Christi posset fuisse[6] individuum speciei hominis et non Christus, tunc posset peccasse ut unus homo fuisse[7] alius. Quorum opposita hic suppono, ponendo quod assumpcio ypostatica a Verbo Dei consequitur[8] ad hominem Iesum, sicut passio consequitur[9] ad subiectum.

Corollary II. The humanity actually thus assumed was the only humanity which it was possible to the Word to assume. The grounds of this corollary to be further discussed later (ch. viii. p. 125).

2°. sequitur quod nullam humanitatem aliam Verbum potuit ypostatice assumpsisse. Patet ex hoc, quod aliter Christus posset[10] fuisse alius et[11] per consequens alia persona, ut post ostendetur.[12] Cum ergo[13] consequens sit impossibile, patet quod antecedens inferius.[14] | [C 61a]

Corollary III. Neither the Father nor the Holy Spirit could have become incarnate. This subject also to be discussed at greater length below (ch. vi. p. 86).

3°.[15] sequitur quod nec Pater nec Donum incarnari potuit,[16] quia aliter Filius posset[17] esse humanitus pater patris. Cum ergo minimum inconsequens[18] sit Deo impossibile absolute, ut capit Anselmus de Incarnacione Verbi cap 6°, patet intentum. Ista tamen dicta erunt magis evidencia postmodum, cum iuxta posite fuerint sentencie modernorum. Nam iste sunt conclusiones Anselmi Cur Deus Homo 6°. et de Incarnacione 7°. et 9°.

All the authorities, such as Augustine and Anselm, which may be alleged in opposition to

Ad omnes[19] auctoritates vel dicta auctorum in oppositum alleganda dicitur, sicut in materia *De Adnichilacione*, quod intelligenda sunt condicionaliter, quod Deus ex se habet

[1] oportet A B C. [2] solita O. [3] correlarie A B C.
[4] sint A. [5] dampnari A B C; dāpnira O. [6] esse A B C.
[7] fuisse *om.* A B C. [8] censetur B C. [9] censetur C.
[10] potuisset A B C. [11] non *add.* O. [12] ostenditur O.
[13] ergo *om.* C. [14] inferens A B C. [15] sic *add.* O.
[16] poterit O. [17] potest A C; potuisset B.
[18] inconues (*i.e.* inconveniens) O M. [19] oppositum A B C.

potenciam sufficientem: unde potest in talia si voluerit, vel si illa possint[1] fieri. Sic enim dicit Augustinus contra Maximinianum, quod Deus potuit alium filium produxisse. Et isto modo loquendi sepe utitur venerabilis Anselmus, ut patet 2°. Cur Deus Homo cap. 5. Et ex hoc processerunt omnes sollicitaciones [2]inanes quid illo posito sequeretur.[2] Verumptamen magna consideracio est et nobis inscrutabilis,[3] unde Deus voluit illum hominem pre ceteris assumpsisse, quod rememorat Augustinus Enchiridion 3°. Profecto modus iste, quo natus est Christus de Spiritu Sancto non ut eius filius de Maria virgine, [4]sic insinuat[4] nobis graciam Dei, qua homo, nullis precedentibus meritis in ipso exordio nature sue, quo esse cepit, Verbo Dei copularetur in tantam persone unitatem ut idem ipse esset Filius Dei qui filius hominis; ac sic nature humane suscepcione fieret quodammodo ipsa gracia illi homini naturalis que nullum peccatum posset admittere.

the author's conclusions, are to be understood as speaking conditionally: they put imaginary cases; but as to the real facts they are at one with the author:

so Augustine in passage quoted.

Oportet ergo theologum capere tanquam principium quod Deus libere[5] contradictorie [6]assumpsit illum hominem sicut libere contradictorie[6] produxit fabricam [7]huius mundi, et huiusmodi effectuum[7] causa est eterna[8] Dei volicio,[9] et per consequens essencia ac bonitas Dei nostri cuius non est [A 85b] querenda causa ulterior. Et sicut respondetur | querenti,[10] 'Quare Deus produxit mundum in illo loco vel in illo tempore pocius quam quocunque alio?'—[11]quod hoc est necessarium ex supposicione, eo quod non posset illum mundum producere nisi ipsum produceret in illo loco et in illo tempore[11]; ita respondetur querenti—'Quare Deus assumpsit illum hominem?'—quod hoc est quia Deus voluit assumere hominem ad complecionem sue fabrice, et non potuit

The ultimate ground of our belief is the eternal purpose of God, *i.e.* his being and goodness, and beyond this we cannot go.

[1] talia *add.* A B C.
[2]–[2] omnes sollicitaciones inanes qui illo posito sequetur A B C; homines solicitantes et amc° (*? anxii*) quid illo posito sequeretur O.
[3] instrumentabilis O.
[4]–[4] sicut filius insinuat O.
[5] liberrime A B C.
[6]–[6] assumpsit . . . contradictorie *om.* A B C.
[7]–[7] huiusmodi et huius effectus A B C; huius mundi et huius effectuum O.
[8] trina A B.
[9] volucio O, *cf. p.* 77, *n.* 8.
[10] querenti *om.* A B C.
[11]–[11] quod . . . tempore *om.* B.

God willed to assume man in place and in time in order to complete his work.

assumpsisse hominem, nisi illum hominem[1] assumpsisset. Sicut enim ille locus et illud tempus individuatur ab illo mundo, sic quod ubicunque vel quandocunque Deus[2] produxerit[3] illum mundum, hoc fecisset in illo loco et in illo tempore. Sic illa humanitas, que est Iesus,[4] sufficienter individuatur a Verbo, sic quod posita illa consequitur suppositacio sui a Verbo; et quamcumque aliam humanitatem per impossibile | [C 61b] Verbum assumpsisset[5] illa humanitas foret Iesus. Dimissis

God having so assumed man, *Scriptura solvi non potest*—the Word cannot be dissolved.

ergo casibus et conclusionibus ex illis inaniter coniecturatis,[6] teneamus confessionem quod dicta 'scriptura solvi non potest[7]'; quia, si non fallor, maior pars heresum circa incarnacionem Christi in isto devio titubavit.[8]

This is the point at which heretics for the most part stumble: saying that Christ is mere man, not God; or pure spirit and not a bodily substance composed of body and soul. Enumeration of heresies in this connection, Ebionitae, Theodosiani, Pauliniani, Photinus, and Philaster denied the divinity of Christ:

Nam aliqui ponebant Christum esse purum hominem et non Deum: aliqui autem e contra dixerunt ipsum esse purum spiritum et non substanciam corpoream ex corpore et anima compositam. In prima parte erant Ebionite tempore beati Iohannis evangeliste dicentes Christum esse purum hominem et non Deum; et ista est heresis 10 quam recitat Augustinus in libro suo de Heresibus. Post eos consecuti sunt Theodosiani heretici, qui divinitatem Christi conformiter negaverunt; et hec est Heresis 33. Post eos consecuti sunt Pauliniani, qui negaverunt Christum semper fuisse,[9] quia non antequam fuit natus de virgine, et, ut verbis utar Augustini, 'Christum non aliquid amplius quam hominem putaverunt'; et illa est Heresis 44. Et post eos consecuti sunt [10]Photinus et Philaster[10] cum suis discipulis eadem heresi dampnati, ut

the Ariani and Apollinaristae denied both his divinity and his humanity: the Meicagismonite denied his consubstantiality with the Father: the Proclianistae and Patriciani his humanity:

recitat Augustinus Heresi 49. Postea consecuti sunt Arriani et Appollinariste negantes tam Christi divinitatem quam [11]eius humanitatem ut[11] recitat Augustinus Heresi 49 et 55. Meicagismonite[12] negant cum Arrianis eandem esse substanciam Patris et Filii,[13] ut recitat Augustinus Heresi 58. [14]Procliauiste et Patriciani[14] negaverunt Christi humanitatem,

[1] hominem *om.* O. [2] deus *om.* A B C. [3] produxisset A B.
[4] Christus O. [5] assupserit (*sic*) O. [6] communicatis O.
[7] possit A C; poterit O. [8] titubant A B C; tutubauit O.
[9] fuisset O. [10] fotinus et siliaster A B C; fotinus et filaster O.
[11–11] eius . . . ut *om.* A B C. [12] Meitangismonte A B C.
[13] patrem et filium A B C. [14–14] Pelianiste et priuciani A B C.

ut patet Heresibus 60 et 61. Et postea consecuti sunt Priscillianiste[1] dicentes cum Manicheis[2] quod nulla caro est a Deo bono sed a Deo malo, et per consequens Christus non est Deus[3] et homo. Hi autem secundum Augustinum [O 223b] Heresi 70 apocrifa sump|serunt tanquam autentica,[4] scripturam sacram vertentes ut hodie ad suam heresim confir- [B 130b] mandam.[5] Sed et Sabelliani erraverunt |[6] in divinitate Christi concedentes confuse Patrem esse Filium et Spiritum Sanctum,[7] seducti paralogismo vocato expositorio, ut ibi recitat Augustinus. Nona heresis,[8] quam Augustinus recitat 73, posuit divinitatem [9]doluisse[9] cum figeretur[10] caro Christi in cruce: et isti, sicut Patripassiani, haberent hodie fautores plurimos.

The Priscillianistae and Manichei, affirming that matter is evil, deny that Christ is God and man: but Augustine refutes them and shows that they give to apocryphal writings the value of holy scripture.

The Sabelliani, confusing the Persons of the Trinity, deny Christ's divinity.

Another heresy which asserted that the divine nature suffered pain at the crucifixion, as well as the error of the Patripassians, would receive much support nowadays.

Nam ut asserunt negantes formas universales, ista foret racio insolubilis lumini[11] naturali—Filius Dei patitur, et ipse est deitas; ergo deitas patitur sive dolet—.Et eadem deduccio valeret Sabellianis—Si Verbum patitur, et ipsum est eadem essencia vel substancia in numero, que[12] Pater vel Donum; ergo [13]uterque eorum[13] patitur; et per idem quelibet persona divina indifferenter fuit homo, nascitur de [A 85c] virgine et suscepit omnem predicacionem temporalem, | quam Verbum suscepit[14]—.Et confirmacio illius est quod [C 62a] maior est unio Verbi ad naturam divinam | ac personarum ad invicem[15] quam est corporis ad animam; sed anima naturaliter compatitur corpori; ergo multo magis tam deitas quam utraque persona compatitur Christo passo.

The Patripassian heresy, as also the Sabellian, arise from the confusion of thought involved in the denial or ignorance of the true doctrine of universals.

Sed constat nutritis in materia *De Universalibus* quod substancia, essencia, vel natura divina, quod idem est,[16] non potest pati ab aliquo vel moveri. Nec est color—si persona, que est communis humanitas, patitur, tunc et illa—cum natura communis abstracta non recipit formaliter predicaciones huiusmodi personales. Et multo evidencius non

For, in accordance with the true doctrine of Realism, a common substance, essence, or nature does not admit predications proper only to individuals: therefore it is not the divine *nature*,

[1] Priolianiste A B C; plalianiste (*sic*) O.
[2] macheis O.
[3] deus *bis* A B.
[4] auteuticam O.
[5] contrigendam O.
[6] errant O.
[7] sanctum *om.* A B C.
[8] heresi A B C.
[9–9] dicentem doluisse A B C; divinitatem dissoluisse O.
[10] fugeretur O.
[11] lumine A B C.
[12] vel *add.* A.
[13–13] utraque illarum O.
[14] suscipit O.
[15] ad idem A B C. A *inter* ad *et* idem *add.* verbum *in margine.*
[16] est *om.* A B C.

but the divine *Person*, who is also an individual belonging to *human nature*; in other words, it is the divine nature differentiated by the assumption of humanity, which suffers; not the Father [nor the Spirit] but the Incarnate Son.

Deity no more 'suffers' than [*abstract*] Humanity laughs, or performs any other act proper only to an *individual* man: a fallacy which is disposed of in the author's *treatise on Universals*.

Such logical sophisms must be explored in order to avoid error.

oportet Patrem pati, etsi Filius, qui est alia persona et eadem essencia paciatur. Nec esset possibile Verbum pati, Patre non passo; nisi Verbum esset tam aliquid quod non est[1] Pater, quam persona alia quam est Pater. Unde, cum, Verbum sit assumpta humanitas plus distans a Patre quam corpus ab anima, patet quod nec est color concludere—Si anima compatitur corpori, cum utraque sit eadem persona hominis; quod[2] per idem Pater compatitur Filio—cum inter eos sit distinccio personalis. Unde tales paralogismi heretici plus placent hodie tam iuvenibus quam adultis quam argumenta solida scripturarum. Unde ignorantibus naturam universalium videtur ista deduccio sophistica insolubile argumentum—Si Petrus ridet, Paulus comedit,[3] et sic de aliis actibus personalibus; et omnis homo est natura specifica; ergo illa natura specifica sic ridet[4] aut aliter personaliter operatur—.Et tales arguecie, locum et tempus occupantes, ponunt placentes[5] plurimis in numerum evidenciarum probabilium, sed indubie ut Tharsites.[6] Alias autem declaravi in materia *De Universalibus*, quod communis humanitas non ridet vel comedit, quamvis sit quelibet persona hominis, que sic facit. Correspondenter communis deitas non gignit nec gignitur, nec gaudet humanitus nec tristatur; quamvis sit Pater qui gignit, Verbum quod gignitur et secundum assumptum hominem[7] supra alios mortales patitur et tristatur. Tales intricaciones sophisticas decet theologis[8] evitando cognoscere, cum sint superficiales colores venenosas hereses pallientes et incautos in logica in errores plurimos inducentes. Et hec est racio quare Augustinus tam sedule recitat hereses de Christo cum suis evidenciis ut caucius caveantur.[9]

The Nestorian and Eutychian heresies

Gal. ii. 6.

Sed inter omnes hereses Nestoriana et Eutichiana sunt hodie eo diligencius precavende, quo theologi eciam 'qui videntur aliquid' sunt iam ad sapiendum predictas hereses

[1] esset B C. *pr. man.* C. *alt. man.* est. [2] et O. [3] comedet O.
[4] vel comedet *add.* O. [5] placenter O; *forsitan* ponuntur placentes *verius legendum*?
[6] tarlites O. [7] omnis O. [8] theologum O. [9] teneantur C.

proniores. Scribit enim Augustinus de Heresi 89 et 90 in fine libri sui De Heresibus, quod Nestorius episcopus contra fidem catholicam dogmatizare ausus est, Christum Dominum Deum nostrum hominem esse tantum; nec illud, quod 'mediator Dei et hominum' effectus est, in utero virginis de [C 62b] Spiritu Sancto fuisse conceptum; sed | postea Deum homini[1] fuisse permixtum, nec Deum-hominem fuisse passum sepultumque[2] dicebat; evacuare[3] contendens omne nostrum remedium, quo Verbum Dei hominem sic suscipere dignatus est in utero virginis, ut una persona fieret Dei et hominis; propter quod sic signanter natus, passus, mortuus, et pro nostris peccatis resurgens, ascendit in celum. Vidit enim iste[4] Nestorius quod humanitas assumpta non fuit divinitas,[5] et hinc paralogisatus credidit[6] quod non fuit Verbum Dei, concedens cum heresi 73 quod Verbum non patitur nisi [A 85d] divinitas[5] paciatur; et sic, cum | [7]illam esse personam sit suppositum,[7] dixit quod in Christo fuerunt due persone; et per consequens Christus vel[8] esset aggregatum ex his, vel persona Verbi non passionata humanitus, ut nec passa, mortua, nec sepulta; quia non vidit quomodo due tam distantes nature possent[9] esse utraque eadem persona. Quidquid autem moderni dixerunt, illo modo intelligunt cum Augustinus, Boecius, Anselmus, et alii capitales doctores concorditer ante Petrum Lombardum.[10] Aliter enim non tam crebro dicerent,[11] quod utraque natura tam corpus quam anima est eadem persona hominis; et quod in Christo tam divinitas[5] quam humanitas est eadem persona Verbi[12]; et quod aliquid,[13] quod nos sumus, recenter factum est[14] Verbum; ut dicit Augustinus super Ps. 80. Omc. 48, 2° de Visitacione [B 131a] Infir | morum et alibi.

Enticiani autem[15] volentes declinare a Nestorianis cum Appollinaristis coinciderant in caribdim, negantes naturam

are most dangerous in our time.

The Nestorians held that Christ is only man; not that the God-man was conceived, born, and suffered: but that [after his conception] God was blended with man;

so that in Christ there were two persons; and Christ is either the aggregate of these, or the Person of the Word did not suffer. Thus the error of Nestorius lay in not perceiving how two most different *natures* may be either of them the same *person*: and Nestorius was so understood by all the chief doctors before Peter, the Lombard;

who, one and all, insisted on the unity of the Person of Christ, [albeit consisting of both a divine and a human nature] being as real as the unity of person in a man, albeit consisting of both body and soul.

The Eutychians with the Apollinarists, recoiling from the Nestorian error,

[1] hominem A B C. [2] que *om.* O. [3] vacuare O.
[4] iste *om.* A B C. [5] deitas A B C. [6] credit O.
[7–7] illam humanitatem esse personam suppositum O; "personam" (*sic cum nota transpositionis signo*) A B C. [8] nec O. [9] posset O.
[10] lūbardum O. [11] docerent O. [12] verbi *om.* O.
[13] aliud A B C. [14] esse O. [15] aliud A B C.

denied the reality of the human nature assumed by the Word: and thus dehumanizing the Head, they deprive the members of Christ's Body of the benefits of the Incarnation and Passion.

nostram cum proprietatibus | et accidentibus ipsam consequentibus per veram humanitatis assumpcionem fuisse in Christo, et per consequens omnes acciones vel denominaciones humanas negant [1] esse in Christo [1] formaliter, nescientes exinde consequi quod [2] toti corpori Christi mistico auferri oporteat que capiti defuissent; ut, si Christus non patitur vel meretur, multo evidencius nullum [3] membrum; cum in capite exemplari oporteat quidquid perfeccionis [4] fuerit esse in posteriores derivatum.[4] [O 223c]

Jews and Mohammedans deny the divinity of Christ.

John x. 33.

Unde Iudei tempore Christi laboraverunt in ista heresi negantes Christi divinitatem; ut patet Ioh. 10. 'Non, inquiunt, de bono opere lapidamus [5] te, sed de blasfemia; quia tu, homo cum sis, facis te ipsum Deum.' Sed in ista heresi exorbitant Sarraceni [6] dicentes Iesum prophetam eximium sed non Deum.

Avoiding these and such like heresies, we should with the Church assert that Christ is two complete substances (*i.e.* natures), viz. God-head and manhood;

1 Joh. iv. 3. *Vulg.*

and that of these indissolubly, personally and formally united in hypostatic identity consists the Person of Jesus Christ.

Iste sunt [7] hereses, quas cum similibus oportet cavere de Christo, confitendo cum ecclesia [8] duas plenas substancias esse Christum, deitatem [9] scilicet et humanitatem; ita quod eadem persona sit perfectus Deus et perfectus homo ex anima racionali et carne in persona Verbi [10] secundum ydemptitatem ypostaticam indissolubiliter coniunctis. Et hinc dicit sanctus evangelista 1 Ioh. 4.[11] 'Omnis, inquit, spiritus,[12] qui confitetur Iesum Christum in carne venisse, ex Deo est; et omnis spiritus, qui *solvit* Iesum, ex Deo non est; et hic est antichristus de quo audistis quoniam [13] venit, et nunc iam in mundo est.' Oportet ergo volentem | infringere [14] latebras antichristi confiteri deitatem [9] et [15] humanitatem insolubiliter, personaliter, et formaliter inesse [15] Domino nostro [16] Iesu Christo. [C 63a]

[1]–[1] inesse Christo A B C. [2] quot A B C. [3] ullum B.
[4]–[4] fuerit esse in posteros derivatum A B C; fuerit in postores dirivatum O.
[5] laudamus C. [6] sarrasseni O. [7] autem A B C.
[8] ecclîs O. [9] divinitatem O *ut saepe* infra. [10] verbi *om.* O.
[11] 40 O. [12] scs̄ O. [13] quam A B C. [14] añfugere. (*Qu.* aufugere ?) O.
[15]–[15] humanitatem personaliter inesse *ceteris om.* A B C. [16] nostro *om.* O.

## Cap. VI.

[*Ostendit quod Christus sit univoce homo cum aliis hominibus; et respondendo obiectibus declarat quod Christus est, secundum multorum doctorum testimonia, creatura.*

*This chapter* (A) *shows that Christ is a man literally and in the same sense as other men are men; and by the discussion of objections to this statement* (B) *illustrates further the thesis of Chap. I., that Christ is a creature, in accordance with the testimony of many weighty authorities.*]

A. — Threefold proof that Christ is a man without metaphor or equivocation, in the same sense as any one of his brethren.

1.—Christ consists of the same elements as we ourselves do, *i.e.* of body and spirit: he is therefore a complete man, and so a man simply, the same in kind (in specie) with his fellowmen.

For (1) neither body nor spirit (which are qualitative parts of a subject) exist in specie (*i.e.* as individuals of a species): but such existence belongs only to the subject of which they are parts.

And since Christ in his divinity cannot belong to a species, nor can his humanity have an individual existence in specie; Christ himself must be the subject having such existence, and the species to which he belongs must be the human species.

Ex istis videtur consequi quod Christus sit univoce homo cum quolibet fratre suo. Probatur tripliciter. Primo sic. Christus est anima eiusdem racionis cum nostra, sicut et corpus eiusdem specifice racionis, que eciam univoce copulatur; ergo est univoce completa humanitas, et sic homo. Non enim est possibile aliquid complete principiari ex principiis omnino similibus cum adequatis principiis, ex quibus principiatur aliquid, nisi conveniat in natura. Cum ergo humanitas Christi et cuiuscunque alterius hominis sic se respiciunt, sequitur quod sunt idem in specie. Aliter enim Christus non esset pocius homo quam ydolum vel ymago; homo enim solum equivoce non est homo.

Confirmatur primo ex hoc, quod nec corpus nec anima, cum sit pars qualitativa suppositi, est[1] per se in specie, sed ipsum suppositum, ad cuius[2] speciem partes[3] huiusmodi reducuntur. Cum ergo Christus secundum deitatem non sit [A 86a] in specie, nec humanitas eius est per se in specie, | ut dicunt negantes ipsam esse suppositum; relinquitur quod Christus sit suppositum per se in specie. Sed in qua, rogo, si non [4]fuerit in humana.[4] Nec audebit catholicus dicere quod corpus et anima Christi erant solum fantastica non consimilis speciei cum partibus aliorum hominum. Quando autem

[1] est *om.* O.
[2] eius O.
[3] per consequens A B C.
[4-4] fuerat in humana A B C.

*Another way of stating this argument adapted to meet Nominalists.*

communicatur cum hominibus ponentibus—'omnia universalia esse signa,'—oportet aliter loqui: ut posito, [1]quod omnis natura[1] humana sit assumpta[2] a Verbo, et ipsum proferat voces et[3] scripta talia—'homo est animal racionale'[4]—et correspondenter eliciat conceptus ut nos facimus; tunc sicut non exinde deficeret species humana ex parte rei, sic[5] forent talia signa univoca vera ut prius, posito quod isti conceptus maneant post assumpciones significantes[6] naturaliter et univoce sicut ante. Aliter enim, solo Christo existente de specie humana, vere sciret ad sensum[7] univocum priorem nedum quod nemo est Deus, sed quod nemo est animal; cum species non esset, deficiente quocunque eius supposito.[8] Quod videtur mihi insanum dicere, cum Christus maxime perficeret genus suum; et per consequens si omnis homo sit Deus, non exinde tollitur species hominis.

*And (2) Christ is formally man with a humanity (i.e. form of man) like the humanity of other men: and when different individuals participate in a common form, that form can be predicated of each of them literally and in the same sense.*

2°. confirmatur ex hoc quod Christus est formaliter homo humanitate consimilis racionis cum humanitate alterius: ergo est univoce homo cum alio. Patet consequencia eo quod, quantumcunque[9] subiecta variantur, dummodo[10] forme, a quibus recipiunt predicaciones huiusmodi, sunt consimilis racionis, predicaciones sunt univoce; ut, quantumcunque [11]subiecta corpora[11] variantur, dummodo habent per totum albedines consimilis racionis, sunt alba univoce.[12] Quod autem humanitates[13] Christi et aliorum essencialiter conveniunt exinde evidet, | quod dimissa humanitate foret [C 63b] illa consimilis racionis cum alia; ergo cum unio sit sibi accidentalis, eo quod potest[14] manere eadem essencia denudata[15]; sequitur quod stante unione erit eiusdem racionis substancialis[16] cum alia.

*And (3) neither the Father, nor the Spirit, but only Christ is man: since Christ is in closer relation to man than the Father or Spirit is,*

3°. confirmatur ex hoc quod Christus est homo, et non Pater neque[17] Donum; quod non esset, nisi Christus plus conveniret[18] cum homine quam Pater; ergo est maior con-

[1] posito natura (*sic cum lacuna*) O. [2] servata B; asserta C.
[3] vel A B C. [4] animal *om.* C; racionale *om.* O. [5] sit B; sicut C.
[6] signantes A B C. [7] sensus O. [8] supposita O.
[9] et *add.* O. [10] dñ nõ O. [11-11] substrata corporum A B C.
[12] unitate A C; veritate B. [13] humanitas A B C. [14] possunt O.
[15] denudata *om. cum lacuna* O. [16] substancialis *om.* O. [17] vel A B C.
[18] inveniret O.

[B131b] veniencia Christi ad hominem quam Patris ad hominem, | vel quam ante assumpcionem fuerat. Et cum [1] non sit pertinens conveniencia nisi vel in genere vel in specie, sequitur [1] quod Christus factus homo convenit in genere cum aliis hominibus, et per idem in specie [2]; quia aliter non foret humanitate nobis similior quam perante, cum conveniencia presupponit unionem.[3] Noto ergo gradu [4] similitudinis [5] vel conveniencie, tunc, cum omnis conveniencia accidentalis presupponit convenienciam substancie generalem, oportet quod secundum humanitatem, qua factus est nobis similis, conveniat nobiscum in [6] genere vel in [6] specie, cum conveniencia in humanitate sit alterius racionis [7] quam conveniencia in aliquo accidente [7] novem [8] generum.

or than he himself was before he assumed humanity: and such close relation is necessarily in genus or in species; and in this case in the genus and species 'man.'

Item omne suppositum speciei humane [9] est homo univoce; Christus est suppositum speciei humane,[9] cum sit filius hominis; ergo est homo univoce. Maior patet ex hoc, quod omne tale suppositum est illa species, et per consequens quiditas vel racio speciei. Et sic eadem est communis racio illi individuo et cuilibet [10] eidem sibi [10] in specie. Cum ergo illa descriptive dicuntur univoce predicata; quibus competit eadem racio predicati, patet quod non potest esse [O 223d] individuum speciei humane nisi sit | homo univoce; aliter enim individuum esset homo, et non diffinicio vel quiditas hominis; et hoc esset ponere hominem non esse hominem. Minor [11] autem argumenti patet ex fide. Nam secundum Apostolum ad Hebre. 2. 'nusquam angelos apprehendit, sed [A86b] semen Abrahe | ut fieret per omnia fratribus consimilis [12];' quia tam secundum naturam corpoream [13] quam incorpoream,[13] et illa sunt omnia. Et consequenter [14] similatus est fratribus suis secundum omnia accidencia positiva [15] naturaliter consequencia [16] has naturas. Aliter enim non esset 'mediator

II.—Every individual (suppositum) of the human species is literally and in the same sense a man: Christ being 'son of man' is such an individual; therefore he is a man.

That Christ is son of *man*, and did not take on him (the nature of) *angels*, Heb. ii. 16, is the catholic faith based upon Holy Scripture.

[1–1] et cum non ptē conveniencia nisi vel in genere sequitur O.
[2] speciei O. [3] univocacionem A B C. [4] gradus A B C; gradû O.
[5] similis C. [6] in *om.* O. [7–7] quam . . . accidente *om.* B.
[8] 9no (= commune) O. [9–9] est homo . . . humane *om.* B C.
[10–10] eidem simili A; idem simili B; idem s. C. [11] maior O.
[12] similis A B C. [13–13] quam incorpoream *om.* O. [14] correspondenter A B C.
[15] posita A B C. [16] conveniencia A B C.

I. Tim. ii. 5. Dei et hominum homo Christus,'[1] ut dicit Apostolus prima ad[2] Thimo. 2.

The doctrine that Christ took Man's nature upon him is taught by Augustine,

Confirmatur primo ex testimonio Augustini. Nam in De Vera Religione 27; 'Ipsa, inquit, natura suscipienda erat que liberanda.' Et 2°. De Visitacione Infirmorum; 'Homo Deus participatus est nostre[3] humanitatis ut nos participemur suo divinitatis;' et sequitur; 'quod tu es, fieri dignatus est.'

Anselm,

Et ad idem vadit processus Auselmi in libro suo Cur Deus Homo; et De Incarnacione Verbi; 'quod aliter non fuisset competens satisfaccio pro peccato primi hominis, nisi individuum eiusdem nature, et sic idem in specie, solveret debitum, quod natura debuit creatori[4] suo.' Nec memini me legisse in scripturis alicuius doctoris famosi oppositum.

Grossteste,

Unde Lincolniensis[5] in suo Exameron dicit quod Christus est homo eiusdem racionis | [6] cum aliis. [C 64a] Et idem dicit sanctus

Thomas Aquinas, and by all Realists: even many Nominalists admit it; as they needs must, inasmuch as even non-Christian philosophers conceive of Christ as specifically human; and, if he was not so, he was the grossest of deceivers.

Thomas et omnes ponentes universalia ex parte rei. Sed et multi non ponentes universalia preter signa; quia multi philosophi, sive fideles sive infideles, conversantes cum Christo et ipsum sencientes, ut apostoli,[7] haberent conceptum specificum in anima, qui signaret illis[8] univoce illum cum aliis; quia aliter fuisset Christus illusor maximus, qui ad hoc ostendit eius humanitatem humanis sensibus, et verbo docuit ipsum esse verum hominem. Philosophi ergo habentes terminos vel conceptus specificos, quos vere predicarent de pronominibus demonstrantibus[9] recto [10]Christum cum aliis, haberent[10] conceptus univocos Christo et aliis: et hoc sufficit ad univocacionem ac ydemptitatem specificam iuxta sic loquentes. Ergo conclusio.

The last statement is thus proved.
(I.) It is a sin to deceive by a sophistical use of words or signs.
Ecclesiasticus xxxvii. 20; LXX. and Vulg.

Confirmatur tripliciter. Primo ex hoc quod peccatum est illudere communicantes per verba vel signa sophistica; sed sic fecisset Christus potissime, si non habuisset aliquam denominacionem univocam cum aliqua creatura; ergo peccasset maxime. Pro assumpto dicitur Ecclesiastici 37. 'Qui

[1] Iesus *add.* O. [2] prima ad *om.* A B C. [3] mater B.
[4] deo. A B C. [5] ut lync'. O; ut patet lincoln B. [6] racionis *om.* O.
[7] philosophi C. [8] i' (= illius) O. [9] in *add.* A B O.
[10]–[10] Christum tum cum haberet C.

Christ often spoke of himself as son of man, and exhibited himself as liable to the accidents of humanity: if these words were equivocal and these acts unreal, Christ sinned as a gross deceiver. As St. Peter, Matth. xvi. 23, was rebuked for supposing that Christ spoke of his passion in an unreal sense, so scholastics nowadays need the same rebuke.

sophistice loquitur, odibilis est.' Et Enchiridion 14. 'Verbis uti ad fallaciam, non ad quod instituta sunt, peccatum est.' Christus autem sepe[1] dixit se esse filium hominis et naturaliter ostendit se esse [2]accidentatum multipliciter; necnon et[2] passionem et mortem et resurreccionem predixit Apostolis ut patet Matth. 16, unde Petro dicenti sibi, 'Absit hoc a te, Domine;' respondit Veritas; 'Vade post me, Sathana: non sapis ea, que Dei sunt.' Et tamen eandem sentenciam Petri dicunt modo scolastici. Sequitur quod vel Christus fuit [3]falsissimus vel illi sunt racionabiliter arguendi.[3]

(2.) If Christ was not in accordance with the reality of his manhood liable to change, sensation, suffering, etc., he had nothing in common with man at all.

2°. per hoc quod Christus non foret mobilis, sensibilis, passibilis, subditus patri vel parentibus secundum quod homo: que tamen glosa est maximum refugium negantibus de virtute sermonis scripturam sacram de Christo [4]enunciantem talia. Et consequens[4] sic probatur. Christus non[5] secundum quod homo est univoce aliquid, nec aliqualiter accidentatus cum aliqua creatura: ergo non secundum quod homo est huiusmodi, ut predicitur. Patet consequencia[6] ex hoc quod non est color concedendi, quod Christus secundum quod homo est sic formatus, nisi vel quia homo est sic denominatus, vel quia illa humanitas est sic formata. Primum non valet, cum non[7] sit possibile Christum sic [A 86c] informari | ut dicunt. [8]Nec secundum prodest,[8] cum illam humanitatem ponunt esse[9] non suppositum, cui soli debetur accio. Et sic nec illam ponunt concipi, nasci, conversari, pati, ascendere, vel quascumque tales predicaciones per- [B 132a] sonales | suscipere. Cum ergo non sit predicacio synecdochica, [10]nisi pars primo et principaliter recipit predicacionem,[11] que exinde secundario toti tribuitur; sequitur quod hec non est construccio synecdochica[10]—Christus secundum humanitatem fatigatur, sicut tristatur aut moritur —cum repugnat illam humanitatem sic denominari; ut

[1] se O.
[2–2] autenticum multipliciter necnon et A B C; accident^a inftitu^t et O.
[3–3] falsum vel arguendi *ceteris om.* O.
[4–4] enunciante talia et consequencia A B C.
[5] enim B.
[6] consequencia *om. cum lacuna* C.
[7] non *om.* O.
[8–8] nec potest O.
[9] esse *om.* B.
[10–10] nisi . . . synecdochica *om.* A B C.
[11] predicacô O.

homo non est albus secundum faciem nisi facies sit alba. Et illa est acuta obex contra negantes | scripturas cum [C 64b] glosa scipsam inficit[1] plus quam textus. Non ergo Christus secundum quod homo est alicuiusmodi,[2] nisi racio hominis univoce sibi conveniat; quia aliter, quid sibi et homini?[3]

(3.) The satisfaction made for the sin of the nature or race of man must have been made by an impeccable individual of that race; but that being impossible for any mere man, the Word assumed human nature in its entirety, and as man redeemed the sin, not of angels, but of men.

3°. confirmatur sic. Ad hoc quod satisfaciat[4] pro peccato nature vel generis,[5] oportet quod natura, que peccaverat, [6]emerendo restituat[6]: sed genus humanum peccavit in Adam et suis posteris: ergo oportet idem genus secundum aliquod eius suppositum ut satisfaciat[7] pro peccato; sed non potuit secundum puro[8] hominem: ergo relinquitur quod suppositum impeccabile satisfaciat assumendo eandem naturam in aliqua essencia singulari: quod et factum est per Verbum,[9] ut superius dixerat Augustinus. Et illam[10] racionem tangit Anselmus 2°. Cur Deus Homo ca°. 8. que, licet non sapiat negantibus universalia, saperet tamen cuicunque pio theologo.[11] Aliter enim non conveniencius assumendo humanitatem redemisset Deus peccatum hominis, quam peccatum angeli; cum plus convenit Christus post [12]incarnacionem secundum humanitatem angelo quam homini.[12] Nam 'dii' solum participative non plus in natura cum Deo conveniunt quam ante participacionem: sed tam equivoce dicitur 'homo' de Deo et de angelis[13] quam equivoce 'deus' de creatura et natura divina dicitur: ergo tam equivoce disconveniunt Verbum et homo post incarnacionem sicut ante: sed ante plus conveniebat angelo quam homini: ergo[14] modo. Quid ergo [15]pertinuit Christi[15] meritum humano generi a quo tante distitit? Non ergo satisfecit illud genus hominum quod peccavit; et per consequens manet in pleno debito sicut | [O 224a] ante; quod est contra Apostolum ad Colos. 2. dicentem quod 'in Christo Deus delevit cirographum decreti, quod erat nobis contrarium.'

Thus the fact of redemption implies the real humanity of Christ.

Col. ii. 14.

[1] interficit B. [2] modi *om.* A B C. [3] hominis O. [4] satisfiat A B C.
[5] ergo A B C. [6] emendando resipiscat A B C; emẽdo restituat O.
[7] satisfacere B; *et altera manu* A. [8] purum A B C.
[9] per sanctum filium B. [10] 2am A. [11] catholico C.
[12–12] incarnacionem cum angelo quam cum homine A B C.
[13] aliis *codd. omn.* [14] et *add.* C. [15–15] participavit Christus A B C

*Argument in support of the assumption made in the preceding argument as to the close relation between Christ and Christian men.*

Confirmatur. Vel est conveniencia maxima, qua Christiani cum Christo conveniunt tantum ex parte signorum, vel tantum ex parte naturarum[1] conveniencium, vel mixtim. Primum dictum est nimium[2] puerile, specialiter cum hoc signum 'homo' summe equivoce significat Christum et alios. Si ex parte signatorum, vel oportet dare eis naturam communem, vel aliter dicere quod in nullo conveniunt, nisi in quo differunt; [3]et sic, ut plus conveniunt, plus differunt[3]; et cum tanta sit conveniencia quanta differencia et e contra; [4]si igitur in infinitum differunt, in infinitum conveniunt, et e contra.[4]

*III. If Christ the subject be not really man, then the accidents of his so-called humanity are not literally such and in the same sense as the corresponding accident in his brethren. But this cancels all faith, hope and love, inasmuch as it reduces the acts and sufferings of Christ to the level of a mimic or artificial arranged performance, instead of regarding them as the natural outcome of his humanity.*

Item, si Christus non sit univoce homo cum aliis, tunc nullum accidens consequens eius humanitatem foret univoce accidens cum accidentibus correspondentibus in suis fratribus. Consequens interimeret totam fidem, spem, et caritatem de Christi incarnacione, et falsificaret scripturas eque nequiter velut Eutichiani et alii heretici supra dicti. Et consequencia patet ex hoc, quod omne accidens individuatur, specificatur, et habet totam essenciam suam a subiecto. Ergo, si subiecta in nullo univoco conveniunt, a maiori vel pari nec accidencia que secuntur; ut, si angelus non sit
[A 86d] eiusdem speciei secundum copullatum corpus cum nostro corpore, tunc nec[5] accidencia, que appropriate[6] consecuntur
[C 65a] nostra corpora, conveniunt eis nisi equivoce; ut, angelus | non dormit, comedit, sentit, gignit, et sic de accidentibus competentibus toti homini: aliter enim essent procreati ab incubis et succubis filii diaboli naturales, et non filii hominum nec proximorum parentum; quod nemo dicit. Si ergo locucio animati[7] [8]psittaci vel[8] inanimati organi non est univoce[9] locucio cum humana, saltem secundum speciem specialissimam[10] propter diversitatem specificam[11] subiectorum; multo magis nullum accidens Christum consequens foret eiusdem

[1] signatorum A B C. [2] intutum O. [3-3] et sic . . . differunt *om.* A B C.
[4-4] si igitur . . . contra *om.* O. [5] nec *om.* O.
[6] appropriate *om.* B; appᵖˡᵉᵗᵉ (*Qu.* a proprietate ?) O. [7] animati *om.* O.
[8-8] siccati (*in marg.* secati) vel A; securati et B; secati vel C; sithaci vel O.
[9] equivoce B. [10] sensitivam A B C. [11] factam A B C.

If Christ be not literally man, then the statements as to what befell the human Christ (the accidents of his humanity), *e.g.* he was born, walked, preached, suffered, are equivocal and used in a non-natural sense. Then he is not like unto us either in *substance* or *accident*: he is not liable to change (mobilis) nor subject to the accidents of humanity, nor a man in any respect 'like unto his brethren.'

racionis cum accidente creato substancie; cum subiecta nec specie, nec genere, nec in aliquo univoco convenirent. Non enim plus convenit Christus nobiscum quam deitas, ut sic opinantes concorditer confitentur; et per consequens, cum accidencia non sint nisi modi create substancie, sequitur quod nulla accidencia de genere[1] Iesu nostro[2] conveniant; ut non pocius conceptus est, vel natus humanitus, ambulavit, predicavit, paciebatur sitim, esuriem, opprobria vel flagella, quam deitas ipsa; et sic fuit obiectum maxime illusivum, cum nec fuit quantus, nec qualis, nec aliquod[3] aliorum[4] encium, cum non sit mobilis aut sensibilis eo quod omne tale accidens univocum | cum aliis[5] requirit primum sub- [B 132b] iectum univocum quod informat. Sed Christus in nullo substanciali est nobis similis, ut dicitur; ergo nec in aliquo accidentali: non enim tantum conveniret sicut elementum, minera, bufo, bestia, vel quelibet[6] creatura.

Ideo dicunt sic opinantes consequenter, sed minus catholice, quod Christus non est mobilis vel accidentatus humanitus. Quod si verum est, tunc indubie non est homo in aliquo fratribus suis consimilis. Quomodo, rogo, haberet fratres, si non sit univoce filius hominis habens eundem patrem et matrem remotos cum filiis[7] aliis, et sic temporaliter conceptus, genitus, atque natus, et sic consequenter, ut canit historia evangelica, conversatus? aut quomodo esset nedum in substancia vel natura vel in aliquo accidente fratribus suis consimilis, si [8]nec in genere,[8] nec in specie, nec in accidente univoco convenirent[9]? Pro certo dicat qui audet! quia ego non audeo tantum subvertere totum sensum historicum scripturarum, cum evangelium sicut et vetus testamentum expresse et absolute attribuit[10] sibi denominaciones accidentales creatas. Quomodo, queso, crederemus[11] aliquid de Christo, si non[12] assercionem propriam,

The author dare not thus contradict Holy Scripture, nor upset the historical meaning of the Old Testament and of the Gospel, both of which expressly and without reserve apply to Christ terms descriptive of the accidents of a creature.

[1] de *add.* O. [2] Christo B. [3] aliud A B C.
[4] illorum B. [5] ~~aliis~~ (antecedens *in marg.*) A; accidens B.
[6] quecunque A B C. [7] filiis *om.* B. [8-8] nec in genere *om.* O.
[9] conveniunt A B; correspondent C. [10] attribuit *om.* O.
[11] credimus O. [12] non *om.* A B C.

qua dicit, 'palpate et videte, quoniam spiritus carnem et ossa non habet, sicut me videtis habere.' Ioh. ult°.? ex qua[1] doctrina hauserat ille celicus paranymphus,[2] quando in principio capituli sui dicit, 'Quod fuit ab inicio, quod audivimus, quod vidimus oculis nostris,[3] quod perspeximus, et manus nostre contrectaverunt de Verbo vite, anunciamus vobis'? Et Apostolus ad Hebre. 4°. 'habentes pontificem [C65b] magnum, qui penetravit celos Iesum Filium Dei, teneamus | spei nostre confessionem[4]: non enim habemus pontificem, qui non possit compati[5] infirmitatibus nostris; temptatum autem per omnia pro similitudine absque peccato.' Quod dictum Apostoli ego nescio aliter exponere quam expositum est a sanctis doctoribus. Per hoc ergo quod Iesus est filius Dei, est 'pontifex magnus [6] superior Aaronitis.[6]' Per hoc quod potestate propria 'penetravit celos,' solus ascendit[7] trahens [A87a] alios secum. Per hoc quod potest compati | nobis in natura communi assumpta, factus est nobis propicius; quia ad Hebre. 5°. dicitur 'cum esset Filius Dei, didicit ex his, que passus est, obedienciam.' Experiencia enim temptacionis multimodis[8] didicit[9] humanitus, que aliter non sic sciret.[10] Temptatus[11] enim erat tripliciter a dyabolo, ut patet Matth 4°; et quadrupliciter[12] a Iudeis de potencia, sapiencia, misericordia, et iusticia, ut patet ex decursu evangelii. Non autem intrinsece a seipso. Quarto fuit illa temptacio nobis pro similitudine exemplari ad docendum nos gratis compati et vincere temptatores,[13] quia capitaneus apostolorum 1 Pet. 2° vere testatur quod 'Christus passus est pro nobis, [14] vobis relinquens exemplum ut sequamini[14] vestigia eius.'

Christ himself expressly uses such terms as imply his real, literal humanity, Luke xxiv. 39; and 'the bridegroom's friend,' (John iii. 29) repeats them, 1 John i. 1.

In the Epistle to the Heb. iv. 14, Christ is described as 'a high priest who can be touched with the feeling of our infirmities': and all the holy doctors expound this passage as a statement of his actual humanity.

For, although as Son of God he is *above* us, and as the unique conqueror (cp. chap. iii. p. 34, l. 24) he is *before* us; yet, having assumed our common nature, he is *one with us* in experience and one in sympathy.

For he experienced (1) from the devil threefold temptation, Matt. iv. 3-9; (2) from the Jews fourfold temptation as to his power, wisdom, mercy, and justice: but (3) from his own inner being no temptation arose; but (4) his temptation was suffered for our sakes to leave us an example, 1 Pet. ii. 21.

Ista est exposicio sana, cui oportet nos insistere non super- [O224b] addendo aliam[15] pre timore impugnacionis sophistice de vi | vocis. Non quod fuit in capite nostro[16] ficta passio et non

To this the only sound exposition

[1] quadam O. [2] peraninphus A C; peranyuiphus B; selitus paraniphus O. [3] oculis nostris *om.* B. [4] confessionem *om.* A B C. [5] compari O. [6]–[6] C *om.* superior; O *om.* Aaronitis, *uterque cum lacuna.* [7] ascendens A B C. [8] multitudine A B C; multi^{do} O. [9] dicit A B C. [10] foret A B C. [11] tempestatus O. [12] quadrupliciter *om.* O. [13] temptaciones A B C. [14]–[14] nobis . . . sequamur A B C. [15] alicui A; aliquam B. [16] nostro *om.* A B C O; *e cod.* M. *inserui.*

of the literal meaning we must adhere, in spite of sophistical misinterpretations which heretics may put upon it.

2 Cor. viii. 9.

And we must maintain that Christ's life, passion, and death were not feigned but actual and real.

For they possessed in detail every accessory of time, condition, and circumstance which could give them most intense reality: and if these circumstances (which are logical *accidents*) are real, the underlying humanity (the logical *subject*) is also real: *i.e.* the humanity of Christ was a real humanity; he was a man.

Lam. i. 12.

vera, ut dixerunt heretici supradicti; sed veram conversacionem, veram passionem, veram mortem, et alias predicaciones sustinuit; ut meminit Augustinus esse de substancia fidei in De Vera Religione 29°. et Euchiridion 4°[1] ca°. 'Nos, inquit,[2] patimur egencias et dolores, sed[3] indubie magis ipse; nam "pro nobis egenus factus est."' 2 Cor. 8°. Et cum in perfecta etate, tenerrima complexione,[4] sensu vivacissimo,[5] non mortificato aliquo membro, in media etate, non supernatante humido[6] infantili[7] sit passus, patet quod in nullo alio est pena vel 'dolor tantus sicut fuerat dolor suus,' ut cecinit Isa. 53°. Secundo fratres sui fossi sunt sub terra vel lapide, sed ipse plus, cum Dominus mundi sepultus est sumptibus alienis, ut meminit Augustinus in De Questionibus Veteris et Nove Legis ca° 59[8]: et, ut breviter dicatur, quicquid debuit facere fecit ad summum, cum oporteat[9] principia exemplaria esse ultima[9]; et eo fecit hec omnia excellencius, quo ipse fuit humanitas copulata ypostatice deitati. Cum ergo omnes ille maneries accidencium creatorum infuerunt sibi formaliter, et omne tale accidens requirit subiectum sibi proporcionatum; | sequitur quod [B 133a] Christus subiectus eis sit idem in specie cum subiectis accidencium consimilis speciei.

Further discussion of the proposition 'Christus est mobilis' (p. 69, l. 11).

Objection.

Sed arguendo contra illud videtur primo tripliciter quod non debet concedi simpliciter quod Christus sit mobilis. [10]Nam non foret evidencia concludendi quod Christus sit mobilis,[10] nisi ex hoc quod secundum humanitatem est mobilis. | Sed talis deduccio non procedit, cum arguitur [C 66a] [11]a *secundum quid* ad[11] *simpliciter*. Ergo non est medium concludendi[12] quod Christus sit mobilis. Sicut ergo non sequitur—Christus secundum humanitatem est creatura; ergo Christus est creatura—; ita non sequitur—Christus secundum humanitatem est mobilis; ergo Christus est mobilis.

[1] 40 O. [2] ergo O. [3] sed *om.* A B C. [4] et *add.* A C; at *add.* B.
[5] vacuissimo A B C. [6] humido *om. cum lacuna* C. [7] infantuli O.
[8] 79 O. [9-9] principalia . . . ultra A B C.
[10-10] nam . . . mobilis *om.* A B C. [11-11] a quo ad O. [12] concedendi A B C.

Reply. It is by reason of his humanity that Christ is (mobilis) liable to change:

Hic dicitur concedendo quod Christus est mobilis cum humanitas sua sit mobilis. Et dicant, qui sciunt, quia pro certo non puto aliam creaturam, sed neque Deum cognoscere quod Deus sit mobilis, nisi ex hoc quod creatura est mobilis que Deo ypostatice copulatur. Et per locum a sufficienti similitudine concedi debet simpliciter quod Christus est creatura, quia tota humanitas eius sibi copulata ypostatice est creatura.[1] Sicut enim negacio includitur in racione creature, que negacio non potest competere divinitati; sic in motu et qualibet forma substanciali vel accidentali in genere: et per consequens, negato quod Christus est creatura, negari debet quodlibet per se inferius; ut, [A87b] quod est homo, animal, corpus, anima, sive substancia, | et multo evidencius quod sit mole magnus, accidentaliter[2] qualis, filius hominis, predicans,[3] passus, locatus, temporaliter natus, sedens, vestitus; quia quodlibet istorum[4] est inferius, indignius, et humilius[5] quam esse substanciam, et[6] presupponit substanciam tanquam subiectum dans eis esse accidentale in genere. Omne itaque per se in genere dicit esse suum possibile esse pro aliqua mensura, pro qua non habet existenciam actualem; et per consequens omne per se in genere dicit se esse creaturam includendo neminem esse primitatis divine.

and this is implied in his creatureship.

B.—The belief that he is a creature is necessary to belief in any statement whatever concerning his humanity: and his creatureship is expressly stated in Holy Scripture: he is not only 'born' but 'made,'

Unde scriptura sacra[7] annunciat Christum simpliciter esse factum, ut ad Gal. 4°. 'misit Deus Filium suum *factum* ex muliere, *factum* sub lege.' 'Non[8] sunt audiendi, inquit Beda, qui legunt "*natum* ex muliere"[9]' Et credo quod nullus dicit hoc determinatum 'ex muliere' esse terminum distrahentem quin sequatur—factus ex muliere; ergo factus—; sicut sequitur—compositus ex corpore et anima; ergo compositus—. Et ideo dicit Augustinus Enchiridion 29, quod illam creaturam, quam virgo concepit et peperit, quamvis ad solam personam Filii pertinentem, tota Trinitas

Gal. iv. 4: and Baeda rightly maintained this reading '*factum*' in preference to '*natum* ex muliere.'

[1] creata O. [2] accut^er (*i.e.* accidenter) O. [3] predicant O.
[4] ñ (*i.e.* nomen) *add.* O. [5] minus A B C; vmis O. [6] sed C O.
[7] sacra *om.* C. [8] notum C. [9] sed factum ex muliere *add.* C O.

*His creatureship is moreover asserted by Augustine,*

fecit; et illam creaturam declarat esse Filium Dei tempore[1] immediate sequente. Et idem dicit in Sermone de Vigilia Epiphanie; 'magnum misterium fuit, quod creator creari voluit': et in Sermone Domini in Monte; 'voluit esse creatura, qui est creator.' Item ad Hebre. 3°. scribit Apostolus: 'considerate apostolum et pontificem confessionis nostre[2] Iesum, qui fidelis est ei qui fecit illum.' Ecce hic dicit absolute quod Deus fecit Iesum. Unde Leo Papa in quodam sermone; 'nova et inaudita convencio, Deus qui eternaliter erat, fit creatura.' Et Lincolniensis in sermone De Natali Domini; 'in spectaculo[3] creacionis[4] conspicitur creator faciens creaturam; in isto spectaculo[3] conspicitur creator factus creatura.' Et Johannes Damascenus | ca°. 50. 'Christus [C 66b] est creatus et increatus:' unde et ca°. 92 concedit quod Christus est creatura.

*Heb. iii. 1.* — *by Pope Leo,* — *by Grosstestc,* — *and by John of Damascus.*

*Again Christ many times admits himself to be inferior to God, and thereby accepts the position of a creature: the expressions of St. Paul, Eph. i. 17: 1 Cor. xi. 3: 1 Cor. iii. 23, and the doctrine of exinanition, Phil. ii. 7, imply it, as Augustine and the older authorities expound it.*

*Matt. xxvii. 46. John xx. 17. John xiv. 28.*

Item nichil habet Deum ut superiorem nisi creatura: Christus sic habet[5]: ergo est creatura. Minor[6] patet ex confessione Veritatis Matth. 27. 'Deus meus'; et Ioh. 20. 'vade ad fratres meos et dic eis: Ascendo ad Patrem meum et Patrem vestrum, [7]Deum meum et Deum vestrum[7]'; et ad Ephes. 1°. 'Deus Domini nostri Iesu Christi, Pater glorie, det vobis spiritum sapiencie'; et 1ª ad Cor. 3°. 'vos[8] estis Christi, Christus autem Dei'; et infra 11°, 'caput vero Christi Deus.' Et ad idem sonat tota scriptura de humanitate Christi; et specialiter illud Veritatis 'Pater maior me est.' Ioh. 14[9]; et illud 'seipsum exinanivit, formam servi accipiens' ad Phil. 2, ut exponit Augustinus primo libro Contra Maximinianum. Non enim audebant[10] sancti doctores inficere scripturam suspicione falsitatis, ut hodie.

*But Duns Scotus says that men were shy of the definite statement of the creatureship of Christ because of the heresies, which affirmed him to be a creature and nothing more than a creature.*

Unde Doctor Subtilis super Distinccione 11. 3ⁱⁱ Sentenciarum dicit quod hec proposicio—Christus est creatura—est concedenda simpliciter, si bene intelligatur, sed negabatur propter hereses dicencium Christum esse pure creaturam:

[1] tempore *om.* O. [2] vestre C O. [3] speculo B.
[4] creaturarum A B C; c^is O. [5] esse *add.* O. [6] maior O.
[7–7] et deum etc. C; deum . . . vestrum *om.* O. [8] nos C.
[9] 15 A B C. [10] audiebant O.

et fingit postmodum responsiones ei, cui non placet sic [O 224c] dicere. Concedit autem | consequenter simpliciter cum Augustino quod Christus incepit esse[1] sicut generabatur ex tempore. Unde Doctor Bonaventura super eadem Distinccione dicit quod doctores magis hoc[2] respiciunt, quod potest esse via in falsitatem vel errorem, quam quod ipsa de se sit falsa vel erronea. Unde concedit[3] consequenter quod Christus [A 87c] est homo creatus | et non[4] homo eternus, cum sit secundus Adam habens multos homines seniores.

*And Bonaventura speaks to the same effect: but both admit with Augustine the creatureship of Christ.*

B 133b] Quandocunque ergo ego dico, quod Christus | est creatus vel factus, intelligo catholice, sicut[5] scriptura sacra et sancti doctores me edocent, quod Christus secundum humanitatem est creatus [6]vel taliter temporaliter denominatus. Et illam regulam dat[6] sanctus Thomas 4°. Contra Gentiles 48. 'Nihil, inquit, Deo proprium enunciatur de Christo nisi racione humanitatis vel expressate vel subintellecte: nec[7] e contrario quoad denominaciones eternas, quas homo ille recipit secundum divinitatem.' Et sic cum gloso ac alios quosdam, quando dicunt quod Christus non est creatura; intelligunt enim quod Christus non est secundum divinitatem creatura: quod est necessarium, cum oppositum sit hereticum. Et quod ille sit sensus suus videtur, quia super 2m. Sentenciarum Dist. 11. Quest. 4[8] dicit quod accidencia creata dicuntur de Filio Dei, non quod ipsa persona eterna his [9]informatur, sed quod natura assumpta[9] his[10] informatur. Quod dictum ego nescio sane concipere nisi intelligendo quod persona Verbi non informetur[11] accidentibus creatis secundum deitatem, sed quod ipsa principaliter informetur eis secundum humanitatem. Nam Verbum predicat et agit actos humanos, informatur virtutibus et beatitudine, sicut substancialiter informatur anima intellectiva et creata racionabilitate.[12] Ideo certum est quod persona Verbi informatur istis accidentibus ac formis creatis, nisi coincidatur in opinionem negantem

*Therefore, when I speak of Christ as created or made, I use these words in their catholic sense, meaning that, according to his human nature, Christ was created. And this accords with the rule of St. Thomas, who elsewhere explains that 'created accidents' are predicated concerning the Son of God, in the sense that the nature assumed by the eternal Person is 'informed' by them. And this I take to mean that the Person of the Word is not so 'informed' in his divinity, but in his humanity: for he performs human acts and is 'informed' with virtues and bliss, even as in his substance he is 'informed' with an intellectual soul and a created reason: and thus it is certain that the Person of the Word is 'informed' with created accidents and forms;*

[1] esse *om.* O. [2] hoc *om.* A B C. [3] concepit A B C. [4] unus A B C. [5] sicut *om.* C.
[6-6] vel (*rasura*) temporaliter denominatus et (*rasura*) dat A; vel creavit vel temporaliter denominatus et (*ceteris ad* enunciatur *om.*) B; vel talis temporaliter denominatus est et illam ram dat C. [7] et A B C. [8] 9 A B C.
[9-9] informatur . . . assumpta *in marg.* O. [10] eis O. [11] informatur A B C.
[12] rōlitate O.

and this follows from the 'mobility' of Christ. Concerning this statement—Christ is a creature — four opinions are held. The doctrine is i. liable to abuse; ii. illogical; iii. heretical; iv. the truth, when the statement is limited to the humanity of Christ; but yet by that humanity must be understood 'whole Christ,' and not a merely formal part of him; as would be the case if the expression were explained as a construction by synecdoche. Those who holding opinions (i. ii. iii.) reject this explanation (iv.), exalt their logic against Scripture and by their mutual contradictions expose their own folly. Rom. i. 22.

mobilitatem Christi simpliciter. | Et illa glosa est evidencior [C 67a] et famosior quam glosa data a modernis ad scripturam sacram et dicta sanctorum.

Quidam enim dicunt quod talis modus loquendi transit[1] in abusum: alii quod doctores desipuerunt ignorantes logicam: tercii[2] quod dixerunt impossibilia et heretica propter [3]devocionem exhortacionis.[3] Sed quarti recte intelligunt quod dicta intelliguntur de Christo secundum humanitatem; et ipsi vere intelligunt, specialiter si ponant quod Christus est illa humanitas et non in construccione synecdochica; cum illa humanitas sit totus Christus, et [4]non pars eius[4] formaliter. Synecdochica enim [5]locucio vel evidencia est[5] a quo[6] ad simpliciter, quando parti principaliter attribuitur denominacio, et secundario suo toti; ut hic homo est racionalis vel quantus. Unde quantum ad priores glosantes dicitur quod affeccione inordinata extraneandi in logica, postposita glorificacione scripture, 'dicentes se esse sapientes stulti facti sunt': in cuius signum vix duo concordant tam in sentencia quam in glosa.

Three objections considered: Objection 1. If Christ is created, he is produced out of nothing, and once was not: which is impossible since he is God. Reply. This argument would equally disprove his generation, conception, and birth: all of which Holy Scripture expressly affirms. Matth. i. 1. Luke i. 31, ii. 6-7. Creation, equally with generation or beginning, may be possible to Christ according to his existence in time.

Sed obicitur tripliciter contra illud. Primo per hoc quod, si Christus creatus est, tunc est productus ex nichilo, et per consequens aliquando non fuit: quod est impossibile, cum sit Deus. Sed rogo sic arguentes attendere quomodo [7]per idem non sequeretur[7] quod, si[8] Christus generatus est ex tempore, conceptus, et natus de virgine, ergo habuit esse post non esse: cum omnis generacio substancie sit produccio a non esse substancie ad esse secundum philosophos. Nec negandus est 'liber generacionis Iesu filii David, filii Abrahe,' ut patet Matth. 1°; vel conceptus[9] aut partus virginis, ut patet Luce 1° et 2°; duplicem enim nativitatem Christi catholici concorditer confitentur. Nec est racio quod creacio non competit[10] Christo secundum esse suum temporale, sicut competit sibi generacio aut incepcio.

[1] transit *om.* C. [2] alii B; *et pr. manu* A. [3-3] devocionis exhortacionem A B C.
[4-4] non per consequens eius C. [5-5] locucio est vel evidencia *codd omn.*
[6] a quo *alt. manu* A; a secundum B; a s' C. [7-7] perinde non sequitur O.
[8] si *om.* O. [9] vel conceptus *om.* C. [10] convent C.

Conceditur ergo quod Christus creatus est nedum secundum animam, que est Christus, sed secundum corpus. Nam gene- [A 87d] ratus est secundum corpus, et hoc generacione | univoca sicut univoce est homo. Sed omnis alia generacio substancie presupponit eius creacionem: ergo et Christi generacio temporalis. Omnis itaque temporalis nativitas, sicut et motus nature create sensibilis aut insensibilis, presupponit creacionem ut causam, cum prius naturaliter sit creacio simpliciter quam aliqua mocio naturalis. Ex quo plane sequitur, quod omne naturaliter motum prius naturaliter creatur quam naturaliter sic movetur. Cum ergo Christus naturaliter movetur, et per consequens accidens creatum inest sibi formaliter; sequitur quod prius naturaliter est [1]creatus: quia aliter[1] indubie non esset denominatus univoce cum ceteris creaturis. Conceditur ergo quod Christus productus est ex nichilo, et sic aliquando non fuit. Primum patet de anima et de corporea essencia in mundi principio; et secunda pars patet intelligendo Christum secundum illam naturam, qua creatus est.

Generation implies creation.

There is therefore a sense in which Christ once was not:

[C 67b] Sed in istis[2] oportet cavere diligenter | et excludere tres sensus erroneos quando dicitur Christum aliquando non fuisse. Primo cavendo ne credatur Christum[3] aliquando secundum deitatem non fuisse, cum Christus eternaliter fuit Deus. 2°. ne credatur Christum secundum esse intelligibile [B 134a] humanitatis ac predestinacionem Dei | aliquando non fuisse, cum eternaliter habet esse intelligibile predestinatum esse Filius Dei. Et 3° ne credatur aliquando non habere esse[4] essencie materialis, [5]cum massa essencie materialis[5] et corporee, que est Christus, sit in mundi principio et non possit deficere. Exclusis ergo istis tribus sensibus erroneis, claret quartus,[6] verus sensus catholicus, quod Christus secundum existenciam humanitatis aliquando non fuit. [7]Quod cum sit verum[7] et implicans Christum aliquando non fuisse, eo quod ipse est illa humanitas, est catholice concedendum.

but this must be so taken as 1. not to apply to him in his divinity;

2. nor as regards the *esse intelligibile* (i.e. *idea*) of his humanity;

3. nor to deny the pre-existence of his material essence:

but (4) in the catholic sense that there was a time when the humanity, which is Christ, did not exist.

Quod si moveat quemquam quod Christus est creatus vel

[1–1] creatus quam aliter quia aliter C. [2] illo A B C. [3] secundum A. [4] esse *om.* O. [5–5] cum . . . materialis *om.* O. [6] quartus *om.* A B C. [7–7] cum tamen est verum C.

Again, if Christ's body had been suddenly created and in the same instant the soul united to it, and then the complete nature assumed; no other term but *creation* would express this sudden process: and this is the right term to apply to the actual, gradual process of the Incarnation.

factus ex nichilo; rogo, quomodo diceretur, si pro instanti incarnacionis corpus Christi subito [1]per totum creatum limitaretur,[1] et anima tunc [2] creata sibi pro eodem instanti uniretur, et pro eodem instanti | natura completa ypostatice [O 224d] sumeretur? Numquid credimus quod Christus non tunc temporaliter produceretur? Baptisemus [3] ergo illam faccionem sive produccionem subitam. Et patet quod non superest nomen competens nisi 'creacio' cum tota humanitas a solo Deo [4] producitur ex puro [5] nichilo precedente temporaliter in effectum: et cum produccio per se et proprie terminatur ad suppositum, relinquitur, quod Christus in illo casu sit factus ex nichilo; et sic omnia argumenta, que viderentur [6] militare contra creacionem Christi in [7] faccione ex virgine, procederent contra illud preter hoc, quod essencia corporea, que est Christus, creata [8] est in mundi principio et interim per patriarchas ac demum per beatam virginem ministerialiter alterata; et revera hoc, licet [9]sit gloriosius,[9] est magis mirabile.

Objection 2. The term 'Christ,' although it speaks of two natures, yet chiefly and taken simply speaks of the uncreated nature; on the principle that an ambiguous term must be understood in its more usual sense.

Quod si 2° obicitur quod 'Christus' dicens duas naturas dicit principaliter ac simpliciter naturam increatam, cum analogum [10] per se sumptum secundum famosius [11] debet intelligi; dicitur, quod si illa evidencia procederet, negandum [12] esset omne predicabile [13]de Christo humanitus,[13] et per consequens totum misterium et fides incarnacionis. Ideo, cum scriptura et sancti doctores concedunt simpliciter utramque maneriem predicatorum de Christo, qui nos sumus ut audeamus [14] tam consolatoriam fidem [15] infringere? Unde Augustinus 2° De Visitacione Infirmorum: 'Cum, inquit, credatur scripture sacre testimoniis sunt alia de Deo Filio [16]nobis [17] propinqua et contigua, et [16] ex ipsa | propinquitate [A 88a] sui et contiguitate nobis familiaria, et ex ipsa familiaritate nobis delectabilia. Delectabile quippe est homini et salutare

Reply. Scripture and the Fathers allow either manner of predicate concerning Christ. As Augustine testifies;

[1-1] crearetur et liniamentaretur M. [2] pro tunc O. [3] baptizaremus O.
[4] Deo *om.* B. [5] ex po (*pro* ex p²o) B C; ex pure O.
[6] videntur A B C. [7] ex A B C. [8] creata *om.* O.
[9] sit graciosius A B C. [10] analogis C. [11] famosma O.
[12] nedum B. [13-13] de Christi humanitatis O. [14] audiamus O C.
[15] fidem *om.* O. [16-16] nobis . . . et *om.* O. [17] modo C.

morienti loqui et saciari de humanitate Christi. Quod enim "Verbum caro factum est et habitavit in nobis," hominis est; quod homo Deus factus est, hominis est: utrumque [C 68a] ergo hoc | ineffabile sacramentum hominis est. Quoniam ergo infirmus hominis intellectus, ex sui ipsius humanitate ponderosa ebetatus, 'videns nunc per speculum in enigmate,' non potest Dei divinitatem, ut dignum est, comprehendere; ad illam, que sua est, Christi humanitatem oculum suum intellectualem reflectat, in illa delectetur, ex illa sacietur, ad illam faciem suam tanquam parietem cum Ezechia convertat.' Et sequitur consilium bonum morbis pestilencialibus fatigatis. 'De homine, inquit, tuo puro fac tibi participem,[1] quia prius fecit Deus de homine tuo puro sibi participem.[1] Ex divinitate processit salvacio et ex humanitate redempcio: utrumque tamen ex utroque:[2] sed, [3]quod unum est michi quadam cognacione et secreta quadam affeccione [et] conglutinio quodam,[3] proprio iure consanguinitatis vendico, tucius et iocundius loquor ad meum Iesum quam ad aliquem sanctorum spirituum[4]: plus debet Christus michi[5] quam cuilibet celestium spirituum[6] quia, quod tu es, fieri dignatus est Deus, non factus est angelus. Nollem, inquit, habere locum angeli, si possem habere locum debitum homini.' Nec dubito quin omnes logici nesciunt offendendo impingere in illam sentenciam de vi vocis, quia cum Christus sit frater noster, ut patet Ioh. 20. 'vade ad fratres meos et dic eis etc.'; et ad Hebre. 2° 'non confunditur eos fratres vocare dicens: "nunciabo nomen tuum fratribus meis"': consequens est quod sit eadem communis humanitas, que est quilibet frater suus; et per consequens debet lege proximitatis diligere fratres suos.

who adduces John i. 14 as referring to his humanity.

1 Cor. xv. 12.

Isa. xxxviii. 2.

which is the plain sense of Holy Scripture in many places.

John xx. 17.

Heb. ii. 11-12.

Ps. xxii. 22.

Objection 3. To hold that Jesus Christ did not exist before his conception by the Virgin is a heresy (compare p. 80, l. 22);

Sed 3° obicitur per hoc quod hereticum est credere Iesum Christum non fuisse ante concepcionem ex virgine, sicut[7] patet de Heresi 44^a^. superius recitata. Ymo cum contra-

[1] participium A B C. [2] utralibet A B C.

[3–3] quod meum est meum quod ex me michi quadam cogitacione et cognacione secreta quadam affeccione conglutinio quodam A B C; quod unum est michi quadam cognacione et cognacione secreta quadam affeccione conclusio (9°) quodam O.

[4] spiritum O. [5] in A B C. [6] celesti spiritui O. [7] et sic A B C.

but if Christ is a creature, he did not so pre-exist: hence he had and had not pre-existence.

dictoria non verificantur de eodem, et Christus Deus est eternaliter post et ante; videtur quod, concesso[1] Christum semper fuisse, negandum est, ut contradictorium, eundem Christum aliquando non fuisse.

Reply.

Hic dico quod, si essem pure gentilis philosophus indifferens omni secte coram capciosissimis | [B 134b] logicis intendentibus[2] michi[3] concludere; dum tamen admitterem gracia argumenti istam philosophicam[4] supposicionem et necessariam fidei Christiane, quod eadem persona Verbi est trium naturarum quelibet; ego concederem conclusionem [5]tanquam sine repugnancia[5] consequentem.

1. No contradiction holds between equivocal terms.
2. Christ as divine, and Christ as a created nature, are equivocal terms.
3. The Person of the Word is body, soul and deity singly.
So the affirmative holds good —Christ (as God) pre-existed —; and the negative also—Christ (as man) did not pre-exist.

Pro cuius declaracione primo[6] suppono quod in equivocis non sit contradiccio: 2° quod summa equivocacio sit inter deitatem et naturam creatam, cum in nullo universali univoco conveniunt: 3° quod persona Verbi sit corpus, anima, et deitas singillatim. Quibus suppositis patet ex posicione[7] tam quod iste Christus fuit in mundi principio. | [C 68b] Affirmativa patet ex hoc quod illa deitas tunc fuit et ipsa est Christus: negativa autem patet ex hoc quod illa humanitas tunc non fuit, et ipsa est Christus. Sicut ergo non est contradiccio quod homo currit et homo non currit, cum multa sunt quorum [8]quodlibet est homo, pro quorum[8] uno verificatur affirmativa, et pro alio negativa; sic in proposito, cum multa sunt,[9] quorum quodlibet est Christus. Et hinc dicit beatus Ambrosius 3° libro De Spiritu Sancto quoad[10] | [A 88b] logicam subtiliter[11] et profunde.

The apparent contradiction is pointedly expressed by St. Ambrose.
Ps. xix. 5.

'Generalis, inquit, est fides ista [12]quod Christus est Dei filius[12] et[13] natus ex virgine, quem quasi gigantem propheta describit, eo quod biformis gemine nature unus consors divinitatis et corporis. Idem ergo paciebatur et non paciebatur, moriebatur et non moriebatur, sepeliebatur [14]et non sepeliebatur,[14] resurgebat et non resurgebat; resurgebat secundum carnem, que mortua

[1] confesso O. [2] intitentibus O. [3] michi *om.* C.
[4] phisicam A C; phô^cam O; *verbum om. cod.* B.
[5]–[5] tanquam repugnancia A B C; tanquam sine (*vel* sive) repugnanciam O.
[6] primo *om.* B. [7] expositorie A B C; expoē O. [8]–[8] quodlibet . . . quorum *om.* O.
[9] sint A B C. [10] quorum ad B. [11] substancialiter A B C.
[12]–[12] quod . . . filius *om.* A B C. [13] ut A B C.
[14]–[14] et . . . sepeliebatur *om.* O.

fuerat, non secundum Verbum, quod apud Deum semper manebat.' Et quando 'sapiebam [1]ut parvulus,' putabam[1] istum sanctum multum ignarum logice.

1 Cor. xiii. 11. (Wyclif's youthful contempt for St. Ambrose's supposed want of logic.)

Et patet quomodo intelligende sunt negative doctorum in materia de Incarnacione. Unde Ambrosius primo De Trini-
[O 225a] tate ca° 6 dicit quod Christus non | est creatura: et tamen constat ipsum[2] expressissime dicere quod Christus suscepit predicaciones humanas univoce cum aliis, in tantum quod dicit eum ad litteram 'profecisse sapiencia et etate,' et ignorasse multa; ut probat, libro 3°. De Spiritu Sancto, auctoritate scripture. Et sic intelligendum est dictum Augustini in sermone De Fide: 'si quis, inquit, dixerit Dei Filium passum, anathema sit.' Exponit enim[3] seipsum ibidem, quod hoc intelligendum est secundum divinitatem, cum affirmativa sit de substancia fidei, scilicet, quod Dei Filius passus est, ut sepe meminit Augustinus. Et ita concordanda sunt alia dicta doctorum, non concedendo contradictoria, sed veritates nedum simul esse veras, sed a quocunque fideli catholice concedendas.[4]

But when he and St. Augustine and other doctors deny the creatureship of Christ; it is with reference to his divine nature that they do so.

Quod si queritur quomodo dabimus contradiccionem in talibus cum negacio preposita toti non sufficit; dicitur[5] iuxta regulam Aristotelis primo Elenchorum ca° 4°, quod enunciando contradictoria de aliquo attendendum est quod illud sit idem ultimum singulare[6] et secundum idem simpliciter et in eodem tempore; ut, quod idem Christus in numero [7]secundum eandem naturam in numero[7] sit simul[8] vivus et mortuus, passus et non passus. Et ita de aliis oppositis est repugnancia.

The propositions concerning Christ which appear to be contradictory do not fall under the Aristotelian definition of contradiction.

Unde concedentes quod Christus eciam[9] secundum altissimam naturam in eo non habuit existenciam ante conceptum ex virgine senserunt,[10] ut Augustinus recitat, nimis heretice. Non autem illi, qui concedunt ipsum non preextitisse subintelligendo secundum humanitatem ad sensum expositum.

1–1 nec parvulus putavi O. 2 Christum O. 3 sicut exponit A B C.
4 concedendas *om.* O. 5 dicit O. 6 simpliciter A C.
7 secundum . . . numero *om.* A B C. 8 et semel *add.* O.
9 eciam *om.* A B C. 10 sencierunt O.

To avoid the mere appearance of a logical contradiction, schoolmen have denied Christ's creatureship.

Contradiccio enim non est nominis tantum, sed et[1] rei et nominis. | Et indubie causa quare scola discessit ab illa [C 69a] logica fuit [2] inanis apparencia [2] sophistica, qua mavult vitare apparenciam redarguccionis vel pucrilis inconsequencie, quam pausare[3] in sensu reali scripture. Prima[4] ad Cor. 4° scribitur: 'nos stulti propter Christum.' Nam apostoli, predicantes Deum[5] crucifixum et mortuum, et[6] simul parem Deo et minorem Deo, reputati sunt nimirum stulti tam a philosophis quam a plebeis. Sed[7] 'siquis videtur inter vos sapiens esse in hoc seculo, sic stultus fiat ut sit sapiens' Deo:' ut precipit Apostolus prima ad Cor. 3°, quia indubie gentiles philosophi ex ignorancia logice et methaphisice reputant sensum illum stulticiam esse.

1 Cor. iv. 10. being unwilling to meet the reproach of being 'fools for Christ's sake,' which the Apostles boldly faced in their preaching.

1 Cor. iii. 18.

It does not follow from the author's position that 'God at some time was not.'

Et si queratur, utrum concedi debet quod Deus aliquando non fuit, sicut generabatur temporaliter vel incepit;[8] videtur michi quod licet illud sane posset intelligi, tamen iste sensus non ministratur ex terminis. Ideo ego concedo negativas solum cum subiectis signantibus geminas substancias in Filio, ut Messias ille homo Iesus aliquando non fuit: quia in illis | intelligo naturam que incepit[9] esse et [B 135a] aliquando non fuit. Non[10] sic autem in nominibus appropriate | competentibus deitati. Conceditur tamen quod Deus [A 88c] fuit natus de virgine, passus et mortuus. Sed illud probabitur resolvendo predicacionem ad hominem sic formatum. Et ex hoc non sequitur quod Deus aliquando non fuit, sed[11] quod secundum hominem aliquando non fuit. Nec est incepcio vel generacio Deo conveniens, Deum esse et ipsum aliquando non fuisse: sed sic ex esse aliquando[12] humanitus et ex negacione, que est,[13] antea humanitus non fuisse, cum instanti et aliis principiantibus illum motum. Et patet quod non sequitur—Christus aliquando non fuit; et ipso est Deus: ergo Deus[14] aliquando non fuit—propter ex-

[1] et *om.* A C O.
[2–2] magis experiencia O.
[3] pensare O.
[4] ii (*i.e.* secunda) O.
[5] Christum B.
[6] et *om.* A C.
[7] sed *om.* B.
[8] incipit O.
[9] cepit O; esse *om.* C O.
[10] non *om.* O.
[11] sed *om.* O.
[12] aliquando *om.* O.
[13] que est *om.* O.
[14] ipse A B C.

trancacionem supposicionis. Unde si concedimus quod Deus genuit Deum et Deus non genuit Deum, licet tantum sit unus Deus propter distinccionem personarum; quanto magis concederemus quod Christus est factus et Christus non est factus, licet tantum unus sit Christus: cum sicut Deus est tres persone, sic Christus est tres nature, longe nobis manifestius disparate.[1] Et patet exemplariter quomodo respondebitur [2]ad questiones et communes[2] obiectus in ista materia seminatos.

*The difficulties and apparent contradictions are solved when we remember that Christ is three natures (cf. p. 3, l. 7).*

---

## Cap. VII.

[*Declarando Christi mobilitatem explanat sensum scripture multis ambiguum, quomodo sapiencia summe mobilis sit habitu inventa ut homo.*

*The sense in which Christ is subject to change* (mobilis) *is defined by discussing* Wisdom vii. 24, '*Wisdom is more moving* (mobilior) *than any motion*,' *and* Philipp. ii. 8, '*found in fashion* (habitu) *as a man*.']

*Having thus far maintained the creatureship of Christ, the author now affirms his 'mobility.'*

Secundo principaliter arguitur non esse concedendum quod Christus sit mobilis. Nam si Christus sit mobilis, tunc Deus est mobilis: sed nullus Deus est mobilis[3]: ergo [C 69b] nec Christus. Minor | sic arguitur.[4] Aliqua res est immobilis: [5]sed nulla, si non Deus: ergo Deus est immobilis[5]: et cum unus Deus sit omnis Deus, sequitur quod omnis Deus et per consequens omnis[6] persona divina sit simpliciter immobilis, et per consequens nulla est mobilis.[7] Si ergo Deus sit mobilis, et omne aliud a Deo sit[8] mobile, sequitur quod omne ens[9] sit mobile, et sic nullum immobile. Ex quo sequitur quod Christus non sit passus, mortuus, aut cum hominibus conversatus, cum tunc esset destructibilis[10] et adnichilabilis.

*The denial of this is grounded on the impossibility of believing that God is 'mobilis.'*

*But this difficulty would equally prevent belief in the facts of the human life and death of Christ.*

[1] disparate *om.* A B C. [2-2] ad consequentes C; ad comunes *sic* O. [3] est mobilis *om.* O. [4] arguitur *om.* C O. [5-5] sed . . . immobilis *om.* O. [6] omnis *om.* O. [7] immobilis O. [8] sit *om.* B. [9] ens O. [10] desinibilis A B C.

Admitted that Christ (who is God) is 'mobilis,' nevertheless it is a necessary truth that God is 'immobilis.' The existence of something 'immobilis,' is necessary. 1. All motion implies a fixed centre.

Hic dicitur quod necesse est aliquam rem esse omnino immobilem: quod patet tripliciter. Primo ex hoc quod omne motum oportet inniti alicui fixo immoto: [1]universitas creata est mota: ergo oportet illam inniti alicui fixo immoto[1]: sicut[2] ergo mixta terrestria innituntur orbi terre, qui non commovebitur secundum centrum fluctuans huc aut illuc, sic omne motum cum sit ordinatum sic moveri ab alio oportet stare in suis limitibus secundum[3] ordinacionem principaliter[4] ordinantis: quia cum moveri sit imperfeccionis et posse movere perfeccionis simpliciter, patet quod prius est pura perfeccio quam imperfeccio exemplata. 2°. patet idem ex hoc quod veritates multe eterne, tam affirmaciones quam negaciones, sunt omnino immobiles; ut 'quod nichil simul est et non est'; 'quod multa encia possunt esse,' etc.[5] Cum ergo omnem rem racionis oportet fundari in absoluta essencia, sequitur quod oportet dare essenciam vel naturam immobilem, cui innixe predicte[6] veritates immobilitatem suscipiunt. 3°. patet idem ex hoc quod illa prima natura est in fine perfeccionis possibilis, quia aliter non esset summe perfecta; sed si posset moveri, posset perfici: ergo moveri non poterit. Si autem[7] moveri posset,[8] hoc foret potissime | [O 225b] obiective: sed eternaliter ordinat omnia, cum non capit suam speculacionem aut[9] praxim a rebus extra: ergo non movetur[10] a suis effectibus obiective; et multo minus localiter,[11] augmentative, vel alterative: aliter enim esset in eo[12] passiva potencia ante actum mixta cum potencia activa, cum aliud sit | posse movere et aliud posse moveri: et sic varie [A 88d] posset[13] perfici et imperfici, quod non competit summe bono. Supposito ergo, quod sit aliqua res et aliquid omnino immobile; consequenter dicendum est quod necesse est quidquid, quod [14]poterit esse,[14] esse mobile. Patet sic. Non est possibile aliquid esse nisi illud sit[15] essencia creata

2. The eternal realities of things (logical axioms) being 'immobiles' are based upon an absolute essence or nature which is 'immobilis.'

3. This first nature is absolutely perfect, and therefore 'immobilis.'

[1-1] universitas . . . immoto *om.* A B C. [2-2] sic C. [3] secundum *om.* C.
[4-4] principalis A B C. [5] etc. *om.* A B C. [6] et *om.* O.
[7] enim A B C. [8] potest A; poterit O. [9] aut *om.* O.
[10] moveri; *add.* potest *in marg.* A. [11] locatur O. [12] ea B.
[13] potest A B C. [14-14] fuerit O. [15] sicud C.

vel essencia[1] increata; omnis essencia creata est mobilis; omnis essencia increata est mobile: ergo conclusio. Minor patet ex hoc quod essencia increata est suppositum mobile:[2] ergo illa est mobile: consequencia patet, quia ipsa est res mobilis[3] eo quod est persona Verbi, que moveri poterit, et nedum hoc, sed habet naturam sibi[4] unitam secundum quam moveri sufficit.

*The person of the Word is 'mobilis;' and also united to a nature which is 'mobilis.'*

[C 70a] Et sic intelligo illud[5] Sapiencie 7°, | 'omnibus mobilibus est mobilior sapiencia': quod dictum, ut michi videtur, potest catholice intelligi et vere ad litteram de Sapiencia eterna[6] suo tempore incarnata; que, cum attrita[7] sit secundum humanitatem assumptam propter scelera nostra, bonificans et vivificans omnia ultra hoc quod sufficeret [8]vel poterit[8] alia creatura, habuit nimirum mocionem fontalem, qua principiat quasi vita omnem mocionem mundi sensibilis et cuiuslibet sue partis. Sicut ergo Aristoteles 8° Physicorum: 'Ymaginatur motum primi mobilis esse quasi vitam viventibus cum mediante[9] illo influitur perfeccio mundo supposito'; sic verissime sine ficticia illa Sapiencia est primum mobile efficacia et dignitate secundum assumptum hominem, mediante cuius motu primo omnium[10] totus mundus ante et post perficitur; cum quelibet alia creatura [B 135b] per Christi passionem ad perfeccionem | primariam,[11] qua Deo serviret [12]placato et[12] homini, instauratur. Non quod propter devocionem finguntur falsa; sed quod verissime[13] de vi sermonis secundum seriem verborum primum[13] mobile sit sapiencia increata; et quod eius motus vel passio perficit *[hominem] plus quam motus celi[14] quamlibet creaturam[15] [aliam] post vel ante. Nam[16] quelibet creatura

*Wisdom vii. 24 explained. Wisdom, i.e. the eternal Wisdom, incarnate in due time, is the source of motion and of life:*

*even as, according to Aristotle, the motion of the primum mobile is the life in things living, and by its influence the world is perfected.*

*Thus by the passion of Christ all creation is perfected.*

[1] essencia *om.* A B C. [2] mobile *om.* A B C. [3] mobilis *om.* A B C.
[4] sibi *om.* A B C. [5] illud *om.* O. [6] eterna *om.* O.
[7] atti^a O. [8] hec (poterit *om.*) A B; hec poterit C.
[9] me^te A B C. [10] omni A B C.
[11] pristinam A; p̄riam (*i.e.* primariam) C O.
[12] et placito A B C; placato (et *om.*) O.
[13] de vi sermonis aut secundum seriem (*in rasura*) verborum (debetur *in margine*) primum A; sermonis sed causacionem verborum primum B. *Cod.* O *om.* vi: *cetera cum cod.* C *ut supra in textu habet.*
[14] ce^l (*forsitan pro* ceteri) O: *at cf. p.* 108, *l.* 11-14.
[15] aliam *add.* O; *forsitan retinendum, et* hominem *post* perficit *addendum.*
[16] nam *om.* O.

citra hominem debet ex institucione primaria servire homini; et sic peccato primi hominis, a quo hodie[1] redundanter[2] haberet perfeccionem ipso stante in originali iusticia, quodammodo peioratur. Cum ergo, per passionem et per consequens per mocionem huius Sapiencie, facta plena satisfaccione,[3] sit natura humana gloriosius restituta; patet quod[4] ista passio rectificat omnem operacionem nature, que humano generi est subiecta: et cum omnis[5] servitus post et ante facta humano generi, non interveniente ista redempcione, foret quodammodo cassata, patet quod compendiosius motu celi [6]vivificat preterita[6] et futura: et cum exinde dolus et peccatum demonum mitigatur, lectum[7] angelorum consorcium augmentatur, patet quod ultra possibilitatem motus celi spiritualem bonificat creaturam. Nec mirum; quia motor[8] intrinsecus huius[9] motus fuit non intelligencia, motrix orbis, sed [10]spiritus preciosissimus[10] Filii hominis et Dei Filii naturalis, qui est 'tanto melior angelis effectus, quanto differencius pre illis nomen hereditavit;' ut dicit Apostolus ad Hebre. primo ca°, quando dicit quod 'Deus proposuit instaurare in Christo omnia, que in celis et que in terra sunt'; ut exponit Gregorius 31° Moralium ca° 38.

Sic ergo intelligendo per Sapienciam personaliter Verbum Dei, ut docent Augustinus et Ieronimus,[11] concedendum est quod ipsa sit summe mobilis; ymo plus | attendendo ad [A 89a] litteram concedi potest quod dicta Sapiencia nedum fuit plus mobilis, sed plus | effectualiter movebatur quam alia [C 70b] creatura quoad velocitatem, quoad compendiositatem, et quoad generalitatem. Quoad velocitatem, quia pro instanti sue generacionis plena carismatum; post verisimiliter in sua ascensione movebatur recte tam velociter ut primum mobile circulariter,[12] vel ut est possibile quod aliquid moveatur, quia causa tardacionis post[13] discipulorum intuitum non est

For by the Passion Man is reinstated in his pristine state of perfection; and in Man's restoration is involved 'the restitution of all things,' inasmuch as to Man was given dominion over all: Gen. i. 26. Ps. viii. 6. moreover by the Passion the sin of demons is mitigated, and the company of angels increased. And the cause of all this 'motion' is not an intelligence which moves the world, but the most precious spirit of the Son of God and Son of Man, i.e. Christ, in Heb. i. 4. whom 'God purposed to gather Eph. i. 10. Col. i. 20. together all things in one.' (This identification of Wisdom with the Word approved by Augustine and Jerome.) Moreover Wisdom is '*summe* mobilis': surpassing in its swiftness,

[1] hodie *om.* C O. [2] redundancia O. [3] satisfaccio A B C. [4] quod *om.* C. [5] omnia O. [6] unificat preterit O. [7] letum (*i.e.* laetum) A B C. [8] mo^r motor *sic* O. [9] cuius A B C. [10-10] species preciosissima A B; species preciosissime C. [11] Iohannes O. [12] circulatur O. [13] post *om.* O.

faciliter fingenda: Christus ergo ex se ascendendo a limbo ad celum ultimum pertransiit velocissime longissimum spacium transmeabile. Quoad compendiositatem patet quod eius brevis passio reduxit totum mundum post et ante ad maius temperamentum quam motus perpetuus primi mobilis suffecisset: prima enim secundum Aristotelem sunt quantitate minima. Quoad generalitatem patet, cum Christus sit creatura corporea et creatura incorporea, quarum utraque[1] multipliciter movebatur, quod sit ceteris plus mobilis: movebatur quidem[2] generacione et morte, augmentacione et alteracione, et demum motu locali multiplici super terram, aquam, et aerem[3] pulsione, traccione, veccione et vertigine, ut actu illo imperfecto reduceret suos ad quietem perpetuam. Unde sicut naturalis philosophus commendat motum tanquam signum efficax nedum ad philosophandum sed ad intentum nature perficiendum, sic nimirum commendat theologus voluntariam passionem. Et constat[4] ex 3° Physicorum quod passio vel est motus vel accidens multum cognatum motui. Sic ergo verissime de virtute sermonis dicitur 'Sapiencia' Dei Patris 'omnibus aliis creaturis mobilior.'

In its summary character,

In its universality.

Thus, as the physicist praises motion, so the theologian extols the Passion; (and passion, according to Aristotle, is a kind of motion;) and it is the literal truth that 'the Wisdom (of God the Father) is more moving than any creature.' Wisdom vii. 24.

Sed obicitur contra hunc sensum per hoc, quod Christus non est ante incarnacionem; et per consequens scriba huius [O 225c] scripture non intendebat ad | litteram mobilitatem Sapiencie incarnate. Hinc dicitur quod, quidquid fuerit de consequente, consequencia non valet; quia, cum apud Deum omnia que fuerunt sunt presencia, certum est quod auctor[5] huius scripture satis cognovit quomodo[6] 'Christus maneat in eternum' iuxta illam vocem vasis eleccionis sue ad Hebre. 13°. 'Iesus Christus hodie et cras ipse et in secula.' Et illud egregie declarat Ieronimus in Epist. De Assumpcione Beate Virginis ad Paulam et Eustochium: 'Christi quidem incarnacionem, hoc est quod Christus suo tempore incarnatur, cognovit patriarcha Abraham iuxta testimonium Veritatis Ioh. 8°. 'Abraham pater vester exultavit ut videret diem

Objection.

As Christ before the incarnation did not exist, the author of this scripture could not refer literally to Wisdom incarnate.

Reply.

To God all things are present; that 'Christ abideth ever;' John xii. 35. 'the same yesterday, to-day, and for ever;' Heb. xiii. 8. was known to the writer of the book of Wisdom; just as, according to Jerome, Abraham knew of the incarnation of Christ: John viii. 56.

[1] tam *add.* A B; *cod.* O *add.* t$^{\hat{a}}$ *forsitan pro* c$^{a}$ (creatura). [2] quadam A B.
[3] et aerem *om.* O. [4] patet B. [5] a$^{or}$ A B C. [6] qm̃ A B C.

meum," id est, tempus incarnacionis et non solum diem eternitatis; "vidit et gavisus est."' Cui Augustinus Omc. 43 adicit argumentum. 'Quando, inquit, Abraham, Gen. 24°., misit servum suum, ut peteret uxorem filio suo Ysaac, hoc cum iuramento obstrinxit, ut fideliter quod iubebatur impleret. Magna enim res agebatur, quando Abrahe semini coniugium querebatur. Sed, ut hoc cognosceret servus quod noverat Abraham, quod nepotes | non [C 71a] carnaliter affectabat, nec de suo genere carnale aliquid sapiebat; ait servo quem mittebat: "pone manum sub femore meo et iura per Deum celi." Quid, inquit, sibi vult "Deus celi" ad femur Abrahe?' Et respondet. 'Cum per femur genus notatur, illa iuracione signabatur de genere Abrahe venturum in carne Deum celi. | Stulti, [A 89b] inquit, reprehendunt prophetam | Abraham tamquam pure [B 136a] puerile gesserit in hoc dicto; sed cum credidit benediccionem sui seminis Messiam credidit de suo semine incarnandum.'

(and in support of the statement that Abraham 'saw his day,' Augustine explains Genesis xxiv. 3 to refer to a foreknowledge of the incarnation.)

Et idem 2°. declarat Ieronimus de prophetia[1] patriarche Ysaac sencientis Christum odore prophetico, Gen. 27. quando dixit, 'Ecce odor filii mei sicut odor agri pleni, quem benedixit Dominus.' Et ita de singulis patriarchis. Cum enim ipsi eadem fide salvati sunt nobiscum, patet quod ipsi crediderunt incarnacionem Domini sicut et nos; et per consequens Dominum suo tempore incarnari. 'Constat, inquit[2] Ieronimus, tempus non preiudicasse[3] sacramento uniti hominis ac Dei.'

(To the same effect Jerome on Gen. xxvii. 27.)

('Time is no prejudice to the mystery of the incarnation.')

Et patet ad obiectus garulos sophistarum, quibus invehunt contra oraciones ecclesie quibus [4]rogat Dominum[4] 'per[5] incarnacionem, nativitatem, circumcisionem, baptismum, ieiunium, passionem, mortem, resurreccionem et ascensionem a periculis liberari'; 'Inanis, inquiunt, est oracio suggesta, cum omnia predicta nec sunt nec possunt esse.' Sed constat quod unumquodque illorum, cum sit nobis preteritum, et futurum suo tempore patribus veteris testamenti, [quod[6]]

(As acts of Christ in the *past* are to us the ground of obtaining mercy, (notwithstanding the futile objections raised against the obsecration in the Litany as referring to acts now not present and impossible;))

[1] philosophia A B C. [2] inquit *om.* B. [3] predicasse O.
[4] orat deum A B C. [5] pro O. [6] *An* quod *sensus causa omittendum?*

so to the O. T. fathers *future* acts of Christ availed;

vere est pro suo tempore et per consequens causa misericordiam impetrandi: non quod quidquam scrupulosum[1] in nostra lege celamus,[2] quod non audeamus disputacioni cuiuscunque philosophantis ostendere. Et illum modum loquendi docet Ieronimus ex illo dicto Iude. 'Iesus, inquit, populum ex Egipto salvans secundo eos, qui non crediderunt, perdidit:' et Apostolus 1ª ad Cor. 10°: 'neque temptemus Christum sicut quidam eorum temptaverunt;' non quod iam esset Iesus Christus natus ex Maria virgine, sed quia illa illa persona, que tempore suo est Christus, est eterna et sempiterno[3] Dei consilio incarnata et[4] materialis essencia semper presto. Sic ergo[5] sancti patres, in quocunque tempore fuerunt,[6] sciverunt vere Christum esse, fuisse, et fore; et[7] proposiciones formate ab eis fuissent vere—Christus est, fuit, vel erit incarnatus—quamvis tunc non fuisset ita[8] quod Christus est incarnatus. Nam, ut sepe dixi, sicut proposicio potest esse hic vera cum hoc, quod hic non sit suum primarie significatum, sed satis est quod ipsum sit alicubi[9]: correspondenter proposicio potest esse nunc vera cum hoc, quod nunc non sit suum primarie signatum, sed satis est quod ipsum sit aliquando. Et sic [C 71b] intelligendus est Augustinus cum aliis | doctoribus quod eadem est fides patrum tam novi quam veteris testamenti. Nam incarnacio, mors Christi, et adventus ad iudicium sunt fides credita, a qua fide absit falsitas, sive ficticia etc. Unde Gregorius 23° Moralium ca°. 15[10] exponens illud[11] Iob. 33°, 'semel loquetur Deus, et secundo ad[12] ipsum non repetet,' ita scribit: 'In Deo ideo dicere quodlibet tempus audacter, licet quod in eo nullum proprie dici[13] licet.' [14]Unde notat[14] causam eius 30°. Moralium ca°. 5° dicens quod Deus preteritorum[15] non reminiscitur, cum ipsa que in semetipsis[16]

Jude 5.

1 Cor. x. 9.

and they knew of the existence of Christ;

and their faith was in essentials the same as ours; as Augustine and Gregory maintain.

Job xxxiii. 14.

The latter expressly teaches that to God everything is present;

[1] scrupulos-(is *in rasura*) A; scrupulos B C.
[2] colamus A B C.
[3] semper in O; semper consilio (*sic*) C.
[4] et *om.* O.
[5] sibi O.
[6] fuerint O.
[7] per *add.* O.
[8] ita *om.* A B.
[9] aliquando A B C.
[10] ca°. 3 A B C.
[11] idem O.
[12] ad *om.* A B C.
[13] dici *om.* A B C.
[14–14] unam vocat O.
[15] preterito O.
[16] ipsis *om.* A B C.

Job x. 5.

so also Anselm;

a doctrine necessary to the understanding of Scripture,

Ps. xxii. 16.

Eccles. xlvii. 11, and fatal to the above objection (p. 109, l. 21).

preterennt eius[1] intuitu semper presencia assistunt: et exemplificat satis notabiliter 34°. Moralium ca°. 5°. tripliciter: unde 9°. Moralium 25 expresserat illud diffusius exponens illud Iob. 10. 'Numquid sicut dies hominis, dies tui?' 'Deo, inquit, nec transacta preterennt, nec adhuc ventura, que non apparent, desunt; quia is, qui[2] semper esse habet cuncta sibi presencia, conspicit.' Et idem dicit Anselmus Monologion 19°. Ideo, ut sepe dixi, nisi omne tempus | preteritum vel futurum fuerit Deo presens, patercntur theologi magnas angustias in exposicione[3] scripturarum ut Ps. 21°. tempore David dicit dicta Sapiencia: 'foderunt[4] manus meas et pedes meos:' et sic de multis scripturis, que pueriliter essent sine racione posite[5] sub ita disparatis temp|oribus nisi ad imprimendum in[6] nobis quod immensa Dei eternitas coassistit omni tempori preterito et[7] futuro. Unde ad istum sensum loquitur sapiencia Ecclesiastici 47°: 'Christus purgavit[8] peccata ipsius.' Et patet quod facta instancia non impugnat sensum datum ad istam scripturam, 'omnibus mobilior est Sapiencia.' [A 89c] [O 225d]

Three other possible senses in which 'Wisdom is more moving than any motion.'

Sunt autem multi alii sensus huic littere adaptati.[9] Ut hi dicunt quod extensive loquendo de motu Sapiencia increata movetur obiective a cognitis terminantibus eius actum. Hi dicunt cum tot sint motus genera quot et entes,[10] et Deus ad omnem punctum mundi continue adquirit dominia, est in illa manerie motus relacionis 'summe mobilis.' Tercii autem dicunt quod in omni motu est dare ordinem prioritatis et posterioritatis[11] secundum successivam denominacionem[12] subiecti in materia motus, et omne tale secundum esse intelligibile ordinatum et descriptum[13] est eternaliter in Sapiencia increata, et secundum illas raciones dicitur figurative 'summe mobilis.' Sed prior exposicio, cum sit literalior de virtute sermonis, verior, et fidei conformior, plus placeret.

[1] eius *om.* O.
[2] his que O.
[3] exposicionibus O M.
[4] fodiunt O.
[5] posita C O.
[6] in *om.* A B C.
[7] vel O.
[8] pugnavit O.
[9] dapnâti O.
[10] entis A B C.
[11] et posterioritatis *om.* A B C.
[12] denotacionem O.
[13] discriptum O.

[B 136b] Unde quamvis auctor scripture intenderit | omnes istos sensus, primum tamen principalius, ut sit introitus ad alios consequentes. Et sic Augustinus de virtute sermonis salvat textus scripture plus imbrigabiles ut illud Ioh. 14,[1] 'Ser-[C 72a]monem quem audistis non est meus, | sed eius, qui misit me, Patris.' Dicit enim illud Omc. 76ª. esse verum de virtute sermonis: 'non, inquit, miremur, non paveamus[2]: non est minor Patre, vel impar sibi: non enim mentitus est; "qui me non diligit, sermones meos[3] non servat:" non est hic sibi contrarius, sed forte non[4] sine misterio ibi dixit pluraliter, hic singulariter; volens hic intelligere semetipsum, qui, cum sit Sermo vel Verbum Dei Patris non autem Sermo sui ipsius, verum dixit ad litteram.' Quod si grammaticus ex accusativo casu offenditur, potest dici quod facta construccione recta non sit[5] anthitesis. Nam qui non diligit Christum, non servat sermones suos, id est,[6] sentencias vel veritates, quas precepit observari. Sed ut manifestet quid ex hoc sequitur, subiungit 'et sermonem quem audistis' (supple[7] 'non servat'); per quam copulacionem docemur mothaphisicam quod omnes huiusmodi veritates eterne sunt idem essencialiter Verbo Dei. Et 3°, ut doceat quod ille Sermo sit idem essencialiter Deo Patri, licet personaliter[8] distinguatur, subiungit 'non est meus sed eius, qui misit me, Patris.' Licet autem sensus catholicus posset esse quod sermo vocalis non sit Verbi ex se, modo quo Apostolus dicit solum Patrem habere immortalitatem[9]; ut exponit Augustinus primò De Trinitate et primo contra Maximinianum ca°. 10; tamen[10] prior sensus est subtilior et mihi[11] carior.

But the first sense (p. 107, l. 10) is to be preferred; thus the literal truth of Scripture is saved; as also in John xiv. 24, according to Augustine's interpretation, which deals with grammatical distinctions of number and case.

1 Tim. vi. 16.

Et sic intelligendus est sensus Apostoli ad Philipp. 2°. quod Christus,[12] 'cum in forma Dei esset, non rapinam arbitratus est esse se equalem Deo; sed semetipsum exinanivit formam servi accipiens.' Pro cuius intellectu notandum quod sicut forma

Similarly Phil. ii. 6. *'being in the form of God . . . he emptied himself, taking the form of a servant,'*

[1] *numerum om.* A B C; 10 O M. [2] paciemus O. [3] sermonem meum A B.
[4] non *om.* O. [5] fit O [6] id est *om.* O
[7] supplendum B C; non *om.* C. [8] pater O. [9] immortalem O.
[10] cum A B. [11] inde A B. [12] Christus *om.* O.

is to be understood by taking 'form' in the metaphysical sense.

Dei est deitas,[1] sic forma ho|minis est humanitas. Utraque [A 89d] enim est forma substancialis; cum quelibet persona divina sit illud quo[2] est Deus,[3] quia Deus formaliter deitate;[1] sicut quelibet persona hominis est illud quo[2] est homo, [4]quia est homo[4] formaliter humanitate. Utramque autem harum formarum habet ut subiectus eis formaliter; unam tamen habet absolute necessario; et aliam accepit[5] ex tempore. Et istam altissimam methaphisicam de formis vellem nostros theologos, etsi non in[6] methaphisica Aristotelis, saltem in verbis Apostoli compendiose addiscere. Ex quo patet, quod non ex propria reputacione vel arbitrio proprio sine veritate substrata vendicavit se esse equalem Patri, quasi[7] raperet sibi honorem Patri debitum, ut facit Sathanas; cum naturaliter et communiter inest sibi cum Patre et Spiritu Sancto[8] esse Deum. Quod co-inest[9] sibi et Patri, ostenderat [10]quando

John x. 30.

dixit,[10] 'Ego et Pater unum sumus.' Augustinus autem

Augustine applies this verbally exact method of interpretation to Phil. ii. 6.

format talem racionem; 'Nichil quod est [11] naturale et essenciale[11] supposito est rapina: [12]sed Christum esse equalem Deo est naturale et per se inest Verbo: ergo hoc non est rapina.[12] Sed faciendo se esse naturam visibilem exinanivit misericorditer semetipsum: *semetipsum* [13] dicit propter ydemptitatem persone que est filius [14] hominis et Dei Filius:[14] *exinanivit* dicit,[15] quia | fecit se ad[16] extra esse naturam corpo- [C 72b] ream, [17]que, [cum] in mundi principio prius originem[17] quam formam habeat, est inanis.' Ad quem sensum, ut exponit Augustinus 12°. Confessionum, scriptura in principio Gen.

Gen. i. 2.

dicit, 'terra erat inanis et vacua.' Nec video quomodo exinanicio[18] pocius[19] possit intelligi quam quod sit[20] res extra facta inanis [21]essencialiter sic ut sit[21] exinanita. Et hoc est verum de Christo ad litteram, cum sit trium natu-

[1] divinitas; divinitate O. [2] quod O. [3] deus *om.* O.
[4-4] quia . . . homo *om.* O. [5] accipit O. [6] in *om.* O.
[7] qui A B. [8] sancto *om.* O. [9] commune A B C.
[10-10] quando dixit *om.* A. [11-11] essenciale et essenciale C.
[12-12] sed . . . rapina *om.* A B C. [13] semetipsum *om.* A B C; sj ipsum O.
[14-14] hominis . . . filius *om.* A B C. [15] dicit *om.* A B C. [16] ad *om.* B.
[17-17] origine C O; *aut* cum *inserendum aut* origine *legendum*. [18] inanicio A B C.
[19] prius O. [20] sit *om.* O. [21-21] essencia sic et sic A B C.

rarum quelibet. Et hinc vere dicit Veritas, Ioh. 14°. 'Pater maior me est:' quia, cum[1] Christus sit tam equivoce divinitas et humanitas, potest respectu predicati absoluti intelligi secundum racionem divinitatis vel secundum racionem humanitatis, sicut exigit predicatum. Et patet ex dictis superius quod non est repugnancia—Pater est maior Christo[2]—et—idem Pater est[3] simpliciter equalis Christo—: ymo, intelligendo personam Christi secundum duas naturas [O 226a] equivoce, non est repugnancia inter ista—Pater est maior | Christo—[4] et—idem Pater non est maior Christo—[4]: nec debent tales predicaciones abici de virtute sermonis quod sunt figurative, quia per idem[5] negaretur hoc—Ego et Pater unum sumus—Pater et Filius et Spiritus Sanctus sunt unus Deus, etc:—cum in prima sit equivocacio, et in secunda concepcio personarum. Ymo, si non fallor, omnis locucio nostra de Deo est figurativa, ut quandocunque dicitur quod Deus est mobilis, natus, passus etc. est construccio non synecdochica sed figura que *antropospatos* dicitur, quando scilicet humana passio Deo attribuitur; ab *antropos* homo et *patos* passio. Non enim habemus nomina, que sine figura Deum signent.

John xiv. 28.

The statements '*I and my Father are one*' and '*My Father is greater than I*' are not really contradictory:

(comp. p. 4, l. 32)

but involve an 'equivocation' as to the Person of Christ.

We cannot speak of God at all except in human and figurative terms, which involve ἀνθρωποπάθεια.

[B 137a] Redeundo ergo ad pro|positum conceditur quod aliqua res, quia natura divina, est omnino immobilis, sic quod nullo modo moveri poterit, licet sit suppositum mobile, ut puta, Christus passus. Patet ista logica in exemplo. Nam natura divina est Verbum tam eternaliter quam temporaliter genitum, et tamen ipsa non est genita, et talis[6] essencia materie prime est suppositum ignis compositum ex materia et forma: et tamen ipsa materia non potest sic componi. Petrus comedit, moritur, vel aliter transmutatur; et tamen [A 90a] natura specifica, que est Petrus, non potest taliter | transmutari. Ideo in omnibus istis similibus oportet diligenter attendere ad predicacionem secundum essenciam et formalem. Et patet quod non sequitur—Deus est mobilis,[7] et omne aliud

To resume the general argument (from p. 107, l. 7), a divine nature in itself '*immobilis*' may be, as in suffering Christ it is, a *suppositum mobile*.

The distinction

[1] cum *om.* B. [2] me B. [3] est *om.* A B. [4–4] et . . . Christo *om.* O. [5] perinde O. [6] et sic C; etc O. [7] mobile O.

between *essential* and *formal* predication saves a contradiction.

a Deo est mobile: ergo omnis res est mobilis—quia aliqua res non est mobilis. Et si queratur—Quid non est mobile?—potest dici equivocando, quod nichil non est mobile, quia natura divina est mobile: et sic, intelligendo predicacionem secundum essenciam non formalem,[1] omne, [2]quod est, est mobile.[2]

Subtle questions in the schools to be deprecated.

Quod si dicatur istam responsionem, cum sapiat contradiccionem, interimere disputaciones theologicas, cum incidit in redargucionem, que est [3] meta vilissima respondentis; dicitur quod multum proficeret modum disputandi sophisticum, | principaliter propter apparenciam arguentis et redargucionem [4] patulam respondentis, ex peccato Luciferi [C 73a]

The devil asked the first question in Scripture.

introductum, esse [5] in scolis theologis pretermissum.[6] In cuius signum prima questio, quam scriptura meminit,[7] est a dyabolo [8]introducta. 'Cur,[8] inquit serpens, precipit vobis Deus ut non comederetis de omni ligno paradisi?' Gen. 3°.

Gen. iii. 1.

Every question is an evidence either of ignorance or of sin:

Unde omnis questio attestatur indubie super ignoranciam vel peccatum. Tamen non negandum est, quin questiones theologice possunt tractari meritorie, cum Veritas quesivit a peccatoribus plurimas questiones.

yet Christ asked questions, and we may do so if our aim is a right one.

Oportet tamen quod utrobique intendatur Dei gloria augmentanda, sophistarum superbia destruenda, et ignota veritas detegenda: omne [9] autem quod amplius est in disputacione theologica 'a malo est:' ideo questio, sicut et iuramentum, occasione vel pena peccati introducta est.

Math. v. 37.

Augustine condemns the contentiousness and vanity of disputants.

Et ista est sentencia Augustini 2° De Doctrina Christiana 31°, ubi docet in disputacionibus cavere rixandi libidinem et ostentacionem frivolam puerilem. Nec [10] ducunt arguicie sophistarum theologos [11] ad metam aliam, sed detegit eorum versuciam arundineam qua prius pompaverant; et hoc ex propriis eorum principiis.

What such men deny absolutely, I accept in a limited sense as catholic truth:

Unde frequenter, ut colores sapiencie sophistice minus appareant, obvio eis negando negativas, que ad sensum equivocum satis catholice concedi potuerunt [12]; ut, dando exclusivam huius

[1] tunc *add.* A B C. [2-2] quod . . . mobile *om.* O; quod est mobile C.
[3] est *om.* O. [4] responsionem B. [5] introductum esse *om.* B.
[6] pretermissis C. [7] invenit O. [8-8] introductatur O.
[9] omnis B. [10] nunc O. [11] theologum O. [12] poterunt O.

universalis—omnis res est mobilis,—formo sic exclusivam, ut apparencia[1] sophistica sit minus evidens—tantum res mobilis est res—quod est falsum pro rebus eternis. Concedi tamen posset quod nichil aliud quam mobile est res, accipiendo 'mobile' essencialiter substantive; et tamen aliud quam mobile est res, posito quod 'mobile' predicetur formaliter adiectivo. Sed Augustinus et alii sancti non curarunt de istis apparenciis sophistarum. Unde in Dialogo ad Felicianum, 'genuit, inquit, et non genuit Maria Filium Dei.'

as in the definition of 'res mobilis.'

Sed ulterius arguitur quod Verbum Dei non sit simpliciter mobile racione assumpti hominis. Nam nulla persona movetur propter habitum [2] vel accidens essencialiter separatum [2]: sed humanitas Christi est habitus Verbo Dei accidentaliter copulatus: ergo propter eius laceracionem[3] vel passionem non sequitur[4] passio Verbi Dei. Confirmatur triplici exemplo. Primo ex hoc quod homo non laceratur vel comburitur, etsi vestimenta eius taliter[5] paciantur. 2°. ex hoc quod humanitas conceditur per tempus notabile non fuisse: quando tamen non conceditur Verbum Dei conformiter non fuisse, non ergo sequitur—si ista humanitas movebatur post a non esse acquirendo essendi terminum,[6] tunc et Verbum—. 3°. confirmatur ex figura Abrahe patriarche, qui cum voluit
[A 90b] Gen. 22°. immolare[7] filium suum Ysaac, | non hunc occidit sed arietem, quem vidit post [8] tergum herentem [8] cornibus. Cum ergo passio Christi fuit per Ysaac allegorice figurata,
[C 73b] videtur quod non persona Christi, sed eius humanitas, | fuit passa.

Objection. The Word is not necessarily 'mobilis' because the humanity assumed by the Word is so. For the humanity is a 'habitus' or separable accident, and the 'passion' of the humanity is not necessarily the passion of the Word.

Threefold confirmation of this objection.

1. Injury to a man's clothes (vestimenta = habitus) does not imply injury to a man's person.

2. Transition from not-being to being on the part of the humanity does not imply a corresponding 'mobility' in the Word.

Gen. xxii. 13.

3. Not Isaac (i.e. the person of Christ) but the ram (i.e. the humanity) was offered by Abraham.

Hic dicitur quod non esset concedendum Verbum pati propter passionem sue humanitatis, nisi Verbum esset personaliter illa humanitas. Sed quia Verbum ex integro est illa humanitas tam secundum corpus quam secundum animam, et acciones ac passiones sunt primo suppositorum; patet quod illa humanitas non pateretur vel ageret,[9] nisi

Reply. If the humanity be not the Person of Christ, Christ did not suffer.

[1] evidencia A B C. [2-2] vel . . . separatum *om.* O. [3] accionem M
[4] est O. [5] tolite (totaliter) O. [6] t'im A B C; tm̄ O.
[7] ymolare A B C; ĩmolale O. [8-8] tergẽtẽ hereutẽ B. [9] ageretur C.

But the Word of God, even God himself, suffered.

quia Verbum, quod est eadem ypostasis vel persona, sic agit vel patitur. Firmiter itaque est tenendum quod Verbum Dei et per consequens Deus ipse pendebat dolens et passus in cruce, et sic de ceteris humanis actibus quos evangelium de Iesu prosequitur. | Et sic, licet humanitas Christi sit [B 137b] essencia, substancia, vel natura separata non conservative sed essencialiter a deitate, que Christus est; | non tamen [O 226b] sic separatur quin sit persona Christi.

Four senses of the word 'habitus' in Augustine on Phil. ii. 8, as—the acquisition 1. of truth,

Sed pro nomine 'habitus' est notandum quod 'habitus' quadrupliciter sumitur, ut exponit Augustinus 83 Questionum Questione 73ª, exponendo illud Apostoli ad Philipp. 2°. 'habitu inventus est ut homo.' Primo pro sapiencia, que est veritas, quam addiscimus, que manens[1] non mota movet animam, quam informat.

2. of food,

2°. pro alimentis habitis mutantibus corpus, quod nutriunt, et digestione mutatis. Omne quidem substanciale nobis adiacens, quod mutat et mutatur adiacendo subiecto, dicitur 'habitus' [2]huiusmodi: 'habitus'[2] quidem, quia denominat subiectum habere quod sibi accidentaliter adiacet.

3. of clothes which take shape from the wearer, (compare p. 119, l. 15.)
4. of things worn, which do not change their shape, as a ring.

3m. genus est quando habituata formantur a subiectis [3]habituatis †perfeccius quam quando membris aptata induuntur.†[3] 4m. genus habitus, ut anulus in digito. Omnia autem hec quatuor, cum[4] denominant substanciam habituari vel habere, dicuntur in predicacione secundum essenciam esse[5] 'habitus;' ut 'motus' dicitur materialiter esse res, que est motu dicto formaliter acquisita, ut patet 3°. Physicorum 9°· 4°. Sumitur autem sufficiencia illorum

Characteristics of these four kinds of 'habitus.'

quatuor penes hoc, quod primus habitus mutat substanciam cui advenit et[6] non mutatur; [7]secundus mutat et mutatur[7]; tercius mutatur et non mutat; quartus nec mutat necessario nec mutatur.

Besides these four senses, philosophers use 'habitus' in two other senses,

Sed preter hec quatuor, [8]que in se sunt[8] substancie, sumitur habitus apud philosophos formaliter ad duos[9] sensus

[1] movens A B C. [2–2] huiusmodi habitus *om.* O.
[3–3] habituatis quam quando membrum aptata induitur A B C; habituatis proficitur quam quando membris aptata induitur O; *lectionem superius in textu datam non sine dubitatione ipse conieci.* [4] cum *om.* B. [5] est O. [6] et *om.* O.
[7–7] secundus . . . mutatur *om.* O. [8–8] que non sunt A B C. [9] suos O.

equivocos. Primo pro qualitate preternaturali[1] de prima specie qualitatis; [2]sive sit[2] corporis habitus, ut sanitas; sive habitus anime, ut virtus intellectualis aut [3]moralis; habitus autem spiritualis ex habitu primo modo dicto[3] materialiter generatur, sicut[4] habitus corporalis efficitur ex secundo. Sed secundo modo sumitur habitus pro forma respectiva de 10°. genere, quod est habere, possessio, vel habicio, et talis habitus causatur ab habitu tercio et quarto modis materialiter intellectis: 'divicie' enim denominant homines divites,[5] possessionatos, vel habentes formaliter.

5 (a) for a *state* of body the result of (2): or of spirit the result of (1).

6 (b) to express the tenth Aristotelian category.

[C 74a] Et patet quod ille sex maneries habitus sunt | satis equivoce. Dicitur ergo quod humanitas assumpta a Verbo est habitus tercii modi, cum accidit enti in actu, non mutans vel faciens ipsam aliam personam quam prefuit. Ideo dicunt sancti quod humanitas est quasi vestis detegens deitatem;[6] et religiosi, qui Christum induunt, habent habitus[7] corporis; hoc notantes, quod[8] accidit Deo humanitas, sed non[9] inseparabiliter. Ideo dicit Augustinus in Dialogo ad Felicianum quod humanitas est accidens Verbo, non quod sit res inherens ut accidencia novem generum, cum sit precipua creata substancia; nec quod sit coëva Verbo vel sicut passio [A 90c] naturaliter consequens[10] ad subiectum; | sed contingenter ex tempore nobis ineffabiliter[11] inest Verbo non mutando naturam, cui advenit, sed formata[12] mirabiliter, quia Verbo Dei ydemptificata vel ypostatice copulata: cum secundum Augustinum primo De Trinitate, 'talis fuit unio[13] incarnacionis, que Deum faceret[14] hominem et hominem Deum.'

Of these six possible meanings, the Word's humanity resembles 'habitus' in the third: it is changed, but does not change the Word.

Explanation of the sense in which the humanity is an *accident* of the Word.

Et patet quod dicta humanitas est forma in tribus conveniens cum formis per se in genere accidentis. Primo in hoc quod presupponit naturam, cui contingenter advenit, longe priorem ipsa naturaliter, quam accidens presupponit creatam substanciam, quam informat. 2°. in hoc quod non facit

Three points in which the said humanity is *forma per se in genere accidentis.*
1. It presupposes a pre-existing nature which it 'informs.'

[1] passionali A B C; pr̄ iili O. [2-2] sumpsit O.
[3-3] moralis aut habitus specialis. Et ille ex habitu primo dicto A B C.
[4] sive A B. [5] divites *om.* A B C. [6] divinitatem O.
[7] habitum B. [8] quod *om.* C O. [9] non *om.* A B C.
[10] consequitur O. [11] ineflicabiliter O. [12] unita C.
[13] unionis A. [14] facere O.

2. It does not change that nature.
3. It cannot exist without the Word as its substance.

naturam, cui advenit, esse[1] quid vel aliud[2] quam absolute necessario semper erat.[3] Et 3°. quod non potest esse sine supposito Verbi Dei, cui inseparabiliter sed contingenter adheret. Et constat quod proprietates proporcionales analogice conveniunt generi accidentis: assimilatur autem passionibus, que dicuntur per se egredi de propriis principiis[4] subiectorum; cum non potest abesse, postquam infuit, cum inseparabiliter consequitur[5] ad Verbum, sicut passio ad subiectum; sed, sicut accidentia separabilia, deesse poterit a subiecto. Convenit 2°. cum accidentibus absolutis per se in genere, cum sit per se substancia motiva et mobilis denominans subiectum proprie et per se moveri formaliter. 3°. convenit[6] cum accidentibus respectivis. Nam, sicut relaciones, habitaciones, et respectus consimiles non exinde movent naturam, cui inherenter adveniunt; sic indubie 'forma servi,' que est humanitas, non potest movere naturam divinam, cum deitas solum denominacione respectiva denominatur ex eius adiacencia summe mirabili.[7]

The humanity is also *accidens absolutum per se in genere*.

Also *accidens respectivum*.

Convenit autem cum ceteris formis substancialibus[8] in his tribus. Primo quod facit suppositum, cui advenit, esse aliud quam prefuit; quia, postquam Verbum fuit pure deitas, nunc est homo. 2°. in hoc quod est idem ypostatice cum subiecto, cui advenit. Sicut generaliter omnis forma substancialis est idem essencialiter vel personaliter[9] cum subiecto forme et composito ex eisdem; sic, inquam, ista humanitas; cum sit eiusdem racionis cum aliis et idem personaliter Verbo Dei, licet Verbum commune sit natura divina, que non potest esse illa humanitas; | sed cum sit individuum humane nature [C 74c] homo Iesus Christus, suscipit saltem in predicacione et secundum essenciam predicata temporalia, que historia evangelica de Christo contexuit, ut post declarabitur. Et patet mira subtilitas in verbis Apostoli quando dicit 'habitu inventus ut homo': non enim video alium terminum, quo

Also *forma substantialis*:
1. because it changes the substance;
2. because it is one hypostatically with the subject;

[3. (?) as being 'habitus.']

The subtlety of St. Paul is shown

[1] esse *om.* A B C. [2] aliquid O. [3] erit A.
[4] principiis *om.* A B C. [5] cum non inseparabiliter consequitur verbum A B C.
[6] conveniunt B. [7] miracli O. [8] specialiter *add.* A C.
[9] personaliter *corr. altera manu* personali A.

[B 138a] posset apcius quoad auditorii intelleccionem, | copiosius quoad philosophicam consideracionem, aut expressius quoad fidei explanacionem, humanitatem Christi exprimere. Ideo respectu [1] sentencie Apostoli, qui fuit prudentissimus predicator, et Augustini sui discipuli, qui fuit scripture sacre subtilissimus explanator, oportet nos ignaros colla mentis submittere.

*In using this expression 'habitus' of the humanity of Christ.*

Quantum ad primam trium confirmacionum [2] patet quod [O 226c] similitudo | non est sufficiens [3]; cum humanitas Christi non solum sit ut vestimentum Verbo, vel [4] ignis ferro, [4] sed vera Christi quiditas, idem personaliter cum subiecto. Ad 2am negatur consequencia quod mocio, passio, et similia positiva, cum sint predicata personalia, sunt [5] persone Verbi [6] racione forme assumpte [6] principaliter tribuenda. Non sic autem negaciones, que non sunt predicata personalia. Ideo [A 90d] dixi superius | quod incepcio non est esse et prius non fuisse, sed causatur ex illis; cum stat illa esse eterna et incepcionem solum instantaneam, et faciens incepcionem non potest facere dictam negacionem. Ideo non oportet, si Deus temporaliter generatur, quod ante [7] non fuit; cum satis est quod sit illud ex vi generacionis, quod non effectualiter fuit ante. Ad 3am patet quod non oportet in toto esse correspondenciam figurati cuiuslibet ad figuram. Unde satis est quod Abraham ducens filium significet Deum Patrem, qui de facto duxit et obtulit super montem Calvarie filium suum unigenitum, sicut Ysaac unigenitus imolatus [8] est super montem ubi templum constitutum est. Ipse quidem fuit forma risus domini nostri Iesu Christi: et satis est quod humanitas idem personaliter Ysaac nostro, sicut aries est idem genere cum Ysaac figurante, [9] sic passa et occisa persona Verbi secundum deitatem et animam semper salva; et sic de aliis, quo huic loco non pertinet [10] applicare. Sed constat repugnare figure quod sit in toto conformitas; quia tunc evidenter

*Reply to confirmation 1 (p. 117, l. 16);*

*to confirmation 2 (p. 117, l. 18);*

*[reference to p. 99.]*

*to confirmation 3 (p. 117, l. 22).*

[1] rtl O. [2] confirmacionum *om. cum lacuna* C.
[3] efficiens C. [4] [4] vitus fio O. [5] sint A B C.
[6] assumpte racione forme A B C. [7] alꝛ (aliquando) B; autem O.
[8] ymo locus C. [9] fugurante O. [10] pertineut A B C.

sequeretur[1] Christi mobilitas; cum Ysaac portavit ligna sicut Christus crucem, ligatus est super[2] struem, sicut Christus affixus est ad crucem. Igitur cum Ysaac noster ex partibus[3] quantitativis componitur, que tam[4] varie movebantur: et, mota parte tocius, movetur et totum, cuius est pars; sequitur quod Christus compositus ex illis partibus movebatur. Nec credo[5] philosophum dicere Deum esse hominem, nisi consequenter dicat eum componi ex partibus, et consequenter moveri ad motum progressivum parcium[6]; [7]cum impossibile sit aliquid non moveri, quod tamen subiective habeat in se motum.[7] Unde Ieronimus exponendo fidem catholicam: 'passus est, inquit, Dei Filius | non putative sed vere.' Et [C 75a] idem docet Augustinus in Enchiridion 40: et Decretalis in Clementinis De Summa Trinitate et Fide Catholica: 'confitemur, inquit, Filium Dei, una cum Patre eternaliter subsistentem, partes nostre nature simul unitas, ex quibus ipse verus Deus in se existens fieret[8] verus homo, (humanum videlicet[9] corpus et animam intellectivam seu racionalem, ipsum corpus vere et per se et essencialiter informantem,) assumpsisse ex tempore in virginali thalamo ad unitatem sue ypostasis[10] seu persone: et quod in hac assumpta natura ipsum Dei Verbum pro omni operanda salute non solum affigi cruci et in ea mori voluit, sed eciam emisso iam spiritu perforari lancea sustinuit latus suum.'

The assertion that God is man implies the mobility of Christ.

In Jerome, Augustine and the Clementine Decretal, the Catholic doctrine is clearly stated.

Ecce primo univocacio[11] Christi cum fratribus [12]propter conveniencium[12] in natura specifica.

Ecce 2°. vera passio Iesu Christi.

Et 3°. cum passus sit et mortuus, sequitur quod fuit homo pro illo triduo.

1. Christ is one with his brethren by his agreement with them in a specific nature.
2. He truly suffered.
3. He was man in the three days' entombment.

[1] sequitur A B C. [2] ad A B C. [3] nostris *add.* A B C.
[4] tu (tamen) B. [5] credo *om.* B. [6] per totum C.
[7–7] cum . . . motum *om.* B. [8] foret O. [9] scilicet B.
[10] ypostatice A B C. [11] unicō (unicio ?) O.
[12] propter convenienciam specificam (*sic*) A; propter pm (propriam *an* primam?) convenienciam O.

## Cap. VIII.

[*Obicit tripliciter contra ydemptitatem specificam Christi cum aliis, et dissolvit.*

*Examination of three objections to the statement that Christ is man in the same sense of the word as other men :* i.e. *that Christ is of the same* species *as other men.*]

Ex istis patet solucio argumentorum factorum communiter ad probandum quod Christus non sit univoce homo cum aliis. Primo per hoc, quod nichil reponitur in specie per aliquod sibi accidentale: sed humanitas Christi est sibi accidentalis: ergo non est in nova specie propter illam: sed ante incarnacionem non fuit eiusdem speciei nobiscum: ergo nec[1] post propter[2] adventiciam unionem. Confirmatur per locum a simili. Nam si homo de novo acquirat albedinem vel quamcumque formam aliam accidentaliter[3] inherentem, non ex hoc[4] est disparis speciei: ergo per idem nec Christus propter humanitatem tam adventiciam.

Principal Objection I. Nothing is in a species owing to some accident belonging to it: humanity is only an accident of Christ: he is not therefore, through the incarnation, in the human species. Confirmatory instance.

Quantum ad illud patet ex dictis quod falsum assumitur. [A91a] Nam Verbum, quod prius erat super omnem speciem, per | assumpcionem humanitatis factum est in nostra specie et 'sub lege.' Et quantum ad similitudinem[5] patet ex dictis racionis diversitas. Si enim per impossibile albedo vel alia forma inherens esset illud, quo subiectum esset aliquid vel aliud quam prius fuerat, [6](sicut humanitate fit Verbum aliquid aliud quam prius fuerat),[6] procederet racio per locum a simili: sed antecedens est impossibile.

Reply. The Word before the incarnation was above every species, by the incarnation is in our species. The instance does not apply.

Et si multiplicentur argumenta sophistica ad probandum quod, quicquid est Verbum, eternaliter fuit Verbum; patet ex dictis de formis solucio. Nam aliquid, quia aliqua

Subsidiary arguments to support objection. 1. Whatever is the Word, eternally was the Word (comp. p. 114, l. 2).

[1] nec *om.* O. [2] propter *om.* O. [3] accidenter O. [4] exinde O. [5] consimilitudinem O. [6-6] ( ) *om.* AB; sic humanitatem fit verbum aliquod aliud quam fuerat prius C.

*Reply. The substantial form or nature of man,*

*John i. 14. Gal. iv. 4.*

*(but not any supposite, hypostasis, or person of man)*

*is the Word since the incarnation:*

forma substancialis vel natura,[1] nunc est Verbum, quod non in primo instanti temporis erat Verbum. Non enim antequam 'Verbum caro factum est' 'in plenitudine temporis,' erat homo; et certum[2] est quod esse hominem est esse aliquid: ideo quando fiebat homo, fiebat aliquid,[3] quod prius non fuerat. | Verumptamen omne suppositum, ypostasis, vel [B 138b] persona, que est, vel que[4] fuit, Verbum, eternaliter erat[5] Verbum. Sed absit ex isto concludere—ergo quicquid.[6] Aliud enim, sed[7] non alius, est Verbum post incarnacionem quam prefuit.[8] Et sic querenti—Quis est[9] nunc Filius Dei, | [C 75b] qui non semper erat?—Idem[10]—dicitur: quod nullus[11] est vel esse potest Filius Dei naturalis, nisi[12] qui absolute necessario semper erat. Sed querenti—Quid est Filius Dei, quod ante incarnacionem ipse non fuerat?—dicitur quod—Natura humana sive humanitas; et illa est quiditas suppositi vel persone—.

*2. Whatever is the Word, is the Person of the Word.*

*Reply. This involves a confusion between quiditas and qualitas, between substance and person.*

*3. If the humanity is the Word and the Word was in the beginning, the humanity in the beginning was the Word.*

*Reply. This involves a confusion between humanity abstract and man concrete.*

*4. If only this thing (i.e. the person of the Word) is now the Word, and eternally was the Word;*

Et patet solucio ad tales argucias—Omnis[13] persona, que est Verbum, eternaliter erat Verbum: sed quicquid iam est[14] Verbum est persona, que est Verbum: ergo, quicquid iam est Verbum,[15] eternaliter erat Verbum. Omnes quidem deducciones tales sophistice sanantur[16] per noticiam fallacie accidentis. Nam persone Verbi accidentalis est quidi|tas in [O 226d] genere, sicut substancie create accidentalis est qualitas.

Et si 3°. sic arguatur[17]—Hoc Verbum in principio erat Verbum, et hoc Verbum est hec humanitas; ergo hec humanitas in principio erat Verbum—patet quod idem est ac si sic argueretur—In principio fuit, quod hoc est Verbum; et hoc Verbum est ille homo; ergo tunc fuit, quod ipsum est homo; sic enim significat humanitas simpliciter abstractive.

Et si 4°. sophista replicet per conversionem ab exclusivis aut exceptivis—Tantum hoc nunc est Verbum—demonstrando personam Verbi—et hoc eternaliter erat Verbum;

[1] ᵘm (materia) O. [2] iterum O. [3] aliud O. [4] que *om.* A B C.
[5] fuit A B C. [6] quicquam *om.* ergo A B; quod quitquam C. [7] et A B C.
[8] ante A B C. [9] esset B. [10] eidem A B C. [11] erat *add.* B.
[12] non qui B. [13] omnes persona O. [14] est *om.* O.
[15] et *add.* A B C. [16] sonantur O. [17] arguitur A; obicitur B.

ergo nichil iam est Verbum, nisi quod eternaliter erat Verbum—constat quod antecedens est verum et consequens falsum. Licet enim tantum hoc sit Verbum, non tamen tantum ista humanitas est Verbum: cum deitas,[1] que est aliud quam illa humanitas, est Verbum et[2] eternaliter erat Verbum. Et patet quod, licet tantum homo et tantum Deus sit Verbum, non tantum humanitas, nec nichil preter deitatem est Verbum. Nam aliud quam deitas et aliud quam humanitas est Verbum; sed nec alius nec aliud quam Deus vel homo est Verbum. Si enim tantum deitas esset Iesus, tunc Pater in divinis non esset aliqualiter[3] maior Iesu. Et constat quomodo exclusive ac exceptive sint suis universalibus adaptande; ut sic dicto—omnis Iesus est humanitas—[4] licet correspondenter dare istam[4] exclusivam—tantum persona, que est humanitas, est Iesus—et proporcionaliter exceptivam et non conformissimam[5] sophisticacionem contingit habere de quolibet alio homine, qui per se est homo, sed adventicie natura corporea.[6] Unde quilibet nostrum in finali resurreccione erit aliud quam erat[7] in morte, quia alia natura; cum in resurreccione erit tam natura corporea quam natura incorporea; in morte autem dumtaxat natura incorporea. Sed non erit alius: ymo solummodo [A91b] idem ipse, cum non potest esse nisi eadem persona. |

nothing is now the Word, but what eternally was the Word.

Reply. The antecedent is admitted to be true, the consequent is false.

The error arises from mishandling exclusive and exceptive propositions.

A change of nature does not necessitate a change of person.

Death and resurrection change our nature; but we each remain the same and 'not another.'

Et illam methaphisicam intexuit[8] ille magnus philosophus sanctus Iob 19 ca°. quando dixit; 'in carne mea videbo Deum salvatorem meum, ego ipse, inquit, et non alius.' Unde Gregorius 18 Moralium ca°. 32. 'Quamvis Christus sit aliud ex Patre aliud ex matre, [9]non tamen est alius ex Patre alius ex virgine: sed ipse eternus ex Patre, temporaliter ex matre[9]; [10]ipse, qui fecit, factus[10]; ipse auctor operis, ipse opus auctoris; manens unus ex utraque et [11]in utraque natura[12]; nec naturarum[11] copulacione confusus,

Job xix. 26-27.

So Gregory maintains the diversity of natures but identity of person in Christ;

[1] divinitas O *ut saepe infra*. [2] et *om.* O. [3] a'q^co (aliquo modo) B.
[4-4] habet correspondenter istam O.
[5] non *om.* A B C; ꝯformiſſia) O. [6] nature corporee A B C.
[7] erit O. [8] texuit A B C. [9-9] non . . . matre *om.* B.
[10-10] ipse qui fecit ipse qui factus est A B C.
[11-11] in utramque natura nec naturam O. [12] natura *om.* A B C.

nec naturarum distinccione geminatus.'[1] Ecce aliud sancti doctoris testimonium [2]de sentencia supradicta.[2] Et sic intelligendus est Augustinus in Dialogo ad Felicianum circa medium et alibi | crebrius, quando dicit: 'quamvis enim [C 76a] aliud corpus, aliud animus, unus tamen atque idem homo et corpus dicitur et animus.'

*and so also Augustine.*

*Principal Objection II. Christ has not identity in species with other men, since he is man only per accidens they per se.*

2°. principaliter arguitur contra ydemptitatem specificam Christi cum aliis ex hoc quod[3] ipse solum per accidens et quilibet alius per se est homo.

*Reply. The accident by which Christ is formally man is of the same kind as the forms by which his brethren are formally men, and not an accident simply. Christ is man per se. The term 'Christ' expresses two forms, deity and humanity.*

Sed patet ex dictis quod non sequitur. Cum illud accidens, quo Christus est homo formaliter, quod Apostolus vocat [4]humanitacionem et habitum,[4] sit eiusdem racionis cum formis, quibus confratres Christi sunt homines formaliter, et non est accidens simpliciter. Sed quia Christus est gigas gemine substancie, scilicet, deitas et humanitas, quarum inferior contingenter inest superiori; ideo dicitur[5] humanitas ad sensum expositum accidens Verbo Dei. Et si queritur[6] utrum Christus[7] sit per se homo, videtur michi quod sic. Nam cum 'Christus' dicit duas formas, scilicet deitatem et humanitatem,[8] ydemptificatas[9] in eadem persona, et potest supponere simpliciter pro utraque: patet quod, intelligendo eum secundum humanitatem, ipse eque per se est homo sicut aliquod[10] individuum sui generis; cum eque vere causatur[11] ex partibus qualitativis et quiditativis consimilis racionis, et eque dependet a corpore et anima a specie et genere cum suis differenciis, sicut Petrus. Nec est color, si Christus sit per accidens homo quia secundum deitatem, quod non sit per se homo: [12]quia extra deitatem est humanitas Christi, que est per se homo,[12] cum de sua essencia sit universalis[13] humanitas. Et ita sicut duplici nativitate nascitur Verbum Dei, sic videtur michi quod duplici

[1] genitus O. [2-2] de sēia sepe dicta A B C; de sīīa sepe dicta O. [3] quod *om.* A B C. [4-4] humanitatem et hominem A B C. [5] debet B. [6] queratur A B C. [7] Iesus A B C. [8] que sunt *add.* A B C. [9] ydemptitas *codd. omn.* [10] aliquid O. [11] causantur O. [12-12] quia . . . homo *om.* C; quia extra deitatem est ~~ho~~ humanitas Christi que est *etc.* A; quia extra deitatem est homo humanitas Christi que est *etc.* B; quia extra deitatem est humanitas Christi qui est *etc.* O. [13] illius A B C.

racionalitate[1] satis equivoce est [2] ipsum racionale. Nam [2] [B 139a] quoad creatam substanciam causatur[3] ab hu | manitate et racionalitate[1] communi sicut alie creature: et hinc competit sibi primus modus predicandi per se ex 2°. posteriorum.

Et quoad diffiniciones hominum dico quod nunquam inventa est a philosophis aliqua probabilis diffinicio sive descripcio hominis, quin illa univoce conveniat Iesu nostro. Est enim animal racionale mortale ante passionem, sicut veteres describebant hominem integrum [4] secundum noticiam imperfectam, quam de ipso habuerant,[5] quos [4] sequitur Augustinus in De Qualitate[6] Anime ca°.[7]: est iterum racionalis substancia ex corpore et anima composita tam post resurreccionem quam ante; sicut Augustinus describit hominem perfectum 15°. De Trinitate ca°. 7°.: est tercio anima racionalis habens corpus ab instanti sue concepcionis et ulterius in eternum. Et sic loquitur Augustinus de homine ut[8] ad personam attinet, Ome. 19,[9] exponens illud Ioh. 5. 'Potestatem dedit ei iudicium facere, quia filius hominis est.' 'Ex virgine, inquit, Maria homo factus est filius hominis; sed hanc potestatem temporalem faciendi iudicium non haberet, nisi acciperet[10] et esset homo prius sine hac potestate. Sed ipse filius hominis, qui et Filius Dei: herendo[11] enim ad unitatem persone filius [12] hominis Filius [12] Dei facta est una persona eadem Filius Dei et [C 76b] [A 91c] filius hominis. | Quid autem | [13] propter quid habeat,[13] dinoscendum est. Filius hominis habet animam, habet corpus: Filius Dei, quod est Verbum Dei, habet animam,[14] tanquam anima habens corpus; et sicut anima habens corpus non facit duas personas sed unum hominem, [15] sic Verbum habens [O 227a] hominem [15] non facit duas personas | sed unum Christum.' Et sequitur. 'Quid est homo? anima racionalis habens

No definition of 'man' fails to suit Jesus.

1. He was before his passion *animal racionale mortale.*

2. He is both before and since his resurrection *racionalis substancia ex corpore et anima composita.*

3. He is since his conception *anima racionalis habens corpus.*

John v. 27.

These definitions proved to apply to Christ by Augustine,

[1] racionabilitate A B C. [2]–[2] ipsum homo. Nam. B.
[3] cãtur *vix per rasuras distingui potest in* A; creatur B.
[4]–[4] secundum . . . quos *in margine* O. [5] habuerunt A; habuerat C.
[6] quantitate A B C. [7] *numerus in omn. codd. om.* [8] aut C. [9] 9 A B C.
[10] nisi per accepcionem O. [11] attendendo A B C. [12] filio . . . filio A B C.
[13] ꝑꝑr (proporcionaliter) habeat A C; p̈biliter (probabiliter) *om.* habeat B.
[14] *Nonne* hominem *legendum*? [15]–[15] sic . . . hominem *om.* O.

corpus. Quid est Christus? Verbum Dei habens hominem.' Ex istis [1] patet quod supradicta sentencia est [1] beati Augustini et Hugonis de Sancto Victore cum aliis; scilicet, quod omnis homo est anima vel spiritus habens corpus. Et credo quod non est possibile hominem completum esse, nisi habeat tempore suo corpus: quia nisi assit corpus organicum, anima non creatur. Unde et Christus habuit corpus in triduo.

and by Hugo de St. Victore.

A soul is never created unless there be an organic body.

4. And no less does Grosseteste's definition of 'man' on

Quod si 4°. volumus [2] describere hominem in sua communitate maxima, patet quod Christus fuit univoce homo cum aliis: cum hec descripcio hominis communissima sit superior ad descripcionem triplicem supradictam. Pro quo notandus est Lincolniensis in suo Exameron de opere sexto diei, qui post exposicionem huius—[3] 'Faciamus hominem ad ymaginem et similitudinem nostram' [3]—sic scribit: 'Quid autem sit homo, ex hic cognitis et auditis diffiniamus: [4] non enim egemus mutuari [4] diffiniciones alienas. 'Homo, inquit, est creatura racionalis, facta ad ymaginem conditoris.' [5] Unde exponens illud Gen. 2°. 'spiravit in faciem eius spiraculum vite,' ita scribit: 'Deus verbo [6] beneplaciti [7] spiraculum vite id est, animam racionalem formavit, et [7] in unitatem persone corpori formando infudit.' Et sequitur: 'per hoc, quod "homo factus est in animam viventem," notatur quod homo interior est homo, et corrupto homine exteriori nichilo minus manet veritas et personalitas uniuscuiusque hominis in subsistencia hominis interioris; quod ex verbis Domini satis insinuatur, cum dicit Matt. 22°. "Ego sum Deus Abraham, Deus Ysaac, et Deus Iacob: non est Deus mortuorum sed vivencium."' Hec Lincolniensis. Quamvis enim Christus sit Deus mortuorum prima morte, non tamen est Deus obiective beatificans mortuos secunda morte. Et hoc sonat *theos* in uno sensu. Cum autem Deus tempore Moysi particulariter dixit se esse Deum illorum patriarcharum

Gen. i. 26.

*creatura racionalis facta ad ymaginem conditoris* apply to Christ.

Explanation of Gen. ii. 2, '*man became a living soul.*' This soul, the inner man (comp. p. 19, l. 1), is the abiding personality,

as in Matth. xxii. 32.

God (Deus Θεός) is in the same sense God both of dead and living.

[1-1] patet supradicta sentencia que est A B C.
[2] voluerimus C.
[3-3] faciamus hô etc. B.
[4-4] non negemus mutuari A B C; non enim egemus mutari O.
[5] auditoris O.
[6] verbo *om.* A B C.
[7-7] spiraculum . . . et *om.* O; in *om.* A B C.

non solum pro lapso tempore cum hodie non daret Moysi evidenciam ad credendum Deum tunc velle iuvare semen eorum; non mirum si isto argumento Salvator imposuit silencium Saduceis de negacione resurreccionis mortuorum. Cum enim ipsi perpetuo vixerant in spiritu, nec desiderium naturale ad naturam corpoream extingui poterat[1]; sequitur quod sancti patriarche non ab hoc perpetuo finaliter sint frustrandi, licet secundum quid mortui sint ad tempus. Alii autem presciti mortui sunt simpliciter morte perpetua; et ista est exposicio beati Augustini Ome. 43. super illud Ioh. 8: 'Si quis sermonem meum servaverit, mortem non gustabit in eternum.'

It is the term 'dead' which has two senses, according as it is applied to those *mortui secundum quid ad tempus*, or to those *mortui morte perpetua*.

John viii. 51.

Nec est negandum a sic dicentibus quin angeli sint [C 77a] *homines*, iuxta testimonium | scripturarum. [2]Quod si obicitur scripturam dicere[2] angelos esse *viros*, et per consequens pari auctoritate concedendum esset fore distinccionem sexuum angelorum. Sed sic arguens non recolit quod 'vir' notat etatem, formam, sexum,[3] probitatem. Concedendum est ergo sine distinccione sexuum omnem creaturam racionalem virentem virtutibus *virum* esse. Unde Ierem.[4] 31. dicitur significanter de beata virgine involvendo[5] Christum duplici matricula, 'femina circumdabit virum'; non quod tunc fuit [B 139b] vir forma corporis vel etate, sed quia omni genere | caris- [A 91d] matum tunc pollebat[6]; vel quia[7] boni angeli | sic virtutibus semper virent,[8] non [9]mirum si[9] scriptura sine implicacione[10] distinccionis sexuum verissime tales angelos vocet 'viros.'

Angels may be called *homines*; even *viri*:

but the latter term need not imply distinction of sex, but as in Jerem. xxxi. 22. *vir* so applied means a being *virtutibus virens*.

Sed ulterius non est negandum quin Christus habet racionem equivocam individuantem, secundum quam est Iesus, que non potest alteri individuo convenire. Aliter enim non esset essenciale principium generis[11] Christiani, nisi in eo quod esset proprietatum collacio addita nature specifice per

Although in species a man Jesus is individualized by properties added to his specific nature,

[1] poterit A B C.
[2–2] quod si obicitur dicere A C; quod obicitur dicere B; et si obicitur scripturam dicere O.
[3] sexuum O.
[4] Ezech. A B C.
[5] inoluen (*an pro* involvente ?) O.
[6] possidebat O.
[7] ergo *add.* O.
[8] vivunt super A B C; semper vivunt O; virent *ex ipso textu paulo superius inventum restitui.*
[9–9] nimirum B.
[10] multiplicacione A B C.
[11] ergo A B C.

which other individuals of the species have not; so Anselm.

But this fact does not necessitate a difference in species.

quam individualiter a singulis aliis distinguitur: ut dicit Anselmus in De Incarnacione 7°., 'Quis alius, queso, est Deus et homo, et[1] ex illis principiis individuantibus temporaliter procreatus,[2] ex quibus efficitur noster Iesus?' [3]Sed procul hoc ad inferendum[3] diversitatem specificam, quia per idem omnia que individualiter distinguuntur different[4] specifice.

Principal Objection III. Christ is not an individual or person in the same sense as other men; because his personality is eternal; other men's is created. If he has also a created personality, he is two persons, and the Nestorian heresy is true.

Tercio principaliter arguitur quod Christus non sit univoce homo cum aliis eo quod non est univoce cum alio homine individuum vel persona. Nam solum personalitate[5] eterna est persona[6]; et illa in nullo univoce[7] convenit cum personalitate creata: ergo Christus non est univoce persona cum alia creatura. Maior patet ex hoc quod aliter, sicut dixit Nestorius, esset in ipso[8] duplicitas personarum, quia una personalitas eterna et alia temporalis: nec[9] dubium quin, si multiplicantur raciones personales multiplicabuntur et persone; quia unius persone una tantum est racio personalis.[10] Et patet minor [11]argumenti ex hoc quod non est maior[11] conveniencia, imo tanta differencia inter personalitatem eternam et quamlibet aliam temporalem [12]sicut et inter essenciam eternam et quamlibet aliam temporalem[12]: sed quelibet essencia eterna[13] non convenit eciam in esse univoce cum alia temporali: ergo per idem nec personalitas.

Reply. Granted that in Christ *personality* is not spoken of in literally the same sense as in other men; it does not follow that *nature* and *species* in Christ are not the same as in other men.

Hic videtur michi probabile quod personalitas Christi sit equivoca vel analogica[14] cum personalitate cuiuscunque alterius fratris sui; et tamen conveniunt summe univoce [15]in specie vel natura. Ideo non sequitur, si Christus non sit univoce[15] cum alio homine individuum vel persona, quod exinde non sit cum isto univoce species vel natura: quia notum est quod univocacio in superiori non arguit univocacionem in inferiori; nec equivocacio inferioris arguit

[1] et *om.* C. [2] procreatus *om.* A B C. [3] licet procul hoc sit ad ferendum O.
[4] different *in rasura alter. man.* A; indifferenter B. [5] personalitas A B C.
[6] Christi *add.* A B C. [7] equivoco A. [8] Christo A B C.
[9] ut O. [10] personalitas C. [11–11] argumenti . . . maior *om.* O; quod *om.* C.
[12–12] sicut . . . temporalem *om.* A B C. [13] eternaliter O.
[14] analoga A B C; ana^{ga} O. [15–15] in specie . . . univoce *bis* O.

For ambiguity in a lower term (person), does not necessarily involve ambiguity in a higher term (species).

equivocacionem communiorum,[1] ut evidet in exemplo.[2] Nam omnia creata per se[3] in genere diverso[4] per differencias [O 227b] opposita univocantur | in genere et non citra; ut substancia [C 77b] et accidens univocantur | quodammodo in analogo transcendente, homo et asinus in genere animalis, et ita de aliis: ydiotes[5] eciam et Hercules equivocantur in signo hominis, et tamen univocantur in genere corporis sive[6] substancie: correspondenter Iesus et Petrus equivocantur in signo[7] personalitatis et tamen univocantur in specie hominis, et in quolibet creato genere plus communi: quia correspondenter, ut aliquid est communius, magis[8] univocat; et ut particularius, sic et minus: in tantum quod persona vel individuum non potest univocare secum personam aliam; ut persona Verbi non potest assumere quamlibet personam hominis, sicut nec aliquam, quia tunc persona esset summe communicabilis. Univocacio enim realis de qua nunc[9] [est] sermo, est quando aliqua secundum eandem racionem communicant vel conveniunt in communi; ut quelibet persona hominis est eadem communis species que est *homo* sub illa communi racione—*creatura racionalis ad ymaginem Dei facta*—persona autem hominis equivoce communicatur naturis[10] oppositis, cum alia sit racio vel individuandi condicio, que est hoc [A 92a] corpus, et alia racio vel individuandi condicio, que est hic | spiritus. Et sic intelligunt illi qui dicunt personam descriptive esse [11]naturam racionalem[11] incommunicabilis [12]essencie vel[12] existencie. Nec[13] est negandum quin sub eisdem signis licet equivoce analogicatur tam increata personalitas quam creata; ut quelibet persona divina est racionalis nature individua substancia, et quelibet persona hominis est raciocionalis nature [14]individua substancia; sed nature[14] sunt multum equivoce tam racionales quam essencie[15] vel nature:

The definition of *personality* is applicable to both divine and human personalities; but in senses which are different although analogous.

[1] ɔ'orꝑ A B C; coĩo4 *pr. man.* coĩorũ *in margine altera manu* O.
[2] Christo A B C; ex° *pr. man. et alt man. in marg.* O.
[3] p^c^ (*i.e.* persone) B.
[4] diviso O.
[5] ydolum A B O; ydiolos (*sic*) C.
[6] sue A B C.
[7] specie A B C.
[8] generalius A B C.
[9] modo B C; nobis O, est *supplendum censeo.*
[10] personis B.
[11–11] naturalem racionalem O.
[12] essencie vel *om.* O.
[13] nunc O.
[14–14] individua . . . nature *om.* O.
[15] encia O.

Petrus eciam est multum equivoce substancia vel individuum respectu persone alterius increate. Sed utrobique est racio creata exemplata analogice in racione superiori eiusdem nominis increata. Ideo laboraverunt priores doctores ad habendum in suis descripcionibus nomina significancia simul licet equivoce tam exemplaria eterna quam eciam exemplata; ut veritas, iusticia, liberum arbitrium; et persona analogicatur[1] secundum Anselmum[2] et Boecium sub istis nominibus.

*Person* is among the terms used in an ambiguous sense by Anselm and Boethius.

Sed obicitur primo per hoc quod Christus est individuum speciei humane, et preter hoc est individuum nature divine: ergo est duplex individuum [3]sicut est duplex[3] natura.[4]

Counter objections to Reply. (1.) If Christ be an individual of the human species, and besides an individual of the divine nature; he is a twofold individual.

Hic dicitur negando consequenciam sicut non sequitur, si Christus sit Filius Dei et filius hominis, quod sit duplex filius; idem enim est individuum nature | humane et nature [B 140a] divine, sed per accidens individuum nature humane, quia secundum naturam assumptam, per se autem individuum, persona, vel suppositum nature divine.

Answer. Christ is son of God and son of man, but not a twofold son. He is *per accidens* an individual of the human nature; *per se* an individual of divine nature.

2°. obicitur per hoc quod universale et singulare dicuntur ad aliquid et per consequens sunt simul natura: sed Christus solum temporaliter est universale: ergo solum temporaliter est singulare; et per consequens aliqua individuatio solum temporaliter inest Christo.

Counter objection (2). It is only in time that Christ has individuation: for *universal* or *singular* cannot be predicated of a divine person.

Hic conceditur prima conclusio. Nam singulare et[5] universale sunt res secunde intencionis que sese mutuo relative respiciunt ita, quod | singulare, ut[6] sic, sit indi- [C 78a] viduum vel suppositum speciei. Ideo nulla persona divina est ad illum sensum[7] quoad deitatem universalis vel singularis, ut patet in De Questionibus Veteris et Nove Legis. Questione 122; sed est[8] individuum suppositum vel persona, Cum ista sint nomina significancia analogice extra genus, ut patet de nomine individui in[9] descripcione Boecii De Persona. Nec est vis[10] quare philosophi sic varie utuntur

Answer. Granted that *singular* (or *universal*) cannot be predicated of a divine person in regard to that person's divinity, since it implies *species*; yet the same objection does not apply to individuality or personality, and

[1] analoga B.
[2] Augustinum ABC; aūs & boy^m O.
[3-3] sicut est duplex *om.* ABC.
[4] nature ABC.
[5] et *om.* B.
[6] ut *om.* ABC.
[7] sensum *om.* C.
[8] est *om.* ABC.
[9] et O.
[10] vis *om.* C.

nominibus. Sicut ergo Christus solum ex tempore est singularis, sic quod singularitas a posteriori accidit suo[1] individuitati vel personalitati, sicut accidit sibi quod sit persona speciei humane: ideo individuitas vel personalitas in Christo non est singularitas que supponitur speciei.

It does not follow that individuality and personality cannot be predicated of Christ.

3°. instatur per hoc quod Christus, quia iste homo, vel in quantum iste homo, est suppositum, individuum vel[2] persona; ergo ista singularis humanitas est causa personalitatis in Christo, sicut est in suis fratribus, et non est causa personalitatis eterne: ergo est causa personalitatis temporalis: ergo in Christo est duplex personalitas, sicut[3] duplex nativitas.

Counter objection (3). The fact that Christ is a definite man makes him a supposite, individual or person: that definite singular humanity is the cause of his personality in time: which added to his existing personality in eternity, makes in Christ a twofold personality.

Hic negatur causalis assumpta eo quod significat circumstanciam cause.[4] Conceditur tamen de Christo vel aliis quod, quia est iste homo, ideo est persona hominis: sed non, quia persona hominis, ideo est persona; cum habet personalitatem nature superioris quam est eius[5] humanitas, quod nulli alii homini potest competere; cum ipse solus[6] sit homo per accidens et cum hoc summe univoce. Est autem in Christi duplex nativitas, una eterna secundum naturam divinam, que eternaliter absolute necessario personaliter nascitur et est natus; et illi accidit alia temporalis non interpellatim[7] sed simul adveniens, secundum quam fuit natura alia et noviter persona hominis. Non enim sequitur—Christus solum temporaliter vel noviter est persona, in- [A 92b] dividuum, vel suppositum humanum: | [8]ergo sic est suppositum[8]—cum arguitur ab inferiori ad suum superius cum impedimento habente vim negacionis.

Answer. The fact that Christ is a definite man is not the cause, only a circumstance, of his personality. He has a twofold nativity, not a twofold personality.

4°. obicitur per hoc quod Christus recenter est tam corpus quam anima, et utrumque illorum est suppositum et persona: ergo Christus recenter est suppositum vel persona: [9]sic enim Christus[9] est corpus et spiritus creatus:

Counter objection (4). Christ at a point in time (*recenter*) is both body and spirit, either of which is a supposite and a person, and those created ones:

[1] sūi A; sui C.  [2] et C O.  [3] et *add.* B.
[4] cause *om.* O.  [5] 9is (*i.e.* communis) O.  [6] solum A B C.
[7] interpolatim A B C.
[8–8] ergo sic suppositum A; ergo sit suppositum B C.
[9–9] sequitur cum quod Christus A B C.

Christ is therefore a created person, and therefore has a twofold personality.

sed utrumque illorum est per se individuum et persona: ergo Christus est persona creata: et cum eciam sit persona increata, sequitur quod duplex personalitas inest Christo.

Answer. Christ did not become a person through taking nature of body and spirit. His personation is unique: in every created person accidental properties are the cause of individuality; Christ is a person *per se*.

Hic dicitur quod antecedens primi argumenti est verum et consequens impossibile. Nec est verum quod aliqua creatura preter Christum est primo per se suppositum vel persona; quia in omni persona creata proprietates accidentales individuant ipsam; et sic idem est sibi personalitas et singularitas que ad ipsam consequitur, sicut passio ad subiectum: Christus autem solum personatur per se primo [1]ex divinitate,[1] et non ex proprietatibus accidentalibus ut alia singularia. Ideo non mirum, si sua personalitas recipit singularitates personarum,[2] ut sibi accidencia, et non ut personalitates. Due ergo nature create eciam in sancto sabato sunt simul utraque eadem persona Verbi. Si ergo persona esset per se superius | ad istam naturam, sicut [C 78b] aliquid est ad *hominem*, tunc sequeretur[3]—si Christus est hoc singulare creatum, [4]tunc est ista persona creata—; sicut sequitur, quod Christus[5] sit aliquid creatum,[4] ex hoc quod est natura creata; et tunc foret duplex persona creata, | [O 227c] sicut est duplex natura creata, quarum utraque est persona.

As every other man is *aliquid* before he is *homo*, so Christ is *persona* before he is *homo*.

Modo[6] autem ille ambe nature, et utraque illarum, sunt eciam pro triduo separate idem individuum, suppositum, et persona: licet enim sint due essencie singulares, tamen sunt unita individua substancia nature humane. Et sophista satis colorate concederet[7] quod illa persona, demonstrando humanitatem Christi, est persona et natura eterna. Ideo in talibus oportet ultra pronomina significancia pure essencias explicare res de quibus loquitur per terminos specificantes formas.

*[8] Quod si arguitur eo ipso quo ponitur aliqua[9] per se

[1]–[1] d'ite A B C. [2] naturarum A B C. [3] sequitur O.
[4]–[4] tunc . . . creatum *om.* B. [5] Christus *om.* O. [6] non A; mō B C; m̂ O.
[7] concederent O.
* [8] *Totus hic locus a* Quod si *usque ad* substancie tales (*p.* 136, *l.* 25) *stellulis supra notatus in Cod.* O. *omittitur*, *sic*—specificantes formas sunt multe arguicie O; *in margine autem alia manus* deficit multum *adnotavit.*
[9] esse *add.* B.

et completa causa causabilis, sequitur illud causabile: sed natura singularis in Christo cum communi creata substancia sufficit per se et complete causare creatum suppositum: ergo illis positis et unitis, sicut est in Christo, sequitur quod oportet ponere creatam personam ex illis principiis resultantem: nam eiusdem speciei specialissime est creata natura atque substancia in Christo, cuius est in quolibet fratre suo. [B 140b] Sicut ergo Christus est univoce cum Petro racionalis nature | individua substancia, sic cum eo univoce est persona: cui enim univocatur diffinicio eciam competit univoce diffinitum.

Objection. All that causes a human person is in Christ: therefore the result (a human person) must also be in him.

Confirmatur ex hoc quod tractantes pollitice[1] cum Christo acceptarent univoce cum aliis personam suam in testimonium et iudicium et quodlibet aliud opus sensibile vel quodlibet personale. Nec potest fingi quod deitas impedit ista principia ad causandum personam.

Christ's person would be accepted as a witness in court.

Hic dicitur quod minor est falsa cum nulla creatura causat naturaliter nisi de quanto a posteriori subicitur voluntati divine prius causanti. Sed voluntas divina non potest ex istis causare creatam personam: nam assumpcio impedit, vel verius iuvat ut natura creata sit suppositum increatum. Cum enim omne recipiens denudatur a natura rei recepte, oporteret Verbum vel esse duas personas, ut dixit Nestorius; vel recipiendo personalitatem creatam personalitatem increatam dimittere; quorum utrumque cum sit summe impossibile, sequitur quod natura rei exaltantis naturam assumptam, ut quasi insorbendo, non permittat[2] eam habere personalitatem creatam. Et hoc intendunt loquentes de supposicione aliena. Et dicitur quod ista natura est persona gloriosissima, [A 92c] | sed illi non competit diffinicio persone create. Pro quo notandum quod *substancia* est commune in Greco ad *ypostasim*, *usiosim*, et *usion*: quando autem diffinitur persona per nomen substancie intelligitur ypostasis, quam alii differenter explicant per nomen *subsistencie*. Et sic Christus non est racionalis nature individua subsistencia vel suppositum,

Answer. Cause does not produce effect except by the will of God.

The Latin word *substancia* represents three Greek words: ὑπόστασις, οὐσίωσις, and οὔσιον. Some translate ὑπόστασις in the sense of *persona* by *subsistencia*.

[1] pollce B; polletice C; pollitice A (*pro* politice = civiliter, *p.* 136, *l.* 12).
[2] permittant A; permittunt B.

nisi suppositum nature increate. Ideo natura assumpta non est formaliter persona sed ydemptice vel ypostatice. Non enim est formaliter ypostasis vel subsistencia, sed substancia vel usion. | Ideo in Christo sunt formaliter tres substancie, [C 79a] sed unica subsistencia, sed ille due nature create faciunt unam naturam completam, que est humanitas, non autem personam, cum deest complementum ex parte cause finalis.

Christ has three *substanciae*, one *subsistencia*.

Ulterius conceditur quod conversantes cum Christo putando eum esse univoce personam cum aliis hominibus ex ignorancia sue divinitatis [1] [acceptarent], univoce personam suam in testimonium.[1] Ideo non potest indicare [2] vel conversari civiliter, ut patet alibi, sed omne iudicium suum foret infinitum maioris auctoritatis quam iudicium persone create. Et ita videtur de omni actu personali quem fecit humanitus: auctoritas enim consequitur personam in dignitate et non naturam accionis pure. Et patet quod descripcio persone signata convertitur cum ista racionalis nature incommunicabilis existencia. *Incommunicabilis* dico quoad supposita, non naturas; et ita subsistencia est contractior quam substancia, ut sumitur ad hec tria. Et ita Trinitas commune principium et commune principatum non est persona vel subsistencia, sed persone vel subsistencie. Nec est color in illa equivocacione, quod divicie sunt substancia racionalis nature, sed substancia restricta ad subsistenciam est consequens ad omne suppositum substanciale. Tales *[3] sunt multe argucie quibus decipiuntur incauti, facte pro stabilienda opinione Nestorii.

Those who would regard him as a person in evidence (p. 135, l. 11) the same as other men, would do so in ignorance of his divine nature.

Sed 4°. principaliter arguitur contra ydemptitatem specificam Christi cum aliis ex parte materie. Nam semen decisum [4] a diversis sexubus et commixtum est alterius speciei quam simplex semen sexus feminei: [5] sed Christus conceptus est puro ex semine sexus feminei,[5] omnes autem alii ex commixtis seminibus maris et feminei: ergo materia ex qua

Principal objection IV. Christ has not identity in species with other men because of the difference of the *materia proxima* (=*semen*).

[1]–[1] *codd.* A B *lacunam xii litterarum exhibent: cod.* C *omnia post verbum* divinitatis *ad* testimonium *sine lacuna omittit.* acceptarent (*cf. p.* 135, *l.* 12) *pro certo supplendum est.*
[2] indicare C. *[3] *vide supra, p.* 134, *n.* 8. [4] decisis C.
[5]–[5] sed . . . feminei *om.* A B C.

factus[1] est Christus est alterius speciei quam materie proxime aliorum: et cum agens semper dat formam secundum condignitatem materie, ut patet philosophis, sequitur quod Christus sit alterius speciei quam alii secundum communem cursum nature univoce[2] procreati. Confirmatur per Commentatorem 8vo. Physicorum 9. 46. ponentem contra Avicennam quod si homo generaretur ex terra, ipse esset homo equivoce propter extraneacionem materie.

of which his body was made by reason of his conception by a virgin.

This objection is confirmed by an opinion of Averroes.

Hic dicitur quod illud argumentum deficit in pluribus. Primo in assumpto quod semen muliebre, quod differt a menstruo, non distat a virili semine nisi secundum maius et minus; sic quod semen virile de communi cursu nature sit in substancia spissius, complexione[3] calidius, et informacione virtuosius. Sed quale magisterium Deo de beata virgine complexione[3] mundissima descindere[4] semen vel sanguinem pro mensura delectationis sue humilime ex gaudio salutacionis[5] angelice, que excedat[6] in [7]bonitate complexionis[7] in proporcione multitudinis et in limitacione virtutis omnem aliam materiam, ex qua fuit persona hominis procreata? quod quia factum est, unde non daretur illi capaci[8] organo spiritus consimilis speciei?

Reply.
1. The divine intervention may have affected the *materia proxima*.

Deficit 2°. in sequela quando infert quod materia proxima, de qua factus est Christus, sit alterius speciei quam materie proxime aliorum. [9]Nam si, sicut est summe[9] possibile, [C 79b] [A 92d] Deus de lapidibus[10] vel quocumque alio mixto vel | simplici | descidisset[11] materiam, et commiscendo athomos[12] in utero virginali dedisset post[13] commixturam ydoneam formam complexionalem[14] humani seminis; adhuc proxima materia, ex qua talis homo fieret, foret eiusdem racionis cum aliis, licet remota materia sit diversa: aliter enim semina hominum generata ex distinctis cibariis in specie forent eo ipso disparium specierum.

2. It is not proven that in this case the *materia proxima* was not made like that of other men.

Ex istis 3°. colligitur quod non refert ex qua materia Deus

[1] natus B. [2] univoce *om.* A B C. [3] commixione A B C. [4] decindere O.
[5] salutatoris O. [6] excedit A B. [7-7] materia commixionis B. [8] capiti C O.
[9-9] si nam perfectum sed summe O. [10] lapide B. [11] decidisset B.
[12] attomos (*i.e.* atomos) O. [13] n⁹ O. [14] commixionalem A B C.

3. To God the *materia proxima* is indifferent: He uses agent or second cause according to His own pleasure.

adaptet[1] materiam proximam ad hominem producendum; dum tamen reducat eam ad temperamentum complexionis seminee,[2] et limitet[3] successive vel subito infundendo humanum spiritum in corpus debite limitatum.[4] Nec refert quo agente Deus ad illud officium utatur pro organo: aliter enim primi parentes, qui sunt principia humani generis, non convenirent cum suis | generacionibus in specie vel [B 141 a] natura: talis tamen error auctoris in principio † caret[5] maximum in processu. Patet deduccio ex hoc quod Adam plasmatus est de limo terre forsitan sine[6] ministerio creature, et Eua de costa viri ab eodem opifice est formata. Sicut ergo non refert utrum ignis ab igne, vel immediate a lumine producatur ad hoc quod sit de natura ignis univoce, et sic de aliis effectibus cuiuscumque speciei vel generis; sic facta de quacumque materia prima complexione et limitacione sufficienti ad animam subiectandam, non refert ad unionem compositi[7] ministerio cuiuscumque agentis secundi hoc factum fuerit, ut[8] sive immediate a Deo, sive ministerio angelorum, sive per se a constellacione celesti, sive a quocumque agente secundo corpus humanum productum fuerit; non refert data anima adesse hominis sicut nec refert a quo artifice create ydolum vel aliud artificiale fuerit[9] fabricatum.

That a thing is strange and in our experience unprecedented is not a disproof of its reality.

Et si dicatur quod Deus, non potest per se, nec cum tam disparibus secundis agentibus, tales effectus producere; tum,[10] quia nec est[11] auctenticum nec expertum; sed raciones seminales forent superflue limitate[12]: quoad illud videtur michi quod talis contencio de Dei persona sit satis superflua, ubi non evidenter scimus racionem pro vel contra producere: unde leve verbum multorum est et satis inevidens—'ego non sum expertus hoc, vel ego non inveni[13] hoc scriptum in historiis michi auctenticis: ergo non est verum'.—Et ex

[1] adept) O. [2] seminis A B C. [3] liniet A B C; *et cod.* O *in rasura.*
[4] liniatum A B C; lîtatû (*i.e.* limitatum) O.
[5] caret *om.* A B C: *forsitan pro* caret *codicis O. lectione* cresceret *vel* foret *legendum.*
[6] tñ (tamen) A B; cû (cum) C; sñ (sine *vel* sive) O.
[7] suppositi A B C. [8] ut *om.* A B C [9] sit A B C.
[10] tamen C O. [11] est *om.* B. [12] linite A B C; lîtate O.
[13] invenio A B C.

alio latere sollicitando fingere quod agens secundum potest naturaliter in talia[1] inexperta excedit limites philosophi naturalis. Sed inter alia opera, que de Deo credimus, partus virginis tenet locum satis probabilem in lumine[2] naturali; cum in multis aliis speciebus animalium narrantur femelle sine commixtione[3] seminis vel tactu maris concipere. Sed admiracio ineffabiliter nobis mirabilis est quod post limitacionem[4] [C 80a] subitam corporis capti[5] de pura virgine copulatus | sit [6]Deus pro instanti generacionis[6] nature complete, et hoc ypostatica unione. [7]Ideo hoc oportet nos ex fide supponere credendo quod nullum aliud tale novum potest fieri, licet hoc fuerit in natura creata analogice exemplatum de ypostatica unione[7] mentis cum corpore. Et hinc tam sepe exemplificat [O 227d] Augustinus cum | simbolo Athanasii quod 'sicut anima racionalis et caro unus est homo, [8]ita Deus et homo unus est[8] Christus.' Decuit enim auctorem nature specialiter post peccatum hominis remissibile per talem assumpcionem viri[9] ex femina speciem hominis innovare: ut, sicut primo formatus est mas ex non-homine, [10]secundo femina ex homine[10] sed ex mare solummodo, tercio autem ex his sexubus commixtis sunt alii communiter procreati; sic quarto pro complemento insticie[11] per se stantis in quatuor[11] compleat Deus virum celestem pure ex femina; cuius [A 93a] necessitas patet alibi. | Nec sequitur ex illis superfluitas limitacionis racionis seminalis diversis mixtorum generibus, ut experiencia philosophorum testatur, quod multa genera animalium, in quibus est distinccio sexuum, tam ex putrefaccione quam ex semine procreantur. Et tamen, cum hoc dicunt philosophi quod nec sexuum distinccio, nec racionis seminalis limitacio est aliquo modo superflua; sic[12] latet in visceribus nature, quid Deus disposuit secundum potenciam obediencialem creature sue per se facere, et quid agens

The real wonder is not that a virgin should bear (there are such cases in animal life);

but that to the body thus generated God should be hypostatically united.

The birth from woman only is a new start for the race of men; which (1) began with a male from non-human matter; (2) then came a woman out of the male; (3) then the race of men from these two together; (4) mankind is perfected by one born of a woman.

Animal life not always *ex semine*, sometimes *ex putrefactione*. In the phenomena of life God works mysteriously.

[1] talis O. [2] lūie A B C. [3] commixione A B C.
[4] liniacionem A B C. [5] capi O.
[6–6] deus per generacionem A B; deus per generacionis C.
[7–7] ideo . . . unione *om.* A B C. [8–8] ita . . . est *om.* O. [9] utri O.
[10–10] secundo . . . homine *om.* O; secundo ex femina ex homine C.
[11–11] persone stantis in quarto A B C. [12] sicut A B C.

Many superstitions are based on this mystery; as demonology, witchcraft, astrology.

creatum a seculis multis absconditum sufficit preter communem cursum nature producere. Et circa[1] possibilitatem talium sollicitantur multi superflue: ut illi, quod demones[2] possunt in aspectu placido celi, mediantibus virtutibus mixtorum sicut herbarum et lapidum, mirabilia vulgo inopinabilia per se efficere: illi quod celum secundum diversas figuras et aspectus astrorum per se[3] potest in talia: et hi quod homines possunt cum iuvamine demonum et constellacione celestium mirabilia inopinata producere. Et in speculacione talium theologizant speculativi inaniter. In practica vero mathematici consumunt tempus figuras celi superflue prestolantes, et demones periculosius consulentes.

The pious theologian is content to know, 1. that strange things may come to pass through second causes; 2 that the power of second causes is restrained by God; 3. that God's incommunicable omnipotence assigns to each work its agent, and to each agent his work.

Sufficit ergo pio theologo quod sciat in genere talia mirabilia ab agente secundo posse fieri: 2° quod sciat istis agentibus secundis a Deo, a quo est omnis potencia, terminos secundum maximum et minimum limitari; nec[4] creaturam aliquam posse in aliquid, nisi secundum eius ordinacionem et benevolenciam limitantem: et 3°. quod Deus ex condicione omnipotencie[5] facit eo ipso quodlibet dandum opus quo vult ipsum a quoquam fieri, et istam condicionem potencie non potest communicari alteri.

As for the opinion of Averroes (p. 137, l. 6) he is not a decisive authority in philosophy, much less in theology.

Quantum ad testimonium Commentatoris patet quod dictum Averrois[6] non debet esse alicui philosopho, et minus theologo, testis auctenticans, cum tam in philosophia quam fide [7]presumptive vel invide sepius[7] deviavit. Fautor autem Commentatoris, cui placeret[8] dictum suum palliare, posset fingere ipsum de Avicenna concipere; quod posset esse homo, cuius proxima materia subiecta anime foret terra, et per consequens corpus alterius speciei | quam mixtum organicum[9] [C 80b] a sibi simili in specie procreatum; et cum forme dantur secundum disposicionem materie, si haberet[10] animam, ipsa foret ab humanitate nostra disparis racionis. Nam in tam

Possibly Averroes, commenting on Avicenna, supposed that the latter meant that unchanged earth might be the material of a man.

[1] ita O.
[2] denōīacōēs (*i.e.* denominaciones) O.
[3] per se *om.* C.
[4] et sic C; ut O.
[5] ōīpo[e] A B C.
[6] aūois A B; auctoris C; aūoys O.
[7-7] p̃supⁿᵒ ve inde septus O.
[8] placet B.
[9] tamen *add.* A B C.
[10] sed haberent O.

But nature does not form even an ape or pigmy of earth, and elaborates man more than any other animal. The superiority of man implies a superiority of 'formation.'

vilem materiam non inducit natura formam [1] simee vel [B 141b] pigmee: [1] vel 2°. quod natura | plus ingenians [2] circa produccionem hominis quam animalis alterius imperfecti, quod corpus sicut et anima [3] non posset produci naturaliter nisi a racionali supposito producatur. Ideo non sequitur—animal imperfectum potest ex putrefaccione produci: ergo homo—qui est finis uniuscuiusque alterius animalis, quia effectum preciosiorem virtus regitiva universitatis plus curat. Unde figuracionem embrionis oportet fieri a virtute informativa ab anima hominis per species triplices dirivata, per fomentum caloris consimilis in matrice, et per nutricionem concepti de sanguine menstruo parientis. Quod si alius sit modus producendi quoad corpus hoc est auctori nature specialiter reservatum. Sed totum illud vix moveret protervum ad credendum possibilitatem negative que petitur.

Others say that, since Adam, no one can be produced otherwise than materially: since on this material link depends the tie of love among mankind.

Tercii autem dicunt quod nemo post primum parentem potest produci nisi materialiter [4] producatur ab homine propter amorem humani generis nutriendum. Nam racione stipitis et cognacionis oportet nutriri amorem inter homines ultra bruta, quia aliter fuisset facile post peccatum Adam totam [A 93b] suam generacionem sicut genus Caim [5] | exstinguere et aliud genus hominum ex disparato [6]principio procreare[6] sine hoc quod Christus paciatur pro salvanda specie. Et tunc esset homo species imperfecta, sine qua mundus posset existere; cum, nullo homine existente, celum posset ut vermes hominem [7] de novo producere; †et multo magis elementum [8] quod est [9] gracia hominis tamquam finis non esset de substancia universali; [10] et, sicut [11] situs spere [12] corruptibilium posset vacuus a corpore.[13]†

To discuss this is beside the point. The catholic doctrine is (compare p. 139, l. 19) that the first man was made of earth,

Sed cum iste tractatus multum [14] distat a puncto proposito, redeundo dicitur quod philosophicum et facile est catholicum sustinere quod primus homo fiebat de terra, secundus sexus

[1] symee vel pigmei A B C. [2] ingenias (*pro* ingeniās) B.
[3] animans B. [4] naturaliter *prima manu correctum e* materialiter A.
[5] cayn A B C. [6–6] principio provocare A; principio hominum provocare B.
[7] hominem *in margine alia manu suppletum* A. [8] elementum *om.* A B C.
[9] est *om.* A C. [10] universi A B C. [11] sicut *om.* O.
[12] spere (*i.e.* sphaerae) *codd. omn.* [13]† *hic locus corruptus videtur.*
[14] membrum O.

the second (sex) from him, the third (man) from both: and so on in the order of nature, until the new and last man of the same species was made of a woman: from him (fifthly) every man is made in spirit, and ultimately remade when the circle is complete (5 and 6 are circular numbers), and by him the human species is to be perfected.

ab illo, et tercius ab ambobus; et sic gradatim de genere consequente quousque novus homo atque novissimus eiusdem speciei cum aliis fiebat ex femina; et quinto[1] omnis homo secundum animam fit ab illo circulariter a quo ultimate reficitur: quinarius autem et senarius sunt numeri circulares. Non enim credo quod species humana peribit, vel quod possit sub tanto auctore eciam quoad perfeccionem illam[2] deficere.

---

## Cap. IX.

[*Epilogat posicionem de humanitate; et, narrando tres radices causantes modernorum discrepancias, dissolvit tres obiectus eorum per ordinem.*

I. *Gives a summary of the author's position concerning the humanity of Christ.*

II. *Explains the three sources from which the modern diversities of opinion have arisen.*

III. *Deals with three principal objections to the author's position.*]

Comparison of the true opinion with errors conducive to clearness.

Consequens est iuxta ponere sentenciam illam senteneiis modernorum, ut diversitas summe veritatis magis appareat et obiectus, quos adversantes invehunt, pla|nius dissolvantur. [O 228a]

I. Wyclif's position. II. Sources of error. III. Objections refuted.

Primo ergo danda est posicio in quodam compendio.

2°. declarende sunt radices ex quibus oritur discrepancia modernorum.

Et 3°. commixtim solventur instancie.

I. Wyclif's position. *The humanity assumed by the Word is perfect man composed of body and a reasonable soul, and by hypostatic union identified with the Word in person, not in nature.*

Stat itaque posicio in hoc—**Quod humanitas assumpta a Verbo sit perfectus homo ex corpore et anima racionali compositus, et per ypostaticam unionem ydemptificatus Verbo in persona non natura**—. Et sic non | est aliud [C 81a] suppositum, individuum, ypostasis, vel persona in Christo ydemptice[3] quam persona eterna Dominus Iesus Christus;

[1] ergo A B C. [2] secundam A B C; illam (*an pro* ullam ?) O.
[3] ydēptito O (*an* Christi ydemptitate *legendum* ?).

cum tam corpus, quam anima, [1]quam eciam[1] humanitas completa sit persona eterna, quamvis sint inter[2] se nature solummodo temporales distincte plurimum ab invicem,[3] et a divinitate[4] a natura, et a substancia vel essencia divina.

Three cautions.

Et sic[5] cavendum est specialiter de his tribus.

1. Not any of his natures (deitas, anima, corpus, p. 3, l. 7) is a supposite other than the Word.

Primo ne credatur aliquam illarum naturarum esse aliud suppositum a Verbo, quod est simul Filius Dei eternus et filius hominis temporalis.

2. There is neither conversion,

2°. oportet cavere ne credatur conversio[6] vel confusio naturarum; cum manet plene natura divina[7] cum duabus naturis incommunicantibus sed creatis constituentibus humanitatem perfectam, omnes[8] et singule eadem persona in numero. Si autem esset conversio tunc natura conversa pro mensura conversionis[9] non maneret; ut lignum conversum in ignem pro mensura conversionis desinit, nova forma inducta et veteri desinente; quod non potest esse de tribus formis incommunicantibus[10] supra dictis. Si autem esset confusio naturarum, tunc forent reciproce quelibet eadem cuilibet, vel omnis vel aliqua incompleta, sicut est de elementis et[11] mixtis integraliter componentibus ipsum mixtum.[12] Modo autem manent tres incommunicantes nature, quelibet plene incommunicans cuilibet; sed utraque creatura per unionem personalem idem ypostatice Verbo Dei.

nor confusion of natures.

3. The humanity and deity are one, not by aggregation, but by hypostatic union, i.e. by personal identity.

3°. oportet cavere ne[13] credatur ex humanitate et deitate fieri unum aggregative, ut est cumulus lapidum, vel accidens et subiectum. Nam unio ypostatica, que est ydemptitas[14] personalis facit quod quelibet istarum trium incommunicancium naturarum est plene eadem communis persona; licet inter se naturaliter distinguantur per totum ex multis sanc-
[A 93c] torum testimoniis supradictis, ut Augustini, Gregorii, | et Anselmi. Unde istam sentenciam colligit[15] venerabilis Anselmus in De Incarnacione Verbi ca°. 7. sub his verbis:

This is the view of Anselm,

[1–1] quantum vel O. [2] in se O. [3] ab ī A B C.
[4] directe A B C. [5] sic *om.* O. [6] conversio *om.* A B C.
[7] divina *om.* O. [8] omnis A B C. [9] conversacionis O.
[10] formis communicantibus A; formis et communicantibus O.
[11] in A B C. [12] mixtum *om.* C. [13] vel O.
[14] unio B. [15] tollit O.

'Sicut, inquit, in Deo una natura est plures persone, et plures persone sunt una natura; sic in Christo una persona est plures nature, et plures nature sunt una persona. "Quemadmodum enim[1] Pater est Deus, Filius Deus et Spiritus sanctus Deus; [2]et non tamen tres dii, sed unus Deus[2];" ita in Christo Deus est persona, et homo est persona, non tamen due persone sed una persona.' Intelligit autem iste doctor | per *Deum* et *hominem* deitatem et humanitatem, [B 142a] quia aliter esset similitudo impertinens, et verba sequencia nimis falsa. 'Non, inquit, alius Deus alius homo in Christo, quamvis aliud sit Deus, aliud homo, sed idem ipse Deus qui et homo.' Quando ergo dicit cum beato Augustino, Ieronimo, Gregorio et aliis quod aliud Deus in Christo et aliud homo, intelligit quod alia natura est deitas et alia humanitas, sed utraque non alia sed eadem persona; quia homo, ut dicit, solum naturam significat, et illum assumptum hominem dicit postea esse Iesum, et eandem personam cum Verbo. Unde non dubium quin per assumptum hominem intelligit naturam humanam | assumptam. 'Verbum, [C 81b] inquit, naturam aliam assumpsit, non aliam personam.' Et ita generaliter intendunt sancti quando dicunt 'aliud Deus, aliud homo; sed non alius,' quod alia natura sit deitas et alia natura[3] humanitas, non autem persona alia sed eadem.

Augustine, Jerome, Gregory; who all maintain a difference of natures in Christ with a unity of person.

II. Three roots of modern divergences: Root 1. The disbelief in universals (*i.e.* the prevalence of Nominalism).

Pro 2°.[4] notandum quod in tribus radicibus stat modernorum variacio ab antiquis. Primo in hoc quod non concipiunt res communes. Noticia quidem[5] universalium secundum Anselmum in De Incarnacione ca° 1°. est medium ad cognoscendum misterium Trinitatis, misterium incarnacionis, et multa alia fidei sacramenta. Sicut enim natura vel forma[6] divina est communis ad tria supposita, sic omnis natura vel forma specifica universalis in actu est communis ad omnia eius singularia; et persona Verbi[7] communis ad

[1] enim *om.* A B C. [2–2] et non . . . deus *om.* B. [3] natura *om.* sit *add.* O.
[4] pro quo A B C. [5] quidem noticie O. [6] vel forma *om* A B C.
[7] videtur A.

naturam divinam et alias duas contingenter extranee ypostatice copulatas: et [1]tolluntur hinc inde[1] sophistica argumenta conformiter.

2ª radix est methaphisica de forma substanciali compositi. Quelibet enim talis forma substancialis compositi est eius[2] quiditas, idem essencialiter vel personaliter cum formato; ut quelibet anima animati, cum sit ipsum vivere et per consequens ipsum esse; et eius essencia, ex 2° *De Anima*, est idem essencialiter vel personaliter cum composito et subiecto; ut anima intellectiva hominis, que est eius humanitas, est eadem persona cum homine sic formato; igneitas est idem suppositum cum igne, et ita de ceteris: et per consequens, cum alique forme sint separabiles a materia que non accidentaliter[3] sunt persone, patet[4] quod personalitas manet cum forma a materia separata.

Root 2. The metaphysical question as to the *substantial form* of a compound existence. Is the *forma* identical with the *formatum*? Yes. Personality resides in this *form* (as in the *anima* in man) apart from the *matter* which may or may not remain part of the subject.

3ª radix est abieccio predicacionis secundum essenciam, ut[5] recte admittentes predicacionem secundum essenciam concedunt cum Anselmo De Incarnacione 7 quod quelibet universalis forma est idem cum omnibus et singulis eius suppositis, et correspondenter de aliis rebus communibus: concedunt eciam quod tam in creatore quam eciam[6] in qualibet creatura omne esse est essencia et e contra, licet in omnibus istis sit formalis differencia vel distinccio racionis.

Root 3. The rejection of predication according to essence, *i.e.* the denial that any universal form is the same as all and each of its supposites.

Cum ergo moderniores variant in istis tribus radicibus, non mirum si variant in germine consequente. Ponunt enim [A 93d] quod non est possibile[7] plures naturas vel res alias[8] singulas | esse unam. Ponunt 2° quod omnis forma substancialis compositi est distincta essencialiter a subiecto, in tantum quod aliqui dicunt omnem formam materialem substancie [O 228b] posse a natura separari. | Et 3° dicunt[9] quod in omni creatura est dare essenciam, que non est esse, sed eius causa, sicut lux luminis vel[10] lucere. Ex istis dicunt consequenter

Positions of the modern doctors. 1. Several natures or other things cannot be one. 2. Every substantial form of a compound is distinct from its subject. 3. In every creature there is an essence which is not its being, but the cause of its being.

[1]–[1] collinitur in O. [2] eius *om.* A B C. [3] accidenter O.
[4] ꝑ (*i.e.* per) O. [5] nec O. [6] eciam *om.* A B C.
[7] impossibile O. [8] aliquas A B C. [9] dicunt *om.* A B C.
[10] et A B C.

As deductions they deny that many natures can be the person of the Word. And as in every man his individual existence and his essence (*homo* and *humanitas*) are distinguished; so Christ did not assume the individual existence of a man but humanity, and this cannot be hypostatically one with the Word. It is necessary in the face of these wide deviations to assume the three propositions called in question above in the three roots, pp. 144, 145, viz. 1. the existence of universals; 2. the identity between the *form* and the *individual formed*; 3. the identity of the (abstract) essence and the individual existence. III. Three Objections considered. Objection I. The Word assumed a person, by assuming humanity which is a person.

quod non est possibile multas naturas esse personam Verbi. Dicunt eciam quod in quolibet homine esse suum et essencia et per consequens ipse homo ac sua humanitas distinguuntur, sic quod omnis homo vel non est humanitas, vel humanitas solum est homo per accidens: unde Christus ut dicunt non suscepit hominem, sed humanitatem, quo non potest esse idem ypostatice Verbo Dei. In istis ergo tribus radicibus et aliis ex eis consequentibus stat modernorum variacio ab antiquis. Magnam [1] quidem vim habent principia, cum eorum variacio | dilatat distinccionem multiplicem posterius [C 82a] dicendorum. Oportet igitur supponere res communes: quod idem est forma substancialis cuiuslibet et formatum; ac demum, admittendo [2] predicacionem secundum essenciam, quod sicut in omni creato vel increato omne esse est essencia et e contra; sic omnis humanitas vel [3] esse hominis est homo sive assumpta sive supposicione propria terminata.

Quibus suppositis restat 3° tollere evidencias ex adverso. Videtur enim primo quod Verbum personam assumpsit, quia humanitatem assumpsit, que quidem humanitas est persona. Nec valet nude negare consequenciam, cum arguitur ordinate ab inferiori ad suum superius. Et talis deduccio a Deo approbatur quod conceditur exinde Verbum sumpsisse aliquid quod prius non fuerat. Et istam racionem Nestorianorum recitat Anselmus in De Incarnacione in principio ca° 7.

Reply. i. The Word already being a person could not become a person.

Hic dicitur quod consequencia non valet, cum idem sit ac si sic argueretur—Verbum fecit se esse hominem, et esse hominem est esse personam: ergo Verbum fecit se esse personam—ubi constat quod antecedente existente necessario | [B142b] consequens est impossibile; cum tantum [4] una persona, que absolute necessario est Verbum, poterit esse Verbum, et per consequens cum Verbum non potest se facere illam personam, patet quod Verbum non potest facere se personam. Sed pro ulteriori declaracione notandum quod assumere personale, de quo scriptura cum sanctis doctoribus in proposito loquitur,

The assumption of personality in the incarnation

[1] Vaguani O. [2] dimitendo A B. [3] est A B C. [4] tamen O.

est duas naturas personaliter unire, id est,[1] duas naturas facere esse unum suppositum vel [2] personam, et ideo vocatur[2] *unio personalis*. Et potest secundum[3] tres gradus active intelligi. Primo pro active principiare unionem huiusmodi: et sic tota Trinitas assumpsit naturam humanam de quanto univit[4] eam ypostatice Verbo Dei. 2° striccius pro activa[5] causancia principali unientis, ut ipsum fiat eadem persona cum natura unita; et sic natura divina univit vel assumpsit in supposito Verbi[6] naturam hominis; quia fecit naturam hominis esse eandem personam non eandem naturam cum persona divina. 3° strictissime dicitur assumere personale pro causancia persone quia fecit[7] naturam creatam[8] esse idem personaliter sibi ipsi. Et illo modo solum Verbum assumpsit hominem. Ex istis patet, cum[9] nulla assumpcio ypostatica sit eterna, quod oportet assumptum esse solummodo creaturam, quia nec alia persona, nec alia natura [A 94a] | est Christi humanitas; licet sit creator, quia persona Verbi, que secundum deitatem non secundum ipsam creat omnia.

Is the uniting two natures in *personal union*.
Personal union may be understood in three senses.
1. A sense in which the Trinity took human nature.
2. A sense in which the Divine nature assumed, in the Word as subject, the nature of man.
3. The sense in which the Word as a personal cause took human nature into personal union with himself.

2° patet, quod non potest esse personalis assumpcio nisi persona naturam assumpserit non personam.[10] Oportet enim personam assumere, quia aliter non esset unio personalis, nisi persona ydemptificaret sibi naturam. Et quod oportet [C 82b] personam | assumentem naturam assumere non personam, patet ex hoc quod personarum personalis[11] ydemptificacio vel naturarum essencialis ydemptificacio est impossibilis, ut nullum unum suppositum potest esse aliud, nec una natura fieri potest alia. Sed sicut persone maxime entitatis uniuntur in suprema essencia vel natura, sic nature maxime distantes ydemptificantur in eodem supposito vel persona. Et patet quod natura divina non potest primo sibi assumere naturam aliam vel personam. Patet ex hoc quod non potest esse alia natura vel persona quam est ab intrinseco necessario absolute, et nullius talis potest esse assumpcio. Oportet

ii. Further, *personal* assumption consists in a *person* assuming a *nature*.

A person cannot assume a person; for nothing can be something else.

[1] id est *om.* O. [2-2] personam non vocatur B. [3] secundum *om.* O.
[4] vīcit (*i.e.* vincit) O. *corr. alia manu in margine* univit. [5] causa *add.* O.
[6] videtur C. [7] facit C. [8] creata O.
[9] quod A B. [10] nec *add.* O. [11] personarum *iterum* O.

ergo naturam divinam uniri[1] Verbo non nature primo quam sumpsit.[2]

iii. The incarnation is not

3° patet quod assumpcio ypostatica, unio, vel incarnacio, aut [3]quomodocunque aliter nominetur,[3] nec est generacio, nec conversio, nec alteracio, sed ydemptificacio; et si est mutacio, tunc est potissima mutacio dextere excelsi. Non

a generation,

enim est generacio, [4]licet generacio[4] ad ipsam consequatur:[5] sicut motus localis ad motum augmentacionis, cum omnis generacio temporalis sit a non-esse ad esse produccio: [6]assumpcio autem[6] videtur esse subsistencie[7] summe minoracio, cum Verbum ex incarnacione minoratum est paulo

Heb. ii. 7.

minus ab angelis, ut exponit Apostolus ad Hebre. 2° illud

Ps. viii. 5.

Psalmi 8[i]; 'minuisti eum paulo minus ab angelis.' Nec est

nor a conversion of substance,

conversio, cum subsistencia Verbi manet summa secundum omnes eius proprietates non composita[8] cum aliquo. Nec est

nor a change into something else;

alteracio, tum quia humanitas assumpta non est inherens accidens; tum eciam quia persona secundum naturam precedentem humanitatem assumptam est omnino immobilis eo quod illi nature non potest accidens, ad quod est motus, formaliter inherere.

but an identification

Ex istis colligitur[9] racio quare sequitur quod Verbum assumendo humanitatem assumpsit essenciam, substanciam,

of an essence or nature, not of an individual or person, with the person of the Word.

aliquid, et naturam; et non assumendo illam humanitatem assumpsit individuum, suppositum, vel personam. [10]Nam illa[10] humanitas est per se inferius ad aliquid, essenciam, vel naturam; cum sit per se quiditas singularis in specie humana; persona autem[11] cum sit extra racionem generis creati est solum accidentaliter superius ad substanciam, aliquid et[12] quodcunque genus creatum. | Cum ergo persona Verbi sit equi- [O 228c] voce Verbum respectu humanitatis, patet quod non sequitur, si Verbum illam humanitatem assumpsit, que non primo per

[1] unisi (*sic*) A; uniri B. [2] sumpserit A; assumpsit B M; naturam quam sumpsit O.
[3] quomodolibet alio nominetur A; quomodolibet nominetur B.
[4]–[4] licet generacio *om.* O. [5] consequitur O.
[6]–[6] assumpcio enim A B; assumptum autem O. [7] sbê (*i.e.* substancie) O.
[8] componens A B C; compos *ad extremum lineae*, -ita *in initio sequentis om.* O.
[9] tollitur A B C. [10]–[10] ñlr̃ (*i.e.*) naturaliter O.
[11] Psori (*i.e.* personari) B. [12] substanciam aut eciam quodcunque A B C.

se sed a Deo equivoce est persona, quod exinde assumpsit personam: ut in exemplo non sequitur—Petrus fecit se septipedalem, album, patrem, et sic de ceteris generibus accidencium: ergo Petrus fecit se esse aliquid—; quia est *aliquid* extra racionem quanti, vel qualis etc. Correspondenter Verbum esse personam est tanquam longe prius extra racionem humanitatis, sed esse aliquid est racio per se humanitatis; cum Christus, in quantum homo, est aliquid eciam quod prius non fuerat: ideo assumendo hominem assumpsit aliquid non personam.

Et si arguatur ex illo sequi quod Christus assumpsit personam hominis, sicut fecit se esse personam hominis: dicitur quod non hoc sed oppositum sequitur ex predictis; cum assumpcio non sit nisi nature per se possibilis, et, [C 83a] [1] nulla | inherente accidente,[1] mutacio est assumpcio. Non enim quelibet faccio, sed solum faccio, qua natura racionalis [A 94b] fit Deus, est assumpcio vel ypostatica | unio; et per consequens solum ydemptificacio est assumpcio.[2] Et patet quod sicut Christus fecit se esse hominem, animal, corpus, substanciam, et aliquid; sic assumpsit hec omnia in illa sub- [B 143a] stancia singulari. Unde idem aliquid, quod fuit eternaliter | est equivoce [3] ad illud aliquid quod[3] assumpsit. Ideo sicut albefactum [4] sit ut sic[4] coloratum et quale, licet perante fuerat coloratum, quia aliter non esset alteracio possibilis: sic in proposito per incarnacionem Christus fit aliquid licet prius fuit aliquid. Sicut enim sufficit ad alteratum, quod ipsum sit alterum secundum gradum quam prius; sic sufficit ad alietatem Christi quod aliquid aliud sit Christus quam prius fuerat.

Although after the assumption Christ was something other than he was before, it does not follow that he assumed a person.

Et patet quod non est assumpcio nisi substancie; et per consequens nullius forme inherentis est assumpcio: ut Christus non assumpsit ypostatice se pati, mori, vel ascendere, quamvis se fecit huiusmodi; quia tunc ydemptificasset passionem, mortem, et ascensionem ypostasi Verbi, sicut fecit

The only assumption possible is assumption of *substance*, not of a *forma inherens*.

1–1 natura inherente accidente A B; natura ente accidente C; nulla inherente in accidente O. 2 est assumpcio *om.* O.
3–3 ab illo quod; *in marg. corr.* ob illud A; ab illo quod B; ab illud aliquid quod C.
4–4 sit ut sit C; tit ut sic O; fit ut sic M.

humanitatem; quod est impossibile. Et sic quelibet nature racionalis accidentalis transmutacio esset assumpcio; quod repugnat supradictis. Persona ergo Verbi accidentaliter est persona hominis. Ergo sicut non assumpsit dominium[1] in mundi principio, nec filium hominis pro instanti incarnacionis; sic nec personam hominis, cum non assumpsit personam. Sed assumendo 'formam servi' fecit se esse personam hominis; licet nullam personam se fecerit, sed illam naturam, quam assumpsit, se fecerit:[2] cum sophisma illud non habet hic locum—Christus fecit se esse hominem, sed nullum hominem—; cum illam[3] humanitatem, et per consequens hoc aliquid se fecit, quod prius non fuerat. Unde si correspondenter esset persona hominis, que tunc et non prius[4] fuit Verbum Dei; tunc concedendum esset quod personam hominis assumpsit: sed assumptum est impossibile.

Objection II. Every man is a person; if Christ did not assume a person, he did not assume man.

2° principaliter obicitur per hoc quod videtur esse distinccio inter humanitatem, naturam, vel formam hominis et personam hominis; cum humanitatem, naturam, et formam hominis Verbum assumpsit,[5] non personam: et hoc sufficit ad inferendum distinccionem. Oppositum tamen dicit posicio, cum dicit naturam assumptam esse personam Verbi; et sic non videtur quod Verbum hominem assumpsit,[6] cum omnis homo sit persona, et nullam personam assumpserit.[6]

Reply. This conclusion follows from pressing needlessly a distinction of *relation* as though it were a distinction of *essence* or of *person*. As in the Trinity the divine nature or essence is distinguished from the divine person, being itself common to the three Persons;

Hic dicitur sicut[7] in materia *De Trinitate*, quod multiplex est distinccio, ut alia essencialis, alia personalis, et alia racionis. Unde distinccio racionis non interimit mutuam predicacionem distinctorum; ut natura specifica hominis, licet a Petro racione distinguatur,[8] cum ipsa sit communicabilis omni homini, Petrus autem non; et[9] tamen Petrus est illa natura specifica, et conversim, sed non ex equo. Et natura vel essencia divina racione distinguitur a persona, cum ipsa communicatur tribus personis producentibus vel

[1] doñ (*i.e.* donum) O. [2] fecerat A B C. [3] ita; (*pro* istam) O.
[4] plus C. [5] assumpserit A B C. [6] assumpserat O.
[7] quod O. [8] distinguitur A B C. [9] et *om.* A C O.

productis; nulla autem persona sic communicari poterit,[1] sicut nec natura divina adintra producere poterit[1] vel produci. Et tamen non obstante distinccione huius racionis omnis persona divina est natura divina et e contra. Correspondenter cum persona Verbi communicatur[2] humanitati et [C 83b] divinitati, patet | quod est distinccio racionis inter personam illam et humanitatem; cum illa persona sit deitas, illa persona est eterna absolute necessaria equalis simpliciter Deo Patri. Illa quidem[3] humanitas non potest esse deitas; sed est necessario temporalis, contingens, et minor simpliciter Deo Patre, licet sit personaliter illud, quod est deitas, absolute necessarium et equale simpliciter Deo Patri. Et patet illa distinccio non tollit predicacionem mutuam forme hominis et persone. Et patet quod assumptum in argumento est verum, sed negatur minor, cum nemo recte dicit oppositum.

*and no Person can be thus made common; nevertheless every divine Person is the divine nature:*

*so the person of the Word is common to the humanity and the divinity, yet there is a distinction of relation between that person and the humanity: nevertheless the* form of man *may be used as a convertible term with* person.

Unde si moderniores admisissent predicacionem secundum [A 94c] essenciam vel personam, licet non formalem, | concedendo tamen cum Anselmo in De Incarnacione 7°. quod natura specifica est singulus[4] hominum, sicut natura divina est singulum suorum suppositorum; et correspondenter quod persona cuiuscumque hominis est tam corpus quam anima, licet ille nature essencialiter distinguantur; et quod inter quamlibet personam hominis et illas naturas sit cum predicacione mutua distinccio racionis: tunc, inquam, saperet illis quod natura divina et natura humana sunt utraque persona Verbi, licet ille nature essencialiter distinguantur, et inter Verbum et utramque naturam sit distinccio racionis; et tunc saperet illis exemplum illud[5] philosophicum fidei in simbolo Athanasii quod[6] Augustinus tam crebro recitat; 'sicut anima racionalis et caro unus est homo, ita Deus et homo unus est Christus.' Diversio autem[7] ab istis principiis facit nimirum variacionem maximam consequenter.

*So Anselm.*

*As the person of man consists of two natures essentially distinct, viz. body and soul;*

*so according to the Athanasian Creed 'God and man is one Christ.'*

[1–1] sicut . . . poterit *om.* O. [2] communicati et O. [3] quieta O.
[4] singłs A B C; siglls O. [5] illud *om.* A B C. [6] et O.
[7] ergo C; gi (*i.e.* igitur) O.

That the Word assumed man is literally true, as the Fathers often say.

Ulterius | concedendum est de virtute sermonis[1] quod [O 228d] Verbum hominem assumpsit, sicut persepe dicunt Augustinus, Ieronimus, et Anselmus, et antiqui qui recte sapuerunt in logica. Cum enim *homo* sit concretum humanitatis, sicut *Deus* deitatis, patet quod potest indifferenter simpliciter supponere pro natura, vel personaliter pro persona; ut sicut *Deus* communicatur omnibus tribus personis divinis, quia deitas est sic communis, et tamen idem *Deus* incommunicatus, cum sit persona gignens; sic *homo* communicatur omni persone hominis,[2] cum sit forma specifica; et tamen *homo* non potest sic communicari, cum sit persona hominis; et correspondenter de aliis secundum supposicionem simplicem et personalem equivoce variatis. Unde quandocunque dicitur quod hominem Verbum assumpsit, intelligendum est simpliciter pro natura; ut humanitatem nedum specificam sed singularem assumpsit, quam Anselmus nominat Iesum Christum. Imo si diligenter attendimus quomodo homo quale-quid vel substancialem qualitatem primo significat, ut dicunt Aristoteles et Anselmus, prius significaret talis proposicio—*hominem Verbum assumpsit*—quod naturam humanam assumpserat[4] quam quod personam hominis | assumpserat.[4] [B 143b] Ideo est talis proposicio ad sensum primarium concedenda et sensus alius est negandus.

*Man* is the concrete of *humanity* and may stand either for the *nature* or the *person* of man.

It is true in the former sense that the Word assumed man, untrue in the latter.

Distinction between *humanitas* and *homo*: *humanitas* like other abstract terms is not always used in the strictly abstract sense

Et si queritur[5] diversitas inter illos terminos *humanitas* et *homo* quoad modum significandi eum, licet de se mutuo predicentur, refert tamen multibi[6] ponere unum vel relicum: dicitur quod more aliorum terminorum quorum unus est concretus aliusque abstractus, concretum supponit indifferenter personaliter | pro persona vel simpliciter pro natura; et hinc [C 84a] recipit formalem predicacionem cuiuscumque generis accidentis: abstractum autem abstractive tentum non suscipit formaliter nisi predicacionem per se et predicacionem secundum habitudinem abiciendo omnem formalem predicacionem

[1] de vi vocis *in margine textus erasi correctio* A. [2] hominis *bis* O.
[3] sumit A B C. [4–4] quam . . . assumpserat *om.* O.
[5] queretur O. [6] multicubi A B C.

*Of the pure essence apart from accidents.*

suppositalem; ut humanitas non est qualis aut quanta accidenter, nec agit, nec patitur, sedet vel ditatur,[1] sed predicaciones respectivas recipit modo quo dictum est de universalibus; ut, si humanitas esset alba, cum humanitas sit esse hominem, tunc esse hominem foret formaliter esse album; et per consequens, ut arguit Aristoteles, homo tunc esset albedo. Et patet quod Verbum solum humanitatem vel naturam humanum assumpsit, non personam hominis; licet secundum alium sensum omnis humanitas sit persona.

*The Fathers use the term humanitas in a less strict sense intermediate between abstract and concrete: as Augustine.*

Verumptamen notandum est quod in materia de incarnacione doctores sancti utuntur isto termino 'humanitas' tanquam medio inter abstractum et concretum: ut Augustinus Ome. 19. super Iohannem dicit, quod 'Maria humanitatem genuit que eciam in cruce passa est'; et Enchiridion 29°; 'illam, inquit, creaturam quam virgo concepit et peperit, quamvis ad solam personam Filii pertinentem, tota[2] Trinitas fecit.' Inseparabilia enim[3] sunt opera Trinitatis, et indubio per 'illam creaturam' intelligit substanciam humanam, que est humanitas, cum paulo ante dicit utramque substanciam, [A94d] divinam scilicet[4] | et humanam, esse Filium unicum Dei Patris. Et sic de multis similibus, que omnia cum eis similibus intelligenda sunt, quod persone Verbi Dei insunt huiusmodi predicata[5] secundum [6]quod homo; hoc est,[6] humanitas est medium vel causa, secundum quam predicata huiusmodi insunt; ut non haberet unde temptaretur, gigneretur, vel meritorie pateretur, [7]et sic de aliis communicacionibus[7] ydiomatum, nisi assumendo naturam hominis. Nec mirum de ista transsumpcione dispari in illa materia, [8]cum [solum] Verbum Dei sit homo per accidens prius persona quam homo[8]; cum solum illa personalitas trahit[9] sibi naturam singularem in suam ypostasim; alie autem persone [10]similis nature sunt cum aliis[10] formis singularibus.

[1] dicatur C O. [2] totum O. [3] non O.
[4] scilicet *om.* O. [5] predicato A B. [6–6] quod homo est quod O.
[7–7] et sic de aliis coîcantibus O.
[8–8] cum . . . homo *om.* A B; solum *c sequentibus correptum omittendum censeo.*
[9] transit O. [10–10] simul nature sunt cum illis A B C.

When the Fathers say that 'the humanity of Christ suffered, etc.,' they mean that 'Christ in his human nature suffered, etc.'

[1]Ideo sic cum dico hoc[1]—'passus est in cruce'—multi fideles sunt indifferentes ad intelligendum[2] illam passionem secundum deitatem vel humanitatem: multi autem proniores ad intelligendum hoc secundum illam naturam secundum quam habet subsistenciam et personam. Ideo racionabiliter ordinarunt sancti specialiter[3] in illa materia ad destruccionem ambiguitatis huiusmodi et certificacionem sentencie pertinentis, quod abstractum[4] limitaret ad sensum expositum. Quandocunque ergo dicitur quod humanitas Christi suscepit[5] predicaciones huiusmodi, intelligendum est quod Christus secundum illam sic suscipit.

Objection III. (If there be no personality nor individuality in the being which is assumed;) then the assumer, the creator, the cause are respectively identical with the thing assumed, created, caused; and so God is assumed.

3° principaliter arguitur [6]deducendo multiplicia inconveniencia[6] que secuntur. Nam primo videtur quod nedum idem est assumens et eciam assumptum, sed quod assumens est assumptum, creans est creatum, causa | suum causatum; [C 84b] ymo si Dominus Iesus Christus sit assumptus, tunc et Deus assumitur, sicut [7]humanitus humiliatur[7]: et per consequens secundum duplicem naturam fuit duplex Christi assumpcio: ymo si nature tam distantes ydemptificari potuerunt, multo evidencius ypostases, que in natura magis conveniunt, tanta ydemptitate uniri potuerunt.[8]

Reply. As in the Trinity there is in the divine nature begetter and begotten, and in humanity (collectively) father and son; so the Word

Ad illud conceditur quod sicut natura divina est generans et generatum, et natura specifica humana cum sit homo pater et eius filius, et per consequens efficiens[9] et effectum; sic Verbum commune[10] ad hec tria deitas, corpus, et anima est simul assumens et assumptum; et racione communicacionis personalis, que distinguitur a duabus prioribus, in quibus est communicacio naturarum, suppositis[11] istis, conceditur quod assumens et assumptum, quamvis in Trinitate non generans, sed illud quod est gignens est genitum; et sic non communis humanitas, sed persona, gignit et gignitur. Ideo aliter

[1–1] ideo cum sic dico homo A B C; ideo sic cum dico hoc O; *forsitan aut* sic *aut* hoc *omittendum*. [2] ad illo intelligendam C. [3] specialiter *om.* C. [4] abstractis C. [5] suscepit O. [6–6] deducendo ad multiplicia inconveniencia A B; deducendo at multi inconveniencia C; deducenda mu tiplicia inconveniencia O. [7–7] humanitas humanatur A B C. [8–8] potuerunt *om.* O. [9] effectus B C. [10] quoad M. [11] istis *om.* C O.

loquendum est in communicacione personarum quam communicacione [1] naturarum eidem supposito. Verumptamen licet Verbum sit assumens et assumptum, tamen non assumitur, sed est natura que assumitur. Et conformiter conceditur quod causans est suum causatum, [2] et creans est suum creatum.[2] Nec ex illo sequitur quod idem [3] secundum idem [3] causat se, cum Verbum solum secundum naturam divinam causat se secundum naturam humanam. Unde non sequitur, [O 229a] quod Deus assumitur, quia predicatum assumpcionis | limitat ad naturam creatam excludendo actum persone vel nature divine assumpto competere: et aliter non esset concedendum quod Deus assumitur, nisi quia vel [4] natura vel persona divina assumitur, [5] quorum utrumque cum sit impossibile docet negandum esse quod Deus assumitur.[5] Et patet quod non est color concedendi quod natura divina creatur, assumitur, patitur, moritur etc. licet Christus, qui est natura divina, predicaciones tales recipiat; cum non secundum [B144a] deitatem sed secundum humanitatem illas sus|cipiat. Et in isto sophismate [6] cecatus est ille Clericus in fide devius,[7] contra quem Anselmus fecit librum De Incarnacione; credidit enim si natura divina sit homo, tunc et omne, quod est natura divina, est homo, [8] et per consequens confuse quelibet persona divina [A.95a] est quelibet, vel tres persone [8] divine sunt tres homines; | ignoravit enim naturam rerum communium. Licet autem negetur quod Deus assumitur, conceditur tamen quod Deus subicitur, humiliatur, et sic de similibus predicatis formalibus; generari quidem vel nasci non solum competit supposito sed nature. Ideo conceditur quod Christus, sicut est duplex essencia vel natura, sic habet duplex esse et duplicem nativitatem: et [9] iuxta illos qui restringunt racionem filii ad suppositum vel personam, tunc tantum una est filiacio in Christo, sicut tantum inest sibi una personalitas, ita quod filiacio

including deity, soul, and body, is both the assumer and the being assumed.

Yet it does not follow that God is assumed; for the assumption is only predicated of the created nature.

Christ, who is a divine nature, is created, suffers, etc.: the divine nature is not created, nor suffers, etc.

The error of Roscellinus, the Nominalist, is answered by Anselm in his De Incarnatione.

[1] personarum *add.* C. [2-2] et creans . . . creatum *om.* O. [3] illud A.
[4] vel quia *codd. omn.* [5-5] quorum . . . assumitur *om.* B.
[6] sophistice A B C. [7] Nestorius *add.* A B; devius . n. contra C.
[8-8] et per vel conse quelibet persona divina est quelibet tres persone O.
[9] et *om.* A B C.

humana accidit[1] filiacioni divine, sicut singularitas hominis accidit personalitati[2] divine. Et sic filiacio humana in Christo simpliciter[3] non est filiacio; cum, multiplicata filiacione que est racio filii, multiplicarentur et filii; sed est genitura temporalis. Aliis autem | plus[4] placet, cum quibus [C 85a] et michi, quod est dare in Christo[5] duplicem filiacionem, sicut et duplicem nativitatem, non autem duplicem personalitatem, cuius racio est nasci, sicut et mori competit persone [6]Christi racione humanitatis et non per se[6] primo illi nature. [7]Ergo per idem vel evidencius filiacio competit supposito primo racione nature, et non primo illi nature.[7] Et hoc sentenciant moderni, qui dicunt, quod natura assumpta non est filius, sed per eius dimissionem[8] Maria potuit[9] duos filios habuisse sine actu giguicionis duplici, vel sine hoc quod illa natura fuit filius Marie pro instanti aliquo vite sue, cum senex inciperet esse filius hominis, quando inciperet dimitti.

Christ has a twofold nativity, a twofold filiation, and a twofold essence.

Licet autem talia ludicria sint impossibilia, tamen videtur probabile quod Christus racione humanitatis habeat filiacionem humanam, sicut racione eiusdem nature habet nativitatem[10] temporalem; potissime cum filiacio sit realis relacio persone[11] in genere sicut alia accidencia Christo humanitus dependent a parente temporali: non sic autem personalitas absoluta, cum *persona* dicitur ethimologice *per se una:* illa ergo non dependet relative ab extremo, nec ab actu temporali, ut nativitas, concepcio, sive giguicio. Unde vel oportet dici[12] quod filiacio eterna accidentaliter sit filiacio hominis, vel quod filiacio hominis non sit filiacio. Secundum non est dandum cum iste terminus *hominis* vel *humanus* non distrahit. Primum autem ex hoc videtur deficere quod filiacio eterna non potest fieri filiacio temporalis. Christus ergo habet in se tot filiaciones quot parentes, sicut Petrus in se tot proporciones duplas et similitudines

Discussion of the *filiatio* of Christ (*a*) eterna, (*b*) humana.

(*Persona* = *per se una.*)

[1] accidat A B C. [2] personali O. [3] simpliciter *om.* A B C.
[4] plus *om.* A B C. [5] in Christo *om.* B. [6–6] Christi . . . per se *om.* O.
[7–7] ergo . . . nature *om.* A B C. [8] dimissionem O.
[9] potuit *om.* C. [10] filiacionem A C. [11] ꝑ se (*i.e.* per se) O.
[12] oporteret dicere O.

quot rebus ipse [1]duplus vel similis est. Et sic[1] cum Ioseph fuit pater eius, ut patet[2] testimonio beate virginis Luce 2°; 'ecce pater tuus et ego dolentes querebamus te;' patet quod Christus habuit ad istum parentem vel nutricium filiacionem legitimam putativam; non autem fuit filius adoptivus, cum non potuit esse filius perdicionis, et illa potencia vel imperfeccio presupponitur ad filium adoptivum. Verumptamen 'predestinatus est Filius Dei,' ut dicit Apostolus ad Rom. 1°. [3]illa quidem creatura ordinata est eternaliter esse Dei Filius naturalis ut[3] sepe dicit Augustinus, et recitat eum Magister 3°[4] Sentenciarum Dist. 6ª.

Luke ii. 48.

Rom. i. 4.

Redeundo ergo ad propositum conceditur quod Christus assumitur, sicut incepit esse et aliquando non fuit; [5]et negatur[6] quod Deus assumitur vel aliquando non fuit,[5] licet ille sit Christus. Et movet me inter alia anathema, quod Augustinus in Exposicione Fidei illud negantibus imprecatur: 'si quis, inquit, dixerit atque crediderit hominem[7] Iesum Christum a Filio Dei assumptum non fuisse, anathema sit.'

To resume the general argument; although God is not assumed, Christ is assumed.

So Augustine, who anathematizes those who deny the proposition that the man Christ Jesus was assumed.

Quod si obicitur quod alius sit sensus quem[8] verba pretendunt, dico quod ad sensum catholicum, quem et[9] ipse conceperat, loquor. Ego puto quidem me in recta logica et philosophia huius sancti dimissis sophismatibus [10]scripture [A 95b] sacre contrariis | educari.[10] Christus ergo assumpsit hominem [C 85b] et non Deum, | licet ille homo sit Deus. Nec est color negandi quod Deus sit exinanitus,[11] passus, humiliatus, et sic de predicatis creatis. [12]Et sic negatur,[12] quod Deus assumptus est; predicatum enim *assumi* limitat ad supposicionem simplicem [13]pro natura, ut—si Deus assumptus est, tunc est deitas[13]—sicut homo assumitur ex hoc quod humanitas est assumpta. Ulterius cum[14] assumpcio respicit

And this is Catholic truth.

[1–1] duplus si} et sic O. [2] ut patet *om.* B.
[3–3] illa quidem creata naturalis ordinata est eternaliter esse filius dei ut A B; illa ordinata est eternaliter esse dei filius C. [4] 3° *om.* O.
[5–5] et negatur . . . non fuit *om.* C O. [6] negetur A B. [7] dominum A B C.
[8] quam A B C; quem *in margine iterum distincte alia manu add.* O.
[9] et *om.* A B C. [10–10] scripture contrariis educare A B; *haec verba om.* C.
[11] inanitus A B C. [12–12] et sic negetur A B C; et si negatur O.
[13–13] pro . . . deitas *om.* C. [14] quod B C.

naturam, conceditur quod, sicut duplex natura a Christo assumitur, scilicet corpus et anima, [1]sic duplex fuit[1] in Christo simplex assumpcio et una completa ad humanitatem principaliter terminata. Nec[2] exinde sequitur quod aliqua illarum posset esse non existente reliqua; [3]sed ordo nature extitit inter[3] illas, ut assumpcio anime fuit prima; et mediante illa assumptum est corpus; et tercio ex his | unita [B 144b est completa humanitas, et totum in eodem instanti temporis, quo iste nature incipiunt esse.[4]

Lastly, in Christ there is a personal identity of different natures, as in the Trinity there is an identity of persons in the *prima essentia.*

Quoad ultimum de ydemptitate constat michi quod numerose evidencie vo|lant hodie[5] ad probandum per locum a [O 229b simili quod quidlibet[6] potest ydemptificari cuilibet, si [7]natura prope nichil potest fieri[7] Deus: exinde enim concluditur quod Deus quamlibet naturam creatam potest assumere, et sic de multis inaniter geminatis. Utrum autem ydemptitas personalis naturarum disparium in Christo sit maior quam ydemptitas personarum[8] in eadem natura simplici, est difficultas. Certum tamen est quod iste ydemptitates sunt disparium racionum et ydemptitas Trinitatis in prima essencia, cum presupponitur ad omnem aliam, est maior quam reliqua, licet non in proporcione racionali.[9] Quoad instancias factas per locum a simili, patet ex dictis quod similitudo non est probabilis.

To explain how this can be, we must leave subtle discussion and fall back on the fundamental facts of the divine nature and the divine will;

Sed dimissis argueiis queritur communiter racio diversitatis, quam est difficile placide assignare, cum sit de fundamento nature; ut quare Deus agens libere contradictorie adextra potuit illud tempus eternum, et non aliud nisi eius partem producere et sic de similibus. Prima ergo pars questionum huiusmodi vel non habet causam,[11] vel consequitur essencialiter ad Deum, sicut passio ad subiectum. Causa autem negative, que est secunda pars questionis, absolute necessaria est per se divina essencia. Cum enim[12]

1–1 sic duplex sit A B C; sicut duplex fuit O. 2 nec *om.* O
3–3 sed est ordo nature inter A B C. 4 cipiunt C; esse *om.* O.
5 hodie *om.* C. 6 ~~quid~~ libet (*sic*) *rasura alia manu add.* A; quelibet B; quilibet C.
7–7 natura proprie nichil potest fieri B; natura prope nichil fieri posset O.
8 personarum *om.* B. 9 naturali C O. 10 parte O.
11 causam *om.* C. 12 enim *om.* A B C.

non potest fieri quod due persone fiant eadem persona in numero, [1]aut due nature eadem natura in numero,[1] vel quod Verbum aliam naturam assumpserat;[2] patet quod solum Deus est causa huius. Quod si dicatur adversarium eque faciliter sustinere oppositum sicut illud a nobis fingitur, dicitur quod tales contenciones sophistice secundum Apostolum sunt nimis inutiles, et ideo debet theologus ipsas abicere[3] tenendo illud quod fides Christiana, scriptura sacra, et sanctorum doctorum consors sentencia ab antiquo nos edocet. Et in omni secta sunt multa credita[4] que nec sufficiunt nec expedit protervo deducere. [5]In hoc tamen[5] excedit secta Christiana quascunque alias, quod maxime archana sue fidei copiose probari [C 86a] possunt, miracula | explanari in naturali lumine evidenciis et exemplis philosophicis, necnon omnes impugnatorum argucie evidenter tolli eciam ex naturalibus et propriis eorum principiis. Ut triplex exemplum[6] ponitur quod fidelis poterit manuduci ad credendum incarnacionis misterium. Primum quomodo duo accidencia diversorum generum, quorum nullum secundum genus potest esse reliquum, sunt idem subiecto ut quantitas et qualitas; non quod [7]sint nature, res, sive substancie[7] que possunt a subiecto et[8] a se invicem separari, sed quod eidem subiecto inest esse quantum et quale; sicut eidem supposito Verbi inest esse tam Deum quam hominem. [A 95c] 2m exemplum propius est, | quod eidem[9] essencie corporee inest posse igniri, quod est materia prima, et accidentaliter esse ignem quod est forma; et sic materia et forma tam dispares sunt eadem essencia, [10]que adventu forme sit aliud quam prefuit; sicut humanitas et deitas sunt eadem persona,[10] que est aliud quam prefuit. 3m exemplum propinquissimum creatorum est de unione ypostatica corporis humani ad animam. Nam eadem persona est tam corpus

Tit. iii. 9.

In accordance with the Christian creed, Holy Scripture, and the concurrent authority of the Fathers. In every 'sect' there are difficulties for the wayward; in the Christian 'sect' the mysteries of the faith can be abundantly proved, explained by light of nature, and illustrated by philosophical evidence and examples, and the subtle objectors refuted on their own ground.

Thus the mystery of the Incarnation may be illustrated by three analogies.

1. Two accidents, *e.g.* quantity and quality, having no separate existence, may be the same as their subject.

2. Matter and form, different in themselves, may be one essence.

3. The union of body

[1]–[1] aut . . . numero *om.* B. [2] assumat O.
[3] ipsas (*corr. al. man.* ipsis) abicere A; ipsis obicere B; ipsis abicere C.
[4] tradita A B C. [5]–[5] et in hoc tantum A B C. [6] exemplum *om.* O.
[7] sint vere res sive substancie A; sint nature res sive substancie B C; sic° n° lmute sbê (sicut nature limitate substancie ?) O. [8] et *om.* A B C.
[9] idem O. [10]–[10] que adventu . . . persona *om.* A B C; que aductû *etc.* O.

*and soul in the person of man.*

quam anima, aliud propter corpus et aliud propter spiritum, sed non alius. Proporcionaliter est de Christo, qui est duarum naturarum utraque. Nam sicut eadem persona hominis nunc est tantum spiritus, nunc cum hoc aliud quia corpus; sic et Christus necessario est deitas sed contingenter humanitas. Raciones autem alias diversitatis et alias conveniencias scit peritus satis elicere et raciones oppositas plane dissolvere.

---

## Cap. X.

[*Suadet 12 evidenciis quod humanitas assumpta sit Christus; et hoc roborat doctorum testimoniis et exemplis.*

*The proposition that the humanity assumed is Christ proved by twelve arguments; and supported by the authority of the Fathers.*]

*The moderns say that the humanity of Christ is not man, although it is a reasonable substance composed of body and soul; (cf. p. 127, l. 12) because by the hypostatic union Christ's humanity is united to an alien substance; and this annuls the negative condition, non suppositata suppositacione aliena, which is a necessary part of the definition of humanity.*

Quia maior pars variacionis in ista materia stat in methaphisica de humanitate assumpta; ideo expedit iuxta ponere sentencias contrarias supradictis. Dicunt enim moderni concorditer [1] quod humanitas Christi nec est homo, nec suppositum, vel persona, licet sit substancia racionalis [2] composita ex corpore [2] et anima, que sunt partes hominis Iesu Christi; sed dimissa illa natura suppositacioni proprie,[3] [4] ut possit per possibile [4] quod maneat non assumpta, tunc foret homo et modo non est homo. Ideo dicunt quod diffinicio hominis negacionem includit formaliter, ita quod descriptive homo sit substancia ex corpore et anima intellectiva composita [5] *non suppositata suppositacione* [6] *aliena.* Et quia ultima differencia deficit nature assumpte cum

[1] concorditer *om.* A B; conco C. [2] goncorpe ex cor^e C.
[3] Pp^c (*i.e.* prope) O.
[4..4] ut posito proporcionale A; ait posito per possibile B; ut posito possibile C.
[5] composit O. [6] suppo~~sitata~~ (*rasura al. man.*) A; supposicione B C.

suppositatur suppositacione Verbi; ideo[1] stante assumpcione ypostatica non est homo.

*This is a harder saying than the older doctrine.*

Ista sentencia[2] iam famosa est michi et forte aliis magis difficilis quam aliqua sentencia antiquorum doctorum superius inculcata. Primo ergo videtur quod Christi humanitas non suppositatur suppositacione aliena: nam[3] nec est nec fit suppositum: et omne suppositari est fieri vel esse suppositum: ergo non suppositatur. Preterea si aliqua supposi-tacione suppositatur cum illa [4]nulli alii creature[4] conveniat, videtur quod sit suppositacio sibi propria, et sic non ali- [C 86b] qualiter | aliena. Confirmatur ex hoc quod suppositacio qua suppositatur formaliter est solummodo temporalis et per consequens dependet ab illa humanitate, sicut accidens respectivum dependet essencialiter ab extremo. Quod si [B 145a] dicatur suppositacionem illam | esse suppositum Verbi, tunc indubie cuiuslibet suppositi creati suppositacio dependet a suppositacione aliena, quia a supposito increato et ad illud finaliter terminatur; et per consequens nullum esset suppositum creatum.

*The hypostatic union does not imply suppositatio aliena.*

*With reference to suppositation Duns Scotus distinguishes three forms of dependence with a negation corresponding to each, 1. actual;*

[O 229c] Sed hic dicit Doctor Subtilis super 3° Senteneiarum | Dist. 1ª Questione articuli 3ⁱ quod est dare [5]triplicem negacionem, sicut et triplicem dependenciam pertinentem. Aliquid enim[6] actualiter dependet a suppositacione aliena, quando est natura completa suppositi nature superioris; ut humanitas Christi[7] non est suppositum, sed natura suppositi Verbi; et si Verbum faceret ipsam esse non naturam persone[8] superioris, tunc esset suppositum et persona. Nichil[9] ergo deficit ad hoc quod sit persona nisi ista negacio quod non est natura suppositi superioris nature. Ideo suppositacio, quam habet in potencia terminatur suppositacione Verbi, que non actu sed potencia est aliena a suppositacione nature humane. 2ª dependencia vocatur potencialis[10]; quando scilicet

*2. potential:*

[1] ymo B C. [2] sentenciam O. [3] et iam O.
[4-4] nulli n^e (*i.e.* nature) O.
[5] dare *om.* B. [6] enim *om.* O. [7] Christi *om.* O.
[8] p^c *codd. omn.: quod compendium etiam* per se *significare potest.*
[9] vel O. [10] personalis A B C.

natura racionalis dependet a supposito increato a quo potest assumi, sed nondum assumitur in unitatem | persone; sed [A 95d] et talem negacionem oportet naturam creatam habere, ut sit persona[1] hominis. 3ª est dependencia obediencialis,[2] qua omne suppositum substancie essencialis dependet a qualibet persona increata, sed eciam[3] potest assumi in unitatem suppositi increati, ut sit communicacio[4] ydiomatum, et ut ipso facto natura persone increate vere Deus sit lapis vel lignum vel cuiuscunque speciei [5]substancie individuum; sicut Deus iam est individuum speciei[5] humane, licet natura talis non possit esse[6] persona divina.

*3. obediential dependence; and applies the last of these to the humanity assumed in the incarnation.*

Dimissa autem contencione verbali, quod supposicacio Verbi non est aliena a supposicacione nature assumpte, cum illa non sit; arguitur primo contra illud[7] per hoc quod omnis homo-non-Deus per se est homo: omnis natura humana completa non assumpta est homo: ergo omnis talis natura per se est homo, et per consequens non potest vicissim nunc esse homo et nunc non-homo. Maior licet sit famosa apud philosophos potest[8] ex hoc patescere, quia aliter humanitas non esset species vel quiditas cuiuscunque persone[9] hominis; cum potest manere idem quod est modo[10] et non homo. Non ergo predicatur homo in quid de aliquo supposito[11] humano; et per idem nulla potest esse per se species in genere substancie, cum omnis substancia potest esse idem quod est, et non esse individuum huius speciei.

*Arguments to prove that the assumed humanity is (the man Christ i.e.) man.*

*i. Every complete human nature is in itself (per se) man.*

Item impossibile est aliquid esse accidentaliter alicuiusmodi[12] nisi sibi insit accidens a quo est huiusmodi formaliter sicut patet ponenti respectus et accidencia distincta: sed omnis homo iuxta hanc | viam accidentaliter est homo: ergo [C 87a] est dare formam accidentalem qua est homo formaliter. Sed et hoc concedunt plurimi dicentes quod in assumpcione ypostatica negacio supradicta corrumpitur et in dimissione

*i. Everything requires an accidental difference to constitute it formally what it is:*

*the aforesaid negation (p. 160, l. 21) called ultima differencia by the objector,*

[1] pars A B C.
[2] obediencialis *om.* A B *relicto xii litterarum spatio*: *et sine spatio om.* C.
[3] et O.
[4] communicacio *om.* C.
[5–5] substancie . . . speciei *om.* O.
[6] posset A B C; possit persona *om.* esse O.
[7] idem A B C.
[8] potest *om.* O.
[9] per se B.
[10] numero C.
[11] supposito *om.* O.
[12] modi *om.* A B C.

ypostatica generatur: et per illam est homo formaliter aliquid positivum, ut nichil, in quantum caret visu vel non habet hoc vel illud, est aliquid. Ex quo sequitur quod nichil in quantum homo vel persona hominis est aliquid vel alicuiusmodi[1] positivum; cum quicquid aut cuiusmodicunque[2] homo nunc est, assistente negacione quod *non suppositatur*[2] *suppositacione aliena*, potest esse adveniente suppositacione aliena ipso facto non[3] homine vel persona. Quod est contra Augustinum 7° De Trinitate 9° volente, quod persona in quantum huiusmodi, est aliquid, non ad aliquid. Si ergo nemo potest fieri qualis aut quantus nisi moveatur, multo magis nemo potest fieri homo cum hoc quod non exinde moveatur; aliter enim non esset generacio.

is not such a difference; for a negation being nothing cannot formally constitute anything: and therefore does not affect the proposition that the assumed humanity is Christ.

Item eo ipso quod forma inseparabilis inest[4] mere formaliter alicui, ipsum denominat[5]: sed humanitas est forma inseparabiliter existens cuicumque nature humane: ergo si inest alicui singulari nature ipsam denominat[5]: sed non potest denominare quicquam primo formaliter nisi hominem: ergo, si inest nature create formaliter, ipsa est homo. [6]Cum ergo humanitas manet continue in natura humana assumpta, videtur quod stante assumpcione erit homo continue sicut prius. Minor videtur ex hoc quod omnis homo est formaliter humanitate homo, sicut mobile movetur motu formaliter, album denominatur albedine, et paciens passione. Humanitas ergo manens post unionem denominat[5] formaliter Christum esse hominem et non dicta negacio: ymo cum ipse sit [7]homo nobiscum univoce et in[7] sua racione, non oportet negacionem ponere, sed ipse humanitate est homo formaliter, videlicet[8] [A 96a] quod eadem sit racio cuiuslibet fratris sui. Ipse enim | non potest suppositari suppositacione aliena, nec negacione; sed humanitate oportet ipsum esse singulare speciei humane formaliter: ergo per idem et alios univoce consimilis speciei.

iii. Humanity is an inseparable form which belongs to every individual man, and to none other:

therefore to predicate humanity of Christ is to assert that he is man.

[1] modi *om.* A B C. [2] supponitur A B C. [3] in O.
[4] inest *om.* A B C. [5] denominant A B C. [6] et *add.* B.
[7–7] homo unitate in (*spatio viii litt. relicto*) A B; homo unitate in C.
[8] vl. (*i.e.* unde) O.

iv. Humanity consists in a human supposite being man; and the Word, by assuming humanity, assumed man; not the nature of any already existing individual man; but *the form of a servant*, i.e. the essence of man.

Item iuxta dicta *De Universalibus* omnis humanitas est suppositum humanum esse hominem: sed, posito quod Verbum assumat ypostatice naturam Petri, manebit ista assumpta humanitas: ergo manebit quod idem suppositum est homo; et sic personam manentem personam Verbum assumeret. [1] Pro assumpto non est facile fingere, quid sit humanitas, | quam Apostolus vocat 'formam servi,' [2] nisi [B 145b] esset [3] hominis vel humana essencia. Et ex isto [4] videtur quod alia nova humanitas [5] incepit esse homo, quando Christus incepit esse homo, humanitate [5] Petri extincta per assumpcionem; quia quod Verbum est homo, tunc incipit [6] esse et quod Petrus est homo tunc desinit. Ex quo | patet [C 87b] quod non assumpsit naturam Petri, cum illa natura manet modo [7] tantum distans a Verbo ut prius. Nam illa res, que prius [8] fuit suppositum Petri, nec est natura nec persona divina, nec est homo modo sicut nec Christus est natura humana: per antecedens [9] vero ista res et Christus conveniebant in specie sic quod uterque fuit homo ut suppono [10]: ergo maior fuit convenienca tunc quam modo. Nec valet dicere quod Christus est homo formaliter non negacione [11] nec humanitate, sed ypostatica unione; quia sic foret racio qua [12] Christus est homo multum equivoca a racione qua quicumque alius est [13] homo; quod indubie sequitur [13] multiplici racione. Nam quilibet alius homo dicitur formaliter homo | negative [14] et per consequens racione increata; [O 229d] Christus autem dicitur homo per unionem ypostaticam, que nulli alii potest competere.

Nor is the Word *man* in any equivocal sense, otherwise than other men.

v. Christ is *per se humanitas* as other men;

Item quilibet alius homo a Christo [15] est per se humanitas; Christus secundum istam viam non potest esse humanitas: ergo non est univoce homo cum alio. Maior patet ex hoc quod licet omnis homo per accidens sit homo, tamen eo ipso

[1] et *add.* A B C. [2] servi *om.* B. [3] esse A B C. [4] quo B.
[5–5] incepit quando Christus incepit esse homo humanitate A B C; incepit esse homo humanitate O. [6] incepit C O. [7] non B.
[8] prius *om.* O. [9] per ante A B C; per aũ O. [10] supp° A B C.
[11] non negacione *om.* O. [12] quia O. [13–13] homo et dubie sequitur quod O.
[14] negacione A B C; netiẽ O. [15] Christo *om.* O.

quod est[1] humanitas, cum iuxta hanc viam post assumpcionem manebit non homo sed humanitas: sed cum illa humanitas non inceperit[2] esse per assumpcionem, sequitur quod prius manserat iste homo. Hoc 2° confirmatur ex eo quod omne per accidens [3]oportet reduci ad aliquid per se[3]: sed Petrus est per accidens homo: ergo est prius per se aliquid, quod potissime foret humanitas. 3° per istud[4] quod ista humanitas adequate individuatur ex eisdem principiis ex quibus iste homo: ergo sunt idem: non ergo potest esse ordo causandi inter eos. Et consequencia principalis ex hoc videtur quod, dato antecedente, Christus et quicumque alius homo non forent eiusdem nature univoce. Nam quilibet alius homo foret natura humana in recto: Christus non potest esse natura humana sed nature humane: igitur sicut Deus non predicatur univoce de creatura, de qua solum dicitur in obliquo, et de persona divina, de qua dicitur in recto; sic nec humanitas dicitur univoce de Christo et aliis: et per consequens non sunt univoce eiusdem nature: ymo cum humanitas sit nomen competentissimum speciei per se predicatum de suis suppositis[5] et non homo, humanitas autem non potest predicari in recto de Christo, videtur quod Christus non sit eiusdem speciei cum homine. Confirmatur ex hoc quod Christus non potest esse [6]alicuius speciei: ergo Christus non est singulare[7] speciei humane. [8]Nam per adversarios non potest esse[6] aliquid nisi deitas, sed[9] [A96b] ipsa[10] non | potest esse aliquid speciei humane[8]: ergo Christus non potest esse aliquid speciei humane. Si enim deitas foret illius speciei, tunc foret causabilis passibilis et activa, sicut alia individua speciei: quod est impossibile. Ideo, si non fallor, repugnat isti vie,[11] quod Christus sit eiusdem speciei cum aliis. Et in ista methaphisica vellem me studuisse, quando sollicitabam[12] me, si quantitas, motus,

else he is not of the same nature as other men; (and then *humanitas* cannot be predicated of Christ *casu recto*, as *Deus* can only be predicated of a creature *casu obliquo*;)

in that case Christ is in fact not of the human species at all.

(The author regrets that in time past, instead of worrying himself about the distinction of accidents, (cf. p. 162, l. 28)

[1] e' (*rasura*) ē A; eûj B; cûj est C.
[2] incepit B; incipit O.
[3–3] oportet alicui per se C; oportet inniti alicui per se O.
[4] ex isto B; per idem O.
[5] compositis O.
[6–6] alicuius . . . esse *om.* O.
[7] simpliciter C.
[8–8] nam . . . humane *bis* A C.
[9] sed *om.* O.
[10] ipse C.
[11] die O.
[12] sollicitabor A B C.

(he did not study the 'metaphysic' of the distinction of the humanity from the Word.) et cetera accidencia distinguantur. | Subtilior enim est distinccio humanitatis a Verbo quam accidentis huiusmodi a subiecto; cum[1] secundum moderniores[2] Petrus inficians[3] in ista hora per assumpcionem et dimissionem potest esse homo et post non homo[4] sine[5] generacione vel corrupcione alicuius rei vel motu aliquo pertinente; quod non contingit eciam de relacione. [C 88a]

vi. If the assumed humanity be not Christ, and if Christ thus differ from it in essence and person; then through the incarnation Christ is not anything other than he was before, being only deity: and there can be no *univocation*, i.e. nothing can be predicated of Christ in the same sense as of any creature.

Item iuxta nunc tacta, si illa humanitas non sit Christus, sed Christus tam extranee differt et essencialiter et personaliter[6] ab illa; tunc Christus per incarnacionem non est aliquid[7] nisi quod fuit eternaliter, cum sit solum deitas sicut ante: sed in deitate non univocatur cum aliqua creatura: ergo nichil vel non aliquid[8] est Christus, in quo univocatur cum aliqua creatura.[9] Sequitur enim—Christus est univoce homo cum aliis: ergo est univoce aliquid cum alio—sicut a simili,[10] si Christus sit univoce albus cum Petro, tunc est univoce coloratus, et qualis cum eo, et ita de aliis generibus quibuscumque. Et sequitur—Christus est univoce aliquid cum aliqua creatura; ergo[11] aliquid est Christus in quo ipse univocatur cum aliqua creatura—quod non esset possibile,[12] si solum deitas foret Christus: oportet ergo speciem humanam, que est communis humanitas, esse Christum; et per consequens non solum naturam divinam, cum illa sit natura plurimum separata a natura humana: ymo cum[13] nulla substancia secunda inest supposito nisi mediante substancia prima, patet quod non communis humanitas foret Christus, nisi singularis [14] humanitas, que natura assumpta foret [14] Christus: patet igitur,[15] si Christus sit eiusdem speciei nobiscum, quod ista species in athomo[16] vel individuo foret Christus; et sic aliquid, quod non eternaliter fuit

[1] tamen A B C. [2] modernos O. [3] inficiens A B; infi in ista C; infinicies O. [4] homo *om.* A B C. [5] sive (*corr. ex* sine) A. [6] potencialiter O. [7] aliud B. [8] aliquando C. [9] ergo non aliquid . . . creatura *iterum* A B C. [10] iuassimili B O. [11] et O. [12] et *add.* O. [13] st (sicut) *add.* O. [14–14] humanitatis (que est natura *in rasura*) humana foret A; humanitatis que est natura humana foret B C. [15] ergo A B C. [16] athopio B; in *cum lacuna* C; attomo O.

Christus. Et sic intelligit Augustinus Enchiridion 29°,[1] 'Utraque, inquit, substancia, divina scilicet atque humana, Filius est unicus Dei Patris omnipotentis, de quo procedit Spiritus[2] Sanctus; utraque[3] unus, sed aliud propter Verbum, et aliud propter hominem.' Unde prius 28°[4] miratur quomodo ille homo fit[5] una persona cum Deo. Et in libro De Predestinacione Sanctorum bene post medium: 'Ille, inquit, homo ut a Verbo Patri coeterno in unitate persone assumptus Filius Dei unigenitus esset! Unde[6] hoc meruit? Faciente, [B 146a] inquit, et suscipiente Deo Verbo[7], ipse homo, | ex quo esse cepit, Filius Dei unigenitus[8] esse cepit.' Ideo ut exponit 13 De Trinitate 37°. 'Gracia Dei in hoc commendatur quod Christus tanta unitate Deo sit coniunctus,[9] ut una cum [C 88b] illo persona Filius Dei fieret, nullis | eius precedentibus meritis.'

Augustine's doctrine is that either substance, the divine and the human, is the Son.

Sed hic datur duplex responsio. Prima quod non est equivocacio vel univocacio nisi in signis solummodo, et sic nulla res est quicquam univoce sive equivoce, sed signa dicuntur quedam equivoce et quedam univoce. 2a responsio modernorum doctorum stat in glosa Augustini et aliorum sic loquencium, quod ipsi non intendunt[10] naturam assumptam esse Verbum sed naturam[11] Verbi.

The author's opponents would reply 1. That univocation and equivocation apply to *signs* (*i.e. words*) only, not to *things*; 2. That Augustine and others mean not that the nature assumed is the Word, but the *nature* of the Word.

Contra primum verbale sophisticum non delector pro[12] nunc [A 96c] arguere, quia intencio loquencium de | rebus univocis est cognoscere, si res similes in racione vel quiditate communicant, vel si de creata essencia Christi est quod ipse sit homo, sicut est de essencia cuiuscunque alterius singularis hominis quod sit homo. Aliter enim secundum verbales logicos non predicaretur iste terminus *homo* in quid de Verbo et secundum rectam methaphisicam; nisi Christus[13] secundum humanitatem, vel secundum quod homo sit aliquid sit[14] sic quod humanitas

vii. The first reply is a sophistical evasion. In using *univocal* terms, people mean to express

[1] nono A B C. [2] Spiritus *om.* A B O; ~~spus~~ scus C.
[3] utrumque O. [4] 28 *om. spatio relicto* C. [5] sit A B C.
[6] cum *add.* A B C. [7] deo ~~cum verbo~~ A. [8] unicus O.
[9] conuictus (*forsitan pro* conviuctus) O. [10] intendunt *in margine* A; *om.* B.
[11] sed natura A B C; secundum naturam O. [12] pro *om.* A B C.
[13] nisi Christus *om.* O. [14] sit *om.* O.

a real identity of being: for substance or *quidity* is as real as *quality* or *quantity*.

sit causa, quare ipse est idem.[1] | Aliter non foret univoce [O 230a] homo cum aliis humanitate specifica. Sicut enim[2] quantitate est subiectum *quantum*, qualitate *quale*, et ita de ceteris; sic substancia vel quiditate est *quid* vel *aliquid* formaliter: et ita, sicut adveniente qualitate fit subiectum [3]eo ipso *quale* quod prius[3] non fuerat; sic adveniente[4] substancia vel quiditate fit subiectum eo ipso *aliquid* quod prius non fuerat. Cum ergo humanitas st per consequens quiditas advenit Christo formaliter, sequitur quod secundum illam fit aliquid quod prius non fuerat, et per consequens est [5]dare, quod aliquid est[5] Christus per incarnacionem, in quo convenit cum homine plus quam ante: et cum *quid* dicit naturam ut *quis* dicit personam, sequitur quod post incarnacionem alia substancialis essencia est Christus, que[6] prius non fuerat: quia aliter indubie in nullo esset univoce vel conveniens creature plus quam ante. Sicut ergo pertinenter queritur et solvitur—[7] Qualis est Petrus post alteracionem,[7] qualis prius non fuerat?—sic pertinenter queritur et solvitur—Quid est Christus[8] post incarnacionem, quod ante non fuerat?—[9] et illud est substancia,[9] natura, et essencia creata Dominus Iesus Christus, que[10] est Verbum esse hominem; quia aliter indubie homo non predicaretur in quid de Verbo: nec Christus, in quantum homo esset aliquid, quod nedum contradicit principiis philosophicis, sed eciam Decretali [11]* *Cum Christus*[12] libro 7° De Hereticis. Quomodo queso dicerent[13] doctores tam veteres quam novi quod aliquid cepit esse Christus, nisi aliquid per incarnacionem fuerit factum Christus? Aliter non oportuit Decretalem libro 7° De Hereticis sic scripsisse: 'Cum Christus perfectus Deus

To deny this is unphilosophical; and contrary to the Decretal beginning *Cum Christus*; which anathematizes

[1] aliud *in rasura* O.
[2] ergo A B C.
[3]–[3] quale eo ipso quale prius B.
[4] sic deveniente A B; si adveniente O.
[5]–[5] dare quod aliquid est A B; dare quod est C.
[6] qui (*al. man. corr.* que) A; qui B.
[7]–[7] qualis . . . alteracionem *om.* O.
[8] et *add.* O.
[9] et idem substancia A B C.
[10] qui A B C.
[11] *Totus hic locus post verbum* decretali *usque ad* confirmatur, *p.* 170, *l.* 15, *in codice* O. *omissus est.*
[12] Cum Christus *om.* O.
[13] debeñt C.

et perfectus homo, mandamus quatenus[1] sub anathemate interdicas—Ne quis de ceteris[2] audeat dicere, *Christum non esse aliquid secundum quod homo*—quia sicut Christus verus [C 89a] est Deus, ita verus est homo ex anima racionali et humana [3]carne | subsistens.'[3]

any who deny the reality of Christ's existence as man (*secundum quod homo*). From which Decretal follow two consequences.

Ex qua Decretali patet primo quod Christus, quia homo, est aliquid quod ante non fuerat; 2° quod sit univoce homo cum aliis. Nam aliter non esset verus homo ex elementis[4] univocis cum aliis principiis fratrum suorum. Aliter enim non esset vere homo, sicut nec Spiritus Sanctus est vere columba. Habito ergo quod sit univoce homo cum aliis, ut dicit Augustinus in quodam Sermone De Trinitate: patet quod est univoce animal, corpus, et substancia cum aliis; et per consequens substancia, que est Christus, est univoce substancia cum aliis substanciis creatis: [5]et cum nulla natura divina sit univoce substancia cum aliis creatis substanciis[5]; sequitur quod creata substancia assumpta est [6]univoce et Christus cum aliis[6] substanciis. Confirmatur tripliciter. [7]Omnis substancia unica univoce[7] subiecta est accidentibus cum aliis creatis substanciis: sed illa non potest esse substancia, essencia, vel natura divina: ergo relinquitur quod alia substancia, ita quod sit gigas gemine substancie, ut canit ecclesia. Item Christus cum sit univoce homo, animal, corpus, et substancia cum aliis est species et genus hominis; et omne tale universale est creatum secundum se totum: ergo [A 96d] Christus | est aliquod creatum. Item si Decretalis solum intelligit Christum esse aliquid *secundum quod homo*; quia omnis homo est aliquid, et, si Christus est homo, ipse est aliquid; tunc conceditur, quod Christus secundum quod quantus, qualis, vel quomodolibet aliter accidentatus foret aliquid; quod notum est repugnare logice, methaphisice, et sensui Decretalis. Sic enim dicerent quod omnis homo secundum quod peccator est aliquid placens: et Christus

1. That Christ, as man, is something other than he was before:
2. That he is man in the same sense (*univoce*) with other men: not metaphorically, as the Holy Spirit is a dove; but as a real created substance;

and thus he is

*gigas gemine substancie*; Ps. xix. 5. Gen. vi. 4. (cf. p. 9. l. 21; and p. 102, l. 27.)

a created thing;

but not a *thing* (i.e. a real existence) only because *created*;

[1] qts A; 9t9 B; 9tmus C. [2] cetero BC. [3] carne assumpta vel subsistens C.
[4] elementis *om. spatio relicto* C. [5–5] et . . . substanciis *om.* B.
[6–6] *an* univoce homo cum aliis *legendum?* [7–7] c̄e substancia univoce C.

secundum quod homo natus ex virgine creavit mundum, cum ut sic inanitus sit equalis Deo[1] Patri; et per consequens secundum quod minor Patre est equalis Patri. Sed quis, rogo, hereticus negaret quin Christus, si est homo, est aliquid? Ideo certum est quod nec Decretalis nec hereticus intelligit sic reduplicativam; sed ut iste terminus *secundum* signat causam formalem specificam, que est causa subiectiva, unde Christus sit aliquid ut pugnarius substancie. Unde videtur michi indubie quod quicunque | concedit de Christo [B 146b] communicacionem ydiomatum et denominacionem univocam accidencium cum creatura, habet concedere consequenter,[2] quod Christus sit duplex substancia et per consequens creatura. Nam increata non potest esse creato accidenti absoluto subiecta; quia tunc foret mole magna et specialis,[3] ut alie create substancie.*[4]

*For the term, secundum quod homo, only indicates a subjective cause.*

Confirmatur ex hoc, quod post incarnacionem fideles sciverunt quid est Verbum, quod per ante nec Deus sciverat esse Verbum: ergo aliquid tunc fuit[5] Verbum quod prius non fuerat. Infideles ergo nescientes ipsum esse Deum sciverunt quid[6] fuerat: ergo fuit aliquid preter deitatem. Cum ergo aliqua racio substancialis | post incarnacionem [C 89b] Verbo conveniat, que non prius convenerat, que non potest poni, nisi hoc quod Verbum est homo; sequitur quod hec sit racio substancialis non aliena a Christo, ut nunc fingitur. Nec sollicitor[7] aptare verba, ut pertineret volenti contendere cum doctoribus signorum[8]; quia ex dictis[9] patet materialiter sentencia et racio Augustini.

*Further proofs that after the incarnation Christ is something other than he was before.*

Illud confirmari potest tripliciter. Primo ex hoc: Verbum assumendo hominem assumpsit aliquid; ergo cum omne assumere sit facere, sequitur, quod faciendo se esse[10] hominem, fecit se esse aliquid; et per consequens per assumpcionem fuit aliquid quod prius non fuerat. 2° confirmatur. Posito quod[11]

*And proofs of quidity in the humanity assumed.*

[1] deo *om.* C. [2] communitur (*al. man. corr.* consequenter) A; communiter C. [3] specialibilis B. [4] *v. p.* 168, *n.* 11. [5] fuerat A B C. [6] quod B. [7] Nolicitor O. [8] terminorum O. [9] signis C. [10] esse *om.* O. [11] quod *om.* O.

pro instanti incarnacionis Petrus fidelis cognoscat Verbum divinum nunc esse Deum et ignoret quod nunc sit homo; tunc patet quod sequitur—Verbum divinum nunc non est aliquid quin iste Petrus nunc[1] cognoscat ipsum esse aliquid: sed Verbum divinum nunc est homo: ergo Petrus cognoscit ipsum nunc esse hominem—. Hic enim non est fallacia accidentis, cum Christus, in quantum homo, sit aliquid: et consequens est falsum: ideo relinquitur quod maior: ex quo sequitur aliquid esse nunc Verbum, quod Petrus nunc ignorat esse Verbum, quod non potest poni deitas. 3° confirmatur ex hoc quod quantitas et cetera accidencia non sunt essencialiter distincta[2] a subiectis: ergo multo evidencius humanitas est homo.

viii. Answer to the second reply of the objectors (p. 167, l. 19). Their gloss upon Augustine comes to a flat contradiction of his plain meaning.

Quoad 2dum[3] patet cuilibet volenti advertere, quod glosa est nimis extranea preter mentem sanctorum; ut quando Augustinus, Gregorius, Ieronimus, Anselmus, et alii dicunt, quod utraque substancia, scilicet divina et humana, est Christus, dicit glosa ipsos per hoc intendere, quod altera non est Christus, sed natura eius, nec conveniens secum[4] in essencia nec persona. Pro certo inter omnes glosas, quas unquam audiveram est hec inculcior, glosare dicta sanctorum directe per sua opposita. Si,[5] inquam, ista glosa sufficeret, quis formidaret auctoritatem sibi oppositam? [6] Sed ut pallient[6] glosam suam, dimittunt verbaliter nega[A 97a]tivam[7] dicentes quod Augustinus intendit utramque naturam esse naturam Christi. Quando autem queritur utrum Augustinus intendit utramque naturam esse Christum, dicunt quod non, sed utramque esse naturam Christi. Et quando ulterius opponitur, si[8] intenderit naturam humanam esse Christum, sicut intendit naturam divinam esse Christum, dicunt quod non: et sic[9] finaliter incidunt in glosam yronicam supradictam. Sed quam sinistrum est dicere quod tam subtiles logici et

[1] nunc *om.* B; non O.
[2] distincte O.
[3] tercium A B C; *sed de* secunda responsione (*p.* 167, *l.* 20) *nunc agitur.*
[4] secum *om.* A B C.
[5] sed C.
[6]–[6] sed plus pallientes O.
[7] negacionem C.
[8] sed O.
[9] quia sit O.

philosophi tam pii et prudentes theologi in precipua materia fidei, capciosissimis hereticis circumsepti, dicerent tam crebro et patule quod utraque natura Christi est Deus, quia persona Christi, si finaliter intenderent quod altera est | Deus, [1]et [C 90a] altera non est Deus.[1] Et nimis leve[2] verbum est dicere Augustinum [3]intendere, quando dicit[3] 'aliud Deus aliud homo sed non alius, quia non alia persona,' [4]quod est[4] quod ipse per hoc intendit, quod non natura alterius persone sit Christi deitas sive humanitas: tum quia glosa illa seipsam interimit falsitate, cum natura divina sit natura alterius persone quam Filii, quia tam Patris quam Doni[5]; tum eciam quia verba essent nimis impertinencia suis sentenciis. Nam Augustinus persepe asserit, quod anima sit Christus [6]et caro Christus, sicut deitas Christus et humanitas Christus,[6] utrumque aliud a reliquo sed non alius[7]; ut patet super Ioh. Omo. 47. 78 et sepe alibi ut patet superius. Et ad hunc sensum ut verba sonant ac raciones concordant, exponunt eum Anselmus, Hugo de Sancto Victore, et alii. Unde De Incarnacione ca° 6° in fine sic scribit Anselmus; 'suscepit Verbum hominem in unitatem persone, ut due nature, scilicet[8] divina et humana, sint una persona.' Et hoc dicit Augustinus in Dialogo ad Felicianum; 'aliud, inquit, Dei Filius, aliud hominis filius, sed non alius:' et primo De Trinitate 9° ca°; 'forma [9]Dei formam[9] hominis accepit, utraque[10] Deus utraque homo'; et sic de quotlibet similibus, ex quibus patet quod sensus datus Augustini primo De Trinitate[11] 16° sit nimis sophisticus,[11] quando dicit, 'talis fuit illa | suscepcio, que hominem faceret Deum et [O 230b] Deum hominem'; hoc est, ut inquiunt, 'illa suscepcio fecit quod homo est Deus, et e contra.' Quis dubitat eciam laicus[12] de conversione illorum? Non ergo oportuit Augustinum

Augustine not only asserts that the human nature is Christ (*i.e.* the Word); but that even its separate parts, soul and flesh, are Christ: and

he was so understood by Anselm, Hugo de Sancto Victore, and others.

So that both these propositions are rightly asserted—*God is man*—and—*man is God*—

[1–1] et . . . deus *om.* O. [2] leve *om.* O. [3–3] intenderet aliud B.
[4] quod est *om.* A B C. [5] dūi A; dōi B.
[6–6] et . . . Christus *om.* B. [7] alius *om.* C.
[8] scilicet *om.* O. [9] forn (*idem verbum in utroque loco*) O.
[10] utrumque B. [11–11] racio sit nimis sophistica A B C.
[12] logicus A B; laycus C.

exponere quod idem sit—Deum esse hominem—et—hominem esse Deum. Intenditur[1] ergo, ut alibi sepe dicit, quod natura illa sit[2] Deus et Deus sit illa natura ypostatice assumendo.[3] Et sic favorabilius et coloracius sunt moderni glosandi, qui dicunt quod humanitas non est Deus. Intendunt enim quod Deus nec per se nec formaliter nec secundum essenciam deitatis sit humanitas.

*by reason of the hypostatic union; although in Himself, formally, and according to the essence of the divine nature, God is not man.*

Et si queratur qualis predicacio sit[4] ista—Deus est homo sive humanitas—, dicitur quod equivocando in nomine acci- [B 147a] dentis | [5]ut supra; hoc[5] est, per accidens; sicut et hoc—Petrus est bipedalis[6]—secundum negantes quantitates distingui est predicacio secundum essenciam; non quod deitas sit natura humana, sed quod persona deitatis sit illa essencia. Est eciam in parte predicacio causalis et formalis, cum humanitas causata a Deo sit 'forma servi,[7] secundum quam Deus est servus obediens Trinitati. Et patet quod humanitas cum sit forma temporalis distinguitur a Verbo, licet sit ypostatice ipsum Verbum. Nec sequitur per locum a simili quod substancia sit sua quantitas; cum non possit esse personalis unio substancie ad accidens inherens formaliter.

*The proposition —God is man or humanity—is logically a predicacio equivoca per accidens.*

[C 90b] Item si sint aliqua | duo, quorum omnes partes sint idem inter se, et[8] ipsa sunt [9]idem inter se: sed Christus et eius humanitas sunt duo distincta quorum omnes partes sunt [A 97b] idem inter se: ergo[9] et ipsa tota | eisdem[10] adequale composita. Minor[11] patet ex hoc quod quelibet pars corporis Christi sicut et totum ipsum corpus et anima est pars humanitatis Christi et e contra; cum Christus non habet partem[12] qualitativam aut quantitativam, nisi secundum humanitatem eo quod secundum deitatem sit indivisibilis omnino. Et maior patet eis qui ponunt omne totum compositum ex partibus esse insimul[13] illas partes; hoc autem

*IX. Things, all the parts of which are the same, are themselves the same: the parts of Christ and of his humanity are the same; therefore Christ and his humanity are the same. It is only in his human nature that Christ has parts; the divine nature is indivisible.*

[1] intendunt A B C.
[2] fit O.
[3] assumenda (*corr. ex* assumendo) A.
[4] est O.
[5-5] accidentis hic (ut supra *om.*) B.
[6] septipedalis A B; bipedalitas O.
[7] servi *om.* O.
[8] et *om.* A B C.
[9-9] idem sed sic est de Christo et eius humanitate ergo A B C.
[10] ex eis A B C.
[11] maior A B C.
[12] partem *om.* O.
[13] in simile A B C; insim] O.

hic supponitur. Et patet cum ista multitudo parcium sit Christus et ista eadem multitudo sit ista humanitas, quod Christus et ista humanitas sunt idem alicui tercio; et per consequens inter se: et cum nulla ydemptitas sit pertinens nisi fuerit personalis, sequitur quod Christus et illa humanitas sunt [1] eadem persona.[1] Et istam sentenciam videtur sapere prima conclusio 5[ti] [2] Elementorum Euclidis: 'si fuerint quotlibet quantitates aliquarum totidem eque multiplices, ut eque maiores aut eque minores, aut singule singulis equales, quemadmodum [3] una illarum [3] ad sui comparem; necesse est totum aggregatum ex his singulariter [4] se habere.' Quod eque evidenter videtur de ydemptitate tocius ad totum, presupposita ydemptitate numerali [5] cuiuscunque partis ad partem sibi correlatam,[6] sicut de [7] paritate proporcionum, sicut patet † applicati.[8] Nam si sint aliqua duo, et quelibet pars unius ydemptificata fuerit parti alterius et e contra; tunc unum [9] ydemptificatur [10] primo alteri.

The major premiss is confirmed by Euclid v. 1.

So the Word assumes every qualitative and quantitative part which an individual man has, and makes every such part a part of himself;

Pono ergo quod Verbum incipiat a pedibus Petri usque ad caput assumendo ypostatice quamlibet partem quantitivam aut qualitativam Petri, sic quod primo in fine hore tam corpus quam anima sit ypostatice assumpta: et patet, posito quod Verbum non aliunde habuerit partem aliquam, nec assumptum dimiserit ante finem, quod quelibet pars Petri fiet idem parti Verbi; et quelibet pars Verbi [11] fiet pars Petri,[11] posito quod in hora alia dimittatur. Nec fingendum quod ydemptificabuntur totali ydemptificacione, nisi Christus et Petrus vel eius natura. Si ergo quamlibet [12] partem humanitatis Christi fecit esse partem sui, tunc se totum fecit totam illam naturam, ut loquitur Augustinus.

he therefore makes himself that whole nature.

Threefold confirmation of this statement.

Et potest confirmari tripliciter.[13] Primo per hoc quod Christus non est [14] infinitum bonus homo, sed tantum

[1-1] idem persona etc. O.
[2] conclusio 7 A B C; 9° 5[ti] O.
[3-3] una illarum *om.* O.
[4] singulariter *om.* O.
[5] naturali A B C.
[6] coloratam O.
[7] de *om.* O.
[8] applicati A B C; appli[ti] O. *an* applicatis *aut* applicacione *legendum?*
[9] una A B.
[10] ydemptificabitur O.
[11-11] fiet pars verbi A B C; fiat pars petri O.
[12] qualibet A.
[13] tripliciter *om.* O.
[14] est *om.* O.

1. As man Christ's goodness is finite; but his goodness and his entity are convertible; therefore his entity as man is finite.

finite bonus ut homo; licet sit infinitum bonus Deus, ut hic supponitur: sed omnis bonitas humana, quam habet, resultat precise[1] ex eisdem principiis ex quibus resultat bonitas humanitatis: ergo precise[1] eadem est Christi secundum quod homo, que est bonitas sue humanitatis, cum bonitas et entitas convertuntur: sequitur quod eadem sit entitas Christi, que et sue humanitatis. Sed et hoc[2] sonat vocabulum et omnia que movent concedere Christum esse [C 91a] creaturam. Non enim est | dare, que creatura esset Christus, nisi foret illa humanitas: bonitates enim non possunt dici incommunicantes; et, si in aliquo communicant, communicant[3] secundum[4] totum; nec est inconveniens sed necessarium, quod Christus habeat quiditatem creatam, cum sit univoce homo cum aliis habens denominaciones accidentales creatas, quod sonat in amplius imperfectum: aliter enim non, in quantum homo, foret aliquid.

2. The quantity and quality of Christ and of his humanity are the same.

2do confirmatur ex hoc quod eadem in numero est quantitas, qua ista[5] duo quantificantur, eadem qualitas qua qualificantur; et sic de motu et ceteris accidentibus quibuscunque, que insunt Christo humanitus, ut patet posterius: quod non esset nisi foret ydemptitas in subiecto: ergo idem est iste homo et ista humanitas. Cum ergo accidens non sit nisi modus subiecti, patet quod ad numeracionem subiectorum [A 97c] oportet accidencia numerari; ut, si aliquid | [6]est *A* motum, aliud est *B* motum[6]; alia est mocio *A* mobilis, et alia est mocio *B* mobilis; neutra [7]autem predictarum[7] substanciarum est pars alterius, cum preter humanitatem vel eius partes non restat signare aliam partem Christi. Ideo humanitas nec est pars quantitativa nec qualitativa Christi; et per consequens, si essent distincte substancie, omnia accidencia, que insunt eis formaliter, distinguerentur; cuius impossibilitatem suppono ex alibi declaratis. Non enim est

[1] pr̄e (*i.e.* pure) O. [2] sed ex hoc A B; secundo C.
[3] communicat *semel* A B C. [4] se *add.* A B C. [5] isti A B C.
[6–6] est ·a· motum ad ·b· moto A; est amotu a'd moto B; est a motu ad a b moto C; est ·a· motum aliquid est ·b· motum O.
[7–7] aliquid predicatarum A B C.

possibile puncta[1] et quantitates, qualitates, et ceteras formas simillimas coextendi. [O 230c

3. Every difference, whether essential or accidental, of the Word is also a difference of the humanity.

Et ex isto capitur 3° quod omnis differencia substancialis vel accidentalis, qua Verbum secundum humanitatem differt ab alio supposito vel natura, est differencia qua humanitas Christi differt ab eodem. Ex quo sequitur ulterius, quod nulla est differencia, qua Christus humanitus differt ab illa humanitate: et cum non sit possibile quod aliquid differat ab aliquo, nisi aliqua differencia differat ab eodem; patet quod non | est differencia inter Christum et illam [B 147b humanitatem assumptam. Patet ex hoc quod omnis substancialis differencia capitur vel a materia vel a forma: sed omnis talis pars Christi est pars sue humanitatis et e contra, sicut et omne aliud accidens absolutum: ergo non superest fundamentum, unde caperetur differencia Christi humanitus, nisi ab illa natura assumpta. Nec valet dicere quod solum secundum naturam divinam differt ab illa; [2] quia [3] sic tantum differret [3] ab illa [2] sicut Pater, et precise[4] convenirent, non obstante unione ypostatica, appropriate[5] ad Verbum: et tunc non plus conveniret[6] Verbum cum aliqua creatura [7] post incarnacionem quam ante; et per consequens non foret eiusdem speciei vel generis cum aliqua creatura,[7] eo quod tantum differt ab ista humanitate cum qua maxime conveniret inter omnes creaturas, quantum differret si esset pure Deus et illa homo, cum differencia amplior non sit fundabilis.

x. The humanity of Christ has causes and denominations peculiar to man: it is therefore man; and no other man than the man Christ.

Item humanitas Christi habet causas completas et denominaciones positivas,[8] que non possunt nisi homini competere: ergo est homo. Et, cum non potest poni alius homo, quam Christus; quia sic Verbum gereret in se monstruose duos homines, | quia personam quam assumeret ad suam [C 91b] personam sed non in unitatem persone, et ipsemet foret alius homo, et illi concurrerent faciendo redempcionis commercium:

[1] pung O. [2–2] quia . . . illa *om.* A. [3–3] sicut differet (*om.* tantum) B.
[4] p̄cie A B C; p̄e O; *cf. p.* 175, *n.* 1. [5] ap̄p̄etate O.
[6] communicaret A. [7–7] post . . . creatura *om* A B C. [8] positas A B C.

oportet ergo quod illa humanitas [1] sit idem homo, qui Christus. Assumptum videtur primo ex hoc quod illa humanitas [1] est substancia [2] corporea racionalis ad ymaginem Dei facta, et hoc [3] sufficit ad esse hominis secundum Augustinum et Lincolniensem ut patet superius. Nec valet ficta [4] negacio, quod sic nemo esset formaliter humanitate homo; nec in quantum homo esset aliquid vel alicuius generis pocius quam in quantum peccator, quod non consonat philosophie vel fidei; ymo nemo sciret an esset homo. Quod autem illa humanitas sit substancia racionalis, omnes concorditer confitentur, cum sit composita [5] ex corpore Christi et eius anima. Ideo, si illa non esset substancia, nesciretur quid esset, aut que alia res esset substancia; et ultra videtur, cum omnis substancia sit substancia prima vel secunda, quod illa humanitas sit substancia prima, et per consequens individuum speciei vel generis. Et cum non solum sit in genere substancie vel corporis, sed [6] inferius in genere animalis, eo quod est sensitiva et racionalis et per consequens substancia animata sensibilis; sequitur quod sit animal. Non enim est racio quod negacio caderet in diffinicione animalis pocius quam in diffinicione cuiuscunque substancie, cum omnis singularis substancia sit suppositum.

*Humanity is a rational bodily substance made after the image of God; (cf. pp. 43, 127, 128) and this description applies to the humanity of Christ.*

Confirmatur. Anima Christi, corpus, et unio eorum cum
A97d] suis consequentibus sufficiunt principiare humanitatem | esse hominem, et non impediuntur propter Verbi incarnacionem: ergo de facto constituunt illam in esse hominis. Maior patet ex quolibet alio homine principiato et individuato per corpus et animam unita cum suis consequentibus: ymo videtur quod absolute necessario sequitur [7] positis istis principiis cum unione predicta, quod individuum constituatur in specie. Nam non est [8] possibile quod forma [9] elementi vel mixti inanimati informet [10] proporcionatam materiam, nisi eo ipso constituatur elementum vel mixtum in sua

Soul and body united constitute humanity; and in the case of Christ the Incarnation does not interfere with this result.

[1]–[1] sit . . . humanitas *om.* O. [2] substancia *om.* A B C. [3] sic A B C.
[4] facta A B C. [5] compositum B; componitur (*om.* sit) O. [6] secundum O. [7] consequitur O. [8] non est *om.* O.
[9] formale A B C. [10] informaret A B.

specie: ergo cum totum genus animalis sit perfeccius et[1] eque plene ab intrinseco principiatum; sequitur quod est dare principia intrinseca et eorum unionem, cum quibus non stat quod individuum illius generis non resultet. Si enim non sit[2] possibile quod albedo informet subiectum, nisi eo ipso[3] constituatur unum album; eque[4] evidenter, si anima informat proporcionatum subiectum, oportet quod[5] ex eis constituitur in signanda[6] specie individuum animalis. Quod autem natura Christi non impeditur ne sit animal, probatur sic. Per assumpcionem est humanitas Christi summe exaltata et in perfeccione ultima creature possibili collocata: ergo non est ab aliqua perfeccione naturali, quam naturaliter appeteret, prepedita: cum ergo omnis perfeccio substancialis sit suppositum, vel presupponit suppositum ut subiectum, et omnis perfeccio | accidentalis presupponit essencialem, et [C 92a] suppositum sic perfectum; videtur quod, si natura assumpta[7] sit, ut sic, a racione suppositi exclusa, et[8] a perfeccione maxima sit prepedita. Quomodo ergo non tristaretur languens circa perfeccionem possibilem a qua deficit per ypostaticam unionem? Maxima quidem perfeccio creature possibilis est beatitudo, sicut philosophi et theologi profitentur concorditer cum scriptura: modo illa beatitudo consistit in clara visione et fruicione divine essencie iuxta vocem Veritatis Ioh. 17[9]; 'hec est vita eterna ut cognoscant etc.'; ergo illa creatura cum[10] non[11] potest esse[11] suppositum stante unione et per consequens non exercere[12] actus suppositales, non potest, ut sic, perfeccionem talem attingere. Sed et hoc[13] concedunt concorditer dicentes quod ista natura, cum non sit suppositum, nec agit nec patitur. Unde et illud Psalmi 44[11] ad litteram dictum de Christo, 'beatus quem[14] elegisti | et assumpsisti,' dicunt esse falsum de virtute ser- [B 148a] monis: sed sic intelligitur—beatus, cuius est natura, quam

Intrinsic causes (principia) and their union constitute an individual.

Christ having the intrinsic causes, *corpus* and *anima*,

Christ has *animal* nature; and this nature is not debarred by the Incarnation from any perfection belonging to it; *i.e.* from the highest bliss of creatureship, the beatific vision:

John xvii. 3.

Ps. lxv. 4.

[1] et *om.* A B C.
[2] est A B C.
[3] eo ipso *om.* B.
[4] que O.
[5] oportet quod *om.* C O.
[6] in assignanda A B.
[7] assumpta *om.* A B C.
[8] quod A B C.
[9] 14 O.
[10] cum *om.* A B C.
[11] pre ê O.
[12] exercendo A B C.
[13] sed secundo C.
[14] quam O.

elegisti et assumpsisti—ista autem natura non est beata, cum non sit suppositum, quia per idem meruit redempcionem generis humani, quod non sufficit creatura, nec est colenda vel latria adoranda: illud ergo, quod nunquam exercuit actus suppositales, non est beatum. Sed rogo attendat lector et iudicet,[1] que istarum viarum[2] sit auribus fidelium magis pia; vel dicere quod natura illa per assumpcionem est beatissima creaturarum; (sic quod[3] non deficit sibi esse [O 230d] hominis vel persone racio[4] per se agendi | et paciendi ac recipiendi formaliter felicitatem et cuiuscunque generis perfeccionem; sic quod assumpcio extollat eam ad omne genus perfeccionis et non vinculat eam excludendo a perfeccione huiusmodi;) quam dicere eius oppositum? quia non dubium quin esse hominem summe merentem ex passione maxime acceptabili Trinitati, et postmodum esse beatum beatitudine maxima[5] possibili creature, est perfeccionis denominacio. Illam autem tollit adversa posicio, et illam ponit expresse [A 98a] nostra posicio | concorditer cum antiquis doctoribus et scriptura.

whereby that nature attains the denomination of perfection.

Sed ne dicatur tales denominaciones humanitatis non posse probabiliter sustineri, cum non sit persona; arguitur primo sic ad illam probandam. Nam illa humanitas est mole magna et accidentaliter qualis cum aliis denominacionibus corporeis accidencium; ergo per idem habet denominaciones spirituales accidentales secundum animam. Probatur consequencia eo quod dato antecedente [6]illa humanitas crevit a quantitate infantili[6] usque ad quantitatem virilem, et [C 92b] hoc[7] secundum omnes | condiciones augmentacioni proprie competentes: ergo augmentabatur, et per idem ambulabat super terram et mare, predicavit, manducavit, et sic de ceteris actibus[8] animalibus, que Christo conveniebant. Nam, cum componitur ex omnibus partibus,[9] ex quibus et Christus; fuit ex se mobilis, sicut et Christus: et per consequens

xi. The absence of a human personality is no bar to the application of *corporeal* denominations to the humanity of Christ. His humanity was capable of *growth* and of the other characteristics of man as an animal.

[1] indiget O. [2] viarum *om.* A B C. [3] quid O.
[4] racio *om.* B. [5] maxime A B C.
[6–6] illa crevit a quantitate infantili C; illa humanitas crevit infacili O.
[7] sic A B C. [8] accidentibus A B C. [9] partibus *om.* A B C.

sufficeret exspirando aerem a suo pulmone secundum suam ymaginativam et[1] [2]cetera vocis organa formare voces simil-

He had human organs of sight, hearing, speech, and so forth;

lime sicut Christus. Non enim haberet organa sensuum[2] et operum suppositalium superflua; sic quod, habendo oculos et aures et instrumenta vocalia, preclusa esset sibi via per positivam[3] assumpcionem ne sufficiat plus sentire quam surdus et mutus; sic quod sufficiencia senciendi et personaliter operandi foret per negacionem,[4] qua[5] imperficitur relaxata. Patet ergo, cum[6] humanitas Christi habet de propriis tam formas quam organa ad humanitus operandum, nec ligatur ex benedicta unione, qua[7] tantum perficitur;

and performed human acts;

quod sufficit, ut loquitur scriptura, humanitus operari. Et confirmatur ex hoc quod Christus non [8]predicat, vel ambulat,[8] nec 'interpellat pro nobis' 'factus obediens,' nisi secundum illam humanitatem.

Rom. viii. 34. Phil. ii. 8.

Sed quandocunque duobus nate[9] sunt inesse denominaciones et non uni nisi[10] per reliquum, sequitur quod illi reliquo denominacio inest primo iuxta illud principium Aristotelis primo Posteriorum; 'propter quod unumquodque et illud magis.' Ergo prius taliter[11] predicavit et ceteros actus humanos fecit illa humanitas quam Christus, cum solum secundum illam sic fecerat: sic enim iuxta sentenciam 5[to] Physicorum: si homo sit sanus secundum thoracem vel moveatur secundum partem, tunc illa pars primo movetur et totum per accidens.

these denominations belong to the Word only as man, and prove the completeness of his humanity as their subject.

Cum ergo denominaciones humane insunt Verbo secundum illam humanitatem, que est primum et completum subiectum eorum; videtur quod prius insunt sibi quam Verbo, cum non possunt inesse Verbo nisi per illam, et sibi possunt inesse cum hoc quod non insunt Verbo; ut signato motu progressivo Christi certum est quod iste non potuit fuisse sine illa humanitate, cum motus ex 5[to] Physicorum individuatur[12] a spacio, a

[1] et *om.* A B C.
[2]–[2] cetera vocis organa formare simillime *etc.* A; cetera organa formare vocis simillime *etc.* B; cetera vocis organa sensuum (formare . . . organa *om.*) C.
[3] propositum A B; perpositam C.
[4] mediacionem A B C.
[5] quia O.
[6] quod A B C.
[7] quam O.
[8]–[8] predicavit vel meruit A B C.
[9] innate B; sunt *om.* C.
[10] unica per (*om.* nisi) A B C.
[11] cûliter (*i.e.* causaliter) O.
[12] indîatur O.

tempore, et subiecto. Si ergo Christus secundum aliam humanitatem moveretur pro eodem loco et tempore secundum quamlibet eius partem quantitativam, alius foret motus. Cum igitur illi humanitati dimisse potest inesse dictus motus sine hoc quod insit Verbo, ut dicitur, et Verbo non possit inesse nisi sibi infuerit[1]; [2]patet quod naturaliter prius sibi inest.[3] Si enim denominacio creata post naturaliter insit Verbo hoc foret[2] secundum deitatem vel secundum humanitatem vel mixtim; non secundum deitatem quia nulla forma accidentalis inest sibi nisi secundum naturam qua est mobilis; si secundum humanitatem sive parcialiter[4] sive totaliter; tunc illi humanitati naturaliter prius inest.

Also *spiritual* denominations *secundum animam* apply to the humanity of Christ; and the human soul of Christ above all other souls enjoys the beatific vision, unimpeded by its assumption in the Incarnation.

Et indubie[5] idem videtur iudicium de spirituali denominacione secundum animam. Nam si anime sanctorum sunt [C 93a] beate in celo, | ymo et corpora; quanto magis completa Christi humanitas, cum habeat in se primo subiective omnem creatam beatitudinem qua Christus humanitus est beatus. [A 98b] Augustinus itaque, qui ponit quod | anima prius nedum intelligit ymo sentit quam totum compositum, diceret quod anima Christi in celo haberet visionem et fruicionem beatificam ultra quamcunque aliam animam. Nec est fingendum quod assumpcio ligat spiritum Iesu ne beatifice delectetur. Et per idem habendo quatuor[6] dotes corporis foret perfecte et complete beata eadem beatitudine, qua est Christus; et [B 148b] idem est iudicium de omnibus | accidentibus creatis que humanitus[7] insunt Christo. Quomodo, queso, aliter adorarem eam latria, si non tantum benefecit michi ut crux Christi? aut quomodo dimissa recoleret de operibus Christi sui, vel maneret inter passionem et mortem dimissa a Deo corpore fatigata[8] si nichil antea[9] fuit passa. Dimissa ergo in uno loco et Christo assumente eam in alio, foret plus quam Christi germanus, ut patet de convenienciis substan-

[1] infuerit *om.* O.
[2]–[2] patet quod si naturaliter prius insit verbo hoc foret (*cett. om.*) A B C.
[3] in esse O.
[4] particulariter O.
[5] et indubie *om.* O.
[6] quatuor *om.* B.
[7] humana O.
[8] fangata O.
[9] auna (*an pro* anima ?) O.

cialium et accidentalium: et non est conveniencia amplior nisi fuerit personalis; in nullo itaque casu Verbum assumeret personam, que esset natura Verbi passa et quomodolibet temporaliter[1] formata; ut patet de comitancia absolutorum conmultiplicatorum cum taliter multiplicatis; et sic facta revelacione illi homini quod adnichilabitur, patet quod dolor redundaret in Christum, nulli autem alteri homini posset sic affici.

xii. Certain accidents (*passiones*) peculiar to man can be predicated of Christ: therefore he is man.

Quo dato, videtur multipliciter quod humanitas Christi sit homo, et sic persona Verbi. Nam nichil est risibile nisi homo; humanitas Christi est risibilis, cum sufficiat predicare: ergo est homo. Maior | patet ex hoc quod risibilitas [O 231a] est propria passio hominis convertibilis cum specie. Et idem est iudicium de passione mortalitatis capta a causa materiali, de productivitate sui similis in specie, que competit sibi passionaliter a causa efficiente, et de beatificabilitate[2] secundum corpus et animam que competit sibi [3]a causa finali.[3]

1. Such accidents can only exist formally in their supposite; they exist in the humanity of Christ, which is itself the supposite of the Word: the Word therefore is man.

2. The possession of *accidental forms* means that a subject is *accidentally* so conditioned. Christ and his humanity are both so conditioned by the same *accidental form*; they are therefore the same subject.

Cum ergo predicaciones huiusmodi solum possunt formaliter inesse suppositis, videtur, cum humanitati Christi insunt, quod ipsa sit suppositum Verbi. Secundo confirmatur idem ex hoc quod omnis forma[4] accidentalis non est aliud[5] nisi subiectum accidentaliter se habere; ut mocio est mobile[6] moveri, locucio est ipsum loqui, et ita de ceteris, ut hic supponitur. Cum ergo eodem accidente informatur Christus et ista humanitas, sequitur quod idem est Christus et illa humanitas: vel[7] si Christus non sit illa humanitas sed movetur secundum illam, alia est mocio Christi et alius motus eius: et ita numerarentur omnes forme complete accidentales in Christo secundum numerum subiectorum: quod[8] est impossibile, cum nullum tale accidens foret pars alterius, sed quelibet pars unius pars alterius et e contra.

3. Nothing which is not God can redeem mankind;

Tercio confirmatur ex hoc quod nichil sufficit redimere genus humanum | perfecte, ut modo redimitur, nisi ipsum sit [C 93b]

[1] temporalis A B C.
[2] et beatificante A B C.
[3-3] a causa finali *om.* A B C.
[4] forma *om.* C.
[5] aliud *om.* C O.
[6] mobile *om.* C.
[7] ut O.
[8] et O.

Deus: humanitas Christi sic redimit: ergo est Deus. Ipsa[1] enim fuit passa omni passione, qua Christus dedit sanguinem in redempcionem ut Christus, et sic de posicione anime ac commercio quo mercatus est Christus. Cum ergo per[2] passionem et tales formas fiebat redempcio, sequitur quod ipsa fecit redempcionem; aliter enim[3] non esset illa humanitas tante[4] diligenda nec latria adoranda. Cum tamen indubie quilibet[5] Christianus debet tantum diligere humanitatem Christi quantum[5] et Christum sub racione qua homo: ymo hec idem sunt et colenda eadem pietate in numero, ut ostendit Magister 3°[6] Sentenciarum Dist. 8. ex[7] testimonio beati Augustini. Christus enim ex hoc quod est ista humanitas et per consequens creatura adorari debet *yperdulia*, et omnis alia creatura venerari debet[8] tantum *dulia*. Nam excellens honor debet Christo attribui, qui ex unione [A 98c] ypostatica est creator ac eciam creatura; | et illa vocatur significanter *yperdulia*; et cum hoc, cum idem Christus sit creator, debet *latria* soli deo debita adorari. Correspondenter humanitas Christi cum sit Verbum, debet adorari[9] latria, et cum in se sit creatura debet adorari[9] yperdulia sicut Christus. Et sic tam Christus quam ista humanitas, que est personaliter ipse Christus, debet secundum duplicem racionem eadem tam latria quam yperdulia adorari: sed absit hoc, nisi illa humanitas foret[10] Christus! Ex quo patet quod non solum deitati, sed soli deo est latria exhibenda. Nec est putandum quod humanitas Christi adoranda sit latria solum secundum ordinem ad alterum, sicut crux, ymago, vel pars Christi quantitativa, sed[11] tanquam corpus animatum, sumptum de virgine, passum pro nobis, dolens et merens, et per consequens vere positum precium pro redempcione humani generis: 'empti enim estis[12] precio

The humanity of Christ redeems; therefore that humanity is God. [The humanity redeems because the *Passion* is the means of redemption, and deity is impassible.]

There are three degrees of worship; viz. *dulia* (δουλεία) which is offered to creatures; *hyperdulia* (ὑπερδουλεία) wherewith Christ as humanity and the highest creature is adored; *latria* (λατρεία) wherewith Christ as the Word is to be adored.

But Christ is not two but one; and as the *latria* is due to that one, it is due to his humanity; which is therefore divine and Christ, and the humanity so adored, is not adored with reference to something else, as is the Cross, an image, or a relic of Christ's body;

[1] ipâ A B C; ipm̃ (*i.e.* ipsum) O. [2] per *om.* A B C. [3] enim *om.* A B C.
[4] tantum tante (*sic*) A C.
[5–5] Christus debet diligere humanitatem tantum quantum B.
[6] 3° *om.* O. [7] hoc *add.* A. [8] tantum . . . debet *om.* O.
[9–9] latria . . . adorari *om.* O. [10] Christus sit B.
[11] sit C O. [12] est O.

1 Cor. vi. 20. 1 Cor. vii. 23. but as the animated body, 'the great price' wherewith we were bought; Rom. viii. 32. Gal. ii. 20. this price was the humanity of Christ: and if that humanity were dismissed (an impossible supposition), it would still be above all angels and men, and demand divine adoration.

magno,' ut dicit Apostolus prima ad Cor. 6° et 7°: et ad id precium atque commercium explanat expressius: 'Deus, inquit, proprio Filio non pepercit, sed pro nobis omnibus tradidit illum': et indubie sic fecit tota Trinitas: unde ad Gal. 2°, 'in fide vivo Filii Dei, qui dilexit me et tradidit semetipsum pro me': et indubie precium traditum fuit Christi humanitas; [1] unde si per impossibile humanitas Christi dimissa [1] fuerit personalitati proprie conversans nobiscum ut proximis, ego diligerem eum ut salvatorem et redemptorem meum, adoraremque eum latria sicut prius: nulli enim alteri hominum adeo potero obligari. Nec video | [B 149a] quin iste homo dimissus, sine peccato vel merito decedens, foret supra angelos et omnes alios homines merito exaltandus propter meritum quo meruit ypostatice copulatus.

These arguments prove that Christ is essentially and substantially man in accordance with Holy Scripture and Augustine. Tit. iii. 4. Baruch iii. 37. Jer. xxxi. 22.

Tales sunt [2] multe evidencie [2] ex quibus | [C 94a] credi debet—si illa humanitas sit aliquid, tunc est Christus—et sic intelligo illud ad Titum 3°; '[3] cum autem benignitas et *humanitas* apparuit [3] salvatoris nostri Dei' etc. Illa quidem humanitas est *mas* de quo Baruch 3° 'in terris vis*us* est et cum hominibus conversat*us* est'; ipse enim est 'vir quem femina circumdedit.' Ierem. 31°. Et hinc dicit Augustinus in De Vera Religione quod 'Verbum virum suscepit nat*us* ex femina.'

1–1 que si dimissa fuerit (per impossibile humanitas Christi *om.*) A B C.
2–2 multe evidencie *om.* A B C.
3–3 cum autem et humanitas apparuerit A C; cum autem et apparuerit B.

# Cap. XI.

[*Solvit instancias quibus moderniores doctores videntur fulcire suam sentenciam, recitando decem ludicra que concedentes possibilitatem dimissionis annuunt consequenter.*

*Discussion of Duns Scotus' theory of the Incarnation including the analogy of Transubstantiation in the Eucharist* (pp. 189-191); *followed by a refutation of the hypothesis that Christ could have assumed many humanities.*]

Superest[1] videre evidencias ex quibus fulcitur opinio huic [2] sentencie mee in verbis contraria.[2] Declarat autem Doctor Subtilis istam opinionem in principio 3[li] Sentenciarum satis subtiliter. 'Accidens, inquit, duplicem habitudinem habet ad subiectum: scilicet, informantis ad informatum; et talis racio includit imperfeccionem subiecti, quia potenciam ad actum quo subiectum perficitur: aliam autem habitudinem ut naturaliter posterius dependens a subiecto causaliter; et ista habitudo attestatur perfeccionem subiecti et imperfeccionem forme dependentis. Sic, inquit, simillime natura assumpta habet duplicem habitudinem ad Verbum, vel sub racione causandi sicut generaliter omnis creatura dependet a tota Trinitate; et illa habitudo presupponit in creatura posse naturale imperfeccionem sapiens, quod oportet habere actum causancie divine inseparabiliter comitantem. 2[a] autem habitudo est, qua natura assumpta secundum potenciam obediencialem potest esse natura Verbi, et illa potencia non potest actuari nisi per miraculum, et dicit quodammodo perfeccionem in persona assumente[3]; terminare itaque dependenciam creature secundum istam racionem est ypostatice [O 231b] assumere dic|tam creaturam.'

The theory of Duns Scotus stated. "As an accident has a twofold relation to its subject, (a) as giving form and so perfection to that which else would be imperfect, (b) as in the order of nature later, and depending on its subject as its cause: So the nature assumed has a twofold relation to the Word; (a) a relation of causation depending like any other creature on the Trinity, presupposing a natural power which smacks of imperfection, and which must have the divine causation in act inseparably accompanying it; (b) a relation of potential compliancy by which the nature assumed can be the nature of the Word, but is only by a miracle actually so made, implying perfection in the person who assumes; and the assumption of the said creature consists in terminating that creaturely dependence in accordance with (b)."

Et ista sentencia placet michi. Nam omne subiectum [A 98d] accidentis | includit in se analogice racionem causantis ad

[1] insuper est A B.   [2-2] huic sentencie contraria in verbis A B C.
[3] assumentem O.

The analogy between the relation of *accidents* to *subject* and that of the created nature to the Word is admitted.

But the eucharistic transubstantiation does not prove the independent existence of accidents apart from subject (v. infra, p. 190).

Scotus' theory suffices to prove that God can be united hypostatically to humanity; but no proof or instance can be adduced to show that God can assume a nature other than that actually assumed.

Scotus asserts that the Word can assume human nature in such a manner as to make it a nature belonging to him, and yet not make it actually the Word. He alleges *five* reasons.

i. Scotus' 1st Reason. No consequence follows incongruous with either the assumer or the assumed.

Reply. This argument proceeds on a false assumption. For personal union implies a oneness of person between the assumer and the humanity assumed.

*Nature* and *essence* are convertible terms: in assuming the *nature* the Word assumes the *essence* of man.

suum causatum quod est in Deo equivoce perfeccionis simpliciter. Verumptamen omnis causancia, qua subiectum causat inherens accidens, sapit imperfeccionem subiecti, quia causanciam materialem vel subiectivam qua est [1]in potencia perfici[1] tali forma. Unde non est dare aliam singularem habitudinem, qua subiectum potest causare accidens sine hoc, quod ipso informetur. Sed quelibet singularis racio vel causa includit racionem analogam, que secundum illud[2] quod est perfeccionis simpliciter, soli Deo[3] potest competere. Nec sequitur ex miraculosa transsubstanciacione in eucaristia quod vel qualitas vel inherens quantitas[4] possit per se[5] existere sine informacione et essenciali dependencia ad subiectum. Ad tantum ergo valet illa sentencia, quod vere ponit in qualibet racione creata lucere potenciam unde Deus potest humanitati Christi[6] ypostatice copulari, sed quod aliam naturam possit assumere probari non poterit vel exempliter edoceri.

Quod autem Verbum potest assumere naturam humanam | [C 94b] faciendo ipsam esse naturam sui et non ipsum Verbum probat Doctor quintuplici racione.

Primo ex hoc, quod nullum ex hoc sequitur inconveniens[7] ex parte assumentis[8] nec assumpti.[8]

Sed in ista racione falsum petitur; cum personalis unio, qua humanitas fieret natura hominis, implicaret[9] illam humanitatem fieri unum personaliter cum sumente. Natura enim completa substancialis cuicumque supposito est generaliter idem suppositum. Et si humanitas sit natura completa Verbi, tunc est [10]essencia et substancia Verbi eo quod *natura perfecta* et *essencia* convertuntur, et si est essencia vel substancia Verbi, tunc est[10] Verbum; cum cuiuslibet rei create vel increate idem est essencia vel substancia et

1–1 ~~in~~ (*sic in rasura alt. manu* A) imposita perficit B; imposita perfici C.
2 idem B C.
3 deo *om.* O.
4 ·n· *add.* O. *quod compendium alibi in hoc cod.* enim *significat, in hoc loco forsitan* non *valet.*
5 per se *om.* O.
6 Christi *om.* O.
7 inconsequens A B C.
8–8 nec assumpti *om.* O.
9 implicat A B C.
10–10 essencia . . . tunc est *om.* B.

res cuius est essencia. Ideo Verbum non potest facere humanitatem esse naturam Verbi, nisi fecerit ipsam esse essenciam ac substanciam Verbi, et per consequens ipsum Verbum. Nec sequitur—ista natura humana est natura Dei; ergo est natura divina—quia talia abstracta cum huiusmodi possessivis convocant[1] possessionem sui primitivi cum quadam racione reduplicandi; ut, si humanitas Christi sit essencia, natura, vel substancia divina, tunc est natura Dei sub racione qua Deus, quod solum est deitas; et si deitas sit natura humana, tunc est natura humana sub racione qua homo; et sic deitate foret Verbum formaliter homo, et humanitate Deus; quod est impossibile. Et patet quod multum refert[2] dicere—deitas est natura hominis—et—ipsa est natura humana; humanitas est natura Dei—et—ipsa natura divina—; cum ille nature tam dispares conveniunt in eodem supposito.

And so the Incarnation consists in the union with the essence and substance of the Word of two natures which have between themselves a great disparity.

2° arguit Doctor per hoc quod persona divina potest terminare quamcumque dependenciam creature, quam dependenciam terminare foret[3] perfeccionis; sed perfeccionis [B 149b] simpliciter est posse facere naturam creatam | esse naturam Dei; ergo Deus hoc potest.

ii. Scotus' 2nd Reason. A divine person can terminate any dependence of a creature, and so bring about its perfection; perfection is to be the nature of God: therefore God can make human nature his own nature.

Sine dubio verum concluditur, sed infidelis diceret quod minor foret pura peticio. Unde quia videmus, quod Deus producit per se multos effectus ut substancias, sicut fide capimus de mundi principio; eliciunt quidam tanquam principium quod deitas vicem cuiuscunque cause secunde supplere poterit. Et ex illo pullulant plurime vanitates; quia certum est quod nullius cause materialis vel subiectivo vicem deitas supplere poterit, hoc est, causare formam eadem causacione sive simillima subducto subiecto; quia tunc deitas posset esse ignea et quomodolibet informata; quod dementis est dicere. Ideo causare materialiter vel [A 99a] subiective | non potest sibi competere; ymo nullum accidens vel formam materialem potest Deus sine causancia[4]

Reply. The conclusion is true: but God does not play the part of a second cause: He produces *substances* as the great first cause: but apart from

[1] *An pro* convocant *in codd. omn. repertum* connotant *potius legendum?*
[2] referret O.
[3] esset O.
[4] communicancia A B C.

*substance* he does not produce *accidents*, which are the result of material or subjective causes.

substancie per se producere: ut, sicut non potest producere motum meum, nisi ego movear hoc causando, sic de qualibet forma materiali. Ymo de accidente spirituali idem dicitur; ut non potest actum volendi creature producere | nisi ipsa [C 95a] creatura nedum concurrat cum eo subiectivo causando, sed et eciam coagendo. Ymo si ultra perspicitur, nullius secundi agentis potest deitas vicem supplere agendo univoce. Ideo vicis suppleecio, cum dicit inferioritatis condicionem vicariam, non potest deitati competere. Quando ergo per se miraculose opus perficit,[1] quod posset facere agens [2]secundum alia[2] accione in genere cum suo regimine instrumentaliter efficere, non supplet vicem agentis; nec e contra cum conformantur in genere.

iii. Scotus' 3rd Reason. The assumed nature is an individual existence before it gains personality: and God can give to that pre-existing existence personality in another than itself.

Reply. This would prove that every person could be somebody else: and it really involves a confusion between first in order of *time* (prius), and first in order of *thought* (superius) cf. p. 193, l. 12.

In Christ (as God) personality, supposition, substantiality precede his individuality (as man).

3° arguit Doctor quod natura assumpta est prius essencia singularis quam suppositatur; ergo pro illo priori potest Deus personare illam naturam in alio.

Sed hic videtur michi quod consequencia sit neganda. Nam iuxta illud sequeretur quod quilibet potest esse quilibet. Nam Petrus prius origine est essencia quam substancia; ergo pro illo priori Deus posset facere eum nonsubstanciam; et, cum prius sit substancia quam corpus, et prius corpus quam animal, et prius animal quam homo, eo quod omne superius est causa sui inferioris; sequitur quod posset indifferenter fieri cuiuscunque speciei substancie tam secundum corpus quam animam.

Sed ulterius pro materia argumenti dicitur quod, quam primo quoad consequenciam humanitas Christi est ista singularis natura, tam primo est ipsa persona Verbi. Non enim posset derelinqui non assumpta, nec post assumpcionem dimitti; quia tunc indubie, sicut incepcio humanitatis presupponeretur prioritate consequente[3] assumpcionem, ita personacio creata, cum esse individuum racionalis nature sit esse personam. Et patet quod Christus prius est persona, suppositum, vel ypostasis quam ipse est natura singularis;

[1] perficit *altera man. corr.* perficiunt A. [2–2] solum illa B. [3] ad *add.* O.

sed generaliter [1] e contra primo, sicut substancia est natura [O 231c] singularis date speciei, ut Christus,[1] eque | primo est suppositum humane nature, sicut est persona hominis. Ideo Christus prius est persona quam est persona hominis vel substancia singularis. Verumptamen non est ordo inter divinum [2] suppositum et personam divinam tanquam inter generalius et contraccius, sicut est in personalitatibus creatis. Sed et in illis non oportet, si Petrus sit prius suppositum substancie quam persona humane nature, quod potest [3] esse suppositum non persona, ut patet ex dictis superius. Singularitas ergo Christi est posterior sua personalitate, et causatur ex condicionibus individuantibus, ut puta ex illo corpore et illa anima cum illa unione ypostatica et aliis que secuntur. Ex quo videtur michi quod Christus non potest aliam naturam assumere, quia tunc posset esse alius homo; et per consequens ista persona, ut post deducetur; quod est impossibile. Et consequencia patet ex hoc quod, si alia fuerint principia individuancia, tunc foret aliud individuum speciei humane et per consequens alius homo. [C 95b] Nec est color quod tempus aut aliud accidens | requisitum individuat substanciam,[4] nisi ut multo evidencius unio ypostatica individuaverat dominum Iesum Christum, ut dicit Anselmus in De Incarnacione 7°. Nec obest quod Christus sit prius suppositum et individuum speciei humane, quam habeat predictam unionem; quia, sicut prius est homo quam iste homo, sic prius est individuum speciei humane, quam *hoc* individuum, et prius est [5] ista unio quam ipse sit hoc [5] individuum.

And it is hazardous to apply to the Divine Being of Christ conceptions which refer to created existence.

4to confirmatur ex hoc quod accidens potest Deus facere [A 99b] per se esse, ut patet de eu|caristia; ergo per idem potest facere substanciam inherere: tantum enim distat de inherente facere non inherens, sicut de non-inherente facere quod adhereat persone nature superioris.

iv. Scotus' 4th Reason. As God can give (as He does in the Eucharist) independent existence to an accident: so is He equally able to bring about the converse result, *i.e.* to make the substance of the inferior nature (man) inhere in the person of the superior (the Word).

Hic dicitur quod loquendo de accidente inherente, ipsum

[1–1] e contra . . . Christus *om.* A B C. [2] individuum A B C. [3] possit O.
[4] nisi *om.* C; ut *om.* O. [5–5] illi unio quam ille hoc O.

Reply. An inherent accident, being only a mode of substance, cannot have independent existence; but every creature is an accident and *adheres* to God as accident to subject; therefore God can only give to an accident independent existence in the sense that it may not formally *inhere* in any substance but actually *adhere* to God alone. The attempt to allow to such accidents as *quantity* and *quality* an independent existence, which is denied to *respective* accidents (such as *relation, action, passion, etc.*), fails altogether; as Aquinas partly admits. In the Eucharist there must be a subject underlying the accidents; what that subject is, I am not careful to define; the attempted definitions in the writings of the saints are ambiguous: perhaps they mean that the essence which after transubstantiation underlies those accidents is that, which before transubstantiation was bread, and which by virtue of transubstantiation ceases to be *substance* at all and remains the same *essence* qualified by the same accidents as before. That essence becomes, not Christ's body, but a sign ineffably signifying to us that at every point it is sacramentally the body of Christ and simultaneously the soul of Christ and also all other qualities (accidents) of Christ whatsoever.

non poterit per se esse, cum omne tale sit modus substancie, sed[1] cum omnis | creatura sit accidens Deo adheretque[2] [B 150a] sibi tam essencialiter sicut accidens ad subiectum; patet quod accidens potest Deus facere per se esse, non sic quin alicui, scilicet Deo, adhereat, sed quod nulli formaliter inhereat; sicut est de toto predicamento substancie, quod non potest sic formaliter inherere. Si tamen racio predicta procederet, argueret direccius quod homo et quelibet alia substancia poterit inherere, sicut quantitas et qualitas creduntur hodie per se esse: quod ego non video. Ideo alias dixi quod, sicut[3] univocando de accidente respectivo, cuiusmodi[4] sunt relacio, accio, passio etc., nullum illorum poterit esse nisi insit substancie ut subiecto: sic nec qualitas nec quantitas, cum sint univoce accidencia sicut illa. De qualitate consentit sanctus Thomas, quod ipsa non potest esse nisi insit quantitati. Et de quantitate est michi evidencius, cum sit substanciam esse quantam, et non potest exspectare rarefaccionem et condensacionem et ceteras mutaciones, quas in benedicta eucaristia oculariter experimur. Ideo, ut alias dixi, esset nimis magna[5] sensus illusio, nisi esset in eucaristia unum quantum diversimode qualificatum et accidentatum ac mobile. Et illud subicitur quantitati, qualitati et ceteris accidentibus que videmus. Sed quoad questionem—quid est de tali essencia?—non sollicitor; licet sint quotlibet dicta sanctorum que sonant quod sit panis vel vinum; que forte intelligenda sunt, quod essencia subiecta illis accidentibus post transsubstanciacionem est panis[6] ante transsubstanciacionem, et virtute transsubstanciacionis desinit esse quid vel substancia, et manet eadem essencia conformiter accidentata. Illa autem non fit corpus Christi sed fit signum signans nobis ineffabiliter quod ad omnem punctum sui sit sacramentaliter corpus Christi et concomitanter[7] anima et omnia alia Christi accidencia absoluta. Nec est

[1] tamen *add.* A B C. [2] adhereret quia B C; et A; *pr. man.* [3] sic A B C. [4] cuiuscunque O. [5] magna *om.* C. [6] cum *add.* A B C. [7] comitanter A B; comicantus C.

de substancia fidei viatorum[1] scire quid est illa essencia; [C 96a] sed satis est cognoscere questionem | si est de ista cum transsubstanciacione et ceteris veritatibus que sacramento eucaristie sunt annexe. Non ergo sequitur—si Christus potest facere corpus suum virtute verborum sacramentalium esse ad omnem punctum illius essencie; ergo potest facere quod humanitas non[2] sit suppositum, vel quomodocunque aliter per terminos magistrales aliter[3] extraneetur racio—[4]in omnibus enim similibus evidenciis est pura peticio.[4] Illud autem quod de eucaristia fides orthodoxa artat nos credere potest catholicus philosophice sustinere. Si enim secundum perspectivos corpus multiplicatur intencionaliter vere presens,[5] ubicunque species eius agitur, et habet ibi efficaciam operandi; quod magisterium Deo facere corpus suum esse ad omnem punctum hostie sacramentaliter et effectus spirituales efficaciter operari!

To define this essence is not necessary to the faith of a pilgrim.

And it does not follow from the analogy of the Eucharist that Christ can make his humanity to be non-essential.

The catholic faith concerning the Eucharist is in accordance with philosophy and with the order of nature shown in the science of Optics.

5[to] confirmatur ex hoc quod accidencia maxime distancia potest Deus facere unitive concurrere in eodem, ut omnia novem[6] genera accidencium sunt idem subiecto. Ergo per idem naturam humanam potest Deus facere inesse subiecto divino cum hoc, quod non realiter sit subiectum.

v. Scotus' 5th Reason. As God can make all the nine accidents concur in one subject, so He can make human nature to be in a divine subject with the condition that it be not in fact a subject.

Sed hic dicitur quod loquendo de unione ypostatica oppositum sequitur ex assumpto. Unde omnes iste evidencie confirmare possunt fidelem credere quod duas naturas potest [A 99c] Deus unire personaliter | in eadem ypostasi ad sensum expositum. Sed quod Verbum assumens non sit natura assumpta, nec iste raciones nec alie [7]possibiles poterunt[7] edocere. Unde quam mirum est quod natura divina et humana tam distantes sint utraque eadem persona, tam [O 231d] mirum est et idem in numero, quod Deus sit homo. Unde | accidencium ad subiecta non est unio ypostatica, cum sint essencie a subiecto generaliter condistincte sine communicacione ydiomatum, ut substancia fiat tale accidens vel e contra. Ideo sicut in materia de Trinitate trinitas creata

Reply. The hypostatic union being the personal union of two natures in the same substance is a different process altogether to the above-named combination of accidents.

As the created trinity

[1] viatoris O. [2] sit non O.
[3] *Nonne* aliter *sic in omnibus codd. repetitum omitti debet?* [4–4] in . . . peticio *om.* B.
[5] prius B C; *et pr. m.* A. [6] novem *om.* A B C. [7–7] po[les] poterint A B C.

of memory, reason, and will is the nearest analogue to the uncreated Trinity (cf. p. 43); so the union of the created spirit to the bodily nature into the person of a man approximates most nearly to the hypostatic union of natures in the Incarnation: and it cannot be proved that such an union is impossible; or that God can assume a nature other than that actually assumed; or dismiss that nature when assumed.

If further it be urged that the *grace of union* presupposes the existence of the nature to be assumed before it actually is assumed; the conclusion is granted: but it does not follow that the humanity can be unassumed. The *grace of union* is twofold; (a) An uncreated grace whereby in essence, or person, or form, the Word willed from eternity to unite the humanity to Himself, be it in essence, or in person, or in form; (b) A created grace, whereby the humanity is formally pleasing to God. The said humanity cannot in time precede so as to deserve the grace of union.

memorie, racionis, et voluntatis anime est inter omnes hucusque inventas simillima pro Trinitate increata viatoribus cognoscenda; sic in materia de Incarnacione ypostatica unio creati spiritus ad naturam corpoream, ut utrumque sit eadem persona hominis, est inter alias plus propiuqua; nec possunt,[1] si non fallor, fieri evidencie ut, vel probetur talis impossibilitas unionis, vel quod Deus aliam naturam possit assumere, aut assumptam dimittere.

Sed instatur per hoc, quod gracia unionis foret gracia maxima possibilis creature, ut illa humanitas fiat Deus; et omnis gracia creata presupponit inesse tam gratificatum quam ipsum gratificans; ergo gracia unionis presupponit naturam assumptam, et per consequens ipsa natura prius est quam de facto assumitur.

Hic dicitur quod conclusio est concedenda, cum omne per se superius sit | prius natura vel origine quam suum [C 96b] inferius; et per consequens et[2] prius quam passio vel accidens sibi inest. Sed ex hoc non sequitur quod illa humanitas potest esse non assumpta, etsi sit | non assumpta [B 150b] pro illa mensura nature sive originis. Sed notandum quod duplex est gracia unionis. Prima increata, qua Verbum voluit eternaliter humanitatem illam sibi ypostatice copulare; et illa potest intelligi tripliciter, scilicet essencialiter, personaliter, sive formaliter, ut patet alibi. 2[da] autem est gracia creata qua humanitas est sic formaliter[3] grata Deo. Et ista gracia licet sit natura[4] vel origine posterior[5] quam subiectum, non tamen est possibile quod dicta humanitas temporaliter ipsam procedat sic quod mereatur graciam unionis; sicut Augustinus innuit Enchiridion 29°, cum non sit possibile ipsam manere per instans[6] temporis non assumptam. Et sicut in aliis hominibus presupponitur gracia preveniens ad meritum, sic in Christo gracia unionis presupponitur naturaliter ad Christi meritum, etsi meritum

[1] putant B. [2] et *om.* O. [3] formaliter *om.* O.
[4] natura *in ras. al. man.* A; ullam B; nulla C. [5] posterius O.
[6] per instanti A C; pro instanti B.

pro instanti unionis naturaliter consequatur. Et istum credo esse sensum Augustini 17° De Civitate Dei ca° . . . 'In rebus, inquit, per tempus exortis summa gracia est quod Deus in unitate persone homini nullis precedentibus meritis copulatur;' non quod gracia sit membrum in corpore vel anima colligans unionem; sed quia ista unio sit gracia non preventa habitu disponente. Unde illa unio cum sit relacio racionis est posterius subiecta humanitate quoad genus cause materialis, et tamen est efficienter[1] prius quam Christus est hoc singulare vel individuum hominis, ut tangitur superius. Sed caveatur de prioritate [2] temporis aut prioritate[2] quoad consequenciam, cum omnia ista pro omni tempore Christi se mutuo consequantur. Unde Augustinus Enchiridion dicit quod ista unio fuit illi homini quodammodo naturalis, cum iste homo non poterit esse sine illa.

And this agrees with the testimony of Augustine.

The union is *after* the humanity regarded as a material cause; but *before* the individual man Christ; for priority in time and priority in causation must be carefully distinguished (cf. p. 188, l. 22).

Et si queritur de subiecto eius primo dicitur quod anima est subiectum primum unionis creati spiritus, non quod sit [A 99d] infusus habitus, sed habitudo relativa. Alia autem unio | corporis ad Verbum subiectatur multiplicative in corpore sicut filiacio temporalis, que est habitudo secundum quam cognitum[3] causatum naturaliter est productum a suo simili in natura. Et per istas particulas patet quod Spiritus sanctus non est Filius Patris, nec vermis est filius hominis, ut docet Augustinus Enchiridion 3°, nec inanimatum est filius sui naturaliter generantis. Correspondenter unio est habitudo, secundum quam una natura alteri ydemptitate ypostatica copulatur; et illa dupliciter secundum diversitatem nature increate assumentis et nature create suppositis copulate. Nec est extraneum vocare illam unionem *graciam* cum sit donum perfectissimum *gratis* datum.

If it be asked, what is the subject of this union? the answer is, that the soul (anima) is the first subject of the union of the created spirit (spiritus); but the body also shares in the union:

and the union is rightly called a *grace*, being the most perfect boon freely (*gratis*) given.

Quantum ad dimissionem nature assumpte patet ex dictis quod Verbum non potest illam dimittere licet contingentissime possit illa[4] | [C 97a] natura Verbo deesse cum sit contingens

(I.) As to the dismissal of the assumed nature,

[1] efficaciter C.
[2-2] temporis . . . prioritate *om.* O.
[3] 9gnitu^m (*? cognitivum*) O.
[4] verba (*sic*) A; verba B.

it is proved to be impossible by the words of Christ discussed in chap. V.; and also because the humanity is in personality identical with the Word, as chap. X. has proved.
Equally impossible are (II.) the assumption of more than one humanity simultaneously or in succession; and (III.) the assumption of the same nature by any other Person (in the Trinity).
Else ten absurd conclusions would follow.

ad utrumlibet Verbum esse hominem vel fuisse. Movent autem ad negandum dimissionem nature assumpte, hoc est ad derelieccionem [1]illius personalitatis non nature[1] ipsius Verbi Dei, argumenta facta superius 5° ca°; et omnia que monent[2] quod humanitas sit idem personaliter Verbo Dei, ut tactum est 10° ca°.

Et ita de assumpcione multarum humanitatum vel simul vel successive; aut quod alia persona eandem naturam assumat. Et placet michi quod ex hoc pereunt modernorum doctorum vocata subtilia et gloriosa sophismata.

1. Primo, posito quod Verbum omnem naturam humanam a mundi exordio assumpsisset que continue viveret assumpta; tunc species humana non salvaretur per successionem suorum individuorum; quia vel tantum unum foret individuum in specie humana, quod foret totum genus hominum[3] et faceret quidquid operatum esset[4] ab homine vel si essent multa individua, tamen posito illo[5] essent nature humane non homines;[6] et sic omne suppositum [7]nature humane[7] foret prius naturaliter quam sua species, a qua tamen non caperet quiditatem.

2. 2[do] dicitur[8] quod potest, quociens libuerit, fieri mutacio a contradictorio in contradictorium sine mutacione aut generacione aut corrupcione veritatis pertinentis. Ut posito quod in qualibet istarum parcium proporcionalium imparium huius hore[9] omnis humanitas dimittatur et quelibet permaneat[10] cum omnibus positivis[11] continue reassumpta; quod est impossibile, cum negacio non potest incipere; ymo unio, que est relacio tercii modi, non potest terminare mutacionem nisi in aliquo | proprio[12] fiat motus. [O 232a]

3. 3° dicitur consequenter quod in fine illius hore fient quotlibet homines, et tamen non fiet [13]aliquid nec alicuiusmodi positivum,[13] posito quod quotlibet nature iam assumpte

[1]–[1] illius . . . nature *om.* A B C; ipsius *om.* O. [2] mouent A B C. [3] humanum O. [4] est A B. [5] ille O. [6] non homines *om.* A B C. [7]–[7] humanum O. [8] dicitur *om.* O. [9] huius hore *om.* O. [10] pi maneat O. [11] pnctę O. [12] proprio B. [13]–[13] aliquid nec alicuius positivi O; aliud nec alicuiusmodi positivum A B C.

dimittantur immote primo in fine hore. Unde subducta omni mutacione preter talem alternam dimissionem et reassumpcionem foret tempus et motus mirabilis successivus. Nec negabunt quin Deus potest, subducto alio[1] motu quocunque,[2] alternare mutaciones huiusmodi, cum dependeant solum a volucione libera Dei; et indubie, cum una foret prius quam reliqua, nedum natura sed tempore foret continua[3] successio temporalis.

4^to^ conceditur de possibili quod iam non est nisi unicus 4. [B 151a] homo, | et infiniti homines ante finem illius hore adnichilabuntur, nec citra generabitur aliquid[4] positivum, et tamen in fine erunt infiniti homines, posito quod Deus ex omnipotencia sua erect infinitas humanitates [C 97b] | in domo illa, quarum infinitum parva sit aliqua, et totidem[5] erect Rome, et assumat omnes illas usque ad[6] finem hore in qua[6] adnichilet omnes Rome et dimittat omnes Oxonie aliter non mutatas. [A 100a] |

5^to^ concedunt in casu quod[7] in ista hora generabuntur 5. vel fient infiniti homines et nichil illorum generabitur vel fiet ab aliquo, sed nec Deus sciet quando aliquis illorum hominum erit, ut divisa[8] ista hora in suas partes proporcionales minores versus ultimum instans et quod in cuiuslibet illarum parcium prima medietate Deus dimittat unam, et in secunda reassumat reliquam dimittendo, servando in eis omnia positiva: tunc patet conclusio, cum nunquam erit ita[9] quod isti homines sunt, et per consequens non erit aliquid de numero istorum hominum.

6^to^ concedunt quod in casu sex filii fuerint in *b* instanti 6. geniti de Maria, in quo instanti non genuit nisi unum, et tamen non potest esse[10] in *b* instanti nec alium filium nisi Iesum suum unigenitum genuisse, posito quod *b* fuit instans in quo genuit Iesum et quod post assumpcionem[11] multiplicata illa humanitate ad sex loca maneat assumpta a

[1] illo A C. [2] quomodocunque A B C. [3] foret *iterum add.* B.
[4] aliud A B C. [5] cottidie C. [6-6] finem in quo O.
[7] quod *om.* A B C. [8] dimissa O. [9] ista O.
[10] esse *om.* A B C. [11] ascensionem O.

Trinitate in tribus locis et in aliis tribus maneat non assumpta: et tunc patet quod sex homines communicant in corpore Christi quod fuit genitum de Maria; ergo sex homines fuerunt ab ea geniti; et patet quod [1] residuum, illi quidem sex homines, forent genus Dei, quia tres persone divine et alie tres creature, hi[2] homines et illi[3] non-homines, hi[2] filii et illi[3] non-filii; et per consequens beata virgo nunquam genuit hos filios, et per idem nunquam fecit ut esset mater eorum; sicut nec corpus pro mensura, qua incepit esse multi homines, incepit secundum aliquid gigni vel esse filius, cum sola negacio non facit filium.

7. 7° concedunt quod stat infinita loca in *b* instanti repleri per[4] istum hominem, qui nec est nec generatur nec generabitur: sed iste idem homo continue usque ad *b* instans distabit a quolibet illorum nec movebitur nec multiplicabitur ad aliquem[5] eorum vel e contra, cum tamen ad situm [6]tanquam ad per se terminum erit[6] motus, posito quod Pater in divinis incipiat assumere naturam humanam glorificatam in celo; et cum hoc, posito quod in *b* ultimo instanti illius hore infinitas humanitates assumeret,[7] que manebunt perpetuo[8] fixe ad modum coree[9] disposite: et patet conclusio. Nam Deus Pater non potest generari divinitus nec generaretur humanitus nisi ad generacionem nature pro tempore quo assumeretur, quod non competit seni vel beato. Sicut ergo Filius adquirit loca[10] movendo humanitus, ita Pater adquirens et replens corporee[11] illa loca quodammodo moveretur. Sed quomodo moveretur aliquid adquirendo locum, qualitatem, | et quantitatem in se [C 98a] subiective, si secundum nullam naturam nec secundum subiectum motus primo motum taliter moveretur?

8. 8° concedunt de possibili quod Petrus in infinitum

[1] quod *om.* A B C. [2] hic A B C; h[1] O. [3] ibi A C; i[1] O; illi B. [4] in A B C. [5] aliquid O. [6-6] tanquam per se . . . erit *cum lacuna viii litt.* A B; tanquam ad per se erit C. [7] assumet O. [8] perpetuum A B C. [9] coree *codd. omn. an pro* choreae? [10] loca *om.* O. [11] corpore A B.

remittetur[1] inmerito[2] et nunquam intendetur[3] quousque fuerit infinitum Deo carior quam est modo; Paulus autem per idem tempus in infinitum intendetur[3] inmerito et tamen[4] in eodem fine temporis[5] sine suo demerito erit Deo quantumlibet minus[6] carus; ex quo videtur quod apud Deum sit excepcio personarum; posito quod Petrus per istam horam remittetur usque ad non gradum meriti exclusive et in fine assumatur a Verbo ypostatice; Paulus autem per idem tempus assumptus continue mereatur et in fine dimittatur: tunc patet conclusio, petito hoc notorio principio quod non est possibile Deum tantum diligere naturam hominis non assumptam sicut naturam propriam quam assumit: tunc posito quod infinitum bonus sit aliquis homo non assumptus, [A 100b] adhuc melior | et Deo carior est quecunque humanitas quam assumit. Et revera[7] talia videntur michi dissona: scilicet quod homo Petrus demereatur continue, quousque fuerit infinitum Deo carus; et Paulus continue mereatur, quousque decidat a summa amicicia Dei sui; cum sceleratissimus peccator contingentissime, ut asserunt, potest assumi[8]; et cum ignorare poterit assumpcionem propriam, non est evidencia dans fidem quin quelibet creatura ypostatice unibilis sit assumpta. Et tunc non video quomodo quis convinceretur ex ydololatria vel cognosceret quiditatem aliquam creature. Concedunt enim quod Deus potest esse lapis et speciei abiectissime creature, potest esse dampnatus, quod est perfeccius. Sed procul a fidelibus ista ludicra venenosa. Unde Augustinus 83 [9]Vet. et Nov. Test.[9] Questionum ques- [B 151b] tione 5ª dicit quod | nullum animal irracionale potest esse [O 232b] beatum, et multo evidencius nulla | inanimata substancia.

(God cannot love any unassumed nature of man so much as He loves a nature which He assumes.)

(Such hypotheses involve impiety as well as absurdity.)

9° videtur de possibili concedendum quod Deus faciendo tres homines eternos, qui non possunt a Deo fieri, tantum perfecit genus humanum, sicut potuit de sua potencia absoluta, licet non plures homines quam illos tres potuit pro- 9.

[1] remitteretur (*corr. in* remittetur) A; remittitur O. [2] merito O. [3] intenditus O. [4] tamen *om.* A B C. [5] temporis *om.* O. [6] nimis A B. [7] revera *om.* A B C. [8] sumi O. [9-9] vet. . . . test. *om.* A B C.

duxisse. Assigno totam multitudinem hominum a Deo producibilium[1] quoad intellectum divinum, et pono[2] quod tota Trinitas quamlibet talem naturam assumat ypostatice; tunc patet quod natura divina fecit trinitatem, tres homines, quos oportet sic opinantes dicere eternos homines, cum non habeant limitandum peryodum temporalem. Et secunda pars gratis conceditur cum dicunt hominem Iesum non posse fieri. | Et tercia pars[3] patet ex hoc quod tam perfectum [C 98b] est genus sicut aliquod individuum speciei; et[4] infinitum perfectus est omnis homo in casu posito; ergo infinitum perfectum genus hominum; ymo, si consideretur, omnis homo foret infinitum perfectus humanitus, quia infinitam perfectam multitudinem tam animarum[5] quam corporum tanquam partes proprias contineret; ergo infinitum perfectus humanitus foret omnis homo, quia infinitum perfeccior quam data anima vel corpus finitum; patet itaque quod non meliores homines[6] vel magis graciosos plus Deum amantes concorditer aut plus beatos in corpore et anima omnino impeccabiles et imperfectibiles perfecciores omnimode quam poterit esse aliqua creatura. Et ultima particula patet illis, qui ponunt naturam assumptam esse hominem. Nam si Deus non potest assumere materiam primam vel formam materialem in unitatem suppositi nisi ydemptificaverit[7] se illi nature, eo quod non est aliquid cuius ipsa est natura; per idem non potest aliam naturam assumere nisi ydemptificaverit se eidem, cum indifferenter cuiuslibet nature create quiditas sit natura. Sed iuxta sentenciam sancti Thome ponent[8] Verbum posse esse multos homines per idem: nam infiniti homines possunt esse isti tres homines, et per consequens non plures istis tribus hominibus possunt esse. 3° confirmatur ex hoc quod unus illorum trium hominum cum sit Pater in divinis, est omnino [9]incausabilis et improducibilis[9]:

[1] productibilium A B C.
[2] posito A B C; *si recte*, assignato *pro* assigno *superius legendum.*
[3] particula O.
[4] quod O.
[5] naturarum A B C.
[6] homines *om.* A B C
[7] ydemptificaret O.
[8] ponentis A B C.
[9–9] incommunicabilis et improductibilis A B C.

ergo non plures quam isti tres poterunt esse; quia, data affirmativa[1] opposita, deficit positum.[2]

10° eliciuntur in casu sic opinanti possibili denominaciones inconpossibiles[3] de eodem; posito quod tota Trinitas assumat ypostatice universitatem creabilem vel creatam. In quo casu videtur primo quod, posita eius possibilitate, non debet a catholico negari[4] simpliciter: cum catholicus debet sustinere ut maximam quod, sicut Deus sit tam bonus intrinsecus sicut aliquid potest intelligi vel eciam cogitari, sic | [A 100c] tante perficit universitatem creatam quante potest sustineri quod ipsam perficiat [5]sine repugnancia racionis, experiencie, vel scripture.[5] Sed sine repugnancia alicuius istorum sustineri poterit quod Deus universitatem creatam ad tantum perficiat; ergo quilibet catholicus debet illam sentenciam sustinere. Non enim[6] repugnat racioni pocius quam ipso de possibili posito repugnaret; nec experiencie repugnat cum nullus sensus humanus sciat discutere utrum Deus [7]sit lapis, asinus,[7] et sic de ceteris creaturis; nec scriptura de dampnacione | [C 99a] hominum vel peccatis aut aliis obviat ne sic fiat, quia post peccatum potest Deus dampnandum assumere; eo quod minus videtur Deo contrarium quod sit racionalis homo vel angelus, quam quod sit omnis bestia *hic* sit quantificatus, figuratus, senex, agens, motus, et sic de aliis denominacionibus tam substancialibus quam accidentalibus, *ibi* autem opposite formatus. Nec valet dicere quod posito hoc de facto scriptura sacra illud exprimeret, quia Paulus 'audivit archana que non licet homini loqui': ymo ut diceretur ex scriptura hoc sequitur,[8] cum Deus summe potens et non invidus vel avarus ex bonitate sua non potest se ab ista beneficiencia continere.[9] Nam iuxta argumentum Veritatis Matt. 7. 'si vos, cum sitis mali, nostis[10] bona data dare filiis vestris; quanto magis Pater celestis dabit spiritum bonum petentibus se?' ista consequencia non valeret, si

10. A pantheistic hypothesis.

(It may safely be granted that the intrinsic perfection of God involves the perfectibility of the created universe;

which, if not expressly stated, is consistent with Holy Scripture.)

2 Cor. xii. 4.

Matt. vii. 11.

[1] m^u (materia ?) *add.* O. [2] positivum O. [3] compossibiles O.
[4] perfecta *add.* A B C. [5–5] sine . . . scripture *om.* A B C.
[6] ergo A B C. [7–7] sit hominis assinus C.
[8] sequeretur B. [9] contrahere O. [10] scitis A; nostis . . . se *om.* B.

homo posset dimittere beneficienciam quam facillime posset perficere instar[1] Dei: tunc enim posset Deus ex libertate de obligacionis nulli [2]hominum sequencium[2] tribuere quamlibet promerenti.

Idle hypotheses based on the divine omnipotence encourage dangerous heresies.

Tales autem dilapsus vani ficti ex amplitudine divine potencie forent nidi[3] hereticis ad hereses periculosissimas seminandum. Descendendo autem in speciali concedunt in tali casu quod Deus est quelibet eius pars quantitativa infinitum modica, et infinitum longa et lata; et ita, sicut est 'primus et novissimus,' (Rev. i. 17.) sic | [B152a] est maximus et minimus possibilis, longissimus, latissimus, brevissimus, et indivisibilis quoad molem. Cum enim sit omnis ignis et omne corpus omogenium et[4] ethrogenium, patet quod foret totus mundus multiplicatus dimensionaliter ubique, et sic nichil per se in genere foret in denominacione aliqua maius aut minus reliquo; cum quidlibet tale sit Deus, et per consequens nichil haberet plures partes quantitativas quam tres, que sunt Trinitas increata, super quibus cuncta sunt posita. Addunt eciam quod in casu posito acciones et passiones et cetere forme personales multiplicarentur concomitanter ubique consequenter ad immensam co-existenciam Trinitatis; et sic non est motus successivus; et per consequens neque tempus, cum prius ac posterius in situ deficiant; et sic de multis quibus ego noc sufficerem assentire. Quomodo queso quelibet pars quantitativa corporis foret essencialiter[5] idem cuilibet? cum tunc pars foret non-pars; quia omne corpus indivisibile, et nulla pars minor | [C 99b] aut maior[6] reliqua; quia essencia divina et Trinitas benedicta, et sic mundus et quelibet pars eius quantitativa | [O 232c] summe perfecta; quia realiter ipse Deus et sic tota Trinitas, si foret quelibet pars quantitativa corporis, differret quotlibet differenciis a seipsa. Deduccio omnium istorum patet ex possibilitate casus et principiis opinionis. Videtur enim multis quod

Many of those who allow such

[1] insticionem A B; iusta et C.
[2-2] bonum sequentis O.
[3] vic A B C.
[4] vel A B C.
[5] numeraliter O.
[6] quam *add.* O.

sicut Verbum[1] potest esse dominus[2] sibimet et minister, ac tota generis humani cognacio, sic potest esse totus ignis [A 100d] et quelibet | eius pars quantitativa: nec credo racionem diversitatis possibiliter assignandam. 2do dicunt quod, sicut Verbum est tantum unus homo,[3] sic quod non multi, ponendo quod mille vel quotlibet humanitates assumpsit sic est tantum unus ignis licet infinitas igneitates assumpserit. Quod non dicunt illi qui ponunt Verbum in casu illo[4] esse multos homines. Et patet plane ranga[5] inconveniencium supradicta, cum omnis substancia per se in genere foret Pater, Filius, vel Spiritus sanctus: et sic utrobique illa tria[6] supposita simul omnes substancie et omnia accidentibus informata sic quod, ubicunque est unus ignis, sunt tres ignes solummodo, qui sunt omnes. Infinitatem autem inconveniencium que secuntur videtur michi stultum deducere, cum gignit sollicitudinem apparencie sine fructu.

*hypotheses go further and admit all kinds of incongruities concerning the Word:*

*which it is not worth while to discuss.*

---

## Cap. XII.

[*Recitando opiniones varias de assumpcione creature declarat quod, si assumeret multas humanitates, foret multi homines, sicut dictat sentencia sancti Thome.*

*Against the several opinions that any divine Person can assume (a) any created nature; (b) every substance existing by itself and only such a substance; (c) every rational creature capable of bliss and only such a creature: it is contended that only the Word could assume human nature, and that only in the man Christ Jesus: and it is argued according to the dictum of St. Thomas that, if the Word assumed many humanities, he would be many men.*]

*What would happen if Christ assumed many humanities? This idle question based on untruth gives rise to manifold error.*

Sed descendendum est ad trimembrem posicionem modernorum qui inani sollicitudine venantur[7] quid contingeret si Christus multas humanitates assumeret. Falsitas enim

[1] non *add.* B. [2] deus A B C. [3] unus homo *om.* O. [4] illud O.
[5] ranga (aren *superscripto*) A; arenga B; ranga *om. cum lacuna* C.
[6] tria *om.* O. [7] variantur O.

As Gregory says untruth involves manifold divergence and perplexity.
Authority, fact (exemplariter), and reason concur in proving that error is inconsistent with itself.
And this is shown to be so in the case of those who deny the (Realist) doctrine of Universals, and other philosophical truths.

dissonat sibi ipsi, teste Gregorio 12 Moralium ca° 14. 'Alius, inquit, relicta veritate mentiri deliberat ut audiencium animum fallat. Sed quantus labor est custodire sollicite, ne ipsa eius fallacia deprehendi queat! Ponit quippe ante oculos quid aliis veritatem scientibus responderi possit; et cum magno cogitatu pertractat quomodo per argumenta falsitatis documenta[1] veritatis exsuperet; hinc inde se circumtegit; et contra hoc, ubi deprehendi potuerit, veritati similem responsionem querit; qui si utrobique verum diceret, hucusque[2] sine labore potuisset. Plana quippe est veritatis via et grave est iter mendacii.'[3] Et indubie, sicut in agilibus, sic in speculabilibus verificatur ista sentencia; et patet tam exemplariter quam eciam racione. Si, inquam, consideremus pictacias quibus negantes universalia, extensionem temporis, et veritates de anima cum sibi similibus pregravantur, in quot errores incidunt, quot subterfugia querunt, et quam onerose locuntur, ut sub | falsitatis pallio [C 100a] simulent veritatem; patesceret in speculabilibus sentencia Gregorii supradicta. Sed et racio illud idem exigit. Veritas enim obiective movet[4] et instruit ad ipsam vere cognoscendum in animo et proporcionaliter proferendum: [5]sed ad exprimendum[5] falsitatem deficit obiectum huiusmodi in natura. Ideo difficultatur falsidicus pallians non existens, ac si absque fundamento vel exemplari aliquis[6] intendit unum non ens vel vacuum fabricare. Unde et illud potest patescere in varietate sentenciarum de incarnacione hodie ventilata.

Reason likewise teaches that the vagueness and non-entity of their object of thought causes endless difficulties in the case of those who maintain erroneous opinions. Thus, those who deny the simple truth of the Incarnation (viz. that *the Word and only the Word can assume the Lord Jesus Christ and none other*) fall into a threefold divergence. For holding that any divine Person can assume a created nature (*a*) some maintain that any created nature without distinction; (*b*) others that only every substance existing by itself; (*c*) others, that only every creature capable of bliss, can be so assumed.

Ponunt enim hi quod quamlibet naturam creatam quelibet persona divina indifferenter potest assumere: hi quod omnem et solam substanciam per se entem: et hi quod omnem et solam creaturam racionalem beatificabilem: et sic de quotlibet subdicionibus et evidenciis, quas nobis, qui ponimus solum Verbum pure Dominum Iesum Christum posse as-

[1] argumenta A B C. [2] utique O. [3] menda^m O.
[4] monet A B C. [5]–[5] sed . . . exprimendum *om.* O.
[6] aliquid B; exemplari tns O.

As to the question whether the Word assumed many humanities, modern doctors disagree.

sumere, non expedit recitare; sed in difficultate, si Verbum multas humanitates assumeret, moderni doctores senciunt satis opposite. Sed pro ulteriori declaracione huius materie iuxta[1] ponam istorum sentencias, ut videatur quomodo exorbitantes a seipsis dissonant, et veritas rectissime in omnibus consonat sibi ipsi.

The opinion of Aquinas is that in that case the Word would be many men.

Ponit enim sanctus Thomas super 3^m Sentenciarum Dis- A 101a] tinccione prima Questione 8^a et 9^a | quod, si Verbum multas B 152b] humanitates | assumeret, foret[2] multi homines; sicut si tres persone eandem humanitatem assumerent, forent omnes et singule idem homo. Et inter omnes veritates, quas laudabiliter de Christo[3] scripserat, non estimo aliquam veriorem. Illa enim veritas connexionis est absolute necessaria, quomodolibet fuerit de extremis. Patet sic. Si aliqua sit humanitas, ipsa est homo; ergo si insint multe humanitates, ille sunt multi homines; et per consequens, si Verbum assumit ypostatice[4] multas humanitates, tunc assumendo facit se multos homines. [5]Antecedens patet quodammodo ex predictis.[5] Ymo ex dictis *De Anima* palam sequitur: quia cum quilibet spiritus hominis per se sit homo, patet quod, si sint multi spiritus tales assumpti, assúmuntur et multi homines. [6]Sed et hoc[6] patet ex eo quod omnis humanitas est personam esse hominem.

The possibility of the assumption of many humanities disproved by several arguments.
1. In that case the body of Christ

Sed quia sanctus Thomas sicut et alii moderni doctores discordant a principiis iam assumptis, ideo oportet arguere contra possibilitatem suppositi aliis evidenciis. Videtur enim quod Christus posset esse quantumlibet monstruosus, quod esse non potest, cum minimum inconveniens sit Deo impossibile; et consequencia videtur ex hoc; quod, mille C 100b] capitibus incommunicantibus existentibus in eodem [7]corpore | humano et[7] proporcionaliter de aliis membris organicis, foret ille homo evidentissime monstrum magnum; sed hoc potest esse de Christo, cum omnem humanitatem potest

[1] antequam O.
[2] forent A C.
[3] de Christo *om.* A B C.
[4] ypostatice *om.* B.
[5–5] antecedens . . . predictis *om.* B C.
[6–6] sicut et modo A B C.
[7–7] corpore ut (*om.* humano) A B C.

would be a monstrous organism.

simul assumere: ergo conclusio. Si enim Verbum totam unam | cognacionem assumpserit tam maris quam femine, [O 23 adhuc foret per adversarios solummodo unus homo, et per consequens tantum unum animal ac unum corpus; et super isto forent omnia dicta membra[1] monstruosa[2] ut estimo. Unde credo quod sanctus Thomas negans multiplicacionem dimensionalem eiusdem corporis, negaret in casu isto quod Christus est solummodo unus homo; nedum quod tunc foret hermofrodita,[3] pater et filius, et tota cognacio; verum quia idem[4] corpus foret dimensionaliter per loca distancia.

But if it is objected that there would be many separate bodies;

Sed hic dicitur quod monstruositas et impossibilitas multiplicacionis dimensionalis intelligitur secundum idem corpus; sed in casu posito foret secundum corpora multum disparia habitus talium situum et membrorum.

it is replied: (a) that 'denominations' of Christ would apply only to one and the same body;

Contra illud tripliciter arguitur.[5] Primo probatur quod secundum idem corpus habeat Christus istas denominaciones; quia secundum eandem naturam creatam et eandem humanitatem, que est Verbum esse unicum hominem; ergo secundum idem corpus. Si enim secundum seipsum habet ista, et ipse sit idem corpus, ubicunque est homo; sequitur quod secundum idem corpus habet ista, ubicunque sit homo.[6]

(b) that the separate union of many single bodies to Christ would produce monstrosity as much as if these bodies were combined into one aggregate before union;

Similiter, si omnia ista corpora essent localiter copulata et adunata stante unione[7] sine generacione vel corrupcione alicuius partis eorum, foret monstrum horribilissimum; quia corpus compositum ex corpore vetule et infantis, viri et uxoris, et sic de tota cognacione. Illud ergo cum fuerit totale et adequatum corpus Christi idem quod prefuit, sicut est modo, sic fuit ante monstruosum. Non enim adquiritur Christo aliqua pars vel partis posicio propter motum localem vel continuacionem[8]; ergo nec aliqua monstruositas secundum se totam. Et hoc est evidencius illis qui ponunt quod omnes partes integri[9] sunt simul ipsum totum.

(c) that the *accidents* due to

Similiter non est evidencia contra multiplicacionem dimensionalem

[1] membra *om.* B. [2] monstruose O. [3] hermifodrita (*sc.* hermaphrodita) O.
[4] illud A B C. [5] arguitur *om.* O. [6] homo *om.* A C. [7] unione *om.* A B C.
[8] *fortasse* contiguacionem *legendum*: *cf. Trialogus*, *p.* 87, *l.* 23. [9] integre A B.

[A 101b] eiusdem corporis | quin consimile contingit reducere contra hoc quod eadem persona sit dimensionaliter multiplicata secundum diversa corpora, ut quod hic sit senex, hic iuvenis, hic mas, hic femina, hic pater et uxor procreans[1] seipsum infantem, et hic adolescens sepeliens seipsum vetulam,[2] et ita de aliis denominacionibus aliorum generum. Unde, cum acciones et passiones personales individuantur primo a supposito non[3] natura, videtur quod multiplicantur ad multiplicacionem suppositi; et sic idem homo foret quantumlibet dissimilis et contrarius sibi ipsi tam secundum [C 101a] accidencia corporis quam | anime, ut sedulus excogitator potest calculare.[4] Et sic contra principia sancti Thome idem corpus in numero foret quantumlibet multis et disparibus formis substancialibus accidentatum.[5]

an indefinite number of incongruous *substantial forms* would belong to one and the same body.

Item, si Christus potest simul habere[6] humanitates tam dispariter accidentatas cum hoc quod maneat idem homo, tunc posset pro diversis sitibus habere denominaciones contrarias; et per consequens, coextensis illis humanitatibus, forent accidencia contraria coextensa; et sic idem simul et semel contrariis accidentibus informatum. Sed hoc modicum videtur modernis, si secundum diversas naturas eidem supposito ista insint. Unde concedunt quod qualescunque forme contrarie per eundem situm et idem suppositum, sed secundum diversas naturas, coextendi poterunt.

2. Also difference of place in these various humanities would involve contrary 'accidents.'

The allegation of diversity of *natures* does not cover this difficulty.

Sed contra illud tripliciter arguitur.[7] Primo posito quod duo corpora coextendantur et utrumque simul pro eodem loco et tempore gradiatur, videtur quod sunt duo motus progressivi,[8] sicut duo quantitates et cetera accidencia coextensa. Oppositum tamen videtur, cum motus individuatur sufficienter a spacio, tempore, et subiecto; sed idem est homo in numero, idem tempus et spacium; ergo cum nulla pars quantitativa hominis graditur, eadem est mocio progressiva. Et per idem posito quod secundum unam humanitatem

(*a*) For to two bodies two motions, two quantities, etc., would belong.

[1] procreatus O. [2] vetulam *om.* A B C. [3] nam O.
[4] 9ñg'e (*i.e.* coniungere) O. [5] actuatum A C.
[6] summe (*fortasse pro* sumere) B. [7] arguitur *om.* C O. [8] successivi B.

penetraret progrediendo multas continuas humanitates[1] quiescentes [2] continue, idem Christus simul et semel secundum idem quiesceret,[2] et motu contrario moveretur.

(b) Moreover, Christ, by the multitude of his humanities, would (as a creature) be infinitely good;

Similiter iuxta illud sequitur quod Christus infinitum bonum animal potest esse, quia mensura bonitatis rei composite capitur a principiis intrinsecis cum disposicionibus formalibus in eadem. Ex quo sequitur quod Christus racione multitudinis humanitatum foret melior homo | quam [B 153a] si solum unam assumeret. Patet consequencia, supposito primo quod Christus sit tantum finite bonus iuxta illam vocem Veritatis, 'Pater maior me est,' Ioh. 14.[3] Ymo si foret infinitum bonus homo racione deitatis, foret per idem infinitum antiquus, et per consequens primus homo, consequens contra Apostolum prima ad Cor. 15. 'primus, inquit, homo de terra terrenus, et secundus homo de celo celestis.' Et ita oportet limitare in Christo omnia alia[4] accidencia, que habet humanitus, sic quod non infinitum bonum corpus vel animam habet Christus; et per idem non infinitum magnus senex vel antiquus homo est Christus, nec infinitum potens ac virtuosus vel sciens homo, quia sic excederet limites speciei eciam secundum hominem assumptum; et per consequens non conveniret nobiscum in specie; que contradicunt supradictis. Quo supposito patet quod Christus existens | bonus homo racione unius humanitatis [C 101b] foret melior homo racione alterius humanitatis incommunicantis coassumpte; cum bonitatem magnam acquireret nullam aliunde deperdens. Nec superest in quo | per [A 101c] humanitatem melioraretur[5] nisi in esse hominis. Et per idem foret in duplo melior homo per assumpcionem duarum humanitatum quam per assumpcionem unius | solummodo; [O 233a] et sic de aliis denominacionibus accidentalibus[6] consequentibus ad easdem. Ex quo videtur primo quod infinitas humanitates assumendo foret eque bonus homo ut Deus, vel unum infinitum foret reliquo maius. Videtur 2do

John xiv. 28.

1 Cor. xv. 47.

which is an impious assertion.

[1] humanitates *om.* O. [2–2] continue . . . quiesceret *om.* O. [3] 10 O.
[4] illa A. [5] melioratur O. [6] accidentalibus *om.* A B C.

quod infinitum melior potest[1] esse asinus quam homo, posito quod infinitas naturas asininas Verbum assumeret naturam hominis dimittendo. Et per consequens sequitur 3° quod species non assimilatur numeris, cum omnis creata substancia magis et minus susciperet[2] ut unus homo[3] esset[4] reliquo in duplo magis homo propter humanitatem duplicem; et sic de qualibet proporcione racionali reali;[5] et per consequens Christus racione multitudinis naturarum excederet in humanitate quodcunque aliud individuum speciei.

(c) Thirdly, Christ would be simultaneously infinitely great and also of a certain definite size (septipedalis).

3° videtur quod ex omni genere accidentis corporei potest esse composicio parcium intensive. Nam coextensis humanitatibus secundum materias possent partes quantitative materierum et suorum accidencium coextendi; et per consequens, cum omnia sunt forme vel materie eiusdem suppositi, sequitur quod per talem composicionem posset unum componi non extensive; ergo intensive; quod est impossibile. Et [sic][6] de materia et ceteris accidentibus, que secundum philosophos[7] non possunt magis vel minus suscipere. Nam eque magnus foret Christus secundum unam humanitatem, sicut[8] foret [9]Christus secundum[9] infinitas equales insimul coextensas. Nec sapit quod Christus sit intensius septipedalis quam prius. Et hic videtur possibile[10] quod infinitum magnus iam est Christus, et nullam quantitatem deperdet, et tamen in fine erit solum septipedalis, posito quod infinitas humanitates equales assumat ad modum coree[11] iuxta positas; sic[12] quod omnes ille sese penetrantes coextendantur in fine sine augmentacione[13] vel diminucione; et patet conclusio. Et sic infinitum magnum potest continue maiorari continue adquirendo quantitatem ac nullam penitus deperdendo quousque infinitum parvum fuerit, ut alibi declaratur. Et conformis est consideracio

[1] potest *om.* B. [2] suscipiat O. [3] homo *om.* C O.
[4] est O. [5] reali *om.* C O. [6] et *om.* O; sic. *in omn. codd. om. suppleri*
[7] philosophum B. [8] simul *pr. man.* A C. [9-9] Christus secundum *om.* A B C.
[10] impossibile B. [11] coree (*an pro* choreae? *cf. p.* 196, *n.* 9) A B C; sese O.
[12] sic *om.* O. [13] alteracione O M.

And as to size, so as to motion, there would be contradictory accidents.

de motu, ut infinitum intensus potest esse motus per motuum incommunicancium extensionem,[1] cum hoc quod mobile quantumcunque tarde ad velocissimum moveatur. Et ex istis potest calculator elicere quotlibet conclusiones nimis mirabiles, quia regularum de velocitate motuum destructivas.

3. Further, a definite body and soul and their union constitute humanity, that is, make Christ to be a man: therefore, the assumption of many humanities would make him to be many men.

Item hoc corpus et hec anima | cum ista unione ypostatica [C 102a] et aliis que secuntur sunt sufficiencia principia ad faciendum Christum esse hominem; cum illis [2]sive aliis quibuscunque[2] positis, hoc sequatur. Sed multiplicatis completis principiis oportet multiplicari effectum formaliter consequentem. Ergo si sint multe humanitates assumpte, sunt multi homines; ut si Christus iam ad humanitatem habitam assumeret aliam humanitatem incommunicantem, illa assumpcio cum sit sufficiens principium, sufficit facere Christum iterum esse hominem; et sic quociens illa principia fuerint geminata.[3] Ex quo sequitur quod si Christus multas humanitates assumeret, foret multi homines consequenter.

For (a) with the variation of the causes, *i.e.* body and soul, the result, *i.e.* the individual man, varies.

Confirmatur tripliciter. Primo si aliqua principia individuant Christum, ut homo potissime foret[4] corpus et anima; et per consequens variatis illis oportet individuum hominis variari. Aliud ergo est Christum esse istum hominem ex hoc corpore et hac anima integratum, et aliud esse[5] istam personam ex alio corpore et alia anima compositum quia aliter indubio non foret Christus aliud per humanitatis | [A 101d] assumpcionem quam foret eternaliter, si solummodo foret Deus. Et patet sentencia sancti Thome, quod Verbum si assumeret multas humanitates ut Iohannem, Petrum et cetera, foret correspondenter multi homines. Verbum igitur esse hominem foret communis humanitas ad ipsum esse Iesum, Petrum etc.

(b) The multiplication of *forms* involves the multiplication of *supposites*.

Similiter impossibile est formas completas eciam accidentales multiplicari simul et semel, nisi eo ipso multiplicentur supposita. Sed omnis humanitas est forma, cum sit illud

[1] coextensionem O. [2] sū plī posit (sive plurimum positis *vel* positivis) O. [3] geminata A; genita B C O. [4] forent A B C. [5] est A B C; *fortasse* est esse *legendum*.

quo substancia formaliter est homo; ergo multiplicatis humanitatibus multiplicabuntur et homines. Assumptum declaratum est de formis, accidentibus, et earum substanciis [B 153b] proximis, | ut si sint multe ambulaciones simul et semel oportet multa supposita ambulare; et ita de aliis; ergo a maiori vel pari, cum humanitas sit suppositum esse hominem non individuata ex successione temporis vel adquisicione adventicii accidentis, quod positis multis humanitatibus multi homines consecuntur.

Therefore from the multiplication of *humanities* follows the multiplication of *men*.

3°· idem patet, posito quod Verbum assumat multas embriones et post completas humanitates[1] animabus congenitis, patet quod anime advenientes, cum sint forme substanciales, faciunt Verbum esse aliud; et per consequens non relinquitur quid[2] aliud nisi illum hominem. Prius enim fuit completus Iesus et per consequens per posteriores animas non fit Iesus. Et si dicatur quod anime advenientes non [C 102b] faciunt Christum esse aliud sed | [3]alterius modi,[3] tunc sunt forme accidentales advenientes enti in actu et non eiusdem racionis cum ceteris animabus, que in quantum[4] huius modi, faciunt corpora animata. Patet igitur, si experiencia et principia philosophica salvari debeant, quod Verbo assumente [O 233b] multas humanitates | est multi homines. Nam numerus hominum, qui est sensibile commune ex 2^do^ *De Anima*, ita patescit sensui secundum quantitates continuas dislocatas et secundum quotlibet differencias accidentales illarum naturarum, sicut innotescit aliquis sensibilis numerus alicui.

(c) Whether the Word assume embryonic or complete humanities, the assumption sooner or later of the corresponding souls, which are the substantial forms of the said humanities, makes him to be other than he was before, *i.e.* add to a complete man Jesus so many animated bodies.

Item posito quod quodlibet suppositum generis animalis servatis[5] omnibus positivis sit Verbo ypostatice copulatum; patet quod non exinde periret genus, species, vel differencia animalis; et per consequens non omne animal foret Christus; ex quo per locum a sufficienti similitudine sequitur quod Verbum assumendo multas humanitates non foret solummodo unus homo. Assumptum patet eo quod Verbum non[6] necessitatur ex unione ypostatica corrumpere aliquod posi-

4. The hypostatic union with the Word does not cancel

[1] humanitatibus B. [2] quin C. [3-3] alterum A B C.
[4] christum O. [5] sciuat *pr. man.* A; sequitur B. [6] non *om.* A B C.

the genus, species, or difference of each 'animal' so assumed.

tivum; et, cum genus, species, et differencia sint plurimum positiva, patet quod non ex assumpcione oportet illas exstinguere; et cum non sit genus in actu nisi habeat species et illa supposita, que specifice[1] distinguantur, patet ex casu possibili illis quos alloquor[2] de facto posito; consequens est quod sint multa individua [3]distincta specifice; non ergo omne individuum[3] de genere viveucium foret Christus; maiorem enim distinccionem oportet esse individuis quam in formis communibus, cum omnia inferiora in suis communioribus uniuntur. Nec potest dici quod manet genus animalis cum suis divisivis differenciis sicut prius, cum indifferenter omnis homo sit asinus, leo, capra, et sic de aliis, si Christus non sit multa animalia racione multarum animalitatum ypostatice coniunctarum. Ubi ergo foret genus distinctum a specie vel individuo secundum communioritatem, si idem individuum cuiuslibet generis animalis sit commune cuilibet animali? Ubi eciam tunc[4] foret | differencia inter racionale [A 102a] et irracionale, rudibile et irrudibile[5] et ita de [6]ceteris, si omne animal racionale sit animal irracionale, rudibile sit irrudibile, et ita de[6] omnibus aliis[7] differenciis assignandis? Omnes ergo termini per se in predicamento substancie nec predicarentur in quid, nec de rebus distinctis specifice cum omne animal sit omne animal, nec forma aliqua est sufficiens medium distinguendi unum suppositum vel naturaliter[8] ab altero eo quod species permixte de se mutuo predicantur; et [9]cum tam species differant[9] quam individua speciei, videtur quod ydemptificatis speciebus individua ydemptificari poterunt. Nec valet dicere quod ex assumpcione huiusmodi species corrumpuntur, quia omnis species, que prius fuit, habet omnem singularem essenciam, quam prius habuit; et Verbum nedum est suppositum hominis sed bovis, leonis, et cuiuslibet animalis. Cum ergo sufficit ad existenciam

[1] specificate A B C. [2] alloquitur O. [3–3] distincta . . . individuum *om.* O.
[4] tunc ergo A B; insuper O. [5] hinibile A B C.
[6–6] ceteris . . . de *om.* A B C. [7] aliis *om.* A B C.
[8] numeraliter M. [9–9] cum species plus differant O.

speciei quod unum suppositum illius nature[1] existat,[2] sequi- [C 103a] tur quod manet omnis species, | que perante. Non enim est hic fallacia accidentis—quicquid fuerit in principio huius[3] hore est modo; species leonis est[4] aliquid quod fuit in principio[5] illius hore; ergo omnis talis species est modo—. Et cum[6] nulla possunt nunc plus differre et nunc minus, manencia omnino immota; sequitur quod, sicut nature per ante differebant specifice, sic et modo; et per consequens modo est species. Confirmatur ex hoc quod omnis species est [7]natura, omnis[7] natura animalis, que prius fuit, modo est; [8]ergo omnis species, que prius fuit, modo est.[8]

Item Deus potest de omnibus hominibus per viam continuacionis facere unum compositum, sicut infinitum magnum et infinitum parvum potest Deus facere hominem. Quo posito[9] videtur primo quod homo potest infinitum maiorari et alias infinitum minorari sine hoc quod quantitatem aliquam adquirat vel deperdat[10]; ut posito quod Verbum quotlibet humanitates seorsum assumat et omnes illas stante unione continuet, et[11] iterum discontinuet, secundum quod exigit conclusio probanda. Nam Christus fuit ante unionem homo medio quantitatis et post continuacionem erit monstrum grandissimum et deforme; et cum ex continuacione nulla quantitas secundum se totam adquiritur, sequitur propositum. Et idem contingit arguere de alteracione; ut potencia[12] naturali tam corporis quam anime tale quidem corpus multiplex sufficeret quantumlibet distanter sentire, et quantumlibet [13]tarde [14]moderando spacium longissimum[15] in brevi[14] describere. Cum ergo cuiuslibet partis illius corporis aliqua pars sit pars corporis Christi, sequitur quod hoc totum corpus sit corpus

5. On the assumption that God can by way of continuation (*i.e.* by joining one to another) out of all men make one compound being, Christ would assume that being in case of his assuming many humanities; and then

(*a*) Any part of this compound body is a part of Christ,

[1] specici B.
[2] existit A B C.
[3] istius B; illius O.
[4] est fuit C; eciam fuit O.
[5] in principio *om.* O
[6] tamen C; tunc O.
[7–7] natura omnis *om.* O.
[8–8] ergo . . . est *om.* A B.
[9] petito C O.
[10] perdat A B C.
[11] ut A B C.
[12] poñ O.
[13] tarde *om.* A B C.
[14–14] moderando . . . brevi *om.* O.
[15] longis A B C; longissimum *aut* longum *sensui necessarium videtur.*

*and this whole body is the body of Christ; which is therefore a monstrosity.*

Christi; | et per consequens Christus, postquam[1] fuit communis stature, iam est ita magnus sicut hoc corpus. Ex quo inferenda sunt alia. [B 154a]

*(b) Any of these humanities is Christ: therefore Christ is any of his quantitative parts: i.e. he is many men;*

2°. videtur sequi quod Christus sit quotlibet partes sue quantitative. Nam ante continuacionem Christus fuit compositum ex qualibet istarum animarum et suo corpore; ex quo sequitur quod Christus sit multe partes quantitative. Nec valet dicere quod natura humana, et non homo, sit pars hominis; quia partes quantitative corporis[2] sunt substancie per se in genere, quod negatur de humanitate; ergo sicut monstrum quod est homo geminus et a dyafragmate versus superius habet hominem eius partem, sic et Christus in casu posito. Non enim desinit esse completus homo secundum illam humanitatem propter continuacionem; sicut nec in|ciperet esse homo secundum istam humanitatem [A 102b] propter discontinuacionem. | [C 103b] Concesso autem consequente videtur primo, si Christus sit quotlibet partes sue, quod multa quorum quodlibet[3] est Christus; et cum Christus non sit aliud quam homo, sequitur quod multi homines | [O 233c] sunt Christus et non propter continuacionem; ergo ante continuacionem fuit Christus multi homines; et non, si non ex assumpcione multarum humanitatum; ergo posito quod Christus multas humanitates assumat, consequitur ipsum esse multos homines, quod est intentum. Nec valet dicere quod Christus non habet partes huiusmodi, cum ex illis denominatur magnus, agens, beatus, et sic de formis ceteris que partibus suis insunt. Et si dicatur quod omnes sunt Christus et non pars eius, sed idem cum toto, tunc restat dicere secundum quam humanitatem Christus a Deo maioratur; cum non sit possibile humanitatem aggregari ex multis humanitatibus, nisi illa a qualibet illarum differat. Et patet quod secundum nullam illarum humanitatum parcialium maioratur; ergo secundum illam totalem; et per consequens est nova humanitas sine correspondenti

[1] preterquam A. [2] corporis *om.* B.
[3] quotlibet *cum rasura alt. man.* A; quotlibet B; quodlibet C; quotlibet quodlibet O.

anima generata; quod est impossibile; cum nec corpus organicum correspondens tali humanitati fingi poterit, nec spiritus[1] implens materiam; nec corpus est maius propter iuxtaposicionem corporis quod non incidit in partem sui. Patet itaque logicis in casu posito quod ad omnem punctum Christi est non gradus augmentacionis, cum non sit motus nisi subiectum aliquod primo moveatur. Et hoc replicatur consequenter contra hoc Euclidis principium, 'omne totum est maius sua parte quantitativa.' Et posito[2] quod Christus assumat[3] omnem naturam animalis; tunc post continuacionem omnium illorum factus monstrum foret alicubi non monstrum, et sic foret multe res, et per consequens multe substancie; quia aliter non foret pars sui, nisi pars et totum ponant in numerum.

which is against Euclid's axiom 'every whole is greater than its part.'

3° potest poni casus de Dei omnipotencia quod infinitas naturas corporeas adaptet infinitis animabus, quarum prima sit dupla ad secundum,[4] et sic in infinitum; et omnibus illis continuatis assumat quamlibet in ypostaticam unionem. Tunc videtur quod Christus sit infinite partes sue, et sic infinitum parvus, et per consequens maior seipso; et cum, ubicunque fuerit, est eque magnus racione multiplicacionis concomitancie, ut patet de eucaristia; sequitur quod in quotlibet locis est minor seipso. Ymo cum infinitas animas Deus potest producere et facere eas incommunicantes[5] materias[6] actuare, sequitur quod sit possibile[7] quamlibet partem quantitativam Christi esse Christum; quod est impossibile, cum tunc non forent multe partes sui quantitative, ut tactum est superius proximo capitulo.

(c) The subdivision of quantitative parts to infinity involves the possibility of Christ being infinitely small, i.e. both greater and less than himself.

[C 104a] Item ex evidencia sancti Thome | videtur quod Christus assumendo multas humanitates sit multi homines. Nam omne nomen appellativum, cuius principalia significata[8] multiplicantur, [9]predicatur vere[9] pluraliter de eisdem. Sed hoc nomen *homo* primo et principaliter significat qualitatem

7. The argument of Aquinas (p. 203) is supported by the use of words,

[1] species A B C. [2] proposito O. [3] assumendo O.
[4] duplam B C. [5] communicantes O. [6] creature *add.* B.
[7] impossibile A. [8] significancia O. [9–9] vere probatur A B C.

*humanitas* predicates the substantial quality of *homo*:

substancialem ut humanitatem: ergo multiplicatis humanitatibus in Christo, [1]et *homo* vere predicatur pluraliter de eodem.[1] Maior ex hoc est evidens quod multiplicatis significatis multiplicanda sunt nomina significatorum; ut si tres persone divine haberent multas divinitates, tunc essent multi dii;[2] et sic de similibus quibuscunque. Minor autem patet ex hoc quod *substancia secunda* secundum Aristotelem in Predicamentis capitulo De Substancia significat *quale-quid* hoc est, [3]*substancialem qualitatem*.[3] Ut patet in methaphisica; *homo* enim principaliter significat | *humanitatem*, [A 102c] *album albedinem*. Concesso ergo consequente et posito quod Verbum assumat omnes humanitates; consequens est quod sint multi homines ex assumpto; et cum Verbum sit omnis homo, sequitur quod Verbum sit multi homines. Negato vero assumpto | de talibus concretis, sed concesso quod [B 154b] principaliter significant talia supposita, oportet dicere consequenter quod iste terminus *homo*[4] omne quod est de sua primaria imposicione significat; et per idem quodlibet nomen appellativum vel concretum quodcunque significat.[5] Nam omnem personam divinam *homo* de imposicione sua primaria significat, et cum hoc singulas creaturas; ergo conclusio. Maior patet ex hoc quod omne suppositum quod potest esse homo, signum significat; omnis persona divina potest esse homo; ergo etc. Et per idem bovem, asinum, leonem, et quamlibet speciem creature; cum omnis natura singularis huiusmodi potest a Verbo assumi stante unione personali ad hominem; quo posito de facto omnem talem naturam significaret, quia omnem hominem significaret; [6]omnis talis species foret homo;[6] ergo omnem talem speciem significaret; et cum nullum nomen significat universaliter formas specificas nisi eo ipso significaverit omnes formas individuas sub eis contentas, sequitur conclusio. Certum est tamen quod non fuit de intencione imponencium terminos ad signi-

If we use one term in the plural number, the other must also be so used: if Christ is many humanities, He is many men.

Any other treatment of words, such as in effect makes *homo* to mean *deitas*,

[1-1] est homo nature personalis personaliter de eodem A B; est homo vere personalis personaliter de eodem C; est homo vere pluraliter de eodem O. [2] dii *om.* B.
[3-3] substanciale qualitate O. [4] homo *om.* A B C.
[5] signat B. [6-6] omnis . . . homo *om.* B.

ficandum, quod iste terminus *homo* significaret *deitatem*; et ita de quolibet designando, quia tunc essent omnes tales termini analogi[1] et equivoci. Perirent eciam superioritas et inferioritas terminorum, et multi sillogismi in terminis substancialibus per fallaciam accidentis; ut sic arguendo—quicquid nascetur ex homine non eternaliter existebat; [2]iste homo nascetur ex homine; ergo non eternaliter [C 104b] existebat[2]; et sic de similibus. Ymo non est verisimile | terminum significare philosopho illud quod nescit sibi significare, ymo quod credit non posse esse hominem. Sed constat quod gentiles philosophi assererent[3] Deum non directe significari per terminos tales specificos, quia tunc concederent Deum posse[4] esse hominem; ergo[5] non significaverat illis Deum; et per idem nec nobis; cum univoce nobis significaret sicut illis nisi[6] per accidens, quia contingit humanitatem esse Deum. Aliter enim cognoscerent [O 233d] et crederent | omnes philosophi in confuso Deum fore hominem in hoc universali—omnis homo erit homo—et nunquam negarent differencias divisivas generi de se invicem predicari, ut sic—omnis homo est racionalis; asinus est homo; ergo est racionalis—. Sic enim concedunt theologi quod homo creavit mundum, quia persona Verbi, que est homo, creavit mundum. Pono itaque quod in mente philosophi ignorantis incarnacionem sit ista intencio specifica '*homo*' naturaliter significans *hominem et solum hominem*. Et pono quod stante illa unione Deus assumat quamcunque naturam specificam animalis; et patet ex dictis et dicendis quod homo foret in qualibet specie animalis; et sic cum veris[7] sequitur quod ista intencio *homo* continue naturaliter significans significaret asinum, leonem etc, sicut modo significat; et ita, ut arguitur in materia de ydemptificacione, quilibet terminus eque indifferenter significaret quidlibet. Quo dato non foret negandum quod homo est asinus; et sic quandocumque

renders language meaningless:

and in this way any word might be made to mean anything else than what it plainly does mean.

[1] anologi A C O.
[2,2] iste . . . existebat *om.* C; ergo *om.* A B C.
[3] asseruerunt A B C.
[4] posse *om.* B.
[5] ergo *om.* A B.
[6] non B.
[7] viris A B C.

predicatur positivum de aliquo positivo, quod idem est directe significatum per predicatum et subiectum, quod sufficit ad verificandum enunciaciones huiusmodi cum paribus que ponuntur. Nec valet dicere quod nullus talis terminus naturam significat; cum sic iste terminus *deus* de sua intencione primaria hominem et omne assertibile significat.

---

## Cap. XIII. | [A102d]

[*Confirmat aliorum sentencias quod, si omnes humanitates assumeret, tunc nec foret unus homo nec multi homines, sed et unicus atque multi; et sic concordat modernorum sentencias cum antiquis.*

*Assuming, as proved in the last chapter* (p. 203), *the truth of the dictum of St. Thomas that if Christ assumed many humanities, He would be many men: the modern view is supported that He assumed* all *humanities, and was thereby both* THE ONE MAN *and also many men; and thus opinions are reconciled and the unity of truth established.*]

Habito quod Christus assumendo multas humanitates foret consequenter multi homines, ut senteneiat sanctus Thomas; probatur quod, si omnes humanitates assumeret, foret unicus homo tantum, ut recentissimi scribentes asserunt satis vere.

1. If Christ is every man, He is still only one man: for *every man* is a term used of each individual man.

Nam hoc posito, omnis homo foret omnis homo; ergo foret solummodo unus homo. Antecedens patet per exponentes, cum homo Christus sit omnis homo; ut patet per conversionem, omnis homo est Christus. Nam si in tali casu non omnis homo sit Christus, cum nulla natura assumpta sit homo, ut dicunt concorditer; sequitur quod aliqua[1] persona de specie humana non sit Christus, et illam personam oportet in casu posito dicere Verbum Dei. Sed constat quod illa

[1] alia C.

est Christus; cum ergo Verbum sit omnis homo, quod quidem Verbum est aliquis homo; sequitur quod aliquis homo sit omnis homo; et tamen[1] nichil est homo nisi illud [C 105a] Verbum; sequitur ex posicione[2] quod omnis | homo sit omnis homo. Quo habito[3] probo quod repugnat huic multos homines esse. Nam si duo homines sunt, [4]tunc duo homines sunt[4] duo homines, et per consequens sunt duo homines differentes, et sic unus illorum non est reliquus; consequens contra datum, cum omnis homo sit omnis homo.

2. The assumption of many natures does not involve the assumption of many men: natures are not yet men (until the individualizing accidents are added).

Item si Verbum in tali casu sit multi homines[5] propter multitudinem formarum, quas predicatum significat; tunc forme ille sive nature plurificate essent Verbum; consequens impossibile sic dicenti; et consequencia ex hoc deducitur[6] quod predicatum nunquam dicitur pluraliter de subiecto nisi quodlibet illorum pluraliter significatorum per predicatum vere dicatur[7] de subiecto; ut natura divina non est multe [B 155a] persone, | nisi quelibet illarum personarum sit deitas.[8] Cum ergo pluralitas in casu posito[9] sit solummodo[10] in naturis, que non sunt homines: [11]videtur quod alienum sit concedere Verbum esse multos homines[11] propter illarum naturarum multitudinem, quarum[12] nulla est homo; ut Petrus non est multa accidencia, licet sit album et musicum, quia tunc esset[13] multe substancie accidentate, et per consequens multi homines, et per idem infinite substancie; et patet prima consequencia[14] eo quod Petrus est precise[15] substancia.

3. If the Word is many men according to the multitude of humanities, and every man is an individual, then He is many individuals, many persons; which is impossible.

Item si Verbum ad multitudinem[16] humanitatum sit multi homines, et omnis homo est individuum; tunc est multa individua, et per consequens multe persone; quod est impossibile. Et consequencia sic probatur. Si Christus est multi homines, et per se homo est substancia; tunc est multe substancie[17] individue racionalis nature non aliene

[1] quod O. [2] expositorie A B C. [3] posito B.
[4–4] tunc . . . sunt *om.* O. [5] homines *om.* A. [6] reducitur O.
[7] dicantur O. [8] deus B; divinitas O. [9] posito *om.* A B C.
[10] modo *om.* A B C. [11] videtur . . . homines *om.* C O.
[12] qua B. [13] est A B C. [14] conclusio A B C.
[15] precise (*an potius* per se ?) *om. cum lacuna iii litt.* O.
[16] multitudinem *om.* O. [17] substancie *om.* O.

The Nominalist theory, which denies the existence of the *homo communis*, complicates the problem.

supposítate[1]; et per consequens multe persone; quod foret absurdissimum, quod Deus esset mille persone, ut puta totus populus Christianus; cum ista posicio negat hominem communem. Minus ergo colorate una persona speciei humane[2] foret communicata tot hominibus quot foret omnis et singuli eorundem, quam quod natura specifica foret unum quodque eius suppositum, quia ibi maneret suppositorum distinccio cum ydemptitate nature specifice. Hic autem est idem singularis homo omnium hominum quilibet; et per consequens omnis homo est[3] omnis homo; persona ergo que communicatur tot substanciis ydemptitate[4] non foret incommunicabilis existencie.

4. If the Word is many different men, wherein do they differ? for each has *corpus* and *anima*.

Item si in casu posito Verbum sit multi homines differentes, ut puta Iesus, Petrus, Paulus; tunc illi homines differunt potissime per sua principia intrinseca, scilicet per corpus et animam; sed non in hoc differunt homines; ergo non restat in eis principium differendi. Minor probatur eo quod omnis homo habet omne corpus humanum vel animam suam partem, et per consequens per appropriatas habitaciones | talium non est | dare distinccionem hominum. Antecedens patet per Doctorem: [5]concedit enim[5] quod Iesus est Petrus, et tamen illi non sunt unus homo, sed duo homines. [C 105b] [A 103a]

(a) Jesus has the body and soul of each individual as his own parts, and consequently every qualitative part of man. *Homo* in the concrete is a personal term: the acts of the Word are the acts of the person Jesus Christ who is the Word.

Ex prima parte sequitur quod Iesus habet corpus et animam Petri tanquam suas partes, et per idem omnem partem qualitativam hominis. Sicut[6] enim conceditur ex posicione[7] quod homo Christus Iesus[8] creavit stellas, quia Verbum, quod est Iesus Christus,[9] sic fecit; et ita de quibuscunque predicatis personalibus, que Verbo conveniunt, cum *homo* concretum sit terminus personalis; ita concedi debet quod iste idem homo componitur ex corpore Petri et eius anima, sicut Verbum, | quod est iste homo, ex eis[10] componitur.[11] [O 234a]

[1] supponente B: suppo^te O. [2] humane *om.* A B C. [3] est *om.* O.
[4] ydempti^te A B C. [5] concedit enim *om.* C. [6] sic AB.
[7] expositorie A B C; *cf. p.* 217, *n.* 2. [8] Iesus *om.* O.
[9] Christus *om.* O. [10] ex eis *om.* O.
[11] ex corpore Petri et eius anima sicut verbum quod est ille homo *add.* O.

(h) *Homines* and *humanitates* are not convertible terms.

Quoad $2^{dam}$ partem non video colorem in dicto, nisi per *homines* appropriate intelligat *humanitates*; et tunc foret proposicio sibi impossibilis; vel aliter concedat quod Verbum est omnes illi homines; et per consequens, Iesus est Paulus, cum hec nomina personalitatem [1] significant. Sed iste homo non est iste homo, cum tale subiectum cum persona Verbi connotat individuacionem, ab isto corpore et ista anima non personaliter sed simpliciter. Sed tunc videtur concedendum quod iste homo non potest istam naturam dimittere vel aliud corpus et aliam animam assumere; nec quod ille homo fuit, antequam fuit homo; et per consequens non creavit mundum, nec est Deus; et per consequens Verbum non est isti multi homines sicut prius, cum non sit eorum personalis assumpcio; cum tunc persona eterna foret quilibet eorundem. Et perirent tales sillogismi in quocunque modo —omne Verbum divinum est Iesus; omnis homo compositus ex corpore Petri et eius anima est Verbum divinum; ergo omnis homo compositus ex corpore Petri et eius anima est Iesus—. Et sic arguendo in $2^{do}$ modo prime figure—nullus homo compositus ex corpore Iesu et eius anima [2]est homo Petrus; sed omne Verbum divinum est homo compositus ex corpore Iesu et eius anima[2]; ergo nullum Verbum divinum est homo Petrus—et sic de ceteris quibuslibet sillogismis. Nec tollit[3] ista responsio raciones predictas quin, si[4] Verbum sit multi homines, tunc est multe substancie vel nature, et sic multe persone; et per consequens simpliciter creatura; quod negat posicio. Nam Deus in casu isto est mille[5] res et quelibet earundem, et per consequens quelibet earundem[6] mille verùm est Deus; et cum non eternaliter essent Deus, sequitur quod[7] inceperant esse Deus; ex quo sequitur quod[7] sunt creature; et sic Deus esset multe creature et quelibet earundem; quod non sapit,[8] nisi concedatur humanitatem [9] esse Christum.[9]

[1] recipiant *add.* B. [2-2] est . . . anima *om.* C. [3] valet B.
[4] sic *pr. man.* A B C. [5] multe A B C. [6] earum A B C.
[7-7] inceperant . . . quod *om.* O. [8] capit O. [9-9] humanitas . . . Christus O.

5. If Christ be many men, then by gradual dismissal of assumed natures, many men would cease to be Christ.

Item si Christus in tali casu sit multi homines, tunc dimittendo paulative naturas assumptas | multi homines per [C 106a] ordinem desinerent esse Christus; quia dimittendo naturam | [B 155b] Petri non remaneret ille homo; quia sic per assumpcionem paulativam non fieret multi homines, sed remaneret precise idem homo. Concesso ergo consequente videtur primo quod aliquid desinit esse Christus, quia aliquis homo, et per consequens [1]natura creata[1] est Christus. Patet deduccio querendo sollicite, quid est illud quod desinit esse Christus. Nam si omnis homo, qui nunc est Christus eternaliter fuit Christus, tunc non multi homines sed solum Deus est Christus. Concesso ergo quod per dimissiones huiusmodi paulativas alique res, quia aliqui homines, desinerent[2] esse Christus; tunc palam sequitur quod multe substancie create forent Christus, cum quelibet illarum rerum, que desinerent esse Christus, non foret natura vel substancia divina, sed alia: et cum non ad dimissionem huiusmodi consequitur alicuius rei corrupcio; sequitur cum veris quod | ille res, [A 103b] que desinerent[2] esse Christus, remanerent non-Christus; et non superest que foret talis res derelicta, nisi foret assumpta humanitas; ergo relinquitur[3] concedendum quod humanitas assumpta foret Christus; et hoc videtur michi sequi formaliter si Christus ex unione ypostatica sit multi homines.

Supposing Christ to have assumed many humanities, Chap. XII. proved that He would not be one man: this chapter, following Scotus, has proved that He would not be many men; He would therefore be neither one nor many: and yet it is certain that He was man;

Propter tales evidencias dicit Doctor Subtilis super 3° Sentenciarum Distinccione prima Questione 3ª quod, si Christus multas humanitates assumpserit, non esset multi homines nec unicus homo; sed et istud[4] debet catholicus concedere tanquam sequens. Nam Christus non esset unicus homo, si multas humanitates assumpserit iuxta[5] proximo capitulo declarata; nec esset multi homines iuxta proxime replicata; ergo conclusio. Certum est tamen quod esset homo, si sic esset. Nam si essent multe uniones ypostatice humanitatum ad Verbum, tunc aliqua humanitas foret ypostatice copulata; et omnis talis unio ponit secundum

[1-1] nulla creatura B. [2] desiverint O. [3] derelinquitur B C.
[4] idem A B C. [5] iuxta *om.* C.

communicacionem ydiomatum Verbum esse hominem; ergo hoc posito Deus foret unus homo, et per idem multi homines.

Item impossibile est Deum esse hominem postquam non fuit homo, nisi per novam ypostaticam unionem. Sed, dimissis omnibus humanitatibus assumptis usque ad unam, foret Verbum homo sine nova ypostatica unione: ergo per ante erat stante ista unione continue idem homo. Si enim Verbum omnem humanitatem assumeret, non exinde periret sed perficeretur species humana, ut patet ex dictis; sed cum
b] non posset[1] esse species hominis | sine individuo hominis, quia destructis [2]primis substanciis[2] impossibile est aliquod aliorum remanere; sequitur quod illo posito foret homo aliquis singularis nullus si non Christus; ergo illo posito Christus foret unus homo. Quod ego non verto in dubium; sed credo quod ex Spiritu sancto diversificate sunt iste tres sentencie per locum a sufficienti divisione.

Quarum prima, ut sanctus Thomas cum suis sequacibus, dicit, quod Christus assumendo multas humanitates foret multi homines consequenter: 2[da] opinio modernorum loquencium dicit quod Christus hoc posito foret solummodo solus homo: 3[a] Doctoris subtilis dicit quod hoc posito nec foret multi homines nec unicus homo tantum. Et quamlibet illarum sentenciarum credo esse absolute necessariam, cum Verbum nullam humanitatem potest assumere preter Dominum Iesum Christum.

Ideo opposito posito est quidlibet formaliter inferendum. Et patet concordancia doctorum in infringibili[3] stipite veritatis; et per idem plane sequitur quod non multe persone divine possunt eandem humanitatem assumere eo
b] quod tunc essent idem homo ad ydemptitatem | humanitatis, ut dicit prima sentencia; essent eciam multi homines propter multitudinem personarum, quarum quelibet foret homo, ut dicit 2[da] sentencia; essent 3° nec unicus nec multi, ut dicit

and he was so by hypostatic union.

6. If the hypostatic union include *all* humanity, the human species would not be cancelled, but perfected thereby; but the *species* cannot exist without an individual; that individual is Christ; therefore Christ is one man.

The Holy Spirit allows of three diverse opinions. 1. That of Aquinas, that in case of assuming many humanities, Christ would be many men; 2. That of the moderns, that Christ would be the only man; 3. That of Scotus, that He would be neither many nor one man. The author thinks each of these opinions absolutely necessary, inasmuch as the Word can assume no other humanity except the Lord Jesus Christ, cf. p. 202, l. 33. Thus the three opinions are brought into agreement. Moreover, it follows that many divine Persons cannot assume the same humanity.

[1] possit O. [2]–[2] priñs (*i.e.* principiis) O. [3] singulari O.

3a sentencia, eo quod denominaciones multiplicantur vel ydemptificantur ex multiplicacione vel ydemptificacione formarum; cum omnis forma sit essenciam vel personam in aliquo formaliter se habere; multe ergo humanitates forent multas personas esse homines, et una humanitas foret essenciam esse unum hominem. Sed certum est, si [1] multe persone divine sunt [1] unus homo, sunt et una persona, et sic eadem creata substancia, et per consequens persona eadem foret quelibet persona diviua; et sic foret nedum confusio personarum, sed persona illa communis creata et assumpta foret cuilibet persone divine ydemptificata; | quod esse non [A 103c] potest.

Nor can either the Father or the Holy Spirit assume humanity.

Et per idem nec Pater nec Spiritus sanctus potest humanitatem assumere; quia non eandem quam Verbum, ut patet ex dictis; nec alias separatas, quia deficit principium iniciantis,[2] mittentis, vel principiantis Patrem incarnandum.

The whole Trinity caused the Incarnation: but there are not three Sons:

John iii. 16.

Quamvis | enim tota Trinitas incarnavit Verbum et misit [B 156a] Spiritum sanctum, hoc tamen solum [3] originaliter fit ex Patre, 'qui sic dilexit mundum, ut Filium suum unigenitum daret,' [4] Ioh 3°; cum sic [4] fuissent tres Filii Dei; et, cum non adoptivi, omnes fuissent filii naturales; quod esse non potest.

nor is God a threefold substance;

Heb. vii. 1.

the three Persons are one and the same essence, and to each the same honour is due.

Et 3° Deus foret triplex substancia, quia tres persone hominum; et de lege evangelica | quilibet subiectus [C 107a] et obediens cuilibet; et in casu Pater in divinis filius vel nepos naturalis Filii vel Spiritus sancti, et sic sibi [5] obediens tanquam superiori, ut Abraham offerebat Melchisedech ad Heb. 7°. Ymo, quantumcunque extraneas cognaciones assumpserint, forent plus convenientes quam cognati aliqui vel germani; cum omnes sint eadem essencia singularissima, eadem latria adorandi. Et sicut in divinitate nullus reliquo plus colendus sit, sic [6] secundum humanitatem nullus honore alteri [7] preponendus; et per consequens non foret eorum facilis cohabitacio propter repugnanciam maioritatis in

[1–1] multe . . . sunt *bis* B. [2] iniciantis *om*. O. [3] solum *om*. B.
[4–4] ioh . . . sic *om*. O. [5] eis O. [6] nec *add*. A B C.
[7] alterius O.

susceptis hominibus, et occasionem date opinionis, quis altero sit melior; cum in doctrina, conversacione, et merito differrent ab invicem, sicut in personalitate et humanitate assumptis secundum quotlibet condiciones individuantes. Que si appareant nobis non sequi vel non esse inconveniencia plus quam Verbum esse hominem, tamen satis est quod sanctis appareat hoc non posse essencie[1] divine competere, nec ex scripturis vel racionibus edoceri sic posse fieri. Ad quid ergo sollicitaremur aggravantes fidem circa illud quod absolute necessarium est non esse? Non,[2] ymo si problema[3] de possibilitate[4] [5]talium non fuerit nichil venturum,[5] ego non vagarer circa conclusiones, que illo posito sequerentur; sed pie dubitarem possibilitatem casuum; nec admitterem casus huiusmodi cum suis sequentibus, nisi aliunde michi fuerint evidentes, ne forte sustinerem repugnans fidei arroganter, pertinaciter, vel aliter viciose.

Such hypotheses involve a needless strain upon faith, and should be avoided: even denied unless evident on other grounds.

Unde miror quomodo moderni negantes Christum esse creaturam, et cum hoc admittentes tres personas divinas eandem humanitatem vel tres omnimode separatas assumere, dicunt quod substancia divina est tres homines et per consequens tres substancie; non enim tres substancie increate, cum tunc eternaliter ita essent. Si autem sit[6] tres create substancie, tunc tres creature forent substancia divina per conversionem; et sic aliquid quod[7] prius non fuerat. Si enim iste tres substancie differunt personaliter, tunc tres persone divine sunt tres substancie, quas notum est oportere distingui a communi divina substancia. Et si dicatur quod, postquam eternaliter erant persone et non substancie, facte sunt substancie, hoc est equivoce ad eternam substanciam
[C 107b] vel personam; | quia aliter unica substancia et non plures foret Trinitas increata. Et multo evidencius si tantum una humanitas sit assumpta a tota Trinitate, non essent tres

The moderns, who deny that Christ is a creature and admit that the three Persons can assume the same or three separate humanities, in effect deny

[1] decencie O. [2] non *om.* A B C.
[3] probleuma A B; propleuma C.
[4] *a verbo* possibilitate *usque ad verbum* aliquid *infra* l. 24, *sequitur alia manus in cod.* A. [5–5] talium fuerint mihi neutram A B C.
[6] siut C. [7] quod *nunc recurrit prima manus in cod.* A, *cf. not.* 4 *supra.*

the unity of the Divine nature:

materiales substancie, ut puta tria animalia vel tria corpora; et sic de ceteris passionibus humanis cum ceteris accidentibus separabilibus; quia adequatum corpus, compositum ex isto corpore et ista anima, est omne animal quod est homo in dato | situ, eo quod eadem sunt principia singulorum, [A 103d] ut deductum est superius. Ymo videtur quod quilibet illorum trium hominum habeat peccatum maximum naturale, cum quilibet caret proprio capite, et sic de ceteris organis quibuscunque; et per idem sunt unum[1] corpus tantum. Licet autem tres persone assumendo tres homines forent indubie tres create substancie; tamen inconveniens est quod increata substancia sic plurificetur[2] in multas substancias, cum divina substancia non in plura dispergitur, sed in ipsam omnis pluralitas creature unite[3] colligitur; quamvis enim Verbum sit due substancie, divina scilicet et humana, divina tamen substancia est tantum una substancia, cum non sit substancia creata: accipiendo enim huiusmodi substanciam pro natura et substanciam personaliter, sic non ponitur[4] in numerum cum divina,[5] cum sit ipsa. Unde videtur quod subiectum abstractum contrahat predicatum ad supponendum simpliciter pro natura, quando sic dicitur—substancia divina est substancia creata—et per consequens proposicio est neganda. Sed cum subiecto personali conceditur quod Verbum est substancia creata, quia homo et humanitas, quod non est deitas. Cuius racionis diversitas est variacio a supposicione simplici in personalem secundum li|mitacionem personalis [B 156b] termini vel abstracti. Et tunc non oportet concedere quod substancia increata sit creata substancia; licet Verbum, quod est increata substancia, sit creata substancia. Trinitas ergo foret | in casu illo tres create substancie; et per consequens [O 234c] necessaria[6] esset [7]ad finem attingendum[7] tanta in Deo pluralitas naturarum; quod est impossibile; cum ad redempcionem humani generis, ad beatitudinem hominis secun-

and reduce it to three created substances: whereas, for the redemption and bliss of man

[1] unicum O. [2] plurificaretur A B C. [3] univoce A B C.
[4] potest A B C. [5] substancia *add.* A B C. [6] necessarium O.
[7–7] ad finem a . . . *cum lacuna* C; ad finem aliquem O.

dum corpus et animam, et quemlibet alium effectum eque sufficit Christi incarnacio, sicut incarnacio horum trium. Sicut ergo non sunt ponendi plures dii propter impossibilitatem superflui, sic nec plurium personarum incarnacio propter causam consimilem.

*both in soul and body, the single Incarnation of Christ suffices.*

Ponunt autem doctores congruenciam[1] in Christo quare incarnatus est et nec Pater nec Spiritus sanctus. Primo [2]quia Verbum,[2] quod est naturalis ymago Patris; per quod factus est homo ad Dei ymaginem, per eandem ymaginem debuit reformari. Unde ex proprietate [C 108a] | ymaginis fuit consonancius quod ymago ymaginem assumeret, quam potencia vel benevolencia alterius persone. Forme enim est reformare deformitatem; sapiencie vincere peccati maliciam remissibilem ex ignorancia contractam; et ymaginis exemplaris fabricam turpatam ad dictam ymaginem prius factam [revocare[3]]. Verumptamen sicut vir non peccavit nisi excitante muliere et dyabolo, et sic iuvamine alterius[4] debuit relevari[5]: sic nec persona Verbi fecit redempcionis misterium sine coefficiencia Trinitatis, aliter tamen Verbum quam duo alii.

*There is a special fitness (congruencia) in the Incarnation of Christ: 1. As the Word is the image of the Father; and man is made in the image of God; it is congruous that the form should reform the deformed.*

2[do] cum Verbum sit Dei Filius naturalis, habet [6]in Trinitate[6] principium a quo mittatur, in cuius auctoritate vel virtute operetur obedienter humanitus. Unde filiacio temporalis habet proprietates analogas in Filio naturali aliter quam haberet in Patre vel Spiritu. Nam utrobique nascitur ex suo principio, et manet Filius faciens nos filios adoptivos[7] [8]et heredes, ut ipse est primogenitus;[8] et hoc sine confusione filiorum[9] cognacionis in Deo, quod Patri innascibili non potest competere. Et si iste conveniencie videntur nobis ignaris modice, tamen sunt apud Deum, qui ponderat cuncta, ad regulam infringibiliter perficiendo.

*2. As the Word is by nature the Son, so filiation in time is appropriate to Him.*

[1] conveniencian A B C.
[2-2] quia verbum *om.* O.
[3] *aut* revocare *aut aliquid simile sensui necessarium est.*
[4] aliter quam dyabolus *add.* A B C; alter quam dyabolus *add.* O. *nempe utraque lectio ut glossa omittenda.*
[5] revelari O.
[6] intrinsece A B C.
[7] adopcionis O.
[8-8] et . . . primogenitus *bis.* O.
[9] vel *add.* C O.

*3. Every 'property' of the Word constitutes a special fitness in Him to become incarnate. The middle person becomes the mediator: the Word proclaims the Father: the Virtue and Wisdom of God overcomes vice and folly, and restores man to his forfeited position: the equality of the Word redresses the inequality of disease into which man had fallen:*

*John xvii. 6. 1 Cor. i. 24. Luke i. 51.*

3° concludendo[1] breviter, non est aliqua Verbi proprietas quin limitat [2]Verbo congruere[2] incarnacionis misterium ultra quam aliis. Mediam quidem[3] personam | oportet esse [A 104a mediatorem Dei et hominum; Verbum eternaliter de corde ingenito eructatum decet verbis predicacionis ostendere Patrem suum Ioh. 17°. 'Pater, manifestavi nomen tuum;' 'Dei virtus atque Dei sapiencia,' prima ad Cor. 1°, debuit vicium ex ignorancia superare; [4]ut homo, qui[4] in sapiencia conditus est per insipienciam perditus appetendo equalitatem increate sapiencie, per illam sapienciam restauretur, et dyabolus usurpando acceptam virtutem et [5]potenciam per dantem[6] virtutem et[5] bracchium deprimeretur, Luc 1°. 'fecit potenciam in bracchio suo.' Et sicut secundum Augustinum est equalitas immediate consequens ad suum principium, sic ab eo specialiter omnis morbi inequalitas ad temperanciam reducatur: ut inequalitas sanitatis in qua dyabolus cecidit, appetendo equalitatem divine auctoritatis sive potencie, secundum iudicium datum Filio per impotenciam puniatur, qua non possit a peccato in Spiritum[7] sanctum resurgere; inequalitas | autem, in qua homo igno- [C 108b ranter peccando in sapienciam, stulte appetendo eius equalitatem, ceciderat, est[8] precise equalitatis terminus,[9] cum sit sapiencia, verbum, virtus, pulcritudo, et species reducenda; et ita de ceteris sacramentis que scriptura de Christo commemorat.

*and so of all the mysterious attributes (sacramenta) of Christ.*

*In the sense that as a fact only the Divine Word assumed the man Christ, these apparently contradictory views may be reconciled.*

Redeundo igitur ad propositum ex dictis colligitur quod quelibet trium predictarum opinionum senteneiat[10] fidei consonum quoad superius recitatum. Et sic concordande sunt apparentes doctorum repugnancie in tam alta materia fidei Christiane.

*The possibility of any divine Person assuming humanity*

Quod si obicitur omnes tres sectas concorditer admittere quod quelibet persona[11] divina eandem naturam assumat

[1] concludo O. [2] congrue (*om.* verbo) O. [3] quippe O.
[4–4] homo autem A B; ut autem C; ut qui O. [5–5] potenciam . . . et *om.* B.
[6] datam A B C. [7] peccatum C. [8] per *add* O.
[9] terminum O. [10] senciat fide O. [11] natura B.

*Is spoken of by the three 'sects' only: 1. as an opinion not an assertion; 2. conditionally; 3. or erroneously.*

vel quotlibet[1] separatim; dicitur tripliciter concordando istam radicem. Primo quod in ista materia opinative locuti sunt nichil temere asserendo, ut patet ex scriptis eorum. 2<sup>do</sup> quod ipsi intelligunt ipsam possibilitatem condicionaliter, *si Deus voluerit*; ad modum loquendi Anselmi. Vel 3° si replicando inutiliter de sensibus eorum argueretur, quod ipsi sic simpliciter sencierunt, potest dici quod non ad laudem eorum opinio eorum forsitan fuit talis. Et taliter glosant ipsi superiores doctores, quorum sensus pocius debet credi. Sed non valet—si isti sic senciunt opinando; ergo verum—cum per idem contradiccio sequeretur; ipsi enim [B157a] discrepant a seipsis. | Sed et sanctus Thomas super Dist. 6. 3<sup>ii</sup> Sentenciarum Questione . . . .,[2] dicit quod sentencia concedens humanitatem assumptam esse Christum non est heretica, licet sit impossibilis in precipua materia fidei. De quo miror, cum tot sancti doctores qui in aliis materiis ambigue sunt locuti, illam sentenciam in materia fidei affirmaverant tam constanter. Cum ergo pium et salubre foret de fide Christiana sentenciam impossibilem tocius fidei corruptivam investigando excludere, videtur quod ecclesia sollicite discuteret quid in ista materia foret catholice sustinendum; quia certum est quod una pars est formaliter impossibilis; ex qua sequitur oppositum tocius fidei, ymo ut noverunt logici, quidlibet inferendum; et talis latens error in principio per vias inopinatas infirmat partes fidei consequenter.

*Although Aquinas does not condemn such hypotheses as heretical, yet as undermining the bases of the faith, whatever in them is found on investigation to be erroneous, should be rejected.*

*Further reasons and refutations of the hypotheses I. that any Divine Person indifferently can become incarnate: II. that the same Person can assume and dismiss at pleasure many humanities: III. that more than one Divine Person can assume the same humanity.*

Sed forte preter instancias factas superius arguitur possibilitas trium casuum abiectorum, scilicet quod quelibet [O 234d] persona divina indifferenter poterit incar|nari; quia eadem persona multas humanitates simul vel successive potest [A104b] assumere et quociens libet potest dimittere; ac | 3° quod multe possunt eandem humanitatem assumere.

*Reason I. General in favour of all three hypotheses*

[C 109a] Primo generatur ex hoc quod precipui moderni doctores | catholici et subtiles in scripturis reliquerant possibilitates

[1] quotlibet (*litt.* t *in rasura al. man.*) A; quidlibet B; quodlibet C.
[2] *lacuna pro numero in codd. omn.*

The chief modern doctors allow their possibility: therefore they may be possible.

omnium istorum casuum cum suis probacionibus et solucionibus obieclorum; quod non est veri simile de talibus ac tantis doctoribus nisi subsit possibilitas eorundem: ergo etc.

Reply. The desire for metaphysical subtlety and the ambition of winning a reputation for novelty may be at the bottom of the matter:

Hic dicitur ut supra quod variacio in methaphisica et honoris extraneandi ambicio est in causa. In cuius signum vix duos invenies quin discordent. Alii autem superiores doctores ut Augustinus, Ieronimus, Gregorius, et Auselmus cum suis sequacibus dicunt concorditer quod Christus post incarnacionem est aliquid, quod prius non fuerat, ut patet superius; et illi concordant cum racione, et verbaliter ac sentencialiter cum scriptura. Nec sequitur ex illo quod posteriores erant heretici, cum sentenciam hereticam potest catholicus sine pertinacia defendere, sicut credo in proposito contigisse. Verumptamen vanum est excludere illos simpliciter a peccato; cum laborando circa [1] veram sentenciam secundum studium bonum [2] de genere contingit catholicum presumptiva superbia vel [3] inani gloria peccare facillime; quanto magis defendendo impossibile, licet intencio secundum aliquid sit recta et vera sentencia: quodlibet [4] enim impossibile disperiret,[5] si per se sine mixtura veri defensum fuerit!

their mutual disagreement points to this source.

Such conduct involves sin even if it fall short of heresy.

Reason 2 for Hyp. I. As Aquinas asserts, every necessity and impossibility is subject to God.

2do obicitur per raciones sancti Thome Questione 7. 3ii et duabus sequentibus. 'Omnis, inquit, necessitas et impossibilitas Deo subicitur.' Cum ergo voluntati Dei omnis impossibilitas subicitur, sequitur quod Patrem incarnari non sit sibi [6] impossibile.

Reply. The argument fails both (a) in matter, (b) in form. For (a) only truth (reality) is subject to God: an impossibility is not so subject. (b) contradiction in terms is

Hic videtur michi quod argumentum peccat tam in materia quam in forma. In materia, quia solum veritas Deo subicitur; nulla impossibilitas est veritas; ergo assumptum peccat. Quod si intelligamus per impossibilitatem signi impossibilis falsitatem vel veritatem negativam, que est absoluta necessitas, nichil ad propositum; sed ad oppositum adducitur. Nam non prodest quod hoc signum sit impos-

[1] circa (*i.e. omittendum*) B. [2] hominum O. [3] vel *om.* A B C.
[4] libet *om.* A B C: *pro* quidem *in omn. codd. inventum* enim *supposui.*
[5] disparet A; disparet B C. [6] sibi *om.* A B C.

sibile—Pater potest incarnari—vel—quod necessario non potest esse quod Pater potest incarnari—ad concludendum propositum. Nec oportet instare pro improbacione argumenti, cum reductum ad formam patenter peteret; sicut facit secundum argumentum, quo capit humanam naturam [C 109b] infinitum distare a qualibet persona divina, et | omnium[1] eque distancium est eque possibilis coniunccio. Nam maior est impossibilis, et sensus minoris petitur.

not the same thing as impossibility in fact.

3° arguitur ex hoc quod posse assumere carnem est dignitatis[2] in Filio; ergo Patri potest competere.

Reason 3 for Hyp. I. The power of assuming flesh is an honourable prerogative, which, if it belong to the Son, cannot be denied to the Father.

Sed iuxta illud sequeretur quod gigni conveniat Patri, cum sit dignitatis in Filio. Dicitur ergo cum isto sancto quod Deus non potest incarnari in persona alia de *potencia ordinata*; sed, *si voluerit de potencia absoluta.*

Reply. Then the Father can be begotten. The truth is, God cannot *de potencia ordinata* become incarnate except in the Person of the Son: there is no limit to His *potencia absoluta*.

Et conformiter dicitur ad argumenta quibus videtur probare quod eadem natura potest assumi a qualibet personarum. Primo ex hoc quod omnis humanitas est indifferenter ad ymaginem Trinitatis, et[3] illa est racio assumendi; ymo cum Verbum humanitatem assumpserit,[4] est ipsa similior et habilior[5] ut ab utraque reliqua assumatur. Constat quidem quod faccio ad ymaginem Dei non est communis racio ut quelibet[6] humanitas a qualibet[6] persona assumi poterit, quia sic omnis homo posset esse Trinitas increata; sed [A 104c] Christo inest racio singularis, unde ille singulariter a Verbo | assumi poterit; et petitur utrobique probandum. Unde multum distat unio potenciarum anime eidem organo[7] et unio humanitatis ad Filium; ita quod non sequitur per locum a simili—si multe potencie anime possunt simul uniri eidem organo,[7] ergo per idem multe persone divine possunt uniri[8] ypostatice eidem corpori—.

Discussion of Hyp. III. Reason. Man is made in the image of God.

Reply. If this is made the ground of Incarnation, every man may be the Trinity.

Quod si queratur[9] racio diversitatis, satis est quod hoc [B 157b] facto | tres persone possent[10] esse unus homo et quelibet

[1] omni A B C.
[2] dignitas A B C.
[3] in *add.* O.
[4] assumpsit O.
[5] humilior A B C; hîlior O.
[6]–[6] humanitas a qualibet *om.* O.
[7]–[7] et . . . organo *om.* B.
[8] *pro* uniri *codd.* A B *ad finem senteneie* copulari *exhibent; cod.* C. *neutrum habet.*
[9] queritur A B C.
[10] possunt A B.

Duns Scotus on this matter refutes himself.

persona divina multi homines; sicut consequenter annuit sanctus Thomas, et [1] hoc posito non sic esset, ut patet ex dictis. Quantum ad argumenta, que facit Doctor subtilis in principio 3[ii] pro hac parte, respondet ipsemet satis claro. Quod si addatur — Verbum divinum liberius copulatum Christo quam aliquam [2] carnem carni ypostatice copulatam; sed anima potest multis carnibus copulari; ergo multo magis Verbum alii humanitati—; dicitur quod consequencia non valet per locum a simili. Nam Verbum liberius produxit hoc tempus perpetuum quam Petrus hunc filium; et tamen Verbum non potuit produxisse aliud tempus, quod nec sit illud nec eius pars, licet Petrus potuit alium filium produxisse, ymo filium qui non fuisset pertinens huic nato. Conceditur tamen quod quamcunque carnem spiritus assumpserit vel sibi personaliter uniret,[3] foret solummodo idem homo. Et sic licet homo posset esse aliud quam est modo, | [C 110a] quia alia natura corporea, non tamen aliud suppositum vel persona, ut patet in materia *De Anima*.

The general result is that statements concerning the Word may be understood of Him 1. as man; 2. as God; 3. as God-man.

Ex istis colligitur quomodo aliqua insint Verbo pure in quantum Deus; [4] aliqua in quantum homo; et [4] aliqua mixtim. In quantum Deus, creavit mundum; in quantum homo, passus est mortem; et in quantum Deus et homo, redemit hominem. Nec debet signum reduplicatum intelligi utrobique, ut dicat [5] consequenciam formalem logicam et causalem; sicut hic Christus in quantum homo est creatura; sed et [6] quomodolibet dicit causam, ut licet potest esse Deus et non produxisse mundum, tamen deitas fuit [7] causa quare pro|duxit mundum et non sua humanitas. Et licet deitas [O 235a] fuit [8] causa quare paciebatur, non tamen secundum illam;

The author defines how far these terms may be used interchangeably as *subjects*

quia tunc fuisset causa formalis [9] vel subiectum passionis; conceditur tamen quod humanitas fuit causa [9] formalis Christi et causa subiectiva mortis: et sic in quantum homo passus est mortem, quia secundum humanitatem. Et

[1] in O. [2] aliam C O. [3] unierit C; vineret O.
[4–4] aliqua . . . et *om.* O. [5] ut dicat *om.* O. [6] in O.
[7] divinitas sint O. [8] divinitas sit O. [9–9] vel . . . causa *om.* C.

intelligendum est *in quantum*, ut dicat[1] generaliter causam[2] quamlibet parcialem vel totalem, completam vel incompletam. Ego non video quin sane concedi poterit quod, in quantum Deus, paciebatur; cum deitas fuit per se causa illius passionis, sed non secundum deitatem, cum tunc deitas principaliter pateretur. Redempcio autem humani generis pro offensa dicit infinitatem precii proporcionaliter ad delictum; et sic oportet redimentem esse precium infinitum; et per consequens Deum; et preter hoc oportet quod distinguatur essencialiter a solvente, cum non sit possibile quidquam[3] mercari primo et immediate secundum seipsum; et per consequens oportet precium, quod secundum deitatem est infinitum, esse naturam alienam[4] creatam. Cum autem nulla alia potuit pertinere nisi illa quo peccaverat, quo compendiosissimo sit[5] et satisfaciens et precium, mercans et mercatum, reconcilians et reconciliatum; relinquitur quod oportet ipsam esse humanitatem 'mediatorem[6] Dei et hominum, hominem Christum Iesum.' Et sic quidquid infuit [A104d] sibi[7] formaliter, infuit sibi[7] in quantum Deus; licet non | omne, quod sibi infuit, inerat secundum quod Deus, nec in quantum homo. Deitas enim fuit per se causa cuiuscunque causati, quod sic infuit Iesu nostro.

to predications concerning Christ:

in what sense Christ as God suffered:

the bearing of this question on human redemption.

1 Tim. ii. 5.

Et si obicitur quod Christus, si in quantum Deus moriebatur, tunc est de racione Dei mori, et indifferenter quelibet persona divina morietur; patet quod consequencia non valet; cum non sit de racione hominis ita mori, cum homo posset esse naturalissime et nec mori[8] nec esse mortalis, [C 110b] id est non habere aptitudinem | naturalem nec necessitatem preternaturalem, ut suo tempore moriatur. Ideo tales reduplicative sumuntur satis equivoce ut patet in logica, quam equivocacionem specialiter in illa materia oportet attendere.

The question—Can God be said to die?—is not involved in the Incarnation.

Ex dictis[9] ergo patet quodammodo qualiter scriptura sacra cum antiquis sanctis doctoribus in materia de Incarnacione

Thus the literal truth of Holy Scripture

[1] dicit *codd. omn.* [2] causam *om.* B. [3] quemquam O.
[4] aliam O. [5] sit *om.* A B C. [6] mediatorem *om.* A.
[7–7] formaliter . . . sibi *om.* B. [8] mori O. [9] istis A B.

as interpreted by the Fathers as to the doctrine of the Incarnation is to be upheld against the various sophistical and discordant modern theories.

Domini ad litteram est sustinenda; et quomodo iacula sophistica modernorum sunt scuto veritatis infallibilis repellenda, ac eorum discordancia equivoca detegenda; ut sic possit theologus in tractando dubia Incarnacionis realia libere sine formidine impugnacionis sophistice procedere in diceuda ad laudem, gloriam, et honorem eiusdem Domini nostri Iesu Christi. Amen.[1]

[1] *In cod.* B. *haec addita sunt.* Explicit tractatus de incarnacione M. I. Wy. anno domini 1433. Scriptori pro penna dentur gaudia sempiterna. Fur huius carte ledatur demonis arte. Et cetera. *Cod.* C. *haec habet.* Explicit tractatus de benedicta incarnacione reverendi magistri Johannis Wycleph. Amen dicant omnia. Si finis bonus est, tunc totum laudabile est.

# NOTES.

Page 1.—Title. *De Benedicta Incarnacione* is Wyclif's own description of this book in the first sentence of the Prologue.

P. 1, line 3.—The *De Anima*, still unprinted, contains the psychology on which this treatise is based. It is referred to infra, pp. 7, 22, 44, 203, 230.

P. 1, l. 10.—The inclusion of Creation as well as Redemption in the scope of the Incarnation is a note of the Scotists. But even Aquinas III. Sent. Dist. i. Quest. 1, Art. 3, speaks of the Incarnation as not only the deliverance from sin, but also as 'humanae naturae exaltatio et totius universi consummatio.' Irenaeus, Athanasius and other Fathers taught the same doctrine, which rests upon such passages in Holy Scripture as Ephes. i. 4, 10; iii. 9-11; Col. i. 16, 17; St. John i. 4; Rom. viii. 19. For the history of scholastic opinion on the subject see Dorner, Doctrine of the Person of Christ, Div. II. vol. i. pp. 361-369, Eng. Tr. Wyclif returns to the subject infra, pp. 79, 108, 199, 230.

P. 3, l. 2.—*viantibus*. In patristic and scholastic language *viator* is a pilgrim as opposed to *comprehensor* or *beatus in patria*. Cf. infra, p. 26, l. 15.

P. 3, l. 3.—*removere prohibens disciplinam* apparently means—to get an obstacle to learning out of the way. Cf. p. 223, l. 15, for a like use of neuter participle, *repugnans fidei* what is in opposition to the faith.

P. 3, l. 6.—Walden, Doctrinale Fidei, i. 39, denies Wyclif's doctrine of the threefold nature of Christ, which is the foundation of the treatise.

P. 3, l. 21.—Walden also denies (D. F. i. 41) that Christ is a creature.

P. 3, l. 26.—Peter Lombard's answer (Sent. Dist. iii. 11), Utrum Christus sit creatura vel creatus vel factus? is as follows: 'Hoc (*i.e.* the affirmative) simpliciter et absque determinatione minus congruenter dici . . . Etsi quandoque brevitatis causa simpliciter denuncietur, nunquam tamen simpliciter debet intelligi.'

P. 4, l. 8.—*ad Felicianum*. The true title is Contra Felicianum Arianum de Unitate Trinitatis. The treatise is not considered genuine by the Benedictine editors, but is assigned to Vigilius Tapsensis. It is quoted as Augustine's in a work doubtfully assigned to Bede; also by Lanfranc, Alcuin, Peter Lombard; and W. follows the opinion of his time. It is in the form of a dialogue between Augustine and Felicianus.

P. 4, l. 21.—*celos* is a gloss on the text of Augustine.

P. 5, l. 2.—*quid et secundum quid.* This formula is also given by Aug. De Trin. I. xiii. 28; Tom. VIII. p. 767. Quid tamen propter quid et quid secundum quid dicatur, adjuvante Domino prudens diligens et pius lector intelligit.

P. 5, ll. 11–13.—Walden (D. F. I. 41) girds at W. for this sentence. Wiclefus ab ista (catholica) fide alienus dicit Christum non esse de necessitate duarum naturarum, sed unam naturam dicit totum Christum. "Non est, inquit, major color . . . humanitas." Vere et specialiter hoc tuum est in ecclesia Dei!

P. 5, l. 15.—Aug. contra Felic. xiii. (Tom. VIII. App. 47). Erat ergo uno atque eodem tempore ipse totus etiam in inferno, totus in coelo.

P. 5, l. 29.—This long passage from Augustine is a good deal condensed and transposed by W.

P. 6, l. 30.—Aug. de Trin. I. xi. 22 (Tom. VIII. 764). Quapropter cognita ista regula intelligendarum scripturarum de Filio Dei, ut distinguamus quid in eis sonet secundum formam Dei in qua aequalis est Patri, et quid secundum formam servi quam accepit, in qua minor est Patre, non conturbabimur.

P. 7, l. 2.—The correct title is Collatio cum Maximino (Tom. VIII. 666, § 13). Maximinus loquitur: Pater enim in illa immensa potentia potentem creatorem genuit. Filius in sua illa a Patre accepta potentia, ut ipse ait, "Omnia mihi tradita sunt a Patre meo," non creatorem creavit sed creaturam constituit.

P. 7, l. 21.—*De Anima.* See note on p. 1, l. 3. *alta* is probably right. Cf. altissimam methaphisicam de formis, infra, p. 114, l. 8.

P. 9, l. 15.—It is worth while to notice that the fact of the *development* of the doctrine of the Person of Christ was not unknown to W.

P. 9, l. 21.—*gigas gemine substancie* is a mystical application of Genesis vi. 4 and Ps. xix. 5. The thalamus is Virginis uterus. Cf. infra, pp. 102, 169. From Ambrose (Migne II. 862) and Augustine (Tom. VIII. 630) downwards, the expression *gigas* is used of Christ. Cf. infra, p. 102, l. 27, 126, l. 24.

P. 9, l. 25.—*ad Galat.* The passage in Bened. ed. is in Epist. to Ephes. i. 2 (Tom. IV. p. 342).

P. 10, l. 1.—*verum esse.* The text of Aug. has *vermem et.* If this is right, the last two words on this page will be *vermem esse* for *verum esse*; and the expression must be based upon Job xxv. 6 and Ps. xxii. 6. Cf. infra, p. 193, l. 24, nec vermis est filius hominis.

P. 10, l. 10.—Aug. c. Felic. vi. 42. Si ex nihilo, creatura; and vii. 43: Creatura ex eo quod non est in id quod est.

P. 10, l. 11.—The Benedictine edd. consider the Quaestiones Vet. et Nov. Test. to be spurious. The passage here referred to seems to be in Quaest. cxxii. (Tom. III. part ii. App. p. 114). Si enim coepit esse, creatura est; si creatura est, Deus non est.

P. 10, l. 23—There is a treatise of Wyclif's *De Trinitate* mentioned in the first Vienna MS. catalogue of Wyclif's works, printed by Shirley, and again by Buddensieg (Polemical Works, vol. i. lxv). But perhaps *declarat* is the right reading, and Jeronimus the subject. Infra, p. 150, l. 25, and p. 191, l. 34, W. seems to be referring to a treatise of his own *De Trinitate.* See Shirley's Catalogue, No. 8, De Ente.

P. 10, l. 29.—Probably *vermem* for *verum* is the right reading. Cf. first line of this page.

P. 11, l. 12.—Aug. de Trin. i. 24 (Tom. VIII, 765). Secundum formam Dei dictum est 'ante omnes colles genuit me,' id est, ante omnes altitudines creaturarum: secundum autem formam servi dictum est 'Dominus creavit me in principio viarum suarum.'

P. 11, l. 19.—Aug. de Trin. xv. 34 (Tom. VIII. 991). Augustine notices the discrepancy between the text of the Psalm and the quotation of it by St. Paul; and forces this very divergence to the establishment of doctrine. 'Cum propheta dixerit, *accepisti dona in hominibus*, Apostolus maluit dicere *dedit dona hominibus*; ut ex utroque scilicet verbo uno prophetico, apostolico altero, quia in utroque est divini sermonis auctoritas, sensus plenissimus redderetur.'

P. 12, l. 13.—Now W. is on his own ground, the necessity of the Realistic theory for the maintenance of Catholic truth. Cf. infra, p. 113, l. 20. Lechler, Wiclif and his English Precursors, ii. p. 11.

P. 12, l. 25.—Walden I. 42. Absit mihi et omni catholico quidquam de Christo asserere nisi quod melius, quod excellentius dici potest. Displicet mihi quod cadaver mortuum dicis Dei Filium, quod cum praedicas morticinum. For *cadaver mortuum*, cf. p. 64, infra.

P. 13, l. 10.—This is the position of many besides Wyclif on many disputed subjects. Compare Life of F. D. Maurice, vol. i. p. 127. 'He came to hold more and more that there was something to be learnt from everything *positive* in each one's faith, and that the mischief lay in the *negative*, i.e. in the denunciation of imperfectly understood truths held by others.' For instances of W.'s application of his principle, see infra, p. 104, l. 17; p. 116, l. 32.

P. 13, l. 16.—*Eusebius.* This must be a quotation from some one of the many continuations of the history of Eusebius. His tenth and last book ends with the victory of Constantine over Licinius at Chrysopolis A.D. 323. Arius died A.D. 336. Accounts similar to this are to be found in Socrates, Hist. Eccl. i. 38, and in Sozomen H. E. ii. 30. Athanasius (Ep. ad Serapionem de morte Arii) is responsible for the main outline of the narrative, and for the parallel with Judas Iscariot. *ὁ δὲ Ἄρειος ἐθάρρει . . . πολλά τε φλυαρῶν εἰσῆλθεν εἰς θάκας (v.l. καθέδρας) ὡς διὰ χρείαν τῆς γαστρός, καὶ ἐξαίφνης κατὰ τὸ* γεγραμμένον πρηνὴς γενόμενος ἐλάκησε μέσος, καὶ πεσὼν εὐθὺς ἀπέψυξεν. The superstitious idea that heretics died by 'visitation of God' was thus applied later to Wyclif himself. "On the feast of the passion of St. Thomas of Canterbury (when he had the intention to preach and allow himself in a blasphemous attack upon the saint) John Wyclif, that organ of the devil, etc., being struck by the horrible judgment of God was struck with palsy, and continued to live in that condition until St. Silvester's day, whom he had often exasperated by his attacks." Walsingham quoted by Lechler, ii. 290-2, 296.

P. 14, l. 4.—Ambrosius de Fide i. 19.

P. 14, l. 10.—See p. 3, l. 26, and note, for Peter Lombard's words.

P. 17, l. 14.—*fontaliter* apparently means—as from a fountain.

P. 17, l. 15.—*eternaliter ad intra.* Cf. supra, p. 10, ll. 21-24. Wyclif is speaking of the *eternal generation* of the Son by the Father, when he speaks of One who utters the Word eternally within Himself.

P. 18, l. 29.—The distinction derived from Augustine of *homo interior* and *exterior* is a favourite one with W. Cf. p. 30, l. 7, and p. 128, l. 24.

P. 19, l. 27.—Anselm de Incarnacione, cii. The passage referred to is important as giving Anselm's opinion on the realistic controversy. 'Illi utique nostri temporis dialectici, immo dialectice heretici, qui non nisi flatum vocis putant esse universales substantias, et qui colorem non aliud queunt intelligere quam corpus, nec sapientiam hominis aliud quam animam, prorsus a spiritualium questionum disputatione sunt exsufflandi. Cf. infra, p. 144, l. 27.

P. 20, l. 10.—The relation of the universal to the individual is discussed infra, pp. 86, 145, and in Trialogus, p. 276.

P. 20, l. 22.—*Multi enim—de vi vocis.* In Fasc. Zizan. p. 20, Kenyngham raises this question of the literal truth of Holy Scripture, and adds that W. makes a distinction between *de vi vocis* and *de virtute sermonis*, whereas he himself regards them as synonymous. On Wyclif's reliance on the literal meaning of Scripture, cf. Lechler's Wyclif and his English Precursors, Eng. ed. vol. ii. pp. 31, 40. In the last sentence of our treatise, W. claims to have shown how 'scriptura sacra de Incarnacione *ad litteram* est sustinenda.'

P. 23, l. 16.—*incarceracione.* This word I doubtfully placed in the text to meet the sense, instead of the uncertain reading of the MSS. *incarnacione* is perhaps supported by p. 36, l. 7 infra, *incineracione* by p. 64, l. 28.

P. 24, l. 14.—*processus evangelicus*, the general drift of the Gospels.

P. 24, l. 21.—Walden falls foul of this passage, D. F. i. 41. 'Sed dicis "ego dico Christum esse Deum in natura, quod Arius non facit, sed dixit Christum pure creaturam: quod ego non facio." Vere jam video doctrinam tuam non esse tutam, quia a fortissima heresi solo distat adverbio *pure*: ita quod si tollatur gracilis duarum syllabarum dictio, id ipsum sine variatione sentiretis utrique.'

P. 24, l. 34.—For Augustine's rule, cf. supra, p. 6, l. 30, and p. 9, l. 6.

P. 25, l. 3.—Walden, D. F. i. 41. 'Dixit Arius dignissimam creaturam, tu dicis eum vilissimam creaturam quia *materiam primam*. Ibi viam Arii superasti, qui hoc dicere verebatur.' Cf. Fasc. Zizan. 2.

P. 28, ll. 22-26.—Walden traverses this statement, D. F. i. 40.

P. 29, ll. 2-6.—Cf. Walden, D. F. i. 40.

P. 32, l. 11.—Aquinas Summa Theol. III. Quest. l. Art. iv. 3. Dicendum quod esse sacerdotem convenit homini ratione animae, in qua est ordinis character: unde per mortem homo non perdit ordinem sacerdotalem: et multo minus Christus, qui est totius sacerdotii origo.

P. 32, l. 17.—Duns Scotus, Sent. Dist. III. xxii. 1. Quaeritur unum, utrum scilicet Christus fuerit homo in triduo? Quod Sic. Christus in triduo fuit Christus: igitur Christus tunc fuit homo. The Subtle Doctor's view as to the triduum is discussed below, pp. 49 seqq.

P. 33, l. 17.—W.'s fondness for triads (Fasc. Zizan. lv.) is strikingly shown here and on the next page. In heaven, earth, and hell Christ is Lord by a threefold descent, viz. in the Incarnation, in the descent of his soul into hell, and of his body into the grave. In hell (p. 34, l. 14) he delivered (eripuit) three sorts of men, viz. patriarchs, prophets, other faithful ones: he let alone (dimisit) and left there other three sorts, the damned, infants, and adults still requiring purgation.

P. 34, l. 28.—*trahentis*. The saying in St. John xii. 32 here and infra, p. 93, l. 15, is strangely applied by W. to the triumphal ascent with 'captivity led captive.' So Rufinus in Symbolum, 29.

P. 35, l. 1.—*tres machinas*. The three platforms or stages, *coelum, terra, inferna* of p. 33, l. 19.

P. 35, l. 8.—*dulia*. The lowest degree of worship, cf. note on p. 183.

P. 39, l. 14.—*synecdochica locucio*. Cf. p. 56, l. 5, for the meaning. The transcribers evidently did not understand the word.

P. 40, l. 6.—*subtilior pars* sanguinis. This attempt to find a material basis for Christ's humanity in triduo is noteworthy. Cf. p. 136, l. 30.

P. 42, l, 4.—*trium naturarum*, i.e. deitas, anima, corpus. Cf. p. 3, l. 6.

P. 42, l. 27.—*unquam* should be inserted after *Deus*.

P. 43, l. 10.—For definition of *homo*, cf. infra, p. 127.

P. 43, l. 14.—On this analogy of a threefold nature in man with the Divine Trinity, cf. Shirley, Fasc. Zizan. lv. Trialogus, p. 58. Also infra, p. 47, l. 30.

P. 44, l. 1.—This passage is quoted in the De Ecclesia (Loserth), p. 126.

P. 48, l. 3.—Peter Lombard's position is defined in S. D. III. xxii. 4. Licet homo mortuus fuerit, erat tamen in morte Deus homo. nec mortalis quidem nec immortalis. Et tamen vere erat homo. . . .

Dicimus ergo in morte Christi Deum vere fuisse hominem, et tamen mortuum; et hominem quidem nec mortalem nec immortalem, quia unitus erat animae et carni sejunctis.

P. 48, l. 18.—For Hugo de St. Victor's definition of *homo*, cf. infra, p. 128, l. 2.

P. 49, l. 6.—The text of the passage in Bonaventura referred to. Sent. Dist. III. xxii. 1, has *aptitudinalis*. For the *triplex predicati*, cf. Trialogus, p. 266.

P. 49, l. 24.—*ibidem* on the same part of the Sentences. Wyclif condenses Duns Scotus, edition of Durand, Leyden, 1639, vol. vii. p. 451.

P. 50, l. 12.—Johannes Damascenus de Fide Orthodoxa III. 3. *τὸ δὲ Χριστὸς* (the name *Christ*) *ὄνομα τῆς ὑποστάσεως λέγομεν, οὐ μονοτρόπως λεγόμενον, ἀλλὰ τῶν δύο φύσεων ὑπάρχον σημαντικόν.*

P. 50, l. 23.—D. Scotus. The substance of Durand, vii. p. 454.

P. 51, l. 4.—Duns Scotus difficult to understand, cf. p. 161, l. 5.

P. 51, l. 7.—*Doctor alius.* Bonaventura, p. 49.

P. 51, l. 16.—The treatise of Anselm, from which W. quotes here more exactly than his wont, is Tractatus De Concordia Praescientiae et Predestinationis, cap. ii.

P. 52, l. 23.—W. is apparently giving in a condensed form the substance of the following passage from D. Scotus, which his transcribers have not unnaturally not understood (Migne's D. Scotus, vol. vii. p. 452): Et si dicatur quod haec est *per se* vera—*Christus est homo*—et si *per se* vera, igitur necessaria; respondeo, si ad *perseitatem* propositionis sufficit subjectum includat in suo intellectu causam inherentiae predicati ad subjectum, et non requiratur quod subjectum dicat haec—*Christus est homo*—semper fuit vera. Sed magis credo quod requiretur hoc et plus, scilicet quod subjectum habeat conceptum unum: vel si non, sed includat conceptus plures, oportet quod ratio ejus sit in se vera, antequam aliquid verificetur de eo.

P. 54, l. 24.—*de Sampsone.* 'So the dead which he slew at his death were more than they which he slew in his life.'

P. 54, l. 27.—The passage in D. Scotus, Migne, vol. vii. p. 454, is as follows: Cum arguitur—Verbum habuit corpus et animam sibi unitam; igitur potuit denominari—dico quod quamvis hoc verum sit, tamen non placuit doctoribus ut denominaretur ab illis.

P. 55, l. 25.—D. Scotus, vii. p. 455. Sed numquid potest aliquo modo denominari ab illis, scilicet anima et corpus? Dico quod sic, si essent nomina imposita; sicut si accidens dependeret ab aliquo sicut supposita tantum, non sicut a subjecto, ut si aliquid supportaret vel sustentaret ipsum accidens, ita tamen quod non informaretur ab accidente, adhuc posset denominari ab illo, si esset nomen impositum: non posset tamen dici albus, nisi informaretur, posset tamen dici habere albedinem. Ita Christus in triduo vel Verbum potuit dici habere animam et corpus; sed nec fuit anima nec corpus, nec animatum nec corporeum propter dictas causas.

P. 56, l. 1.—Here and below, p. 83, l. 24, W. practically admits the failure of scholasticism. 'Before Peter the Lombard' these questions did not arise. Excessive definition created fresh difficulties: the simpler statements of the older doctors were more satisfactory.

P. 56, l. 4.—Wyclif will have the words understood in their literal sense, *Christus est anima—Christus est corpus* (cf. p. 39). This was the fifth of the 'haereses quas primo jactavit in aera; . . . quod Christus est sua humanitas, et est sua anima et ipsum corpus.' Kenyngham in Fasc. Ziz. p. 2. Walden, D. F. i. 40, quotes the passage, 'nec valet—tibia,' and insists that W. has defined *synecdoche* incorrectly. He adds: Si hic non sit synecdoche, fallimur: quia ab antiqua grammatica non solum quando a parte totum, sed et quando pars a toto denominatur, est synecdoche. . . . Nos autem meliores imitantes grammaticos Hieronymum, Isidorum, Bedam, Augustinum, et Magnum Gregorium, dicimus esse synecdochicam figuram conceptionem cujuscunque partis de quocunque suo toto, etiamsi transumpta quacunque denominatione dante plenum intellectum totius in sua parte vel e contrario. Et per hoc Christum fuisse carnem sepultam, verum esse synecdochen et non appropriato sermone sic dictum.

W. defines synecdoche again, infra, pp. 59, 89, 98. In the last passage he again maintains Kenyngham's 'fifth heresy.'

P. 57, l. 18.—*septipedalis*=of a certain definite size, in extension. A stock illustration. Cf. infra, p. 207, l. 23. Fasc. Ziz. pp. 117, 120 and Shirley's Glossary in F. Z. p. 538, *septipedalitas*. Also Arnold, Select Eng. Works of Wyclif, vol. iii. p. 500.

P. 57, l. 24.—*abreviator suus Cowtonus.* Who is this Colton or Cowton who abridged Duns Scotus? I can find no certain trace of him. In Fasti Ecclesiae Hibernicae, vol. iii. p. 15, there is a notice of J. Colton, a native of Norfolk, educated at Cambridge, the first Master of Gonville and Caius College, Prebendary of York, Dean of St. Patrick's, Archbishop of Armagh, 1382-1404; Lord Chancellor of Ireland. He wrote Constitutiones Provinciales, and also a work on the Papal Schism. In his University days had he whetted his wits in abstracting the Subtle Doctor?

P. 60, l. 4.—Peter Lombard, S. D. III. 21, B. Quis nisi hostis veritatis dicat animam a Verbo depositam?

P. 60, l. 11.—Joh. Damascenus De Fide Orthodoxa iv. 1 (in Migne Gt. Patr. vol. xciv. p. 1105): *οὐδὲν τῶν τῆς φύσεως μερῶν ἀπέθετο, οὐ σῶμα, οὐ ψυχήν.*

P. 60, l. 17.—Aquinas Summa III. l. ii. 3. Corpus Christi non fuit in morte a divinitate separatum.

P. 62, l. 7.—*Doctor Solempnis.* This is the distinguishing name of Heinrich Göthals of Ghent, flor. 1293. Cf. Lechler, John Wyclif, vol. ii. p. 7, Eng. ed., and Loserth's De Ecclesia, p. 317, l. 27, note, where Gandano is misprint for Gandavo. The Solemn Doctor 'had preceded W. in the path of an Augustinian Church-Platonism conjoined with Aristotelian method.'—Lechler.

P. 64, l. 11.—*incorrupcionem.* Possibly *interrupcionem* is the word intended.

P. 65, ll. 3–16.—This passage illustrates W.'s personal humility, his reliance on the authority first of Scripture, then of the Church Fathers and doctors, then his grotesque humour, and withal his strong personal clinging to faith, and his robust common sense.

P. 65, l. 9.—The question was seriously entertained by Scotus whether God could have assumed the nature of a lower animal. Wilberforce on the Incarnation, p. 209, ed. 3 (1850), glances at this strange hypothesis. Cf. infra, p. 197.

P. 65, l. 19.—*Quod Filius Dei non potest desinere esse homo* is one of the 'earliest heresies' of W., apparently attacked by Kenyngham at Oxford. The position which W. takes up in this chapter in proof of the continuous humanity of Christ, *Quod Deus de potentia sua absoluta non potest damnare illam creaturam, demonstrando illam quae est unita Christo*, is also condemned. Cf. Fasc. Ziz. p. 2.

P. 67, l. 18.—*Cesarem semper Augustum* here seems to refer to God the Father. W. also applies the title to Christ. Lechler, ii. 69 and 91; De Ecclesia, p. 124. Bryce, Holy Roman Empire, ed. iv. p. 219, note, says—'imperatore domino nostro Jesu Christo' is a form not uncommon in the Middle Ages—especially during vacancies of the imperial throne.

P. 67, l. 28.—Aristotle, Phys. II. 3. *ἔτι δὲ τὸ αὐτὸ τῶν ἐναντίων ἐστὶν αἴτιον· ὃ γὰρ παρὸν αἴτιον τουδὶ, τοῦτο καὶ ἀπὸν αἰτιώμεθα ἐνίοτε τοῦ ἐναντίου, οἷον τὴν ἀπουσίαν τοῦ κυβερνητοῦ τῆς τοῦ πλοίου ἀνατροπῆς, οὗ ἦν ἡ παρουσία αἰτία τῆς σωτηρίας.*

P. 68, l. 4.—Aquinas, S. T. III. l. ii. 3 (Migne, iv. 462). Cum igitur in Christo nullum fuerit peccatum, impossibile fuit quod solveretur unio divinitatis a carne ipsius.

P. 69, l. 23.—*carismatum*=*χαρισμάτων.*

P. 70, l. 26.—That Christ was at once *comprehensor* perfect in grace and felicity, one who has reached the goal (1 Cor. ix. 24; Phil. iii. 12). as well as *viator*, one who is hastening toward it, was the traditional scholastic view from St. Thomas downwards. Dorner, Person of Christ, Div. II. vol. i. p. 333. Duns Scotus questioned it, Dorner l.c. p. 348. On this subject, Bruce, Humiliation of Christ, p. 79, remarks: "The Christ of Aquinas is after all not our brother, not a man, but only a ghastly simulacrum. Not to speak of his material part which, according to the author of the *Summa*, was perfectly formed from the first moment of conception, and born without pain: the soul of Christ differed from ours to an extent which makes us feel that between Him and us there is little in common." W. seems to be trying to save the reality of the *weakness* of Christ after the flesh by the limiting word *arraliter*.

P. 70, l. 29.—*dotes corporis* (cf. infra, p. 181, 231), the four endowments of the glorified body, subtilty, agility, incorruptibility, transparency, of which 'Christ toke ernes here in this world,' are dwelt on in an interesting passage in Wyclif's English Sermons, Arnold, vol. i. p. 142. In Trialogus, p. 394, W. hints at a correspondence between the *quattuor dotes* and the *quattuor elementa*; and accepts Anselm's list of *septem dotes, pulcritudo, velocitas, fortitudo, libertas, sanitas, voluptas et diuturnitas* as not inconsistent with the former list, which is as old as Aquinas. These four gifts are also the dower of Christ's *mystical* body, Eng. Works, ii. 234.

P. 73, l. 13.—Wyclif (Trialogus, p. 238) distinguishes *three* meanings of *scriptura*. "Primo scriptura sacra signat Jesum Christum librum vitae in quo omnis veritas est inscripta juxta Johannis x. 35. Secundo modo signat veritates in ipso libro vitae inscriptas, sive sint rationes exemplares aeternae sive veritates aliae temporales. Et tertio modo famosius quo ad vulgus signat aggregatum ex codicibus legis Dei et ex veritate quam Deus ipsis imponit." In Trialogus, p. 244, God Himself is liber vitae. Deus etiam est signum cujuslibet rei signabilis, cum sit *liber vitae* in quo quodcunque signabile est inscriptum.

P. 73, l. 13.—*liber vitae.* In W.'s view here Christ, *i.e.* the Word containing *rationes quotlibet exemplares* (supra, p. 12, l. 15). 'Everything which was created was originally and before its creation in time livingly present, was ideally performed in the eternally preexistent Logos.' Lechler, ii. 11.

P. 73, l. 31.—W. seems to mean that *semini* tui *qui* is another instance where change of gender is of doctrinal significance. W. notices below, p. 113, ll. 3–17, Augustine's attention to grammatical forms. Also p. 184, l. 22, where W. puts a strain on the text of Augustine.

P. 75, l. 6.—W.'s theory of Annihilation was among the 'earliest heresies' attacked. Fasc. Ziz. 2. Quod Deus non potest annihilare creaturam. Cf. Trial. p. 50.

P. 75, l. 7.—*libere contradictorie.* W. condemns (Trial. p. 72) as a mere scholastic quibble (terminus magistralis erronee introductus) the *libertas contradictionis* or hypothesis of God's denying himself, *i.e.* doing otherwise than he has done. Cf. infra, pp. 228, 229.

P. 78, l. 21.—*Donum.* W. adopts from earlier writers this term for the Holy Spirit; cf. p. 86, l. 31.

P. 78, l. 23.—*inconveniens* should have been in the text as it is in the passage of Anselm referred to. De Inc. Verbi, V. c. 5. Quoniam ergo quamlibet parvum inconveniens in Deo est impossible, non debuit alia Dei persona incarnari quam Filius. Illo enim incarnato nullum sequitur inconveniens.

P. 79, l. 9.—Aug. Enchir. c. 36 (Tom. VI. p. 210). Hic omnino granditer et evidenter Dei gratia commendatur. Quid enim natura humana in homine Christo meruit, ut in unitatem personae unici Filii Dei singulariter esset assumpta?

P. 79, l. 30.—W. seems to mean that the Incarnation was necessary for the completion of God's work in creation. Cf. p. 1, l. 10, and note.

P. 80, l. 21.—Pauliani is the correct name.

P. 80, l. 26.—W. has tripped here. *Philaster* is several times quoted by Augustine as the author of a catalogue of heresies, not as himself a heretic, *e.g.* De Heres. xli. (Tom. VIII. p. 12). Philaster Brixianus episcopus in prolixissimo libro quem de heresibus condidit et cxxviii haereses arbitratus est computandas.

P. 80, l. 30.—*Meicagismonite*. Aug. de Her. LVIII. (Tom. VIII. p. 20). Metangismonitae (*μεταγγισμός vas in vase*) dicentes sic esse in Patre Filium quomodo vas in vase.

P. 81, l. 5.—*apocrifa* as opposed here to *autentica* and to *canonica* (supra, p. 11, l. 4) means in W. the writings of Fathers and Doctors, as distinguished from Holy Scripture, which latter would of course include 'the Apocrypha' of our old Bibles. Trialogus, p. 239. Scriptura sacra infinitum magis autentica et credenda—scripta aliorum doctorum magnorum quantumcunque vera, dicuntur apocrifa. From the use which W. makes of the books of Wisdom, Ecclesiasticus, and Baruch (v. Index I.) in this treatise, one infers that in his earlier days he gave them the full value of Holy Scripture. But only four years after his death, in the revised Wycliffite version, put forth by Purvey in 1388, the same distinction between canonical and apocryphal books is made as in our Sixth Article. Among 'apocrifa that is bookis withouten autorite of bileue' are placed 'ii bookis Ecclesiastici and Sapience which the Chirche redith to edifying of the people and not to conferme the autorite of techingis of Holy Chirche.' Madden and Forshall, i. 1. Probably this represents W.'s own view towards the close of his life; and if so we have another instance of his gradually shaking himself free of Roman tradition.

P. 81, l. 9. —*expositorio*, a logical fallacy 'deceptorius paralogismus.' Trial. 273. Cf. also Trial. p. 64, and De Ecclesia, p. 31.

P. 82, l. 18.—*Tharsites*, apparently another logical fallacy.

P. 83, l. 1.—*Augustine's* Treatise according to the Benedictine editors (Tom. VIII. p. 28) ends with Heresis 88, the Nestorian and Eutychian heresies not being known by those names until after the death of Augustine. The passage quoted below, l. 2–12, is from the spurious appendix to Aug. de Heresibus.

P. 83, l. 29.—The passage from De Visit. Inf. is quoted at length infra, p. 100.

P. 84, l. 28.—Hooker, E. P. V. liv. 10, sums up the doctrine of the Incarnation in four adverbs like these three of W.'s.—ἀληθῶς, τελέως, ἀδιαιρέτως, ἀσυγχύτως. An earlier attempt had ἀτρέπτως, ἀχωρίστως for the first two.

P. 85, l. 22.—This was Docetism, that Christ had only the appearance [δόκησις] of man.

P. 86, l. 20.—W. returns to this argument, infra, p. 155.

P. 88, l. 8.—*processus*, general drift. Cf. p. 24, l. 14.

P. 89, l. 27.—*synecdochica*, p. 56, l. 4, note.

P. 91, l. 26.—*procreati ab incubis et succubis*. W. means such as Grendel in Beowulf, and Robert le Diable. A touch of medieval superstition.

P. 93, l. 3.—*celicus paranymphus.* W. applies to St. John the Evangelist the title which St. John the Baptist used of himself. St. John iii. 29.

P. 94, l. 9.—*humido* is a noun. Mr. Matthew supplies me with a good parallel from the De Statu Innocentiae (MS. Trin. Coll., Dublin, C. I. 23, p. 333a.). Magis bonum est Petro adulto quod privetur humido superfluo membris corporis solidatis quam foret fluxus humorum cum illa qualitate membrorum.

P. 94, l. 10.—The passage quoted is from Lam. i. 12: the reference in *sumptibus alienis* to Isa. liii. 9, caused the mistake.

P. 95, l. 27.—Bede contrasts *factum* ex muliere and *natum* ex Patre. Thus, Hom. I. x. (Migne, Bede, vol. v. p. 53) factum ex muliere, hoc est ex maternae carnis substantia, and in Hom. I. vi. (Migne, Bede, vol. v. p. 36) commenting on Luke ii. 15: *Et videamus hoc Verbum quod factum est.* Quam recta et pura fidei sanctae confessio! In principio erat Verbum. . . . Deus erat Verbum. Hoc Verbum *natum* ex Patre, non factum est, quia creatura Deus non est. In qua nativitate divina videri ab hominibus non potuit; sed ut videri posset, *Verbum caro factum est et habitavit in nobis. Videamus ergo*, inquiunt, *hoc Verbum quod factum est*, quia antequam factum est, hoc videre nequivimus. Bede is arguing from the Vulg. and misses the distinction between *λόγος* and *ῥῆμα*.

P. 95, l. 31.—The same passage of Aug. is quoted below, p. 153, l. 15.

P. 96, l. 4.—*in Sermone Domini in Monte.* I cannot find the quotation there.

P. 96, l. 13.—Damascenus De Fide Orth. III. iv. (Migne, Patr. Gr. xciv. 997) *καὶ γὰρ ὁ Χριστὸς, ὅπερ ἐστι τὸ συναμφότερον* [quae vox utrumque complectitur] *καὶ Θεὸς καὶ ἄνθρωπος λέγεται, καὶ κτιστὸς καὶ ἄκτιστος, καὶ παθητὸς καὶ ἀπαθής.*

P. 97, l. 23.—The reference is to Lib. iii. S. D. 11. 4.

P. 98, l. 12.—*synecdochica locutio.* See above, p. 56, l. 4, note.

P. 99, l. 23.—*esse intelligibile.* W. distinguishes three forms of existence. 1. Ideal, in the divine intuition. 2. Potential, in second causes. 3. Actual, in the individual. Cf. Trialogus, p. 86. Unde creaturae habent triplex esse notabile. Primo *esse intelligibile* vel ydeale eternum in Deo; secundo *esse-exemplare* in suis principiis, quomodo creaturae productae posterius creantur in principio mundi in suis principiis; et tertio *esse individuum* in suo completo existere, quod fit opere administrationis. Cf. De Ecclesia, p. 126. Also Fasc. Ziz. p. 34, where the third is called *esse existere in genere proprio.* W. says that there was a time when in the third sense *Christus homo* was not.

P. 101, l. 17.—Aug. De Vis. Infir. ii. 2 (Tom. VI. 256). Aude igitur, fili mi, de homine tuo Deo facere quoddam participium, quia prior fecit Deus de homine tuo puro sibi participium . . . sed quia meum est meum, quia et ex me mihi quadam cogitatione et cognatione, et secreta quadam affectione conglutino, quodam proprio jure consanguinitatis mihi vendico, etc.

P. 101, l. 33.—*superius*, p. 80, l. 22.

P. 102, l. 15.—*singillatim*. Walden, Doctr. Fid. I. 42, attacks this passage thus: Numquid aliquis ante nostrum Wyclefum sic solvit Jesum et tripartiebatur eum, dicens Christum esse trium naturarum quamlibet singillatim et omnes eas conjunctim? . . . igitur tripartitis Verbum aliter quam antiqua ecclesia, quae ista tria dixit esse Christum solum.

P. 102, l. 27.—*gigantem*, v. supra, p. 9, l. 21, gigas gemine substancie.

P. 106, l. 13.—That God is *immobilis*, cf. Trial. p. 52.

P. 107, l. 17.—Passages resembling this are to be found in Arist. Phys. viii. 6, 7; Metaphys. xi. 7.

P. 108, ll. 10–12.—This passage is expanded in one of W.'s Christmas Sermons, Arnold, i. 320. Possibly *dolus* should be *dolor*. Compare Sermon referred to: 'all the fendis in helle ben beterid agens their wille; for their cumpany is maad lesse and thei have harm (=loss) of many felowis.'

P. 109, l. 14.—The reference is to the passage, supra, p. 107, l. 13.

P. 110, l. 28.—Here, as above, p. 42, l. 23, W. defends 'the Litany' against its impugners. But who were these Rationalists or Puritans?

P. 112, l. 17 —*Christus* purgavit, a forced rendering of LXX. *κύριος*.

P. 113, l. 14.—W. ignoring the idiom which occasionally attracts the antecedent into the case of the relative (*e.g.* Virgil, Aen. i. 573, urbem quam statuo vestra est), gives a naïve reason for the accusative *sermonem*, thus surpassing even Augustine's strained explanation of the words. Et fortasse propter aliquam distinccionem, ubi suos dixit, dixit pluraliter, hoc est *sermones*: ubi autem *sermonem*, hoc est Verbum, non suum dixit esse sed Patris, seipsum intelligi voluit. Tract. in Joh. lxxvi. 5 (Tom. III. part ii. p. 696). W. has already claimed Augustine as his model in the exact grammatical interpretation of Scripture *de virtute sermonis*, supra, p. 73, l. 28.

P. 113, l. 20.—This '*metaphysic*,' already introduced, p. 12, l. 13, is the basis of W.'s system of thought. Its scriptural warrant he finds in the opening verses of St John's Gospel, where (verses 4 and 5) he adopts the rendering *quod factum est in ipso vita erat*, cf. Westcott, St. John, p. 29. In Trial. p. 62, W. thus states his position that all 'ideas' are in 'the Word.' Omnes ydeae quae sunt formae exemplares secundum proprietatem aliquam sunt in Verbo quae est forma ac sapientia Dei Patris . . . omnes dictae ydeae distinguuntur inter se formaliter et a Deo, sunt tamen omnes essentialiter ipse Deus. Cf. Fasc. Ziz. pp. 80-83.

P. 115, l. 18.—*antropospatos*=*ἀνθρωποπάθος*. Cf. Trial. p. 175. This bold admission of the necessity of anthropomorphism in our conceptions of God is an example of W.'s insight and robust good sense.

P. 116, l. 32.—Cf. p. 13, l. 10. *modificare negativas* was a principle with W., *i.e.* to endeavour to find the germ of truth in inaccurate statements.

P. 118, l. 20.—Aug. loc. cit. (Tom. VI. p. 64) defines the third kind of *habitus* thus. Tertium genus est cum ipsa quae accidunt mutantur ut habitum faciant, et quodammodo formantur ab eis quibus habitum faciunt, sicuti est vestis: nam cum reposita vel projecta est, non habet eam formam, quam sumit cum induitur atque inducitur membris. Ergo induta accipit formam, quam non habebat exuta: cum ipsa membra, et cum exuuntur et cum induuntur, in suo statu maneant. Aug. thus applies it to the Incarnation. Isto autem *habitus* (Phil. ii. 8) est ex tertio genere; sic enim assumptus est ut commutaretur in melius, et ab eo formaretur ineffabiliter excellentius atque conjunctius quam vestis cum ab homine induitur. W. or his predecessors (for Peter Lombard (III. S. D. vi.) also quotes this passage from Augustine) has condensed Aug. so briefly as to be obscure and apparently unintelligible to his copyists. Cf. Dorner, Person of Christ, Div. II. vol. i. 315.

P. 119, l. 18.—W. gives the substance of Aug. ad Felic. cap. xii., but adds the logical technicalities.

P. 121, l. 27.—*risus*, Gen. xxi. 6: also Gen. xvii. 17, and xviii. 12.

P. 122, l. 13.—The date of this Decretal, Clementis V. in concilio Viennensi, is 1312.

P. 127, l. 27.—*animam*. Since the text was printed I have found that *hominem* is the word in Aug.

P. 129, l. 17.—*Vir notat etatem formam sexum probitatem* should have been printed as a leonine verse.

P. 133, l. 2.—W. professes to give the meaning of Anselm in the preceding passage. Walden, Doctr. Fid. I. 42, denies that W. can claim Anselm's authority. Nihil tibi et Anselmo qui dicit naturam quam Christus assumpsit non esse Christum, nisi quando ponitur cum collectione proprietatum personalium in eadem persona Verbi, et tunc est *iste homo*, id est, Jesus non natura abstracta composita. Non est enim idem *homo* et *Jesus homo*. *Jesus homo* persona Christi est; *homo* vero simpliciter, natura est quae assumpta est, cum Verbum caro facta est.

P. 132, l. 6.—*exemplaria . . . exemplata*. Ideas or forms and individuals respectively.

P. 132, l. 8.—Anselm De Inc. Verbi ii. Omnis individuus homo persona est. Again, De Inc. V. vi. Personam designamus quae cum natura collectionem habet proprietatum quibus homo communis sit singulus, et ab aliis singulis distinguitur. And again, Monologion lxxviii. 78: Persona non dicitur nisi de individua rationali natura.

*Boecium*. In a work ascribed to Boethius, entitled De duabus naturis et una persona Christi, c. ii., the author discusses the difference between *natura* and *persona*, and concludes thus: *Natura* est cujuslibet substantiae specificata proprietas: *persona* vero rationabilis naturae individua subsistentia. Dorner, Div. II. i. 151.

P. 136. ll. 11–13.—Possibly *indicare . . . indicium* is the better reading.

P. 136, l. 30.—This repulsive discussion is not without value as showing W.'s desire to include physical science in his studies.

P. 137, l. 5.—*Commentatorem.* This title is given to Averroës as the author of the Commentaries on Aristotle. Cf. Trial. p. 78. Aristoteles et Averrois commentator suus. The schoolmen owed their knowledge of Aristotle mainly to the Arabic scholars, whose Arabic paraphrases were translated into Latin.

P. 139, l. 24.—*alibi*, p. 142, top.

P. 139, l. 27.—*putrefaccione.* Spontaneous generation was held not only by the schoolmen, but even by Bacon, Advancement of Learning, i. p. 39, Kitchin's edition: 'Many substances in nature which are solid do putrefy and corrupt into worms.' And similarly of plant life (p. 60), 'moss which is but a rudiment between putrefaction and a herb.'

P. 141, l. 16.—Among the *tercii* would be found Wilberforce, On the Incarnation, p. 46, where he argues for Traducianism, except in some part of our spiritual nature, which is due to Creatianism.

P. 148, l. 2.—Cf. Wyclif's Sermons, Arnold, vol. i. 160: Sith there ben foure manere of bryngingis forth of man, and the fourthe and the laste, apropred unto Crist, is that man cometh clene of womman without man.

P. 145, l. 19 —For W.'s theory of the relation between the *general* and the *individual*, cf. pp. 20, 86, 145, and Trial. 276.

P. 145, l. 19.—W.'s formula is 'quelibet universalis forma est idem cum singulis ejus suppositis' (p. 145, l. 19). Hence it follows, that 'unica communis humanitas est quelibet persona hominis' (p. 20, l. 10); and hence also Christ who assumed *humanitas*, that by which men are men, the *nature* or *form* of Man, is identified with *men*; and so whatever by virtue of their participation in the *form* (p. 86) is predicated of men generally, may or rather must likewise be predicated of Christ *secundum hominem.*

P. 155, l. 19.—*ille clericus in fide devius.* This is Ruzelinus, or Roscellinus, Compendiensis, the preceptor of Abelard, a native of Armorica, educated at Soissons and Rheims, Canon (clericus= canonicus) of Compiegne, the first medieval exponent of Nominalism. Against him Anselm wrote his treatise on the Incarnation, A.D. 1094, which he entitled *Epistola de Fide Trinitatis et de Incarnatione Verbi contra blasphemias Ruzelini.* Anselm's account of his work is as follows (De Inc. V. c. i.):—Cum ad huc in Becci monasterio essem abbas, presumpta est a quodam *clerico* in Francia talis assertio. '*Si in Deo,* inquit, *tres personae sunt una tantum res; et non sunt tres res unaquaque per se separatim, sicut tres angeli aut tres animae; ita tamen ut potentia et voluntate omnino sint idem; ergo Pater et Spiritus Sanctus cum Filio est incarnatus.*'

Quod cum ad me perlatum esset, incepi contra hunc errorem quandam epistolam; quam, parte quadam edita, perficere contempsi, credens non ea opus esse; quoniam et ille contra quem fiebat, in concilio a venerabili Remensi Archiepiscopo Raynaldo collecto errorem suum abjuraverat; et nullus videbatur, qui eum errare ignoraret; partem tamen illam quam feceram quidam fratres me nesciente transcripserunt atque aliis legendum tradiderunt: quod idcirco dico ut si in alicujus manus pars illa venerit, quanquam ibi nihil falsum sit, tamen tanquam imperfecta et non exquisita relinquatur; et hic quod ibi incepi, diligentius inceptum et perfectum requiratur. Postquam enim in Angliam ad episcopatum nescio qua Dei dispositione captus et retentus sum; audivi praefatae novitatis auctorem in sua perseverantem sententia dicere se non ob aliud abjurasse quod dicebat, nisi quia a populo interfici timebat. Hac igitur causa quidam fratres precibus suis me coegerunt ut solverem questionem, qua ipse sic irretitus erat, ut nullo modo se expediri ab ea posse crederet; nisi aut incarnatione Dei Patris aut Spiritus sancti, aut demum multitudine se impediret.

And so the great medieval controversy between Nominalism and Realism was launched.

Anselm refers to Roscellinus also in Epist. II. xxxv. and LI.

P. 156, l. 23.—*persona.* W. gives the same etymology in Trial. p. 60. Another given by P. Lombard is *per se sonans.*

P. 157, l. 16.—*The Exposicio Fidei* is Sermo incerti auctoris, Benedictine ed. Tom. V. App. 283.

P. 159, l. 13.—*lumen nature.* Cf. Trial. pp. 55, 56. 'Not only in matters of action and duty, but also in matters of faith, Wyclif recognizes a *natural light*, only he most distinctly pronounces to be erroneous the notion that the light of faith is opposed to the light of nature, so that what appears to be impossible in the light of nature must be held for truth in the light of faith, and vice versa.' Lechler, ii. p. 16. W. attempts, infra, p. 191, l. 10, to bring the 'eucharistic miracle' (p. 216, l. 10) under a scientific parallel.

P. 159, l. 30.—Cf. supra, p. 18, l. 25.

P. 161, l. 20.—For those who wish to try to understand the argument I transcribe the passage from Duns Scotus, vol. vii. p. 15; D. S. III. iii. 1:—Sed distinguendum est inter dependentiam actualem, potentialem, et aptitudinalem: et hoc vocando aptitudinalem, quae semper quantum est de se, esset in actu: quomodo grave aptum natum est esse in centro, ubi semper esset, quantum est de se, nisi esset impeditum. Et potentialem voco absolute illam, ubi nulla est impossibilitas ex repugnantia, vel incompossibilitate terminorum, et ista possibilitas potest esse quandoque respectu potentiae activae supernaturalis, non tamen naturalis. Licet igitur sola negatio dependentiae actualis non sufficiat ad rationem personae, neque independentia tertia posset poni in natura creata ad Verbum. Nulla enim est natura, vel entitas creata, cui repugnet contradictorie dependere ad Verbum:

tamen negatio dependentiae aptitudinalis potest concedi in natura creata personata in se ad Verbum; alioquin violenter quiesceret in persona creata, sicut lapis violenter quiescit sursum; et ita ista negatio scilicet non dependentia, non quidem actualis tantum, sed etiam actualis et aptitudinalis, talis complet rationem personae in natura intellectuali, et suppositi in alia natura creata; nec tamen haec dependentia aptitudinalis ponit repugnantiam ad dependentiam actualem, quia licet non sit aptitudo talis naturae ad dependendum, est tamen aptitudo obedientiae: quia natura illa est in perfecta obedientia ad dependendum per actionem agentis supernaturalis; et quando datur sibi talis dependentia, personatur personalitate illa ad quam dependet; quando autem non datur, personatur in se ista negatione formaliter, et non aliqua positivo addito ultra illam entitatem positivam, qua est haec natura.

Dorner, Div. II. vol. i. p. 340 seqq., attempts to unravel the Subtle Doctor's meaning. Most readers will agree with W. (pp. 51, 161) in finding 'this doctor's Latin difficult'

P. 163, l. 10.—*ad aliquid.* I now think *aliud aliquid* the right reading. The words of Augustine are—Tres personas ex eadem essentia non dicimus, quasi aliud ibi sit quod essentia est, aliud quod persona. De Trin. vii. 6, 11.

P. 168, l. 25.—Why are the quotation from the Decretal and the comment on it absent from the English copy? Had English students already begun to discount the value of Papal decisions?

The Decretal is among those of Gregory IX. from a letter of Alexander III. to the Archbishop of Rheims.

P. 170, l. 6.—*reduplicativam*, v. Fasc. Ziz. Glossary, p. 538.

P. 170, l. 8.—*pugnarius.* I can find nothing in Du Cange or elsewhere to explain this word.

P. 170, l. 26.—*doctores signorum.* One of W.'s titles for the Nominalists who followed Occam. Similarly in Fasc. Ziz. 125, sectae signorum; p. 117, cultores signorum; p. 105, baptistae signorum. These expressions are based upon the theory that common nouns are only *signs* of thoughts, which latter are *signs* only of particular things.

P. 170, l. 11.—*Doni.* For this title of the Holy Spirit, cf. 78, l. 21.

P. 181, l. 23.—*dotes corporis.* Cf. p. 70, l. 29, and note thereon.

P. 183, l. 11.—Peter Lombard, S. D. III. ix. 4. Est cujusdam modi *dulia* quae creaturae cuilibet exhiberi potest; et est quaedam soli humanitati Christi exhibenda non alii creaturae, quia Christi humanitas super omnem creaturam est veneranda et diligenda. Aliis autem placet Christi humanitatem una adoratione, quae *latria* dicitur, cum Verbo esse adorandam non propter se sed propter illum cujus 'scabellum' est, cui est unita. Neque ipsa humanitas sola vel nuda, sed cum Verbo cui est unita; nec propter se, sed propter illum cui est unita, adoranda. The reference is to Aug. de Verbis Domini, Ps. xcviii. 5. *Adorate scabellum pedum ejus quoniam sanctum est.*

Sciendum quia in Christo terra est, id est, caro quae sine impietate adoratur.

Aug. De Trin. I. vi. 13 (Tom. VIII. 757) defines *latria* thus: Eam servitutem qua non nisi Deo serviendum est quae Graece appellatur *λατρεία*.

P. 184, l. 7.—Wyclif is unsparingly condemned by the Roman doctors for this adoration of Christ's humanity, which follows necessarily from W.'s principle — *Christus est trium naturarum quaelibet.*

Walden, D. F. I. 44, after quoting this passage of Wyclif, 'Si per impossibile . . . obligari,' delivers this sweeping condemnation: Procul absit illa logica ab ecclesia sancta Dei, quae est merae idololatriae tam affinis . . . Wicleffus prohibente Augustino in carne Christi cogitatione manet quando illam jam actu per casum suum a Verbi persona suspendit, et sic adorat etiam adoratione illa, qua scriptura dicit *Dominum Deum tuum adorabis, et illi soli servies.* . . . In hoc toto nil distas ab idolatra.

Two centuries later Petavius (circ. 1644), vol. v. p. 215, De Incar. lib. xv. c. 4, himself apparently ignorant of this treatise of Wyclif, repeats Walden's censure: Foedissimus primum error fuit Joannis Wicleffi, qui, ut Thomas Waldensis refert, asseverabat carnem Christi a Verbo disjunctam adoratione latriae venerandam esse. Hoc autem non ex eo concludebat, quod aliquando fuisset assumpta, ut quasi pristinae dignitatis vestigium aliquod retineret, ut erudito theologo visum est, sed alia de causa; nimirum quod ut ibidem Waldensis ait, carnem solam verum Christum et verum hominem esse diceret . . . Quod heretici delirium absurdum est, et ab Augustino aliisque patribus refellitur.

P. 184, l. 9.—*proximis.* Petavius after Walden reads *proximus.*

This theological or rather scholastic dispute, and the cognate question of the *triduum*, is probably glanced at by Spenser, who was not without some scholastic lore, Faërie Queene, I. 1, 2, *And dead as living ever him adored.* As a corollary W. says that since the exaltation of humanity by the Incarnation, 'aungelis in heaven wolden not take kneling of John' (Engl. Works, i. 390), *i.e.* the *dulia* offered to angels in the O. T. was henceforth inadmissible, the angels being only fellow-servants (*σύνδουλοι*) with men of the God-Man. Cf. supra, p. 35, l. 6.

As to *adoration* of Christ incarnate Wyclif is near to Damascenus, *εἷς τοίνυν ἐστὶν ὁ Χριστὸς Θεὸς τέλειος καὶ ἄνθρωπος τέλειος· ὃν προσκυνοῦμεν σὺν Πατρὶ καὶ πνεύματι, μιᾷ προσκυνήσει μετὰ τῆς ἀχράντου σαρκὸς αὐτοῦ, οὐκ ἀπροσκύνητον τὴν σάρκα λέγοντες· προσκυνεῖται γὰρ ἐν τῇ μιᾷ τοῦ Λόγου ὑποστάσει, ἥτις αὐτῇ ὑπόστασις γέγονεν. οὐ τῇ κτίσει λατρεύοντες. οὐ γὰρ ὡς ψιλὴν σάρκα προσκυνοῦμεν, ἀλλ' ὡς ἡνωμένην Θεότητι, καὶ εἰς ἓν πρόσωπον καὶ μίαν ὑπόστασιν τοῦ Θεοῦ Λόγου τῶν δύο αὐτοῦ ἀναγομένων φύσεων.* — De Fide Orth. III. ch. 8.

P. 184, l. 22.—The words of Aug. De Vera Rel. xvi. 30 (Tom. I. 757) are—Ne quis forte sexus a suo creatore se contemptum putaret, virum suscepit natus ex femina. *Verbum* as the subject is placed several sentences before: and the grammatical form of the sentence scarcely bears the strain which W. puts upon it. Cf. supra, p. 73, l. 28, for Augustine's enforcement of doctrine by grammatical forms. Possibly, however, W. was laying the stress of his argument only on *virum*.

P. 185, l. 4.—Duns Scotus, III. S. D. i. 1 (vol. vii. 6). Accidens enim ad substantiam sive ad subjectum suum duplicem habet habitudinem scilicet informantis ad informatum, et ista necessario includit imperfectionem in subjecto informato, eo scilicet quod potentialitatem habet respectu actus secundum quid scilicet accidentalis. Aliam habet ut posterioris naturaliter ad prius, a quo dependet: non ut ab aliqua causa: quia si habet subjectum pro aliqua causa, habet ipsum pro causa materiali, et hoc est, inquantum informat ipsum. Si igitur istae duae habitudines accidentis ad subjectum ab invicem distinguantur, altera necessario est ad subjectum sub ratione imperfectionis in ipso subjecto, scilicet potentialitatis. Altera nullam imperfectionem necessario possit in eo, sed tantum prioritatem naturalem, et sustentationem respectu accidentis. Huic simillima est ista habitudo, quae est dependentia naturae humanae ad personam divinam, quae est extra omnem dependentiam causati ad causam.

The next article, Explicit quomodo non repugnat personam divinam terminare dependentiam naturae humanae.

P. 186, l. 10.—Here W. introduces the analogy between the Eucharist and the Incarnation, which he follows up, pp. 189, 190.

P. 189, l. 23.—Cf. Lechler, ii. p. 202. Select English Works of Wyclif, iii. 502.—Cf. p. 130, l. 2.

Walden, D. F. vol. iv. discusses at length W.'s sacramental theory.

P. 190.—For the stages of W.'s opinion as to the change which takes place in the Eucharist, cf. Shirley, Fasc. Ziz. lx. and xv. note 4. Lechler, ii. pp. 172, 217. Matthew, Eng. Works, xxiii. He is here in the stage intermediate between belief in transubstantiation, and his final belief in 1381 that the bread remains bread. F. Z. p. 115; Trial. p. 251. In the present passage (l. 22) he allows that the bread ceases to be bread: what the 'substance' then is he knows not, and cares not to inquire: but he does not believe now any more than in the final stage of his opinions that there is in the Eucharist *accidens sine subjecto.* Cf. supra, p. 186, l. 10.

P. 191, l. 12.—*perspectivos* seems to mean *students of optics. Perspectiva* est mathematica disciplina quae circum visum versatur. Boethius in Du Cange sub voc. Cf. De Ecclesia, p. 99, l. 10.

P. 193, l. 24.—*vermis.* Cf. p. 10, l. 1.

P. 194, l. 6.—Walden, D. F. I. 44, condemns W. for asserting that the humanity actually assumed was the only humanity possible to be assumed. Alia quaedam documenta circa humanitatem recenter inducit, et doctoralibus casibus responsa nova et satis peregrina supponit. Ubi enim quaeri solebat utrum Christus aliunde potuit vel aliam humanam naturam, quam illam quam assumpsit sibi unire; ipse celeri pede negationis omnes difficultates ejus excussit, dicens casum impossibilem: et Dei Verbum humanitati isti tam fortiter colligavit ut putetur dici de eo, quod alligavit Regem Coeli in compedibus, et nobiles Christi partes, scilicet corpus et animam, in manicis ferreis. Unde dicit cap. vi. De Incarnat. "Secundo sequitur, quod nullam humanitatem aliam Verbum potuit hypostatice assumpsisse. Quod patet; quia aliter Christus poterit fuisse alius homo, et per consequens alia persona: consequens est impossibile: ergo et antecedens."

P. 195, l. 16.—Rome and Oxford were the common scholastic illustrations of places, as Peter and Paul of persons.

P. 200, l. 6.—*nidi*, the distinct reading of the Oriel MS. is confirmed by Fasc. Zizan. p. 14, where Kenyngham quotes Wyclif's 'three *nests* logical, natural, metaphysical,' and amuses himself with the metaphor.

P. 201, l. 9.—*ranga*, the reading of A.O. There is no such word in Du Cange. Of our MSS., C. omitting the word with a lacuna, shows there is a difficulty about it. B. has *arenga*. Of this latter Du Cange says: *arenga* v. *arengua* = oratio publica, declamatio, concio = harangue. *arengaria* (Ital. ringhiera et aringheria = locus editus unde concionantur publice). Hickes thence derives English 'ring' of spectators.' The sense here requires some word signifying *crowd*.

P. 202, l. 14.—*pictacias*. Du Cange: *pittacium* schedula de membrana decisa: corii particula quae soleae repeciatae (pecia = piece, patch) insuta est. Joshua ix. 5. Calceamenta perantiqua quae ad indicium vetustatis pittaciis consuta erant. Clouts, *i.e.* unauthorized additions. Polemical Works, Buddensieg, i. p. 44, l. 44. In Trial. p. 377, quamvis ista secunda particula sit iners pictatia a fratribus adinventa, the meaning seems to be an unsound argument. So likewise in Trial. p. 246, on which Lechler notes, *Pictacia* proprie *pittacium* = panniculus unguento illitus et vulneri impositus. Forcellini gives the meaning of a medical plaster.

P. 202, l. 24.—Aquinas (Summa Q. iii. Art. 7) admits the possibility of the manifold assumption: Persona divina non ita assumsit unam naturam humanam quod non potuerit assumere aliam.

P. 218, l. 21.—*Doctorem*, apparently Aquinas, p. 208 supra.

P. 207, l. 23.—*septipedalis*, cf. supra, note on p. 57, l. 18.

P. 223, l. 15.—*repugnans*, apparently *neuter accus.* something inconsistent with the faith. For similar use of participle of *prohibens disciplinam*, p. 3, l. 3.

P. 229, l. 14.—"W. conceives of the Divine omnipotence as a power self-determining, morally regulated, ordered by inner laws."

Lechler, ii. p. 42. This is *potencia ordinata: potencia absoluta* is a fancy of men, not a reality. Cf. supra, pp. 75, 77, and also De Dominio Divino, iii. 5, quoted by Lechler. Thus *Si voluerit*, if otherwise than the fact, is an impossible supposition. Cf. Trialogus, p. 154. Deus non potest quidquam producere vel intelligere nisi quod de facto intelligit et producit. Cf. Trial. p. 157 and p. 231, where W. says, Non est Deus mobilis ut homines in agendo, sed si quidquam fecerit, rationes priores aeternae necessitant ut sic fiat. Cf. also supra, p. 76, l. 22. W.'s doctrine of divine omnipotence being limited by the perfection of the divine nature is already in St. Augustine and St. Paul. Cf. Aug. De Symbolo Sermo ad Catechumenos, § 2. Deus omnipotens est, et cum sit omnipotens mori non potest, falli non potest, mentiri non potest, et, quod ait Apostolus, *negare se ipsum non potest*. 2 Tim. ii. 13.

P. 232, l. 1.—*ad litteram*. Cf. note on p. 20, l. 22.

# INDEX I.

## REFERENCES TO HOLY SCRIPTURE.

### OLD TESTAMENT.

# INDEX II.

## REFERENCES TO OTHER AUTHORS.

[Where nothing else is given but in Column 1, the page of this edition, the author is only named or referred to by Wyclif without quotation. Where Columns 3 or 4 are blank, I have failed to identify the quotation or reference.]

### St. Ambrose.

| Page of this book. | Wyclif's citation. | Where found. | Ed. | Vol. | Page. |
|---|---|---|---|---|---|
| 14. | 1 De Trinitate, 9. | De Fide, i. 9. | Migne, | ii. | 917. |
| 102. | 3 De Spiritu Sancto. | De Incarn. V. | ,, | ii. | 862. |
| 103. | 1 De Trinitate, 6. | De Fide, iii. 9. | ,, | ii. | 626. |

### St. Anselm.

Ed. Gerberon. Lutetiae Parisiorum. MDCCXXI.

| | | |
|---|---|---|
| 19. | De Inc. Verbi, 1. | Epistola De Inc. Verbi, ii. |
| 26. | ,, ,, 6. | ,, ,, vi. |
| 51. | De Concordia, 5. | De Concordia Praescientiae, ii. |
| 78. | Cur Deus Homo, 6. | Cur Deus Homo, ii. 9. |
| 78. | De Inc. Verbi, 7, 9. | De Inc. Verbi, v. 5. |
| 79. | 2 Cur Deus Homo, 5. | Cur Deus Homo, ii. 5. |
| 83. | | |
| 88. | Cur Deus Homo. | ,, ,, ii. 6, 8. |
| 88. | De Inc. Verbi. | |
| 90. | 2 Cur Deus Homo, 8. | ,, ,, ii. 8. |
| 112. | Monologion, 19. | Monologion xx. (aliter xix.). |
| 130. | De Inc. Verbi. | De Inc. Verbi, vi. |
| 132. | | |
| 143. | De Inc. Verbi, 7. | ,, ,, vi. |
| 144. | ,, ,, 1. | ,, ,, ii. |
| 145. | ,, ,, 7. | ,, ,, vi. |
| 146. | ,, ,, | ,, ,, vi. |
| 151. | ,, ,, | ,, ,, vi. |
| 152. | De Inc. Verbi. | De Inc. Verbi, vi. |
| 155. | | |
| 171. | | |

| Page of this Book. | Wyclif's citation. | Where found. | Ed. Vol. Page. |
|---|---|---|---|
| 4. | Ad Felic. | Ad. Felicianum xi. xiii. | viii. App. 45-47. |
| 4. | Ad Pasc. Ep. 12. | Epist. 238. | ii. 857. |
| 4. | Ad Dard. Ep. 40, 7. | Epist. 187 (8) | ii. 680. |
| 5. | Omc. 47. | Tract. in Joan. Evang. xlvii. 13. | iii. pt. ii. 613. |
| 5. | Omc. 8. | ,, ,, ,, viii. 9. | iii. pt. ii. 357. |
| 6. | Contra Maxim. 1, 2. | Collatio cum Maximino ii. 14. | viii. 661. |
| 7, 8. | Ad Volus. Ep. 3. | Epist. 137. (9-14) | ii. 405. |
| 10. | Dial. ad Felic. | Ad. Felic. 5. | viii. App. 42. |
| 10. | De Quest. Vet. et Nov. Test. 122. | Quaest. cxxii. | vi. pt. App. 1114. |
| 11. | Ep. 31. | De Trinitate i. 24. | viii. 765. |
| 11. | Expos. Eph. 4. | ,, ,, xv. 34. | viii. 991. |
| 12, 13. | | | |
| 14. | Ad Bonifac. Ep. 33. | Epist. 185. 1. | ii. 643. |
| 15. | Omc. 48. | Tract. in Jo. Ev. xlviii. | iii. pt. ii. 617. |
| 17. | ,, | ,, ,, ,, | iii. pt. ii. 617. |
| 17. | ,, 47. | ,, ,, xlvii. | iii. p. ii. 611. |
| 17. | De Heres. 49. | De Heresibus xlix. | viii. 18. |
| 17. | ,, 55. | ,, ,, lv. | viii. 19. |
| 18-21. | Ad Pasc. Ep. 127. | Epist. 238 (10-21) | ii. 856-860. |
| 22. | Ad Dard. Ep. 40. | Epist. 187 (4). | ii. 679. |
| 22. | Omc. 47. | Tract. in Jo. Ev. xlvii. 9. | iii. ii. 610. |
| 24. | Contra Maxim. 11. | Contra Maximin. ii. 14. 3. | viii. 704. |
| 27. | Omc. 78. | Tract. in Jo. Ev. lxxviii. 3. | iii. ii. 700. |
| 30. | ,, 50. | ,, ,, ,, li. 4. | iii. ii. 635. |
| 31. | ,, 47. | ,, ,, ,, xlvii. 10. | iii. ii. 611. |
| 39. | | | |
| 40. | ,, 52. | ,, ,, ,, lii. 13. | iii. ii. 643. |
| 40. | ,, 78. | ,, ,, ,, lxviii. 1. 3. | iii. ii. 699. |
| 41. | ,, 78. | ,, ,, ,, lxviii. 1, 3. | iii. ii. 699. |
| 43. | De Trin. 17, 7. | { De Trinitate vii. 4. 7 | viii. 858. |
| | | { ,, ,, xv. 7. 11. | 973. |
| 48. | Ad Dard. 40. | Epist. 187. | ii. 679. |
| 55. | | | |
| 59. | Contra Simplic. 1. | | |
| 60. | | | |
| 62. | Omc. 119. | Tract. in Jo. Ev. cxix. 6. | iii. ii. 803. |
| 65. | | | |
| 67. | Omc. 47. | ,, ,, ,, xlvii. 10. | iii. ii. 611. |
| 73. | Omc. 44. | Tract in Jo. Ev. xlviii. 9. | iii. ii. 617. |
| 79. | Enchir, 3. | Enchiridion 36. | vi. 210. |
| 80-82. | De Heres. | De Heresibus *passim*. | viii. 1-28. |
| 83. | ,, 89, 90. | ,, ,, | viii. 14, note *d*. |
| 83. | Omc. 48. | Tract. in Jo. Ev. xlviii. | iii. ii. 615. |

| Page of this Book. | Wyclif's citation. | Where found. | Ed. Vol. Page. |
|---|---|---|---|
| 83. | De Vis. Inf. 2. | De Visit. Infirm. (*incerti auctoris*) ii. 2 | vi. App. 256. |
| 88. | De Vera Rel. 27. | De Vera Religione xvi. 30. | i. 757. |
| 88. | De Vis. Inf. 2. | De Visit. Infirm. ii. | vi. App. 256. |
| 89. | Enchir. 14. | Enchir. 22. | vi. 205. |
| 90. | | ,, ,, | vi. 205. |
| 94. | De Vera Rel. 29. | De Vera Religione xvi. 31. | i. 758. |
| 94. | Enchir. 4. | | |
| 94. | De Quest. Vet. et Nov. T. 59. | | |
| 95. | Enchir. 29. | Enchir. 38. | vi. 211. |
| 96. | Sermo de Vig. Epiph. | | |
| 96. | ,, Domini in Monte. | | |
| 96. | Contra Max. | Contra Maximin. ii. 14, 7. | viii. 707. |
| 100. | De Vis. Inf. 2. | De Visit. Infirm. ii. | vi. App. 256. |
| 101. | De Her. 44. | De Heresibus, 44. | viii. 13. |
| 103. | Sermo de Fide. | Sermo, 233. | v. App. 383. |
| 108. | | | |
| 110. | Ome. 43. | Tract. in Jo. Ev. xliii. 16. | iii. ii. 588. |
| 111. | | | |
| 113. | ,, 76. | ,, ,, lxxvi. 5. | ,, 696. |
| 113. | De Trin. 1. | De Trin. i. 6, 10. | viii. 755. |
| 113. | Contra Max. 1. | Contra Maximin. i. 5. | viii. 681. |
| 114. | Confess. 12. | Confession, xii. | i. 212. |
| 116. | De Doctr. Chr. 31. | De Doctr. Christi., ii. 31, 48. | iii. i. 38. |
| 117. | Dial. ad Felic. | Ad Felicianum, xii. | viii. App. 46. |
| 118. | Quest. 73. | De Div. Quaest. Quaest. 73. | vi. 64. |
| 119. | Dial. ad Felic. | Ad Felicianum, xii. | viii. App. 46. |
| 119. | De Trin. 1. | De Trinitate, xiii. 28. | viii. 767. |
| 122. | Enchir. 40. | Enchir. 52. | vi. 215. |
| 126. | Dial. ad Felic. | Ad Felicianum xi. | viii. App. 45. |
| 127. | De Qualitate An. | De Quantitate Animae. | i. |
| 127. | Ome. 19. | Tract. in Jo. Ev. xix. 15. | iii. ii. 445. |
| 129. | ,, 43. | ,, ,, ,, xliii. 11. | iii. ii. 586. |
| 132. | De Quest Vet. et Nov. T. 122 | Quaest. cxxii. | iii. ii. App. 1115. |
| 139. | | | |
| 143 | | | |
| 144. | | | |
| 151. | | | |
| 152. | | | |
| 153. | Ome. 19. | Tract. in Jo. Ev. cxix. | iii. ii. 802. |
| 153. | Enchir. 29. | Enchir. 38. | vi. 211. |
| 157. | Expos. Fid. | Sermo (de Fide Cathol. *incerti auctoris*) 233. | v. App. 383. |
| 163. | De Trin. 7, 9. | De Trin. vii. 6. 11. | viii. 863. |
| 167. | Enchir. 29. | Enchir. 38. | vi. 210. |
| 167. | De Pred. Sanct. | De Predestin. Sanctor. xv. | x. 809. |

| Page of this Book. | Wyclif's citation. | Where found. | Ed. | Vol. | Page. |
|---|---|---|---|---|---|
| 167. | De Trin. 13, 37. | De Trin. xiii. 17. 22. | | viii. | 943. |
| 169. | Sermo de Trinitate. | | | | |
| 170. | | | | | |
| 171. | | | | | |
| 172. | Dial. ad Felic. | Ad Felician. xi. | | viii. | App. 45. |
| 172. | De Trin. 1, 9. | De Trin. i. 7. | | viii. | 758. |
| 172. | „ 1, 16. | De Trin. i. 13. | | viii. | 767. |
| 174. | | | | | |
| 177. | | | | | |
| 181. | | | | | |
| 183. | | | | | |
| 184. | De Vera Rel. | De Vera Relig. xvi. 30. | | i. | 757. |
| 192. | Enchir. 29. | Enchir. 36. | | vi. | 210. |
| 193. | De Civit. Dei. 17. | De Civ. Dei x. 29. | | vii. | 264. |
| 193. | Enchir. 3. | Enchir. 39. 40. | | vi. | 212. |
| 197. | Quest. Vet. et Nov. Test. | De Diversis Quaest. Quaest. 5. | | vi. | 4. |
| 226. | | | | | |
| 228. | | | | | |
| | Averroës (Commentator on Aristotle). | | | | |
| 137. | | | | | |
| 140. | | | | | |
| | Avicenna. | | | | |
| 137. | | | | | |
| 140. | | | | | |
| | Bede. | | | | |
| 95. | | | | | |
| | Boethius. | Ed. Simler, Tiguri. MDLXXI. | | | |
| 83. | | | | | |
| 132. | De Persona. | De duabus naturis et una persona Christi, c. ii. | | | |
| | St. Bonaventura. | | | | |
| 49. | 3 Sent. Dist. 12. | iii Sent. Dist. xxii. 1. | | | |
| 60. | „ „ 21. | „ „ xxi. 1. | | | |
| 97. | „ „ 11. | „ „ xi. 1. | | | |
| | St. Chrysostom. | | | | |
| 66. | | | | | |
| | Cowton or Colton (abbreviator D. Scoti). | | | | |
| 57. | | | | | |
| | St. Damascenus (Johannes). | Migne. Patr. Gr. xciv. | | | |
| 46. | | De Fide Orthodoxa, iii. 3. | | | 990. |
| 50. | Cap. 49. | „ „ 27. | | | 997. |

| Page of this Book. | Wyclif's citation. | Where found. | Ed. | Vol. | Page. |
|---|---|---|---|---|---|
| 60. | | De Fide Orthodoxa, iii. | 27. | | 997. |
| 96. | Cap. 50, 92. | ,, ,, | 27. | | 1097. |
| | DECRETALS. | | | | |
| 122. | In Clementinis. | (v. *Notes*). | | | |
| 168. | De Hereticis, vii. | ,, | | | |
| | DUNS SCOTUS. | Ed. Durand, Leyden, MDCXXXIX. | | | |
| 32. | iii. Sent. Dist. xxii. 1. | vol. vii. p. 441. | | | |
| 49. | ,, ,, | ,, 441. | | | |
| 50. | ,, ,, | ,, 451. | | | |
| 52. | ,, ,, | ,, 452. | | | |
| 57. | | | | | |
| 96. | iii. Sent. Dist. xi. 1. | ,, 240. | | | |
| 161. | iii. Sent. Dist. i. 3. | ,, 15. | | | |
| 185–191. | ,, ,, 1. | ,, pp. 3–35. | | | |
| 218. | | | | | |
| 220. | ,, ,, 3, 3. | vii. 45. | | | |
| 221. | | | | | |
| 230. | | | | | |
| | EPIPHANIUS. | | | | |
| 17. | | | | | |
| | EUSEBIUS. | | | | |
| 13. | Eccles. Hist. 10, 13. | (v. *Note* ) | | | |
| | EUCLID. | | | | |
| 174. | v. 1. | | | | |
| 213. | i. axiom 9. | | | | |
| | ST. GREGORY. | | | | Ed. Antwerp. 1615. |
| 108. | xxxi. Moralium, 38. | | | | |
| 111. | xxxiii. ,, 15. | | | | Tom. ii. p. 597. |
| 111. | xxx. ,, 5. | | | | |
| 112. | xxxiv. ,, 5. | | | | |
| 112. | ix. ,, 25. | | | | ii. 256. |
| 125. | xviii. ,, 32. | | | | ii. 482. |
| 143. | | | | | |
| 144. | | | | | |
| 171. | | | | | |
| 202. | xii. ,, 14 | | | | |
| | GROSSETESTE (LINCOLNIENSIS). | | | | |
| 88. | Examcron. | | | | |
| 96. | De Natali Domini. | | | | |
| 128. | Examcron. | | | | |
| 177. | | | | | |

| Page of this Book. | Wyclif's citation. | Where found. | Ed. Vol. Page. |
|---|---|---|---|
| | HENRY GÖTHALS OF GHENT (Henricus de Gandavo) Doctor Solemnis. | | |
| 62. | Quodlibet, 12. | | |
| | HUGO DE ST. VICTOR. | | |
| 18. | | | |
| 55. | | | |
| 65. | | | |
| 128. | | | |
| 172. | | | |
| | ST. JEROME. | | Migne, xi. 132. |
| 6, 7. | Epist. ad Paul. et Eustoch. | | |
| 9–11.1 | Ep. ad Gal. | Comm. Eph. ii. 10. | |
| 13. | | | |
| 28. | | | |
| 30. | | | |
| 53. | Ep. ad Paul. et Eustoch. | | Migne, xi. 132. |
| 108. | | | ,, ,, |
| 109. | ,, ,, | | ,, ,, |
| 110. | | | ,, ,, |
| 111. | | | |
| 122. | | | |
| 144. | | | |
| 152. | | | |
| 171. | | | |
| | ST. LEO. | | |
| 70. | | | |
| 96. | | | |
| | PETER LOMBARD. | | |
| 3. | iii. Sent. Dist. 11. | | |
| 14. | ,, ,, 11. | | |
| 48. | ,, ,, 22. | | |
| 56. | | | |
| 60. | ,, ,, 21. | | |
| 83. | | | |
| 157. | ,, ,, 6. | | |
| 183. | ,, ,, 8. | | |
| | ROSCELLINUS. | | |
| 155. | | | |

# INDEX III.

## RARER LATIN OR GREEK WORDS.

| | |
|---|---|
| *magistralis* | scholastic, 191. |
| *maneries* | manner, 34. |
| *nuncupative* | opposed to *autonomatice* and *per se* of a term applied in a non-literal sense, 21, 48. |
| *omagium* | homage, 35. |
| *omogenius.* | (ὁμογενής), 200. |
| *parasceue* | (παρασκευή, St. John xix. 42), 71. |
| *paralogisare* | to deceive by a logical fallacy, 83. |
| *paranymphus* | (παράνυμφος) friend of the bridegroom, 93. |
| *paulativus* | gradual, 200. |
| *peryodus* | period, 198. |
| *pausare* | to pause, 104. |
| *pictacia* | patch? (*v.* Notes), 202. |
| *plasmare* | to form, 76. 138. |
| *pollitice* | politice = civiliter, 135. |
| *pompare* | to exult, 116. |
| *praxis* | (πρᾶξις) action (opp. to *speculatio*), 106. |
| *pugnarius?* | (in the Vienna MSS.), 170. |
| *ranga* | v.l. in MS. B. *arenga*, or *arangua*? (harangue), hence a ring, crowd, 201. |
| *secta* | Christiana, 159. |
| *septipedalis* | possessing extension, 57, 207, *v.* Note. |
| *sesina* | seisin, legal possession, 33. |
| *spera* | sphaera, 141. |
| *tharsites* | v.l. Oriel MS. *tarlites*, apparently a logical fallacy, 82. |
| *theos* | Θεός, 128. |
| *usion* | οὔσιον } substantia (in logic), 135. |
| *usiosis* | οὐσίωσις } |
| *ypostasis* | ὑπόστασις (*passim*) } |

# INDEX IV.

## GENERAL.

D.

T.



U.



V.



W.



STEPHEN AUSTIN AND SONS, PRINTERS, HERTFORD.

☞ **The Society's Issues for 1885 and 1886 will be sent only to those Members who have paid their Subscriptions. The Subscriptions for 1886 became due on Jan. 1, and should be paid at once to the Hon. Sec., J. W. STANDERWICK, Esq., GENERAL POST OFFICE, LONDON, E.C. Cheques to be crost, 'London and County Bank.'**

---

# The Wyclif Society.

*Third Report of the Executive Committee, for* 1885.
(*March*, 1886.)



1. Since the Committee's last Report (June, 1885), the Society has issued to its Members one of its two Books for 1884, Dr. R. L. Poole's edition of Wyclif's *De Civili Dominio*, vol. i., and its two Books for 1885, Prof. Loserth's edition of Wyclif's *De Ecclesia*, and Mr. A. W. Pollard's edition of the Reformer's *Dialogus, sive Speculum Militantis Ecclesiae.* The second book for 1884, Mr. Rudolf Beer's edition of Wyclif's *De Composicione Hominis*, has been kept back by its editor's illness and other causes; but the text of it is in type, and Mr. Beer hopes the volume will be ready for issue in June next.

The first of these works gives Wyclif's theoretico-communist view of property, his theory of government, and the right of civil rulers over church property. He maintains 1, That, as dominion implies a true use of the thing possessed, it is incompatible with mortal sin, while, on the contrary, every one in a state of grace has a real lordship over the whole universe.' As a consequence it follows that, in an ideally perfect community, all goods would be held in common. 2, That the law of the Gospel is by itself sufficient for all the purposes of human life and government.

3, That, although monarchy has, under present conditions, many advantages, the best form of government is aristocracy, of which the typical example is the rule of the Hebrew judges. 4, That the Church, that is, the whole Christian community, of England may righteously deprive the clergy of their endowments.

The two next books state more at length Wyclif's view of the Church, both in idea and realisation. In *De Dominio Civili*, ch. xliii., he had shown shortly that the Church 'is the entire body of the predestinate, past, present and future, whose head and eternal director is Christ.'[1] In *De Ecclesia* he restates and developes this view; divides the Church into three parts,—1, the triumphant (the blessed in heaven), 2, the sleeping (the souls in purgatory), 3, the militant (the Christians fighting with the world),—shows that no mere man, and so Pope, can be Head of the Church; that it is impossible for us to know who is a member of the Church, and that the Canonization of Saints is therefore a groundless and mischievous practice. He then lays down the relations which should subsist between Church and State, contends that no abbey or church lies outside the King's jurisdiction, and strongly upholds the civil authority of the King over the clergy, and the duty of the laity to deprive the clergy of their temporalties if they misuse them. The book concludes with an argument and protest against the abuse of Indulgences, which were adopted (in the main) by Hus.[2] To the scholar who discovered the full extent of Hus's great debt to Wyclif, Prof. Loserth, of Czernowitz, the Society is indebted for the edition of *De Ecclesia*. Miss Alice Shirley was so kind as to english his Introduction, and Mr. Matthew to write the English side-notes.

The *Dialogus* or *Speculum Ecclesiae Militantis* is mainly on the endowment of the Church, and teaches that all property held by it in direct ownership must be abolished, though tithes are not condemned, if used properly. The Pope is Antichrist's vicar rather than Christ's; and 'it might be good for the Church to be without a Pope.' The *Dialogus* is also important as fixing an earlier date than was before known, 1379, for Wyclif's reaching his final opinion on Transubstantiation, that 'Consecration is not material, but spiritual; and the Host, although at every point in it verily and indeed

[1] Mr. Poole's Introduction, p. xxix.
[2] See Prof. Loserth's Introduction, pp. v xvi.

Christ's Body, remains bread as to its substance as well as in its accidents.'[1]

2. The year 1885 ended with a balance in the Society's favour of £327 odd, after paying £178 for the printing (and in 1884, £21 for the binding) of *De Civili Dominio.* Of this balance, £250 odd has since been paid away—£178 for *De Ecclesia* (£156 printing, £22 binding), and £72 odd for *Dialogus* (£51 printing, £21 binding)—leaving £77 available for the 1884 *De Composicione Hominis*, with the right to increase that sum by part or all of the £50 paid in advance for *De Benedicta Incarnacione* in 1884.

The Society has now 368 Members. If they all pay their subscriptions, two volumes—one, thick; one, thin—can be issued by the Society for 1886. But it cannot be too strongly imprest on Members' minds, that on them, and them only, depends the extent of the Society's issues. If they will but find the money, and canvass all Library-Committees and friends within their range, to join the Society, its Editors will give them the books.

The present state of the Society's work is this:

I. The Rev. Edward Harris's edition of the *De Benedicta Incarnacione* (232 pages, with full side-notes and collations) is all printed; but various causes have prevented as yet the completion of the notes and indexes, and (as mentioned in last Report) 'the difficulty of the subject, and the subtlety and intricacy of Wyclif's argument, with the necessity of giving an historical sketch of the views of his near predecessors on the Personality of Christ, will cause some further delay in the issue of the book. Messrs. Austin of Hertford are printing it.'

II. Mr. Rudolf Beer's edition of the *De Composicione Hominis* has its text all in type at Carl Fromme's press in Vienna. Mr. Matthew is revising the English side-notes to it. Miss Alice Shirley will english its Introduction. Mr. Beer hopes to finish the book by June.

III. The following works are copied, and in Editors' hands, preparing for publication:

**Summa Theologiae.**

Book I. **De Mandatis Divinis**, ed. F. D. MATTHEW (nearly ready for press).

„ II. **De Statu Innocentiae.** Ditto.

„ IV.-V. **De Civili Dominio**, ed. R. L. POOLE, M.A., Ph.D. (Book III. has been issued.)

[1] See Mr. Pollard's Introduction, pp. xviii, xix.

Book VI. **De Veritate S. Scripturae**, ed. Dr. R. BUDDENSIEG.
(Book VII. **De Ecclesia**, has been issued.)
" VIII. **De Officio Regis**, ed. Dr. AUERBACH.
" IX. **De Potestate Papae**, ed. A. PATERA.
" X. **De Simonia**, ed. Dr. HERZBERG-FRÄNKEL.
" XI. **De Apostasia**, ed. F. D. MATTHEW.
" XII. **De Blasphemia**, ed. T. A. ARCHER, M.A.

**Sermons**, ed. Prof. J. LOSERTH (all copied. They will fill four volumes).

**Miscellaneous Tracts**, ed. F. D. MATTHEW (43, 44, Shirley); **Expositio S. Matth.** c. xxiii. xxiv.; (54) **Contra Magistrum Outredum de Ornesima**; (55) **Contra Willelmum Vynham**; (48) **De Servitute civili et Dominio seculari**; (64) **De Paupertate Christi**; (77) **De Ordine Christiano.**

**Responsiones** etc., ed. Dr. AUERBACH; (57) **ad. Radulfum Strode**; (58) **ad argumenta cujusdam emuli veritatis**; (59) **ad xliv quaestiones**; (60) **ad decem quaestiones.**

**De Dominio Divino**, ed. R. L. POOLE, M.A.

**De Actibus Animae**, ed. J. H. HESSELS, M.A.

The following works are copied only, and wait for editors. The copies were made by Dr. Buddensieg (except Nos. 1, 18, and 24), and he kindly places them at the Society's disposal:

(1) **Logica.**
(18) **De Eucharistia tractatus major.**
(23) **De Eucharistia et Poenitentia**, sive **De Confessione.**
(24) **De Prophetia.**
(39) **Sermo Pulcher.**
(47) **De Oratione Dominica.**
(48) **De Salutatione Angelica.**
(61) **Epistolae Octo.**
(84) **De Concordatione Fratrum.**
(89) **Descriptio Fratris.**
(92) **De Praelatis Contentionum.**
(94) **De Graduationibus.**
(95) **De Gradibus Cleri Ecclesiae.**

Mr. J. H. BULLOCK has copied part of the **Tractatus de Tempore**, the 6th Treatise of Book I. of **De Ente**, sive **Summa Intellectualium**, and Book I. of the **Opus Evangelicum**, sive **De Sermone Domini in Monte.**

Mr. RUDOLF BEER will shortly copy **De Materia et Forma**, **Replicatio de Universalibus**, and **Differentia inter Peccatum Mortale et Veniale** (Shirley, 6, 9, 28).

3. The Society's books for 1886 will be (the Committee hope and believe)

1. *De Benedicta Incarnacione*, edited by the Rev. E. Harris, M.A.

2. *Sermones*, Vol. I., edited by Prof. Loserth, Ph.D., Czernowitz.

For 1887, 1888, and 1889, Prof. Loserth hopes to edit successively Volumes II, III, IV, of Wyclif's Sermons. He (with his industrious copier) has been good enough to work hard during the past year at the examination, copying, and collation of the Sermons, and has found that all but about four of the *Sermones Mixti* in Shirley's Catalogue are included in one or other of the four collected Parts of Sermons. These four unique Sermons will therefore be added as an Appendix to Part IV. of the Collection. He expects to have 15 sheets of Vol. I in the Fromme press by May 1 next.

During each of the three years 1887, '8, '9, the Committee hope that one of the Society's Editors will have ready either a short Book of the *Summa*, or a set of the Miscellaneous Treatises, so as to keep the Society's issue up to two volumes a year. But as the copying of the Logical and Philosophical Works is still going on, more money is wanted to enable the Society to keep up its yearly two volumes. As time goes on, lukewarm subscribers fall off, good friends die. The continuers and survivors who care for Wyclif's memory, must show that care by getting fresh Members for the Society, which has yet at least ten years' work before it, possibly fifteen. Members must look their undertaking full in the face, and resolve to 'put it through.'

4. The Executive Committee repeat their thanks to the Society's Editors, Copiers, and Helpers, and specially to Messrs. R. L. Poole, J. Loserth, F. D. Matthew, A. Pollard, R. Beer, E. Harris, S. Herzberg-Fränkel, Patera, J. H. Bullock, and Miss Alice Shirley. The Society's thanks are also due to the Governing Bodies of Trinity College, Cambridge; Trinity College, Dublin; Oriel College, Oxford; and the University Libraries of Vienna and Prag, for loans of MSS. for the use of the Society's Editors.

5. The Subscription to the Society is One Guinea a year, payable on every First of January. The payment of five or ten years' Subscriptions in advance will help the Society's work. All Subscriptions and Donations,—which are much desired,—should be paid to the Hon. Sec., J. W. Standerwick, Esq., General Post Office, London, E.C., and Members will save both him and themselves trouble by sending him an Order on their Bankers, in the following form, to pay their subscriptions:—

________________ 1886.

To Messrs. ____________________

Till further order, pay to the London and County Bank, for The Wyclif Society, One Guinea now, and on every following First of January.

(*Signed*) ____________________

# THE WYCLIF SOCIETY.

*Patron*—His Grace the Lord Archbishop of Canterbury.

*President*.—His Grace the Lord Archbishop of York.

*Vice-Presidents*.—Most Rev. Lord Plunket, Archbishop of Dublin; His Grace the Duke of Devonshire, K.G.; His Grace the Duke of Buckingham and Chandos; Rt. Hon. Viscount Eversley; Right Rev. Lord Bishops of Bath and Wells, Carlisle, Durham, Down and Connor, Liverpool, London, St. Davids, Sodor and Man; Rt. Hon. Lord Ebury.

*Executive Committee*.—F. J. Furnivall, 3, St. George's Square, Primrose Hill, London, N.W., *Director*; Prof. Montagu Burrows, 9, Norham Gardens, Oxford; F. D. Matthew, Quarryton, Hayne Road, Beckenham, Kent.

*Honorary Secretary*.—J. W. Standerwick, General Post Office, E.C.

*Local Honorary Secretaries*.—*Ireland*—The Rev. C. H. H. Wright, D.D., Cliftonville, Belfast; *Scotland*—The Rev. James Kerr, 53, Dixon Avenue, Crosshill, Glasgow; *Wales (North)*—Principal Reichel, University College of North Wales, Bangor; *Cheshire*—Rev. A. MacKennal, Highfield, Bowdon, Cheshire; *Devonshire*—Rev. E. Harris, Wellswood Park, Torquay; *Gloucester*—The Rev. J. J. Mercier, Kemerton, Tewkesbury; *Lancashire*—Jos. Thompson, Esq., 23, Strutt Street, Manchester; *Lincoln*—The Rev. Canon Pennington, Utterby, Louth; *Middlesex (West)*—The Rev. E. Chester Britton, Hermosa, Ealing; *Norfolk* — Rev. O. W. Tancock, Norwich; *Somersetshire* — Rev. Aubrey Townshend, Puxton; *Yorkshire (East Riding)*—The Rev. Horace Newton, Driffield; *Yorkshire (West Riding)*—Rev. J. N. Worsfold, Haddlesey, Selby.

*Bankers*.—The London and County Bank, Aldersgate Street, London, E.C.

---

*The Society's Publications for* 1882 *and* 1883 * (£2 2s.) *are*:—

Wyclif's *Latin Polemical Works*, 2 vols. (with Facsimile of MSS.) edited by Dr. R. Buddensieg.

*The Society's Publications* (£1 1s.) *for* 1884 *are*:—

Wyclif's *De Civili Dominio*, Lib. I., edited by Dr. Reginald Lane Poole.
Wyclif's *De Composicione Hominis*, edited by Rudolf Beer.

*The Society's Publications for* 1885 (£1 1s.) *are*:—

Wyclif's *De Ecclesia* (with Facsimile of the MS.), edited by Prof. Loserth, Ph.D.
Wyclif's *Dialogus, sive Speculum Ecclesiæ Militantis*, edited by W. A. Pollard, M.A.

*The Society's Publications for* 1886 (£1 1s.) *will be*:—

Wyclif's *De Benedicta Incarnacione*, edited by the Rev. E. Harris, M.A.
Wyclif's *Sermones*, Part I., edited by Prof. Loserth, Ph.D.

* The very heavy outlay for copying in these years made the issue of more volumes in them impossible.

# RECEIPTS AND PAYMENTS OF THE WYCLIF SOCIETY,

## FOR THE YEAR 1885.

### RECEIPTS.

| | | | | £ | s. | d. |
|---|---|---|---|---|---|---|
| Balance brought forward | | | | 326 | 17 | 9 |
| By 7* Subscriptions of 5 guineas each | | | | 36 | 15 | 0 |
| Other Subscriptions (319*) | 334 | 19 | 0 | | | |
| Less cost of collection | 0 | 5 | 0 | | | |
| | | | | 334 | 14 | 0 |
| Donations | | | | 10 | 2 | 0 |
| | | | | £708 | 8 | 9 |

* Subscriptions made up as follows:

| | | | |
|---|---|---|---|
| In respect of 1882 | 24 | | 334 |
| 1883 | 29 | 1887 | 7 |
| 1884 | 44 | 1888 | 5 |
| 1885 | 214 | 1889 | 4 |
| 1886 | 23 | 1890 | 2 |
| | | 1891 | 2 |
| | 334 | | 354 |

N.B.—This item was made up subsequent to the Audit.

### PAYMENTS.

| | | | | £ | s. | d. |
|---|---|---|---|---|---|---|
| Copying, &c. | | | | 177 | 15 | 0 |
| Printing *De Civili Dominio* | 178 | 0 | 3 | | | |
| Binding, etc. | 4 | 6 | 3 | | | |
| Circulars, etc. | 15 | 15 | 8 | | | |
| | | | | 198 | 2 | 2 |
| Commissions | | | | 0 | 3 | 7 |
| Incidental Expenses | | | | 5 | 7 | 9 |
| Balance | | | | 327 | 0 | 3 |
| | | | | £708 | 8 | 9 |

Examined and found correct, 15th February, 1886, { ETHELBERT W. BULLINGER. GEORGE SMITH.

*Chaucer*, founded by Dr. Furnivall in 1868, to print all the best Chaucer MSS., &c. *Editor in Chief*, F. J. Furnivall. *Hon. Sec.* W. A. Dalziel, 67, Victoria Road, Finsbury Park, N. Subscription, Two Guineas a year.

*Early English Text*, founded by Dr. Furnivall in 1864, to print all Early English literary MSS. *Director*, F. J. Furnivall. *Hon. Sec.* W. A. Dalziel, 67, Victoria Road, Finsbury Park, N. One Guinea a year for the *Original Series* of Prints of MSS. only, and One Guinea for the *Extra Series* of prints from MSS. or black-letters of Texts before printed.

*New Shakspere*, founded by Dr. Furnivall in 1873, to promote the intelligent study of SHAKSPERE, and to print his Works in their original Spelling, with illustrative Treatises. *President*, ROBERT BROWNING. *Director*, F. J. FURNIVALL. *Hon. Sec.*, K. Grahame. 65, Chelsea Gardens, Chelsea Bridge Road, London, S.W. Subscription, One Guinea a year.

*Ballad*, founded by Dr. Furnivall in 1868, to print all early English MS. Ballads, and reprint the Roxburghe, Bagford, and other collections of printed Ballads. *Editor in Chief*, The Rev. J. W. Ebsworth, M.A., F.S.A. *Hon. Sec.* W. A. Dalziel, 67, Victoria Road, London, N. £1 1*s.* a year.

*Shelley*, founded by Dr. Furnivall in Dec. 1885, to promote the study of Shelley's Works, reprint his original editions, and procure the acting of his *Cenci* and *Hellas*. *Chairman of Committee*, W. M. Rossetti. *Hon. Sec.* S. E. Preston, 86, Eaton Place, London, S.W. Subscription, One Guinea a year.

*Browning*, founded in July, 1881, by Dr. Furnivall and Miss E. H. Hickey, to further the study of ROBERT BROWNING's poems, and to print papers on them and Illustrations of them. Subscription, One Guinea a year. *Hon. Sec.*, J. Dykes Campbell, 29, Albert Hall Mansions, Kensington Gore, London, S.W.

*Philological*, founded in 1842, to investigate the Structure, Affinities, and the History of Languages. *Hon. Sec.*, F J. Furnivall. One Guinea entrance, and one a year. Parts I. and II. of the Society's English Dictionary, for which material has been collecting for 28 years, have been lately issued, edited by Dr. J. A. H. Murray, and publisht by the Clarendon Press, Oxford.

*Wagner*, to promote the study of his Musical and other works, and the performance of his Operas at Bayreuth. *Hon. Sec.* for England, B. L. Mosely, 55, Tavistock Square, London, W.C. Subscription, Ten Shillings a year.

---

Shakspere Quarto Facsimiles, 10*s.* 6*d.* each, or 6*s.* if the whole series of forty is taken, edited by F. J. Furnivall, Prof. Dowden, Mr. P. A. Daniel, Mr. H. A. Evans, Mr. Arthur Symons, Mr. T. Tyler, and other Shakspere scholars. B. Quaritch, 15, Piccadilly, London, W. (Twenty Facsimiles have been published, and ten more will be ready soon. The Series will be completed in 1886.)